DEADLINE VEGAS

– His Obsession – Casino Revenge

– Douglas Stewart –

Deadline Vegas: First published 2020
Copyright © Chewton Limited, Douglas Stewart

The right of Douglas Stewart to be identified as the author of this work has been asserted by him in accordance with the Copyright, Designs and Patents Act 1988 and other current legislation.

You may not copy, store, distribute, transmit, reproduce or otherwise make available this publication (or any part of it) in any form or by any means (electronic, digital, optical, mechanical, photocopying, recording or by any other manner whatsoever) without the prior written consent of the author and of Chewton Limited. Any person or body who does any unauthorised act in relation to this publication may be liable to criminal prosecution and civil claims for damages.

All rights reserved.

ISBN: 979 8637739 318 (paperback)
ASIN: B087629NG7

Chewton Books, an imprint of Chewton Limited

BOOKS BY DOUGLAS STEWART

Fiction
Deadline Vegas
Dead Fix
Hard Place
Hard Place – The Prequel
Undercurrent
The Dallas Dilemma
Cellars' Market
The Scaffold
Villa Plot, Counterplot
Case for Compensation

Contributions
M.O. – an anthology
Capital Crimes – an anthology
Death Toll 3 – End Game – an anthology

Non-Fiction
Terror at Sea
Piraten (German Language market)
Insult to Injury
A Family at Law

Non-Fiction under the name Brett Morton
Roulette – Playing to Win

DEDICATION

To my wonderful family who make everything worthwhile.

ACKNOWLEDGEMENTS

Thanks to the many people in London and Las Vegas who provided me with vital details on which to build the plot. Thanks also to those, like my wife Bridget, my son Fraser and my good friends Alan & Sharon Bath and Ros Gale for their eye for detail when editing and correcting.

Praise for Douglas Stewart's Books

"A clever blend of villainy" –
Sunday Times, London

"Stewart's writing is fast-moving and laced with that natural British sarcasm that comes so effortlessly. Tough to put down" –

Richard Marcus – Author and Gambling Expert

"Do read this superb novel" –
Sunday Independent

"He makes us think but entertains us" –
Evening Telegraph

"Gripping, action-packed thriller."

PETER JAMES
Best-Selling Thriller Writer
Voted by WH Smith readers: *The Best Crime Author Of All Time*

"In Dead Fix, Douglas Stewart takes you as close as you'll want to get to the high-stakes, high risk world of top-level match fixing."

SIMON TOYNE
Best-Selling author of SANCTUS – a trilogy

TABLE OF CONTENTS

Prologue	xv
Chapter 1	1
Chapter 2	4
Chapter 3	9
Chapter 4	12
Chapter 5	16
Chapter 6	18
Chapter 7	24
Chapter 8	26
Chapter 9	27
Chapter 10	30
Chapter 11	34
Chapter 12	36
Chapter 13	38
Chapter 14	43
Chapter 15	45
Chapter 16	47
Chapter 17	51
Chapter 18	54
Chapter 19	56
Chapter 20	59
Chapter 21	61
Chapter 22	65
Chapter 23	68

Chapter 24	71
Chapter 25	75
Chapter 26	78
Chapter 27	81
Chapter 28	83
Chapter 29	86
Chapter 30	90
Chapter 31	92
Chapter 32	96
Chapter 33	98
Chapter 34	99
Chapter 35	103
Chapter 36	107
Chapter 37	111
Chapter 38	113
Chapter 39	116
Chapter 40	119
Chapter 41	124
Chapter 42	127
Chapter 43	130
Chapter 44	132
Chapter 45	135
Chapter 46	139
Chapter 47	142
Chapter 48	144
Chapter 49	150
Chapter 50	153
Chapter 51	155
Chapter 52	157
Chapter 53	162
Chapter 54	165

Chapter 55	172
Chapter 56	177
Chapter 57	182
Chapter 58	187
Chapter 59	190
Chapter 60	193
Chapter 61	199
Chapter 62	202
Chapter 63	204
Chapter 64	208
Chapter 65	210
Chapter 66	212
Chapter 67	217
Chapter 68	221
Chapter 69	227
Chapter 70	230
Chapter 71	232
Chapter 72	234
Chapter 73	236
Chapter 74	241
Chapter 75	244
Chapter 76	249
Chapter 77	253
Chapter 78	256
Chapter 79	262
Chapter 80	265
Chapter 81	268
Chapter 82	273
Chapter 83	275
Chapter 84	277
Chapter 85	280

Chapter 86	283
Chapter 87	289
Chapter 88	293
Chapter 89	297
Chapter 90	300
Chapter 91	307
Chapter 92	311
Chapter 93	316
Chapter 94	320
Chapter 95	327
Chapter 96	331
Chapter 97	336
Chapter 98	344
Chapter 99	346
Chapter 100	352
Chapter 101	355
Chapter 102	357
Chapter 103	364
Chapter 104	366
Chapter 105	371
Chapter 106	375

Prologue

Beth Dexter slumped in her leather seat. Her ice-cold eyes were fixed on her remaining chips as the dealer swept away her losing bet. Beside her, the roulette wheel was still spinning, the white ball nestling in number 22 black. Never before had she hit such a losing streak. She looked at her remaining stacks of multi-coloured chips – worth £800,000 or around one million in US dollars.

In that fleeting moment, Beth kicked herself for playing alone at the table. Nobody to be her witness. *Damn you. Finlay Dexter.*

She silently cursed her brother for refusing to join her in Dukes Casino.

With her huge loss, there was no turning back now. She pushed out all her chips.

Another black number and I'm cleaned-out.

Now the ball was circling the wheel. Beth stood up to get closer, her trim figure leaning forward. Her full lips were now razor-thin and her fists were clenched. The ball was still moving fast, tight beneath the wheel's rim. She could scarcely breathe, her heart pounding as the ball hissed above the numbers, red, black, red, black and the green of zero.

Any red number please.

Playing the Martingale staking system, Beth had always won big.

Until tonight.

The bouncing ball had been the kick, her buzz.

This was stepping into thin air on a bungee.

This was free-fall parachuting before the chute opened.
Beth had tried them both.
No turning back now.
The ball slowed.
Shit-or-bust time.
A crazy risk.
Especially when I'm playing in a bent casino.

- 1 -

Ding!
Five miles across London from Dukes, a text arrived.
Finlay Dexter scowled at the intrusion. Reluctantly, he checked the message. *Dex: Must meet. We're going to Vegas. Beth. xxx.*
He returned the phone to his pocket without replying.
Vegas?
More about her bent casino crap again.
Get lost, Beth.
Casinos don't need to cheat.
With dawn breaking and big carp to be caught, images of his sister in a glitzy casino were unwelcome. Out here was a different world. Here, in the silence and with the smell of damp grass, he was immune from Londoners going about their 24/7 business.
Better still, perched on his canvas stool, he could escape his own demons – the screaming nightmares and waking in sheets soaked with sweat.
Here, as he watched a moorhen glide over the silvery sheen of the water, he never questioned his sanity.
He could almost believe he was sane.
Some of his psychiatrist's advice had stuck
Avoid stress!
Try fishing!
Keep taking your medication.
Give it another year.
"Imagine your brain as a bruised tomato," Wilfred Grierson had

explained. "Mistreat it and it won't just be a bruise. Keep taking the *med-i-cation*." The Scot's last word, like most of them, came out slowly, something Dex reckoned was to extend the time and cost of each consultation. Doc Grierson was big on tablets, big on *med-i-cation*.

Two years on since the murders.

Two years since my life was destroyed.

As he waited for the tug-tug of a carp nosing around the bait, the text still grated.

Me? Go to Vegas?

Well ...bollocks to that!

He checked the time: 5:17 a.m.

Beth must have just left the casino. For someone so intelligent, what his younger sister saw in chucking money at roulette wheels was beyond him. In her day job at Canary Wharf, Beth gambled *other people's* millions – far more sensible, as he'd told her.

Yet she'd been winning big money.

Now, something about Dukes had spooked her.

No. I won't come with you.

If they're crooked, don't you go either.

But she had.

Unable to relax, he reeled in and folded the stool for the trek along the dusty towpath to Hammersmith. As he broke into his powerful stride, a hint of a smile creased his healthy features as he anticipated the day ahead – a six-mile jog followed by sizzling bacon in warm bread. After that? More research into the death of Diana, Princess of Wales. A friend in diplomatic security had tipped him off. There had been a cover-up of *irregularities in Paris.* Delving into archives had become a welcome distraction.

Tonight? That was okay too. Bar-tending at the Black Sheep pub off the Fulham Palace Road, another step in his rehab. And not, *definitely not*, planning a trip to Vegas.

He crossed over Hammersmith Bridge. With the sun now rising over Docklands, he could see *Who Cares,* his bright red and green barge moored upstream beyond the two pubs.

Grierson had approved of his choice of a floating home. "A wise decision Mr, er, er, Finlay. Womb-like, wouldn't you agree?"

"Doc, you only ever get my name right on your bills. The name's Dexter. Finlay Dexter. My close friends call me Dex. *You may call me Finlay or Mr Dexter.*"

While on the medical treadmill, he had decided months ago that Wilfred Grierson's strong point was extracting fees from every orifice. If Grierson were right, *a big if* as Dex reckoned, recovery was still a huge stack of medical bills away.

"*Injured Wallet Syndrome.* That's what I'm suffering from," Dex had suggested during the previous one-thousand-pound consultation. Except for a sniff, Grierson had ignored the comment.

As he clambered onto the deck and then ducked into the accommodation, thoughts of Beth returned. Unwelcome images of the Vegas skyline filled his mind.

Me?
Go to Vegas, baby?
No way.

– 2 –

In the hush of the casino-floor, Beth's *Balade Sauvage* perfume drifted across the wheel in the direction of the inspector. Her knuckles were white as she pressed down on the green baize, watching the erratic dance of the ball as it hit the strikers. Reality and the outside world had disappeared. The opulent surroundings meant nothing. She was oblivious to the three Saudi princes losing their millions at blackjack or the two Moroccans playing baccarat just a few steps across the squelch of expensive carpet.

For now, nothing mattered but a white ball landing on a red number.
11 Black.
36 Red.
Stop! Stop!
13 Black.
Fuck!
But no!
It's trickling on!
27 Red.
It's stopped
27 Red.
I've won!
I've won!
Thank Christ!

Distantly, Beth became aware of Jeb Miller's voice. From his high-stool behind the wheel, the portly, self-important little inspector had spoken. He had an absurdly rounded mouth beneath a thick black moustache that did nothing to disguise his baby face. Whatever Miller was saying never penetrated Beth's bubble. She felt breathless, drained and exhilarated all at once. She stared, almost transfixed as the ball circled on number 27.

Miller's tone was sharper now. What was he saying? Beth looked up. "Ms D, I'm sorry but that was a late bet, a no-bet. I had to get it taken off. You must get your bets on earlier. The ball had dropped before you placed it."

Beth looked at the Oriental dealer. His name badge showed Wun Yee but regulars knew him as One-Eye. She saw that he had pushed her chips off the layout. "That is so-o-o wrong! I bet long before the dealer said *no more bets*."

Miller edged his fat bottom off the stool to continue the conversation "Not so."

Damn you Dex. "Mr Miller, don't cheat me. I won and you know it."

Dukes' management hated noisy scenes and on hearing Beth's raised voice, Nigel Forster-Brown, the manager, sidled over along with a Maltese pit boss and a shift manager. FB, as he was known to everyone, waved his arms soothingly. "Ms D. Please keep your voice down. If there's a problem, a slight misunderstanding, I'm sure we can sort it."

Beth looked at the tall, stooping figure with contempt. "You'd better, FB! This place stinks! Mr Miller called my bet *late*. In his dreams!" She spat out the words.

FB spoke quietly, trying to defuse the position. "Please, now please be quiet. Our cameras will resolve it." Forster-Brown moved away to a telephone out of Beth's earshot as Miller eased his overfilled trousers back onto his stool, the seams of his dinner jacket straining at every move.

"Normally, we'd spin," Miller puffed "but as you're the only player at the table, it's your choice." Beth looked round the ornate room and saw the smoked-glass domes. Behind them were the cameras capturing every detail of every moment. Known as the *Man-in-the Sky*, she knew they would have recorded everything.

"I'll wait," Beth snapped as she watched FB talking on the phone, his head nodding. Then, eyes lowered as usual, he returned. He rarely met anyone's gaze and now was no exception. "I'm sorry, Ms D. I'm afraid the inspector was right. The cameras caught it all. After the dealer said *no more bets*, you finally pushed out all your chips. But the ball had dropped. Not onto number 27 at that point, you understand. But it had reached that slow speed where no casino allows any more bets. You didn't lose but unfortunately you didn't win."

"This is unbelievable!" Beth wanted to let rip with expletives learned at Roedean. "Show me the recordings."

By his gentle and almost effeminate standards, FB's tone was frosty as he stared at the thick pile of the Turkish carpet. "Not possible. Ms D. I'm sorry. We are not running the Odeon Cinema."

Beth thought for a moment. She knew the battle was lost. Except for the shouting. "I want the boss. Get Pepe here."

FB looked at the wheel as he replied. "Mr Carmino is having dinner. I'll tell him." He turned to One-Eye. "Carry on. Spin the wheel."

"Hold it," commanded Beth. Her voice was taut. "I decide when One-Eye spins. Got it?" She glared at both FB and Miller in turn.

FB nodded okay and then scuttled through a door with a tap-in code. Seconds later, after climbing a flight of stairs, he was admitted to the Surveillance Room, where three employees were studying several banks of monitors with ever-changing views.

"Wipe everything for Roulette Table AR3 and the ones covering Baccarat Table BC6. Technical problems." The listeners laughed as one of them set to work.

Downstairs by AR3, Beth fingered her chips, still indecisive. At that moment, Pepe Carmino appeared, slithering across the carpet like a snake, his dinner-jacket expensively cut and his white shirt immaculate. Aged mid-forties, he stood just over six foot with dark, Latinate features. With movements as smooth as silk, his tongue was designed to match. The only blemish to his matinée-idol image was a faded scar down one cheek. Even that only added an air of attractive mystery.

"Ah, Pepe," Beth volunteered. "I've a serious…"

He patted her arm. Beth flinched, disliking an oily charm that other women found irresistible. To his international members, he may have sounded like one of the braying elite who graced Glyndebourne, the Royal Enclosure at Ascot or who watched polo in Windsor Great Park. But on Dex's only visit to Dukes, he had spotted the accent of an Essex Boy made good. "I know," Carmino soothed her. "FB told me. I've just viewed that spin. It was indeed a late bet. We was…were perfectly in our rights to remove it."

"Let me watch it then."

"Club Rules. Nobody gets into our Surveillance Room. I wish it were otherwise because I would far rather have you convinced. But I cannot make exceptions. The cameras don't lie."

Beth stood silent for a moment. "No." She glared at the casino owner. "Not the cameras."

Carmino never flinched at the implication. "But Ms D, you didn't lose. You just didn't win."

Beth turned to One-Eye as she pushed out every single chip to bet on red again. "Spin the wheel," she commanded.

Twenty-one revolutions later, the ball trickled to a stop.

"Ten, black, even," said One-Eye.

Beth turned to face Carmino. She spoke quietly yet the menace was obvious. "You have just made the biggest mistake of your life. I never forget. I never forgive."

-3-

His breakfast plate cleared away, Dex was at his desk, surrounded by cuttings about the Alma Tunnel in Paris. On a shelf were several silver trophies, reminders of his sporting prowess before big business had consumed him. Stacked beside him were notebooks and articles dating back to Paris 1997. On the wall was a photo of him on an ecology protest march. A cut-out from a newspaper pinned to a corkboard proclaimed **GREED NO LONGER GOOD**. Beside it was a newspaper headline: **Princess D – it *was* murder**.

On the TV, a twenty-four-hour news programme was running. A summery-looking journalist ended her piece to camera. "This is Tiffany Richmond from the Euston Road for BTC-TV." Dex had always admired her – fancied her too in a long-distance way. There had been some great reviews of her book about African child starvation and corruption in foreign aid. He empathised with that big time.

As he fingered his phone, he agonised over letting Beth down. At thirty-one, she was two years his junior and usually, for her he would do anything. *But Vegas? Not on, sis.* He imagined her somewhere high up in a Docklands tower with her team of forty surrounding her like battery hens. In his darkest days after the murders, despite her high-powered job, Beth had always been there for him, although recently she had become increasingly brusque.

"Time you put the past behind you, Dex. You're wasted in that pub pulling pints."

"The doc says I need another year," he had reminded her with a cheeky grin that plenty enough admirers found engaging. With his dark hair flopping across his forehead, he had retained a youthful charm that even the murderous events had failed to age. His eyes were wide-set and blue-green, his nose strong and his chin square and prominent. Only what was inside was brittle.

"Snap out of it," Beth had persisted. "Your management skills. Your success. Don't waste them." And then, *big mistake*, she had added. "And after Father now wants to kiss and make up."

"Don't ever come the Father bit again," he had snapped back. That last sour exchange had ended a recent convivial evening.

Decision time – banter with the drinkers at the Black Sheep? Or rub shoulders with oil-rich gamblers being fawned over by Dukes' obsequious staff?

He autodialled and reached her voicemail. He listened to her soft tone inviting callers to leave a message. "Hi, Beth. Sorry. No Dukes. Big job on. I'm washing an elephant's testicles. Love you!"

Twenty minutes later, Beth picked up the message and shook her head at her brother's irreverence. With slim fingers racing, she texted him. "Okay, Dumbo. I'll come to the pub. Must see you." She turned to the window looking towards London City Airport, her thoughts still angry at being screwed. Just then, a colleague, Jason Rodway, stuck his head round the door. "You wanted a word?" She liked the New Yorker and wondered sometimes whether she fancied him too.

"Jason, I'm leaving for Vegas tomorrow, so I need you to take care of these." Beth pointed to a bunch of market reports she had just printed off.

"Sure. No problem." He picked them up and was about to leave when she called him back cocking her head to one side as an impulsive thought struck her. "Remember I told you I'd picked up vibes that Dukes was as bent as a corkscrew?" She saw him nod.

"Last night, Dukes cheated me for nearly a million." She nodded towards her cellphone. "Now, I've got a pointer to Vegas."

Rodway's deep voice rose. "Holy crap! A million!" He paused and moved closer in an act of solidarity. "But stirring up shit in Vegas? You gotta be kidding me. Smart that is not." He leaned against her desk. "You won't go alone?"

"Dex hates me gambling. He despises Dukes and his aim is never ever to go to Vegas again. He went about eleven years back."

"Your brother had my sympathy but now he needs to snap out of it."

Beth's tone was suddenly sharp, quick to defend Dex. "He's been to hell with no return ticket."

Rodway shrugged. "You know him best. But anyway," he pulled the door open, "you take care. Didn't you say Dukes is tied up with building Space City Casino?" He saw her agree. "Those Vegas guys won't be pussycats. Don't tread on the wrong toes. There's plenty enough stiffs already buried in the Mojave Desert."

Beth fingered a silver picture frame showing her at the Cheltenham Gold Cup with Pepe Carmino. "Space City's a five-billion-dollar project but it's way behind schedule and over budget." She put down the photo. "It'll maybe launch in two or three months." She turned the frame over as if shutting out Carmino. "I've discovered that Dukes has a big stake in it. Keeping the project alive has been tough."

Rodway looked concerned. "I never took to Carmino. His smile had all the sincerity of a whore's ecstasy."

"Didn't realise you were an expert in that area, Jason." Beth's infectious grin was similar to her brother's as she returned to her desk. "I'll see you after my long weekend. Ciao!"

Once she was alone, Beth turned over the photo and shivered, wondering about that scar down his cheek.

-4-

From the canned music system, the strains of Beyoncé could be heard above the mid-evening noise of the mainly young clientele who sat at chrome tables or stood in cliques, toes tapping as they chatted. Behind the bar of the Black Sheep pub, Dex was just adding Red Bull to a blonde's pink gin when Beth appeared. On seeing her, he waved cheerfully and moved to an empty part of the counter so that he could lean across and kiss her. As she shimmied across the room, in her expensive outfit of cream jacket, red blouse and shortish black skirt, she oozed panache. Once again, Dex felt guilt at denying his help.

She stretched across the bar to add a hug to his kiss. "Where's the elephant?"

"Out the back, drying off. Tomorrow I'm on rota for shampooing a skunk's scrotum. Can life get any better?" As he spoke, he poured her a vodka and slim-line and nothing for himself.

"Any better? Not unless you're talking Formula One, cricket, crackpot Princess Diana theories or chatting up blondes."

"Guilty as charged but don't forget the fishing."

"But no help for your little sis."

Dex whistled. "You know my views on gambling. But somehow you always won? This Martingale system. You thought it gave you easy money."

She nodded. "Last night, I won again except I lost everything. A million. Just like that." She snapped her fingers to highlight the speed. "Fucked something rotten. All my previous winnings."

As she sipped her drink, Dex recognised the hatred in her eyes. "With you there, they could never have used their late bet trick."

"A million quid could have fed a load of orphans." Much to Beth's irritation, Dex picked up a couple of bottles and started to juggle them. "Anyway," he continued as he deftly caught a falling bottle behind his back, "how in hell could I have stopped you losing all that dosh?"

"By being there." Quickly, she explained how, on a previous visit, she had been suspicious of a *late bet* call on a Lebanese player.

"More fool you for risking it then."

Beth made no admission, though her eyes conceded her mistake. "I've a lead to nail these bastards. It takes us to Vegas."

Dex opened his wallet and pulled out a couple of fivers. "You're broke. Will that help?"

"Be serious, Dex. I'm onto something big, seriously big."

"Look, you know what that nutter Doc Grierson advised."

"Lifestyle gurus, psychiatrists, quacks, shrinks – forget them! You're over it! Do something useful. Come to Vegas."

"After my days at Harvard, you know my views on America ... too full of Americans. Plus I've a ton of pills to prove I'm ill. Besides which I quite enjoy being a bum." He waved cheerily at two new arrivals, now seated along the bar. "Back in a mo. The brunette, Molly, is, well ... tonight ... I'm taking her back to *Who Cares*."

Dex juggled his way along the bar to serve the two women. The process turned into animated chat and raucous laughter – much to Beth's irritation as she tapped on her smartphone. When Dex came back, she moved straight into overdrive.

"Listen, Dex. This is not just about me last night. This is mega-fraud."

"Casinos don't need to cheat. They get rich anyway – mugs like you."

"Remember Pepe Carmino?"

Dex nodded as he dried and polished glasses still hot from the dishwasher. "I've been given a contact in Vegas – a dealer called Tavio. There's a skeleton rattling around Dukes that's bigger than your elephant's backside."

Dex was more interested now than he appeared but said nothing.

Beth fingered the chunky gold brooch that dominated her lapel. "I fly in the morning." She paused, knowing the next bit was tricky. "On the return flight, I'm routed via Chicago where Father joins me. He's doing a property deal on Michigan Avenue."

"Then it's a no. It would be no even without Father. With him, it's no, no, no…not bloody likely no." He leaned across the bar and held her hand. "I'll never forgive him."

"But to help me? Couldn't you? Wouldn't you?"

"Sorry Beth but no."

She looked across at him, a hint of tears welling up in her eyes. "Dad's knocking on a bit and feels very alone."

"After what he did to me? Fuck him!" Dex's voice had taken on a throaty edge like a dog's deep growl. He lowered his eyes, the downturn in his mouth emphasising his feelings. "The best thing Mother ever did was dumping him."

Beth knew better than to debate that point. "If Tavio comes good, I'll hold the nuts on Carmino. Help me when I bring back the evidence. I can't handle this alone."

"I'll think about it."

"You're big on conspiracies like Princess Di and JFK, yet you won't take me seriously?"

Dex shrugged. "So far, I'm underwhelmed."

"Please come. I'm scared."

"Don't go, then. Dukes is not your problem. Forget gambling. Forget casinos. Forget Pepe Carmino. Find yourself a husband, have a couple of kids. With your looks, you could take your pick."

Beth frowned as she flicked her hair, the colour rising in her cheeks. "Surrender to Dukes? Never."

Dex recalled their childhood and knew there was no stopping her.

"Calling *late bet* a few times a week could save Dukes twenty million a year. Blackjack scams could add another ten mill."

"Dukes doesn't need the money."

"Wrong! They're bankrolling Space City like crazy." Beth scowled as Dex returned to his juggling—this time with three bottles, much to the delight of Molly whose skirt had ridden high up her thighs. "This Tavio guy has something on Pepe. Something about Panama."

"Must be a hat, Beth." Dex chuckled.

Beth drained her vodka angrily but then her face softened and she stretched out to give him a hug. "Dex. I need you there."

He went around the end of the bar and pulled her next to him. He was shocked to find her small frame trembling. "Don't go, please."

"I can't let go." They shared a lingering hug.

"Love you, Sis." Dex watched her exit before going to the back, his eyes welling up. There he downed three of Grierson's pills with a gulp of water before returning to the bar.

At least I can now resist swilling down a bottle of whisky.
Beth alone in Las Vegas?
God! If anything happened to her.
What have I done?

"Same again, Dex." Molly's voice was a welcome interruption.

-5-

The digital clock by the bed showed just after 2 a.m. Molly and Dex lay entwined on his queen-sized in the almost dark confines of his bedroom. As she stroked his ear, Molly purred sleepily with contentment, "Where have you been all my life?"

"Sex on a boat. The earth always moves." For a few moments, he continued to run his fingers down her cheek and was about to offer more of the same. Then he realised she was already asleep. Moments later, he was gone too, arm still cradled around her neck.

Everything changed an hour later.

"Fire! Fire!" As he shouted, Dex was half-raised on one elbow. Molly awoke terrified. Dex's shouting seemed to be right in her ear. He was now screaming, one arm waving in every direction. His body was twitching and shaking out of control. Now fully alert, Molly jumped out of bed, aware too that she was soaked with his sweat. She stood naked, arms across her generous breasts staring at Dex's haunted features. In the greenish light from the clock's face, he looked like a hunted animal, teeth bared and snarling. "Call 999. Fire! Fire!" His anguished voice filled the confined area.

Molly looked around the narrow surroundings and knew at once there was no fire. "Wake up, Dex. You're dreaming. F'Chrisake, wake up!" She switched on the bedside light and after a few seconds, she saw his eyes flicker open. Gradually the world according to Dex came into focus and he too rose from the bed, his lean body dripping with rivulets of sweat.

"Christ, Molly! I'm sorry. I'm okay now."

Molly was already pulling up her purple panties and hastening to get away. "You scared the hell out of me, Dex."

"I'm sorry. I sometimes get these terrible nightmares. But don't go. Please. Let me get you a coffee, water, brandy. Whatever."

Molly sat on the corner of the bed. She shook her head as she adjusted her tight skirt and then pulled on her tall black boots. "I'm out of here. That was too weird for me."

Dex grabbed his dressing gown and wrapped it around him as he followed her into galley. "Let me walk you to your car."

"I don't want you anywhere near me."

She never waved goodbye as Dex shut the entrance and headed for the bathroom, where he kept his tablets for his *psychotic disorder*, as Grierson loved to call it. He took two with a glass of water and then flopped onto the soaked and rumpled sheets, his hands now clenching and unclenching. The room smelled stale. He got up and opened the small porthole to let in the chilly night air.

Maybe I never will be cured.

Maybe those memories will always haunt me.

"Fuck you, Father." The shouted words made him feel better.

– 6 –

Just under a mile off the Las Vegas Strip on West Sahara Avenue, Enzo Letizione emerged from the Nevada & General Bank. It was nearing noon. The heat shimmered off the sidewalk and glinted on the roof of his black BMW sedan. The sky was cloudless except over the Spring Mountains to the west. The exceptional heat, even by Nevadan standards, suggested a storm by late afternoon.

Letizione was wearing a lightweight pale blue suit with a striped shirt but no tie. Beneath his wavy, thinning hair, there was a hint of moisture due more to the meeting than the sun beating down on him. As he walked the few steps to his car, his heavy jowls were unusually taut and his eyes were hard enough to cut glass. There was a frown on his tanned forehead as he wrestled with the aftermath of the uncomfortable meeting. Eagerly, he swung his bulk into the car, slammed shut the door and set the air conditioning to full blast.

Before pulling away, he reset the radio station from the heavy beat of the blues channel which he had played on the way to the bank. Now he needed something different. He chose a cool jazz station as background for his drive to the Venetian Hotel, a few minutes away. Letizione, a youngster during the bad old days of mob rule in Vegas and now in his late sixties, phoned Pepe Carmino, who confirmed he would be waiting under the canopy.

Letizione spotted him at once. The Englishman was talking on his phone. In a lime-green shirt and yellow slacks, he looked like a golfer on the first tee. They greeted each other with profuse but false sincerity before heading toward the towering edifice of Space City. Just before reaching Caesars Palace, as they rounded the curve on the Strip, the new casino's tower could fleetingly be glimpsed way south beyond the MGM.

By the time they were snarled up at the Flamingo intersection, the banal pleasantries had been concluded. "Enzo, we're in this shit because you screwed up." As he spoke, Carmino leaned slightly toward Letizione, who could smell an expensive aftershave, hinting at musk and driftwood.

"We been unlucky."

"Bullshit! You're the boss in Vegas. Due to your lousy management, London's being bled white. We're working our backsides off, throwing money at your bankers. Till the strikes, the cost overruns, Dukes was legit. Life was sweet."

"Don't blame me for the unions."

"But I do." Carmino's voice conveyed menace, causing Enzo to look ahead to avoid the stare. "Your job is to fix problems. Your job is to deliver. We've busted out on our covenants." The Englishman unwrapped a piece of gum and started to chew vigorously as at last they crossed the intersection. Outside the Bellagio, they took in the crowds gathered to watch the sway of the fountains. "We okay for the Grand Opening? On time, is it?"

"You got it."

"And those leeches at the bank? Sorted this morning?"

"Purring. That extra moola you're sending, they're pussycats." Letizione could see from the corner of his eye that Carmino was not buying into this. "They're sure purring," he added, increasing the listener's disbelief.

Carmino tugged the American's sleeve. "I don't buy that shit. I can smell your sweat. There's more. There's *a but*."

"No big deal. They're calling for another slug of capital. Fifty mill."

"Fifty million dollars!" Carmino thumped the dashboard. "You think my name is David Copperfield producing that kind of money from a rabbit's butt? Where the hell do I find another legit fifty?" Neither of them had an answer to the rhetorical question. There was silence except for the strains of Brubeck from the surround sound. "Going belly-up is not an option. Firing you is."

At the entrance to the Space City site, a security guard in a peaked cap and navy-blue uniform recognised Enzo Letizione and waved the car through into the nearly finished Grand Entrance. No sooner had they stepped out than Letizione's gofer appeared offering bottles of water, hard hats and the opportunity to stare upwards at the nearly complete building.

It was truly magnificent and from the outside, looked ready to open. It towered over the Strip – sixty-three floors of shimmering metallic blue in a gentle curved design. Inside, however, there were dozens of electricians, electronics engineers, carpenters and supervisors scurrying in every direction. Everywhere was movement. Overhead, were multi-coloured cables awaiting the ceiling tiles to complete the finish. The floor was still uncarpeted so that the sounds of jackhammers, cutters, welding equipment and circular saws made talking impossible.

They walked up the long staircase to Letizione's office. To a fault, it was spacious and comfortable. Modern artwork adorned the walls and figurines on plinths nestled between fronds of greenery that softened the boxy squareness. From a drinks-cabinet with sink unit, the host poured large Bombay Sapphires slopped over ice and lime but easy on the tonic. Here in his own domain, the American felt more at ease and was pleased that maybe Carmino had mellowed after seeing the building.

"Look, Enzo. I've sweated most Dukes' regulars dry—used all the usual scams. But if just a few members get suspicious, then gossip could spread quicker than a broad's legs. There's a woman. She's a ball-breaker. The word *feisty* would undersell her. She was rolled over the other day and knew it. She couldn't prove it, of course. No witnesses. But she's here now. My system picked up something about the Cosmopolitan Hotel."

"Staying in the Cosmo? Doing what?"

"I'll find out." Carmino moved on. "Given the mess here, there's only one option. It comes at a price. And you'll pay. With my balls on the line, not all the cash I transfer here will arrive. You got me? We top up our offshores, you and me both." Carmino was in no mood to negotiate as he snapped his punchline. "Ninety-five percent skim to me, the rest is yours."

Letizione saw the dead-eyed look and decided to be grateful for the miserly five percent. "So, you doing a deal with that tight-assed Geneva lawyer? The guy you said was so mean he even cuts his own hair?"

Carmino laughed for the first time since his arrival. "That's him. Pudding-bowl style. But he's smart. His clients are bent Brussels politicians, Government insiders on the take, industrialists, people-smugglers. They all got the same problem. Untaxed wealth, maybe bribes, maybe stolen money. And now Swiss Banks' secrecy – that's just about gone. He wants to be several jumps ahead of the law. Banking secrecy everywhere will soon be dead like the bleeding dodo. The buzz word in banking is *transparency* – tax havens sharing information. Whistleblowers will get pay-offs for stealing data and snitching about bank customers and their hot money."

"I'd heard ... but the Swiss bankers won't surrender easily."

Carmino shrugged. "I'm not persuading him differently. Panic among Swiss advisers suits me. I reckon when surrender happens, the Feds will be opening up Swiss Bank accounts quicker than a can of beans."

"Meaning for us?"

"This lawyer knows of a shed-load of money that's hotter than a bitch on heat. It's from Europe, Africa, Russia and the Japanese Yakuza – all hidden behind anonymous companies, foundations and trusts in remote islands but they is ... are, all manipulated through this lawyer's office. And he wants to shift it quick. Wants to retire and sleep easier at night."

Letizione pressed a switch and a floor-to-ceiling mirror suddenly became two-way. From his office on the mezzanine level, the two men stared across an atrium, dominated by a mock-up of a Space Shuttle on a launch pad. "Full piggybanks like that need emptying. Go get it, Pepe."

"We done plenty of good stuff back in London. Like Boy Scouts—we're well prepped with a second set of books, new bank accounts." The smile was sly as he continued. "Coupla months back, I fixed the guy from the Gambling Commission." He slapped Letizione on the back as he concluded. "Money, a couple of hookers, Viagra and a few blow-jobs."

"What's the deal on laundering?" The chins on Letizione's jowly face wobbled.

"Pudding-bowl wants a big cut but the sums passing through Dukes will be mega." Carmino's smile was greedy, showing a lot of whitened teeth. "Under the deal, each guy he introduces leaves Dukes with only 80% of what he introduces."

"I get it. So a shyster arrives with a million and leaves with eight-hundred thousand?"

"We keep 20%. He leaves with a Dukes' cheque – good clean money to present to carefully identified banks in Limassol, Dubai and Mauritius – no questions asked." He saw that Letizione was impressed. "Plus, with the scams we got running at the tables, we'll keep those cocksuckers at the bank happy."

Letizione nodded whilst thinking more about his next question. "You ever work in Panama?" Without success, the American tried to sound casual.

Carmino's eyes narrowed for a second before he responded. "Never been there. Why do you ask?"

"I was playing Texas Hold 'Em, low stakes stuff, down at the Golden Nugget. I met an off-duty dealer there. He deals blackjack in that joint beside the Trop. Name was Tavio. The guy was playing loose. He'd had a few drinks."

Carmino swirled the tonic with a swizzle-stick and then pointed it at Letizione. "So?"

"Reckons he knew you way back in Panama."

"Guy's mistaken. Like I say. I've never been there."

Enzo Letizione's smile was forced. His years of experience shouted that Carmino was a lying shit. "Ain't no big deal. I guess the guy was even drunker than he seemed." He sat down at his U-shaped desk and pulled out a slim folder from a locked drawer. "Here's the schedule till launch: detailing the ongoing work; the A-List celebs to be invited, the headliners and the high rollers we're comping." He turned to the final page. "And that's the plan for the soft opening. You got it all there."

Carmino looked distracted, as if lost in the details. He grabbed a handful of peanuts and washed them down with the remains of his drink. "I'll take the file. We can talk over dinner tonight." He paused and Letizione noticed the sinister look as Carmino sucked in his cheeks and narrowed his eyes. "I'm leaving. Something to sort."

- 7 -

That evening, as Letizione and Carmino settled down for dinner in the Picasso Restaurant at Bellagio, Beth was barely eight hundred metres away in the Nine Fine Irishmen bar in the New York, New York Casino. She hadn't moved for twenty minutes though her eyes had been watching everybody who had stayed, left, or arrived. Almost satisfied that nobody was tracking her, she drained her spritzer and re-joined the throng among the tables and slots on the maze of the casino-floor.

Taking no chances, she decided not to return directly to the Cosmopolitan. Instead, she rode the escalator up to the bridge over the Strip to the MGM-Grand Casino. As she walked with short, bustling steps, a maroon bag slung over her shoulder, a solitary man who had been playing the slots but watching the bar, stood up and slipped into the endless tide of people. Moments later, he was on the bridge, mingling with the crowd toing and froing above the fumes from the evening traffic.

Before entering the cool of the MGM, Beth paused in the cauldron-hot night to look around her. Fifteen paces behind her, the follower kept his face lowered and turned away and spoke into his cellphone.

Am I paranoid or is that guy I saw playing the slots on my tail?

Uneasy, Beth went through the automatic doors and hit the cold blast from the air-conditioning. She descended the escalators and almost immediately exited into a quiet back-street. There, she entered a gift emporium stacked with souvenirs and toys and jostled between the shoppers till she hit The Strip and turned towards the Cosmopolitan Hotel. After a few paces, she paused to look around but of the solitary man, there was no sign.

Relax! There's nobody following.

Unseen by her, the solitary man had nodded to a woman wearing a blue tank-top and jet-black jeans. As he peeled away, the woman hurried across the street and into the emporium.

By the time Beth reached her bedroom and locked the door it was nearly 10 p.m. She let out a sigh, suddenly sheepish at her fears. Even so, she placed her red-hot documents in the safe before calling room-service. After showering, a change of clothes, a rare steak and a Californian red, she could risk hitting the tables downstairs.

– 8 –

It was pushing toward noon when Dex returned from the supermarket and settled down to read a novel called *Family Legacy*. The author seemed to have a pretty strong insight into how and why JFK was murdered in Dallas. He had just reached a chapter about the sighting of Lee Harvey Oswald in New Orleans when his phone rang.

"Beth! How's Vegas?" He checked the time. "God! It must be around four in the morning over there. You had a big win?"

"Listen, Dex." He heard a sob at the other end of the line.

"Beth? You okay?"

"I'm scared." There was a long pause while he heard more sobs. "That guy, Tavio Sanchez? Y'know about Panama?"

"How did it go?"

"He's dead. Gunned down."

– 9 –

Dex spent an anxious afternoon trying to concentrate on the JFK book while his mind kept replaying the rest of the call. On several occasions he looked at the bottle of Glenlivet. He kept it beside the TV as a reminder that he was still fighting his demons. Somehow, he resisted, instead taking several red pills for what Grierson had also called his *acute depression and personality disorder*.

In his head, he could still hear Beth's frightened voice. "It was on the local news. The cops reckoned a contract killing. No known motive. Dex," she whimpered "it'll be me next."

He wanted to say he had warned her but now was not the time. *Now*, she needed him. *Now*, his little sister was alone in a city of two million people, one of whom was a hired killer. Stunned at the implications, Dex fought to gather his thoughts. "Where's Pepe Carmino?"

"I don't know, Dex. I've locked the door of course but I'm scared to death." Her voice broke again.

"Does he know you're in Vegas?"

"I mentioned the Cosmopolitan to Adam." This was a reference to their godfather, Adam Yarbury. "We had dinner in Dukes, so maybe yes, if Carmino has everywhere bugged."

"Did you tell Adam about Tavio or cheating?"

"No."

"That's good but get the next flight to Chicago or to anywhere."

The reply was a long time coming. "Maybe I'm being over-dramatic. I'll stick to meeting Father in Chicago. We land at Heathrow at 7:15 a.m. tomorrow. Father's limo will meet us there." There was a brief pause and he heard rustling paper. "Write down these letters – G A D E C H. My password is Z A Y B X C W B. I'm backed up on the Cloud."

"Done but I'm not into all this Cloud stuff. Anyway," he tried to sound reassuring, "I'm sure nobody is coming to get you. But if you're that scared, move hotels." Dex heard another sob and a sniff and he imagined her lying on a bed in a foetal position, clutching her phone.

"Dex, write down this name too. Maria-Elena Sanchez. Panama. Got it? Okay. Let's meet tomorrow night. Drinks in the Rivoli Bar at the Ritz. 6p.m."

"You'll tell Father?"

"Confide in him? Never." The old Beth shone through for a moment.

"Love you, Beth. Safe flight."

"Together, we'll bring down Dukes. But if…" again Dex heard her voice breaking. "…but if I don't make it back, promise me," momentarily, her voice gave out completely "you'll destroy Carmino and get back what Dukes stole."

"You'll be just fine, Beth. But if it makes you feel better, then yes, I promise. I'll never rest. Drinks at 6 p.m."

Now, as he looked at his notes, it all seemed unreal. Had she met this Tavio? It seemed probable. What had she learned about Panama?

The afternoon dragged, his imagination running wild and it was a relief when it was time to head for the Black Sheep. That evening, pulling pints and mixing absurd yellow or pink cocktails helped time to pass quicker. He was just ending his shift when his phone rang. It was Beth, sounding much better. "I've left Vegas. I'm fine now."

"Where are you?"

"At O'Hare, Chicago. Father's in the bar downing a double Jamesons. We're boarding in two minutes."

"I told you. See? Love you, Beth."

"Love you, Dex. See you at the Ritz."

Unseen by Beth as she had cleared Immigration at McCarran in Vegas, a solitary figure had been watching, intent on making sure that she was boarding – an anonymous man who then spoke rapidly into his phone. In London, Arnie Fisher, a weasel-like figure, took the call that Pepe Carmino had told him to expect. Fisher and Carmino had been at school in Essex but ever since, their careers had taken very different routes. To Carmino, Arnie Fisher was indispensable – ideal for taking care of a problem like Beth Dexter.

− 10 −

With Beth now safely away from Vegas, Dex had slept remarkably well. On awakening, he looked out at the blue horizon beyond the river. A rowing-four skimmed by, the cox bellowing instructions. It was a wonderful summer morning. Days like this had been too rare. Later, as he stepped out of the shower, a text from Beth arrived. "Chauffeur's arrived. Getting in the limo now. I'll call you from home. Must speak soonest."

Twenty-five minutes later, he was in the galley frying eggs and turning the bacon. The local TV news was on but he was barely listening. His attention was on tracking down a witness beside the Alma Underpass in Paris. As a lawyer, his statement could be vital. The Establishment had done a great job of slamming shut doors and closing ranks to prevent investigators.

As he savoured the smoky flavour of the bacon, he heard the wail of sirens from emergency vehicles. With the busy Great West Road close by, he was well used to that. He munched contentedly on the toast, beside him the scribbled note with Beth's username and password. He tucked it into the JFK book and returned to planning the afternoon. *Maybe some trout fishing over at Brentford?*

From across the galley, the words *Hogarth Roundabout* and *Great West Road* on the TV grabbed his attention. "For drivers in West London, there are reports of a major accident on the eastbound carriageway of the A4 on the approach to Hammersmith. First reports are that at least two vehicles are involved, with one of them on fire. Both carriageways are closed. Drivers are advised to take an alternative route. Expect severe delays in the Hammersmith and Chiswick area during the morning rush hour."

He glanced out to the north and saw that the blue of the sky was now tainted by a rising plume of thick black smoke that paled gradually as it rose and spread, darkening the horizon as far as he could see. He imagined his father's face, puce with rage that even with all his wealth, London traffic still left him helpless at moments like this.

He called Beth with no response. He had no number for his father, an arrangement that suited them both perfectly. Uneasy now, he found it impossible to enjoy his hot wheat toast with lashings of Oxford marmalade. Beth's phone was invariably switched on. He tried LBC radio. At the end of an interview with a Labour politician, they cut to Hammersmith. "Traffic on the Great West Road between Hogarth Roundabout and the Hammersmith Flyover is at a standstill. Unconfirmed reports suggest that an HGV loaded with aggregate has struck a saloon car on the eastbound carriageway. Four vehicles are now on fire. So far, there is no word about casualties. Our reporter…"

With Beth's phone not responding, Dex had heard enough. He could sit still no longer. Like a man possessed, he was away, striding through the galley and onto the deck. He gathered speed Chiswick Mall, a street lined with expensive homes with prime Thames views. From there, he raced into Eyot Gardens, pounding the pavement toward the pall of black smoke. The Great West Road had become a giant parking lot with both directions at a standstill Looking westward, and covered by drifting black smoke, he saw a mass of blue flashing lights. Fire, police and ambulance crews were everywhere.

Fists pumping furiously, he raced beside the jammed vehicles until blocked by the blue and white tape preventing access.

Both arms held high, he waved at a WPC who was standing just beyond the central barrier. Although she saw him, she turned away to talk into her phone. Above the noise, all Dex could see was dense smoke and steam rising from where fire crews were hosing down the remains of several vehicles.

The air was acrid and flecked with burning particles. Even with a hand across his mouth, there was no escaping the pungency of the morning air. It filled his mouth and lungs and his eyes were stinging. Above the shouting, he could hear the whine of cutting equipment but except for the very obvious burned-out cab of a truck, his view was limited. Its remains pointed skyward like a giant praying mantis, seemingly on top of another vehicle.

Dex was about to ask a West Indian driver of a flatbed if he could clamber on for a better view when he saw a TV crew crossing the central barrier in his direction. He recognised the reporter as Tiffany Richmond's two-tone chestnut hair cut short. She was wearing a navy blouse under an off-white jacket with black slacks. A simple silver chain hung around her neck. She looked smaller than when on the TV, maybe five foot six and daintily built.

"Hey, Tiffany!" he yelled at the top of his voice against the hubbub. He tried again and then the West Indian beside him tooted to catch her attention. She saw Dex waving furiously. For a moment she hesitated but then changed direction and approached him. Without words, her elfish face asked what he wanted.

"Heh! Thanks! Is there a black stretch-limo involved?" His words were tumbling out. "My sister. My Father, they were in his limo heading into London. Anything you can give me?" He barely took in that she needed scarcely any makeup, her pale skin being smooth, her eyes almond-shaped and watchful. Her sympathetic look came more from her eyes than her shapely mouth, which had the slightest hint of pink lipstick.

"You tried phoning?"

"No answer." From his height, he looked slightly down to her up-tilted face.

"No names have been released. I doubt they're even known yet. And yes, there is a limo involved. Three occupants were taken to Charing Cross Hospital, Fulham Palace Road."

The word *three* hit Dex like a hammer-blow. "And their condition? I mean, were they…?" Dex could not bring himself to finish the sentence.

He was vaguely aware of her perfume as he hovered close to her, "Removed just before I arrived."

"Did you get the limo's registration?" Dex spotted from the flinch that she knew the answer but there was a delay while she decided whether to tell him.

"Your name is?"

- 11 -

"Dexter. Finlay Dexter. Known as Dex." He saw Tiffany's immediate shocked reaction. Her oval face puckered, her jaw tightening as he continued. "Father's limos both had a personalised number-plate. He owned CHAS 111 and DEX 911."

Tiffany paused. "The car's front number plate was partially destroyed." She lowered her eyes. "Look. I mean…I'm sorry." Dex saw a slight hint of tears as she glanced up at him. He found himself amazed that reporters who saw and heard so much suffering could get emotionally hung up. Especially someone like Tiffany Richmond who had watched countless children dying in Africa. "Dex, I'm sorry. The registration was DE something. The rest was unreadable."

He felt faint and swayed alarmingly. Instinctively, she grabbed his bare arm to steady him. Concern etched across her face, she continued. "Would you like a lift? You don't look too good."

Dex clenched his fists, took a deep breath and forced himself to stay calm despite his brain pumping out despairing messages.

Is fire destroying my life again?

He tried to appear stiff-upper-lip. As he fought to meet her gaze, his voice was strangulated. "Thanks. I mean yes. I mean no. I can walk back. I only live just over there." He pointed vaguely toward the river. "I'll head for the hospital. The Chelsea & Westminster, you said. Right?"

Tiffany corrected him gently. "The Charing Cross. Much

nearer." As she spoke, she pressed her card into his hand. "If I can help, let me know. Sometimes we hear more sooner than the public – and that includes family. But we don't always report it. Or not at once, anyway." She gripped his arm. "And I hope you get some good news at the hospital." Her face told Dex to be prepared for the worst. "And maybe we can talk later. By the way – your sister's name and your father's?"

Despite his hatred of journalists, Dex was in no mood to tell her where to stuff her question. Without hesitation he told her it was Beth Dexter and Sir Charles Dexter CBE. But instantly he regretted his cooperation as she followed up.

"When I get further ID confirmation, of course I'll be mentioning their identities. On the basis of *unconfirmed reports suggest*, you understand. And I'll mention that you were at the scene."

He gave her a feeble despairing smile. "I have reasons to despise the media. But thanks. Yes, go on, report what you like."

Tiffany looked puzzled but said nothing as he turned away.

As he jogged homewards, there was just one thought on his mind.

Perhaps it had not been an accident.

-12-

It was over seven hours later when a weary but distinguished looking surgeon entered the small room. where Dex had been waiting for news. "I believe you're Sir Charles Dexter's son?"

"Correct."

"You've had quite a wait. Simon Morrison. I'm a neuro-surgeon. We're alone in here, so let's just stay put, shall we? Take a pew." As Dex seated himself on the utility chair, he wondered how many times Morrison had brought bad news to families in this windowless green-painted room. There was a no smoking sign on the wall, yet there was a cheap tin ashtray and the air was fusty. Dex placed Morrison at about fifty-four, as slim as his delicate fingers, greying at the temples and with small eyes. The face was watchful, the beard neat and well-trimmed. "Your father is in a coma. He suffered a severe head injury but his spine is intact."

"He'll come around okay?" Dex was surprised at how concerned he felt about someone he had reason to hate beyond measure.

"Oh yes. I'd say so, yes. But it was quite a bang, so it may be some while before we can assess the long-term effects." He raised his hands defensively.

Dex stood up and circled the small room. "You heard that my sister and the chauffeur were both killed?" Dex spoke without emotion, as if he were passing on news about strangers, yet inside he was being ripped apart.

"Oh God, no! I had no idea. My team work in our own bubble." He stretched out a consoling arm but made no attempt to touch him.

"They were travelling together, were they? Do you want to talk about it?"

"Thanks, but no. So—a long haul for Father? Months, years?"

Morrison was non-committal "For now, caution is the word."

-13-

Had it been his father's funeral, no doubt Sir Charles's pin-striped solicitors would have had instructions for a big send-off. There would have been choirs, processions and a string of eulogies. London's fat cats would have filled every pew, most of them glad to see the back of him. But he and Beth had hated pomp and so Dex had fixed a private ceremony for her, by invitation only.

This sunny but unusually chilly morning, just fifteen people had passed through the lych-gate and walked along the flagstones into St Martin's Church in Bladon, a small Oxfordshire village. Six were aunts and uncles. Their mother had flown in from her Italian villa near Sorrento and had arrived on the arm of her twin sister.

Adam Yarbury was there, his normally beaming face looking sombre. Besides being a godfather to Dex and Beth, he had been a valued friend. Semi-retired from the City, Adam had never needed to work anyway. His preferred newspaper was *The Racing Post* and his haunts were racecourses and Dukes where occasionally he had met up with Beth. The other mourners were four of Beth's school friends and two colleagues from work. Still in hospital, Sir Charles was unaware of Beth's death.

The village of Bladon is nearly two hours northwest of London and had become famous because Sir Winston Churchill and others from his family had been buried there. The Churchill ancestral home at Blenheim Palace was close by. Dex and Beth had spent their childhood in the village and had known Reverend Hillyer most of their lives. With his gold-rimmed spectacles, silvery hair tufting out around his ears and a cheerfully rounded face, he had the jolly look of someone more suited to weddings than funerals.

As they exited the small church, Dex spotted an absurdly lavish wreath. Among the many floral tributes, it stood out. It was nearly a metre across and was a tasteful blend of chrysanthemums, carnations and pink and white roses. He bent down and opened the message: *From Pepe Carmino and the team at Dukes – with deepest sympathy.*"

Shocked onlookers saw Dex's face harden and his eyes narrow with rage. In a sudden move, he ripped the card from the wreath and tore it into small pieces. Then, to the jaw-dropping looks of the bystanders, he stooped again, picked up the wreath and after taking a few steps, hurled it Frisbee style over the wall and into the meadow beyond.

Dex could see that an explanation was expected but said nothing, simply joining the vicar on the short walk to the grave. Hillyer gave him a raised eyebrow look before intoning the final internment formalities. They were standing beside Beth's grave next to where, just two years before, Dex had also buried Caroline and Jamie, his wife and infant son.

The service concluded, Hillyer led the mourners toward the wooden lych-gate. The churchyard was lined with evergreens and hawthorns. Butterflies flitted and hovered. The air was filled with the cheerful chatter of sparrows. Swallows were catching summer flies. Carmino's wreath had been an unwelcome reminder of his promise to Beth. Saddled with the burdens he now faced, Dex envied the birds their freedom to swoop and soar at will.

Only the Reverend Hugh Hillyer knew of his inner torment. As the mourners drifted toward their cars, he tapped Dex on the shoulder and stopped him beside Sir Winston's grave. For a moment, they stood in respectful silence. "Winnie stood alone. Defiant."

The slate-grey eyes turned to Dex. "But *you* cannot emulate that great man. Nor should you try. Not with your health problems. You've told me your fears. Or some of them. I think you could tell me more, much more."

Hillyer's words were accompanied by a hurt look, the eyes delivering the message. "Dex, I remember your courage as a boy. Defying that tyrant of a father. You have nothing to prove to yourself – or to anybody. Don't be ashamed to do nothing. Revenge will do nothing for your recovery. Revenge is an unruly beast and can have unforeseen consequences." He pointed back toward the three family graves. "Beth would understand. After the tragedy of Caroline and Jamie, you have your own life to lead. And getting you better is a priority."

"But," Dex faltered. "Isn't that selfish? I made promises. I *never* break promises."

"Dex—if Beth had *known* what lay ahead, she would never have burdened you. If she had truly known of the dangers, then yes, *that* would have been selfish – selfish of her. Do nothing hasty. But if you must do something, don't carry the burden alone. I know what you went through when Caroline and Jamie died.."

"They did not die." Dex interrupted sharply. "They were *murdered by persons unknown*."

Hillyer acknowledged his hurtful understatement by an immediate apology. "And now this…" he struggled for words "…this horrendous tragedy." Dex held back from saying that Beth too had been murdered and let the vicar continue. Hillyer shook his head slowly, his voice fruity and mellow. "We cannot know precisely what Beth had got herself into but you know enough to understand my warning. Don't try standing alone." He turned to Sir Winston's grave. "Even he needed the Americans … and he knew it."

As Hillyer finished and Dex was about to comment, he spotted one of his aunts approaching. She was whispering to her husband rather louder than she thought. He caught the words *that hell would freeze over before she would ever look after her brother*. The husband's grunt and nod of agreement said it all. Dex knew that his father had been respected by some but loved by nobody. Not one family member had visited him in hospital. The relatives had sided with his mother when she had fled the family home after being battered, kicked and punched once too often. Even so, his aunt's remark was an untimely reminder of another decision Dex had to wrestle with —that of his father's welfare.

Dex stood with Hillyer's comforting arm across his shoulders as the last of the mourners headed to the wake at The Bear in Woodstock. At that moment, he became aware of someone standing just beyond the lych-gate. For a moment, he did not take in what he was seeing. As the vicar shook his hand and declined the invite to the wake, Dex left the churchyard and saw that it was Tiffany Richmond.

"This was strictly private. No media." Dex regretted sounding quite so severe. He took in that she was dressed entirely in black, a colour she wore well.

"Look, I'm not here as a reporter. I came here…" She sounded embarrassed. "I came out of *solidarity*. But…" She nodded to the security man who stood bolt upright a few paces away. "No access."

"Solidarity?"

Tiffany looked towards the cemetery. "Explanations can come later."

Dex was intrigued yet wrong-footed. He scuffed the gravel with his highly polished black shoe. "The wake is not the place. Here's my address. Maybe Thursday? Around 7 p.m. I could rustle up pasta."

"Can we say 8 p.m.? By then I'll have finished my book-signing in Leadenhall Market." Her smile was underpinned by the quiet sincerity in her gentle voice. It was unlike her matter-of-fact style on screen. For a second, Dex thought she was fighting back tears but that seemed unlikely. Why would she cry? He decided he must have been mistaken. "You're right, Dex – now is not the time for us to talk but we have a bond as I'll explain."

A bond?

What does she mean?

His look was still curious as he lowered himself into the driving seat. "I'm sorry they wouldn't let you in. It was good of you to come. If I had known…"

"And, Dex – I've picked up something else. That's for Thursday too." He spotted concern in her tone as he nodded goodbye and slowly pulled away. His thoughts as he drove toward Woodstock were uncomfortable.

Carefree days of fishing, juggling beer bottles and slopping around the barge were over. But what would replace them?

Nothing good.

That was for sure.

- 14 -

His mind still in torment, Dex gave up trying to sleep. Instead, he treated himself to a bacon butty with oodles of brown sauce, leaving the bacon to grill while he dressed in his waterproof jacket and trousers. Lastly, he grabbed his fishing tackle, hoping at last to lure one of the big carp. Even though now murder filled his mind, he had never worried about safety on the isolated towpath. He had no fear of darkness. As he padded along under the drizzle, not another soul around, the familiar but distant sounds of London at night surrounded him – the hum of traffic, barking dogs, the yelp of an urban fox and a church clock striking three. The first hint of dawn was yet to appear as he listened to the pleasing hiss and swish of the Thames flowing by.

Usually, when fishing all that mattered was the tug-tug of a suspicious carp. But not this morning. His agenda seemed endless – what to do with Father for starters. How to keep his promise to Beth? Where to start? *Beth's laptop? Her phone?* Never found. Presumably swept away or destroyed in the blaze. Tavio had been executed but Metro had no leads. Had Beth spoken to him in time? Or had he been silenced? Who knew Beth would be speaking to him? Maybe her password to the Cloud held the answers?

And never far away was the recurring image of the huge DAF tipper-truck reared up over the limo like a stallion servicing a mare. His thoughts honed in on Sir Charles, his biggest worry. Soon, Father would be released. There would be nothing more the hospital could do for him.

What then?
No way could Father live alone.
Maybe a specialist care home?
Somewhere out of sight, out of mind?
You mean dump him?
So, must I leave Who Cares?
Return to the family home?
He had no happy solution as his mind turned to his promises. Get back Beth's losses. Do-able? He had no idea. Destroy Carmino, Dukes and Space City? It seemed unreal, absurd even. Yet Beth had been convinced they could do it.
If I do nothing, how do I live with myself?
Life had to have a purpose.
And mine is what?
Juggling bottles?
Beth deserved better.
Am I up to it?

Note to self: Don't ask Doc Grierson this.

-15-

After the morning rush, Dex visited a gambling bookshop run by an extrovert Scotsman called Gus McKay. Beth had once said that he had cleaned out a casino playing roulette.

"You ought to read this book." The dapper little Scot, resplendent in his tartan trews, headed toward the fifty or more books on roulette. He looked all of his seventy-plus years. His small shop was tucked away in a Dickensian back street behind the Aldwych. McKay returned clutching *Gambling Scams* by Darwin Ortiz. "Essential reading, that one. Here's another – *Thirteen Against the Bank* by Norman Leigh. He organised a coup against the casino in Nice. I expect Norman's dead now. With three pals of mine from Glasgow, we used his system called Reverse Labouchère. We rolled-over a casino in Germany. Later, we were banned."

"Banned? Just for winning?"

McKay's watery blue eyes above an aquiline nose showed his astonishment at the ignorance of his customer. "You've a lot to learn, pal."

"I intend to beat a casino, bring it down." Dex stood beside the counter and nodded at the little man with his lined face. He was rewarded with a mocking smile.

McKay's laugh was throaty and the right side of his face twitched. "Aye, right enough, I've heard that before. Casinos have gone bust but never by players winning!" He laughed again. "They go belly up from mismanagement or to cheat the taxman."

He looked at his half-hunter watch that was draped across his tartan waistcoat. "Look, pal. It's my pie and pint time. We need to talk. I'm sorry to say it but your sister was a daft gambler. She was a bonnie lass but she played the Martingale system." He shook his head. "I warned her that one day it would bite. But," he shook his head sadly, "she never believed me."

Dex sounded almost shrill as he defended her. "It never failed her. She only lost because the casino cheated." Dex regretted sounding too defensive.

"I ken that fine. But playing the Martingale—doubling up after every lost bet till you win or hit the table limit – that's a mug's game. No disrespect. She got lucky for months."

Dex said nothing as McKay double-locked the door and pocketed the key. Then the Scot's eyes narrowed as he wagged a finger. "If you want to end up a millionaire by gambling, start with two million. I've plenty to tell you."

~ 16 ~

Dex laughed as the small but spritely figure took off down the narrow street, leading him to a poky timbered pub that was filling with students. As they waited for the barman, Dex decided to ask a question that had been puzzling him. "You became a millionaire, so it *can* be done. So why are you now flogging books from a Holborn back street?"

McKay looked at Dex with renewed respect. "Fair point. I lost it all playing poker in Vegas. A cash game. I was out of my league. I then tried to win it back playing blackjack."

Dex was suspicious. "After you won big in Germany with this Reverse thingie, you could play anywhere else – London, Edinburgh, Holland, Australia, Vegas. Do it all over again. Easy. Then don't lose it at the poker tables." Dex saw from the bored amusement on the Scot's face that he was not the first person with that suggestion.

Having ordered, they sat down in a booth made from former church pews. "I'm banned. I'm in the Griffin List subscribed to by the Vegas casinos. My mug shot is shared globally."

"Griffin?"

"Griffin Investigations. They gather the names and details of anyone who is a known cheat or who is regarded as bad for casino business. Their records are called the *Black Book*. Card-counters playing blackjack can beat the casino. If caught, they are blacklisted and labelled as *advantage players*. Besides identifying card-counters from the way they play and how they wager, casinos also use continuous shuffling machines and other tricks to beat the counters. But their ace is the Griffin List containing details of the player, the style of play used and, of course, their appearance."

"A wig and a false moustache."

As they waited for their steak pies with peas and mash, McKay downed a generous slurp of his ale while Dex sipped from a pint of orange juice. "You've a lot to learn." The words were accompanied by a war-weary expression and a shake of the head. "Face-recognition software sees through a disguise."

"Was this reverse thingie cheating?"

McKay's grey hair shook with the vehemence of the denial. "I card-counted at blackjack. Pure skill. Reverse Labouchère – pure skill but potentially expensive for the casino. Casinos don't tolerate players getting an edge."

"Card-counting? Legal or illegal?"

"Legal…but get caught card-counting, expect to be banned and named in Griffin."

Dex was warming to the dapper little man who looked too puny even to lift a set of bagpipes. The expression *comfortable in his own skin* seemed apt. At his age, he had accepted that *shit happens* but the occasional sparkle in his eyes suggested he not lost the will to fight that. As Dex watched him tuck his low-slung brown tie under his waistcoat, the guy's crackle of electricity was still captivating.

"Break the bank? Going to tell me why?"

"Not why, no." Dex was not ready for that explanation and McKay shrugged as if it was of no concern. "I promised Beth to get revenge against two casinos, one in London, the other in Vegas."

"Impossible. You'd be as effective as a flea biting a rhino's bum." For a man who stood less than five foot four, he had a rich, resonant voice. He wiped a watering eye. "Look laddie, casinos are too cunning, too rich to be broken. They're run by mean bastards."

McKay spat out the last word with surprising vehemence. "They're not good losers, ye ken. A smile from a casino boss is another man's lie."

Dex sat silently, not sure how to react.

McKay looked across the narrow table and his eyes held a warning. "If you're a big loser, casinos smarm and grease you until they've bled you dry. If you're a big winner, they red-carpet you to win back what they see as *their money*. Once you've been cleaned out, they drop you. The smiles, the handshakes, the freebies. They disappear." He peered watchfully at Dex from over the rim of his pint. "Which casinos?"

"I'd rather not say."

"Good answer, son. Take care. Not just what you do but *who you confide in*. Casinos are all ears. Careless talk costs lives." His eyes narrowed. "You've the hands of an accountant, not a street fighter."

"I want your help, not your opinion," Dex intervened sharpish, stung at the accusation.

McKay looked at him as if appraising a prize bull. "Well... surprise me! Maybe you have balls of steel! You'll need them when the gorillas get to work with wire cutters or pincers."

Dex blinked, uncertain how seriously to heed the warning. "Are you kidding? Gorillas?"

"The heavies that are paid to scare you shitless." The Scot pointed his fork toward Dex. "You're going all-in. *All-in* means you're staking your life."

"But you broke the bank." Dex realised his tone was too strident. "And what about that song—*The Man who Broke the Bank at Monte Carlo*."

"Charles Wells in 1891." McKay shook his head ruefully. "He won a fortune but died broke. But the casino wasn't bust. Not even close. When Charlie boy had won all the chips *at his table*, they closed it – placing a black cloth over it like a shroud. The casino was never busted. These days, they would keep the table open, topping up with more chips."

Dex's face showed disappointment. "You mean the Monte Carlo casino never did go belly up?"

McKay laughed but not unkindly. "Dream on! You'll never win enough to break a casino." He wiped some beer from his mouth with the back of his hand. "If you want to destroy a casino, you need to find out what they're hiding, their dirty little secrets."

Dex liked that but did not volunteer what Beth had discovered about Space City's finances. "But your roulette system was infallible?"

"Reverse Labouchère? Yes…and no! You could win a fortune but you need deep, deep pooches – that's pockets to you Sassenachs. Most folk run out of money first."

"Could I do what you did—but on my own?"

"Better with at least two of you. We had four covering even-chance bases. You can win big, huge even."

"I'm listening. Explain Reverse Labouchère."

-17-

Five thousand miles away, as Dex chatted in the Holborn pub, Enzo Letizione changed his position in his deep recliner. He was seated in Pepe Carmino's suite at the Venetian Hotel, about a mile from the Cosmopolitan. During a long and difficult evening, Carmino had kept Letizione on the defensive. Sweat stains circled under the American's armpits after over twelve hours under the cosh. A stale smell hung over him.

"I gotta be going." The American tapped his watch. "I'll hardly get my head down before them dumb-fucks from the union are banging on my door."

Carmino swirled a balloon-glass of seventy-year-old Champagne Cognac. He stood by the window, legs crossed, every inch of him oozing command. After the long hours chewing the fat over two bottles of Barolo, a huskiness in his voice kept Letizione on edge. "Nobody here shits on us again. Not unions, no motherfucker, nobody. Do whatever it takes! Got it?" He saw Letizione's startled eyes show resentment before he nodded without enthusiasm. "Got that, Enzo? *Do whatever it takes.*"

Enzo Letizione rose stiffly from his chair to stare out at the neon lights far below on the Strip. "You still with that Hungarian blonde? Irenke, was it?"

"Ever porked a corpse?" Carmino fingered the scar on his cheek as if in recollection of something and then continued. "Forget Irenke. I'm done with her opening her legs for me. Now, she's only good for opening the blackjack tables. Know what I mean?"

Letizione looked thoughtful. "Sure I do."

"I got the Gambling Commission inspector and several of his team …" He pressed his thumb hard onto the table-top and rotated it slowly. "Exactly where I want them. Irenke's tricks won't be sussed!"

Enzo looked less impressed than he was. He watched the flashing lights of a cop car weave a path toward Downtown and thought of his own pocket aces. The problem was when to play them. Not now, for sure. He turned to face Carmino. "Extracting the dough from this Swiss lawyer's clients? You reckon to raise fifty mill plus our cut?"

The Englishman jabbed his finger into Letizione's chest. "Two hundred million. Easy. We got legit reasons to move money to Vegas. The second set of books. Like I said, the inspector's our man now. The Gambling Commission can go fuck themselves. Their bean-counters will never spot this." He drained the last dregs from his glass. "I'll sucker the eighty-percent from these rich guys. Maybe more from some. Besides Irenke, I've someone else able to make their dicks rule their brains."

"Anybody I've met?"

Carmino shook his head, yawned and stretched. "She's an Aussie. Worked in a Sydney hospital. She headed to London a couple of years back. She's been hanging out in the best bars, the top hotels."

"A hooker?"

"Jude? No. Just a good-time girl and greedy for the high life with the face, tits and bum to get her there." He glanced across to Letizione. "And she'll go down a treat with these rich bastards, if you get my drift."

The dirty chuckle brought a rare smile to Letizione's wrinkled face which was now in need of a shave. "Seems you got all bases covered, Pepe." The words carried no conviction but short of playing those pocket aces, for now Carmino had his balls on a plate. "You take care now, Pepe." The meaningless words hung between them as the American waddled toward the door.

-18-

"Reverse Labouchère. Simple concept, difficult maths. With two of you playing roulette, one only bets on red and the other on black. One bet will always lose. If zero hits, you both lose at least half your stakes. Sound crazy?" The Scotsman winked and started to explain. "The secret is in the staking system—the amount you bet."

For the next thirty minutes and while sinking another London Pride, McKay waltzed through the explanation, scribbling ever larger numbers on Dex's notepad. "Try tossing a coin one hundred times. It should come down fifty heads and fifty tails. But it won't. It might be forty-six heads and fifty-four tails. But occasionally it could be thirty-seven heads and sixty-three tails. Roulette is the same. That imbalance lets you win big."

"Terrific! But how long could that take?"

"Till you get a big imbalance?" He shrugged. "It could happen in the first hour. It could be ten days. In my case, we played for seven days. Nearly cleaned us out too."

"And this is not cheating?" Dex saw the emphatic denial before continuing. "Know someone who can team up with me?"

McKay's already twitchy face went into twitch overdrive as he ignored the question. "In London, they might say they don't like your style of play and invite you to stay away."

"Ban me?"

McKay laughed. "Why not? They make the rules. They might close the table or lower the maximum bet limits once you started winning serious loot. In Vegas, it's different. If they don't like you, the gorillas will encourage your departure. It's *shit-yourself time*, trust me. Those Vegas heavies have voices like they gargle with gravel."

"Happened to you?"

"My gorilla moment? Aye! In Vegas. Card-counting." Dex noticed that McKay's hands were now shaking at the memories. "That's when I was put in the Griffin. After that, you can run but canna hide." He looked wistful for a moment. "Forget winning big at blackjack. If you card-count, you'll be caught."

- 19 -

Dex stared at a legal cartoon on the pub's wall. "Anything positive for me, Gus?"

McKay nodded thoughtfully. "I may have saved your life. That's a positive." He beckoned Dex to lean forward, although nobody could hear them in their secluded booth. "It's Dukes, isn't it? And Space City?" His face suddenly looked young again, the wrinkles almost fading for a fleeting moment.

Dex had no need to say anything. His shocked look was a clear admission.

"How did I know? Elementary! You mentioned London and Vegas. I never did trust Pepe Carmino. Dukes is funding Space City. Your sister played in Dukes. It's a private company. That means they have a better chance of fiddling the books, hiding their crimes. You want to destroy them? My advice: fight dirty. Find their weakness." McKay paused to stir the coffee. "Keep it secret. Top, top secret until you have all the evidence. Any leak and Carmino will have you."

"More on him?"

"He's a total shit but a magnet for women. I wouldn't trust him or his casino. But don't quote me!" He chewed the side of his finger before continuing. "There's a rumour, some story behind Pepe's scar. What it is, I've no idea."

Dex was unsure whether the Scot was withholding something but let it pass. Instead, he was tempted to mention Panama and Dukes' *late bet* scam but something held him back. Perhaps it was

McKay's earlier warning about careless talk. "Assuming Dukes is bent, what am I looking for?"

The Scot nodded. "Prove cheating. Best of all, prove breaches of the Gambling Commission's rules. If they lose their licence, they're dead, buried, kaput!" He leaned forward and grasped Dex's sleeve. "Closing down Dukes equals no cash for Space City. Job done. Total destruction."

"You make it sound so easy."

"No way! Watch your back. If Carmino learns you're after him..." He ran his finger across his throat. "Careless talk, remember?" The Scot drained his beer and, as he put down his glass, his face twitched again. "Come to the back room of the shop tomorrow. I'll show you some tricks used by bent casinos or bent dealers."

Dex nodded. "And someone to help me—a real expert who isn't banned? You never answered that."

"There is someone – a good card-counter. He loves beating the casino at anything. He might switch from cards to Reverse Labouchère. His name is Billy Evans. He's never counted cards in London and is not in Griffin."

"I can sense a *but* in your voice...a big but. Right?"

"Billy got himself hooked on the white stuff." McKay tapped the base of his nose. Without saying more, he eased himself from the bench seat and brushed the crumbs from his trews. "It's time for me to open the shop."

Dex motioned McKay to wait a moment as he opened his backpack. From it, he removed a brown envelope and showed the Scot a photo of Enzo Letizione at the topping-out ceremony for Space City. "Know him?"

Dex knew the answer even before the reply came. McKay's face said it all. "Letizione. Enzo Letizione. Looking older with fatter cheeks than when I used to come across him."

"A gorilla?"

McKay shook his head. "No. But casinos where he cut his teeth, they gave out a fair few beatings. Now, he's a Vegas insider. In a city that runs on juice, he has plenty enough. But the unions at Space City – they've been a right pain in his arse. They have juice too."

"Form? Violence? Convictions?"

"I doubt it. Letizione wouldn't be approved to run Space City without a robust CV. Maybe around thirty, nearer forty years back, he worked Downtown. Mob-rule was ending. He'd have seen or heard most things. Executions, torture, beatings. Like the car bomb attack on Lefty Rosenthal. Aye, to survive back then, Letizione would have known never to cross Tony Spilotro. He knew to show respect to *the made men*. That's how he survived." McKay looked deadly serious. "A lesson for you too, son."

"But Letizione's not a mobster?"

McKay signalled uncertainty. "Don't underestimate him. Not all sharks live in the sea." He paused for emphasis. "But their victims end up in the desert or feeding the fishes. Just outside Vegas is Lake Mead. Many a corpse has been dumped in there."

− 20 −

Despite Gus McKay's warnings, Dex had no intention of backing off. He had gone straight to the Black Sheep to tell the boss he was leaving. "We'll miss you," the manager volunteered. "As will those young women downing their fancy cocktails. Come back if you change your mind." He had then phoned Adam Yarbury to fix dinner at *L'Escargot*, a favoured haunt of Adam's in Soho.

Back on *Who Cares*, Dex sprawled out on the sofa, one end piled with cushions for comfort. Everything about Princess D was now piled up on a shelf. In its place was a stack of books on gambling scams. He had already started on Norman Leigh's *Thirteen Against the Bank* and was captivated. That team had cleaned up in a French casino using Reverse Labouchère. A quick reader, Dex had devoured nearly fifty pages before the disturbed night and the steak pie caught up with him. The book slumped to his chest as he drifted off into a deep sleep.

It was nearly five p.m. when he awoke, sitting up in torment. "Fire! Fire! 999!" It took a few moments for the narrow strip of cabin to come into focus. He flopped back, his wet shirt clinging to him and his chest heaving. He lay still, gasping for air until his breathing had calmed down. Every nightmare ended the same way – always with him helpless as the flames raged through the cottage.

Slowly, he rolled off the sofa to head for the bathroom, where he saw the rows of pill bottles. For a moment, he was tempted to take one, two or even three. Then he paused.

Had the pills and potions ever done any good?

Damn you Grierson.
Was it your cocktail of med-i-cation causing the nightmares?
Wind back the clock.
Live normally.
Except for the booze.
Okay, that had been out of control.
But in moderation? Was drink such a crime?

With a fierce backhanded swipe, he swept every pill-bottle and pack crashing to the floor. He felt better already for that. Then, he tipped every pill, hundreds of them, white, red or pink onto a towel which he took to the porthole. As he tipped them into the fast-flowing river, he laughed manically as he imagined Grierson's face.

– 21 –

Still undecided about Father's future, Dex finished dressing. Despite knowing that Adam Yarbury would probably wish even to be buried in a pinstriped suit with his old-school tie, Dex selected a charcoal open-neck shirt with a fawn sports coat. Forty minutes later, he reached *L'Escargot* and mounted the steps into the historic restaurant. He saw Adam at once, or rather saw someone sitting behind *The Racing Post*. "Hello, Adam."

The paper was immediately dropped. The city-suit was enhanced by a rose in the lapel. Yarbury's face beamed enthusiasm. "Just planning my selections for Newbury tomorrow. A trainer reckoned Sentosa Serenade is coming good. Seven-to-one. Good odds in a mixed field."

"I'll think about it. I never seem to get much luck."

"Horse racing, dear boy? Not luck. It's knowledge. Who you know, what you hear and from whom you hear it. Otherwise, pick with a pin. Like I do. I'm on G&T. A double of course. Can I tempt you? What's your poison?"

"You can. As of today, I'm drinking again – in moderation."

Adam nodded approvingly. He summoned the waiter and ordered doubles. "Moderation in everything. Excellent philosophy – women, drink, horses, blackjack. Never been too good at it myself though."

As usual, Adam's laugh was self-deprecating. His face had a baby-like innocence and, despite having lost most of his hair and what remained tufting silvery-grey, he appeared years younger than pushing seventy. Laughing heartily, he had once explained that he only took risks in his personal life – slow horses, bad cards at Dukes and unsuitably young *but delectable* women. "Is that godfatherly advice or what?" he had added with a thump on the table. Adam had never married – but women who had passed through his revolving doors had always left with a smile and on good terms. In the private bank where he had risen to be chairman, his creed had been *anticipate the risks, have no worries.*

After they had ordered French onion soup and rare steaks, Yarbury selected a Chambertin from a good year. "No point dying rich is there, old chap," he volunteered. "Oh God! Sorry! Not a time to be mentioning death!"

Dex waved his arm over his gin dismissively. "I need to talk about Beth and Dukes, whatever pain that causes."

"You? Talking about casinos? My dear chap. So out of character." He removed his heavy black spectacles and huffed on them, his rosy cheeks swelling like bellows. "I thought we'd be talking fishing or crackpot theories on Princess Diana in Paris."

"Another time, perhaps." Dex grinned. He knew that Adam Yarbury was far too Establishment to contemplate that death in the Alma Tunnel had been anything other than an accident. "Still doing a bit of banking?"

"Not so you would notice. I'm non-exec now. I just tootle in for occasional board meetings. Most days, I toddle down to the club – that's Dukes, of course. Have a spot of lunch with some acceptable claret, lose money at blackjack or watch the nags on their big screen."

As the soup was served, Dex waited till they were alone again. "You sound very cheerful about losing at blackjack. Or are you being modest? You win often enough, I expect."

"Win?" Dex was rewarded with a look of incredulity. "My dear boy, blackjack's my vice, a legacy of pontoon played in the dorm at school. Winning is not the point. I don't play to *win*. I play for the *fun* of it, for the *gamble*. I don't expect to win and rarely do."

"What about card-counting? Basic Strategy?"

"Quite beyond me, dear boy. Don't laugh! I may be a banker but adding up numbers was never my strong suit." He selected a brown roll with olives. "Of course, I've *heard* of card-counting. The chaps tell me you can work out whether the remaining cards are mainly tens and aces." He sighed. "That baloney would take the fun out of it. Anyway, don't they shoot you if you get caught? Bit like a fallen horse, what?"

"Casinos don't approve, no." Dex spoke with all the authority of an expert despite having never heard of card-counting before meeting McKay. "Did Beth ever play blackjack?"

Adam gazed up at a large chandelier as if that would jog his memory. "No. She played roulette and that was never my game. Too complicated with all those coloured chips being placed everywhere. I like the turn of a card. Shit or bust. Usually bust in my case! If I'd won every time my cards added up to 22 or 23, I'd be a rich man."

Dex nearly chipped in that Adam *was* a very rich man, but refrained. He leaned forward to share a confidence. "I want to join Dukes. I suppose you must propose me?"

"Lordy, lord! Well, bless my soul!" Adam Yarbury swirled the burgundy in his glass and sniffed approvingly. "Chambertin! The king of red wines, truly noble. But you, joining Dukes? Splendid! We can dine there another time. They have a pretty decent Richebourg."

"Maybe," Dex replied with caution. He was thinking of McKay's warning that everywhere, the bars, dining room and cloakrooms, was probably secretly bugged by Carmino. "Tell me, did Beth ever talk about Pepe Carmino?"

"She volunteered that he made her flesh creep. Unctuous. That was the word she used. Nothing special. Why do you ask?"

Dex ignored the question. "And you? Your opinion?"

"Of Pepe?" He grimaced as he measured his answer. "Works his favourites like Lothario at a tea dance. And his hands—soft and smooth but always ice cold. If you'll excuse the expression, shaking his hand is like caressing a corpse."

Dex admired his fillet steak and mixed salad. "Ever been cheated in Dukes?"

-22-

Yarbury's head rocked back with laughter. "Cheat me? Good heavens, no. Why would they? Casinos always win anyway – especially with players like me. With my play, I've paid for their electricity for years."

"But you do win? I mean, you were joking when you said you always lose?" Yet even as Dex said it, he saw that same shocked look on the listener's face, so he continued. "I mean, not always win…but…well, quite often." He finished lamely on seeing Adam Yarbury's bemused look.

"You really don't understand casinos my dear chap!" The tone of voice was very much that of godfather to godchild, except that the Bible had never featured in what Adam preached. "I've been playing for damned near fifty years, so I dare say I might have won once or twice." He rolled his eyes as his head rocked back with a snorting laugh.

"You never play to win?"

"My dear Dex, you have a lot to learn if you're going gambling." He topped up Dex's glass. "Stick to good wine and naughty women. And if I may say so, never drink more than half a bottle of wine. Now, where was I? Oh yes. Of course, I get lucky and win a few hands but I'll always go on and give it all back. So, no, I don't have the *occasional good day*. I do get the occasional good hand. You see I don't stop if I'm up a few thousand. Where's the fun in that? What would I do for the next couple of hours? When my last chip has gone, I stop."

"You enjoy losing?" Incredulity was evident in Dex's voice and his frown.

"I enjoy *gambling*. Losing is the price of my pleasure. Can life get better than splitting a pair of tens when the dealer has an ace and beating him twice over? I know its naughty to split tens but that's the buzz. Sometimes, I'll even take a card on 19 just for the sheer hell of it. Because once in a while I'll get a 2 and hit 21."

"Dukes must love you."

"They do. I get a load of freebies—trips to Silverstone, Ascot, Cheltenham. Even Longchamps in Paris. Last week Carmino had a dozen of us up at Wembley to watch England v Germany."

"I watched it. Two nil to us for a change."

"Mick Glenn scored them both. He's a regular in Dukes. Plays big." Adam's lip curled in disdain. "He's a good footballer, but the man's an oik, a noisy oaf. A bad loser, what? I'm sure Dukes only tolerate him because he drops most of his weekly wage."

"What does he play?"

"Roulette. Usually with some popsy wearing what we old fogeys call a pussy-pelmet. When he's losing, his effing and blinding carries round the room." He shook his head so that the remains of his silvery-grey hair rose and fell. "I'm darned if I know what women see in him."

"Maybe his income of £200,000 a week? The bling? The Armani suits, his Lamborghini, his huge pad in North London, the villa in Florida."

Adam took a deep breath. "Put like that… call me old-fashioned. To me, he's just a boorish yobbo who ought to stick to greyhound tracks."

"You ever chatted to Pepe about his background?" Yarbury was still on a roll about the footballer. "Sort of chap who swigs beer from a bottle. Vulgar tattoos on his arms."

Dex laughed. "Adam—you've got to loosen up."

"Fashion and trends pass me by," he guffawed, head rocking back. "But no, whatever his background is or was, he would have a smooth explanation."

"Ever hear him mention Panama?"

"Can't say I have."

"Rumours of how he got his scar?"

"Someone suggested it was over a woman. There again, I also heard he was in a car accident on the M25." Adam pushed the remains of his salad to one side. "But you said this was about *Beth* and Dukes."

"It is. Everything tonight is top, top confidentiality?"

Dex saw the slight hurt on his godfather's face at the suggestion that any conversation would be anything else. "Mum's the word, old chap. Anything you say is strictly *entre nous* – all secret squirrel and Chatham House Rules."

"Beth was cheated – around a million. But she never understood why a casino would need to cheat. Then, someone in the City explained that without Dukes stoking the boilers, Space City would go into Chapter 11."

"Go on, dear boy!"

-23-

Dex floundered as he wrestled with what to say. Adam though waited patiently, ever the true gentleman that he was. Then in a torrent, the story tumbled out. "A poker player recently back from Vegas suggested she meet a dealer with dirt on Pepe Carmino." As Dex rattled through the little that Beth had told him, he found Adam to be a good listener. "She went to meet the dealer but he was shot dead while she was there. And Beth? She had just landed from Vegas when…when she was … killed." He choked on the words and wiped a tear from his eyes. "Was that sheer coincidence? Or was she silenced for finding out too much?"

Adam Yarbury said nothing but his eye movements signalled that the cogs were turning. They closed tightly shut, then opened briefly before closing again. All the while, he swirled the red wine in his glass. "Dex, I don't like the sound of this. Not one little bit." He suggested they attack the ripe stilton before he continued. "A late bet call, eh? That could happen if there was no witness."

"Thanks for that."

"But poking her nose into Pepe Carmino's past?" He shook his head in resignation. "And then asking questions in Vegas. Bad call. Inviting trouble." His eyes fixed on Dex. "Did she meet this Tavio fella?"

Dex selected a crunchy piece of celery to add to the stilton. "I don't know. It wasn't clear. My guess? Yes, she did. That would explain why she was petrified after he was murdered."

"Who knew she was in Vegas? Pepe?"

"Maybe. FB did."

"Nigel Forster-Brown?" The sniffy way Adam said the name showed his disdain. "Pepe's poodle."

"There's something else. Beth gave me password access to all her computerised data but I can't get in."

"You got her laptop back from the police?"

He shook his head. "Gone but backed up in the Cloud."

"Quite beyond me, dear chap. Or perhaps I should say *good heavens above*!" He laughed at his own joke, hands slapping on his knees. "I can't even work a TV remote."

"Anyway, the password doesn't work."

Adam positioned his fingers in front of his lips as if in prayer. "If I get your drift, you think that…?" Dex rocked his head from side to side, so that Adam continued. "Another conspiracy? Beth was another Diana? Murder disguised as an accident?"

Dex spoke slowly and his voice was lowered. "I've no evidence. One helluva coincidence though." He saw his godfather was not instantly dismissive. "The police think the trucker was blinded by the sun and then slammed into Father's stationary limo."

"But you think he was paid to …?" Adam reached for the port decanter, as if in shock. "Has the driver been charged? He survived, didn't he?"

"Yes. No sign of any prosecution. Early days, I guess."

Adam frowned, and scratched behind his large ear. "So, I mean, what's this all about?"

"I promised Beth. She *made* me promise that if anything happened to her, I would not let it rest."

"Let what rest?"

"What she was working on."

"Meaning?"

"Get back her million and bring down Carmino's empire."

Adam gulped and reached for his schooner of port. "And so… your intentions?" His placid features were now creased by a deep frown.

"The same … revenge with knobs on!" Dex's response came quickly. "And I need to know if Beth was murdered."

Adam exhaled a long sigh. "You've always been loyal to a fault. Look where it left you with Caroline and Jamie. Dex, trust me. Please leave it."

"I'm sorry Adam but I can't."

"You need help from me?"

"I don't know yet."

"Do you have a plan?"

"Yes. Listen to this."

– 24 –

"Cheating by dealers then," McKay's commented as he led Dex into the stock room at the back of the shop. Dex took in the roulette wheel with the green baize layout. There was barely room to sit down. Unsold books lay everywhere, stacked in boxes or on metal racks. The air was stale and there was no window, the only light coming from a naked bulb that hung from the ceiling.

"Roulette books used to sell well," McKay explained, waving an arm at the dozens of brown-paper parcels. "But suddenly poker became the rage. That and the on-line book market left me with enough unsellable books on roulette to feed every camel in the Sahara."

Dex shared McKay's resigned laugh as he seated himself on a typist's chair beside the layout, several stacks of chips in front of him. McKay explained that they had a nominal value of one hundred or one thousand pounds each.

"I'll be the dealer," McKay prompted. "I want you to bet ten one-hundred chips on black – that's a thousand pounds in total." He then dropped the ball on 17, a black number on the wheel. "You win! That's an even chance bet and you're paid out equal money. So how much?"

"I staked a grand, so I win a grand." Dex replied after some hesitation.

"The dealer pays your win like this." McKay grabbed a stack of one-hundred cash chips from his side of the layout and pushed them across the green baize. "I now match the height of your stack with mine to pay you ten chips. The casinos call this *sizing into the bet*. Now, watch." Dex did so and saw his single pile of ten chips get matched. "You now have two-grand in front of you—two equal stacks. Correct?"

"Agreed. Two-thousand quid."

"Count them." Dex did so. He stopped at nine and stared across at McKay. "There are only nine chips in each stack. I've only got eighteen hundred. I'm two-hundred short."

McKay nodded, his tic working overtime. "I've just cheated you and you saw nothing." He grinned with satisfaction. "You get a busy table, lots of players chatting, laughing, drinking – some are careless about counting their win. Most would spot if the casino paid them *one* short because the height of the two stacks wouldn't match. That's called a *short stack*. But, done well, this cheating technique called *bumping* is hard to spot and very profitable."

"I'm staggered. What did you do?"

Dex watched as McKay re-created Dex's stack of ten chips. "This is a replay. What I should do is get ten, eleven or even twelve chips and slide them across the layout to match your staked bet." He winked. "What I should do is *to size into* your stake running my finger across both stacks to level them and take away any in excess of ten. Got that?"

McKay saw Dex was with him before carrying on. "What I actually did was to judge your stake at ten chips. I then built a stack of only eight chips which I slid across the table. Done honestly, your winning chips are pushed across, sliding along the green baize. But if I am cheating, I deliver the eight chips holding them slightly raised, like this." He showed the daylight between the bottom chip and the green baize. "This is called *going in high*. When my eight chips are beside your ten, with my hand positioned over the two stacks, I bump the two stacks together so that the bottom one from your stack slides under my eight—and *voila*—both stacks are equal but with only nine in each. Result: the casino saves two hundred quid and too many mug players will never notice."

"In Dukes, Beth said plenty are betting thousands, so cheating would be even more profitable."

"Aye, right enough! If a player does spot the shortage, he'll probably assume it was his own mistake." Dex saw that McKay was enjoying himself as he continued. "Now here's an even more profitable scam." He pointed to Dex's cash chips each worth one-thousand pounds. "Put eight of those on top of the 11 on the layout." When Dex had carefully counted out the chips and positioned them, McKay looked satisfied. "You have bet eight grand. If the ball lands on 11, you win 35 times your stake – a cool £280,000."

McKay then dropped the ball onto 11 on the wheel. "You win, Dex! I don't say this but I know I must pay you £280,000." His grin was sly as he placed a small glass ornament on top of Dex's stake. "That's called the *dolly*. Casinos always place it on top of the chips that have backed the winning number."

Dex nodded and watched intently hoping to spot whatever trick was about to be performed. "Go on."

"Remember that on a busy table, several players may also have bet on 11. You wouldn't necessarily be the only player being paid out. But for this demo, it makes no difference." He lifted the dolly and assessed the chips staked by Dex and then proceeded to gather and count out several large stacks of chips as winnings. Then he pushed them across the baize.

Dex grinned confidently. "You're banking on me not bothering to count them. I'm too lazy to do the maths multiplying 35 times eight thousand. I just accept the winnings without thinking about it."

McKay rewarded him with a silent smile and a wink. "Many do."

Dex smirked. "I'm not falling for that." With a cocky look, he continued. "I'm going to count the winnings." With pedantic care, he did so and ended with a triumphant "Yeah! Caught you! You only paid me £245,000. You owe me another £35,000."

Gus McKay, cocked his head, sparrow-like, to one side. "Aye, even honest casinos make mistakes. Usually the inspector spots them and sorts it." It was now McKay's turn to smirk across the layout. "Go on. What do you do now?"

"I say – hey! You owe me another £35,000. The pay-out should have been £280,000. There's only £245,000 here."

"Let me check again, sir." McKay again lifted the dolly from number 11 and counted out the chips staked. Then he replaced it. "I'm sorry, sir. You only staked seven chips. I correctly paid you 35 times seven thousand equals £245,000. The pay-out is correct."

"Hey. I staked eight chips."

"I'm sorry, sir. You *thought* you staked eight but it was only seven." McKay wiped a watery eye.

"Okay, Gus, I surrender. What did you do?" I *know* I bet eight chips."

McKay grinned. "As I raised the dolly to count your chips staked, I *palmed off* your top chip from the stack. That is, I secreted it out of sight in my palm as I pulled away and replaced the dolly. I then surreptitiously dropped the stolen chip among the hundreds beside me. Net profit of £35,000."

"I'm not satisfied." Dex looked indignant. "I'm sure I bet eight chips. Check the cameras." Dex had barely said the words before he saw the futility and a rueful look filled his face.

McKay nodded. "Of course, we'll check. Then back comes the message: sir, you only staked seven."

McKay moved to his blackjack layout. "Want to learn some more tricks?"

~ 25 ~

Pepe Carmino showed no signs of jet lag after his private jet flight from Vegas to London via Geneva. Indeed, he was feeling exhilarated as he bounded into Dukes. True, the Swiss lawyer's terms had been fierce but within hours, the first hot money would be flowing across the tables downstairs. Carmino locked his office door and slid aside a large original painting of a racehorse by George Stubbs.

He tapped in the code for the safe and from inside removed a box of tricks that controlled his own personal surveillance system. This operated secretly and independent of the official cameras that operated the *Man-in-the-Sky* system. Using old mate Arnie Fisher and two overpaid technicians, he had the restrooms, back-offices, every seat in the bar and every table in the dining room secretly bugged and filmed.

The wizardry had served him well. He had overheard card-counters boasting over dinner. He had tipped off Security to nab a youngster snorting cocaine in the Gents. listened in as Nigel Forster-Brown moaned about him to Terry O'Keefe, the Finance Director. He had heard FB moaning again. That time the moans had been rather different as the camera had caught O'Keefe engaging in a frenetic act of sodomy with FB across the end of his desk. The image of FB's fingers scratching helplessly on the polished wood surface gave Carmino lingering pleasure.

And both of them married men too. Tut-tut! Shocking!

The knowledge had been invaluable. Ever since, both men had

preferred full co-operation with Carmino's plans to the threatened alternative. When not on other *special duties*, Arnie Fisher and an assistant would spend hours checking the recordings and reporting anything of significance. Today, Carmino noticed with a wolfish smile as One-Eye and Jeb Miller pulled the late-bet trick on a wealthy Nigerian diplomat, saving the casino two million. Like Beth, the bent politician had also lost on the following spin.

No witness.

No complaint.

Carmino sucked in his cheeks and laughed as he watched Miller commiserate with the drunken diplomat who shrugged away his bad luck and left the table, swaying slightly as he walked.

Carmino put away his wizardry and called FB. "That footballer Mick Glenn in tonight?"

"He's in the restaurant with a brassy bit of stuff. He told me, *nudge-nudge-wink-wink,* that he won't be playing tonight. He's in tomorrow to play *roully*, as he calls it."

"Make sure that Jeb Miller and One-Eye look after him well." Carmino laughed unpleasantly. After ending the call, he reached deep into the back of the safe and removed a framed photo of himself as a young man. He was wearing flip-flops, a Che Guevara T-shirt and green shorts. Next to him stood a smiling young woman aged about twenty-two, her arm around him. In the background was an ornate church and perched around the roof were several vultures, their backs bent as they watched the scene below. He relived memories of his time dealing blackjack at the Casino Sienna. The young woman had also been a dealer. Scrawled across the foot of the photo in thick blue ink was his caption *Spot the Vulture!*

Looking at the old photo, he could almost smell the sultry heat rising from the Panamanian street. Gently, he stroked the woman's face as he recalled their passion. Slowly, and with obvious reluctance, he removed the photo from its frame. "Time for you to go, Maria." He then raised it to his lips and kissed the smiling face before slowly feeding the picture into the shredder.

− 26 −

About six miles west of Dukes, Tiffany Richmond parked her two-seater Mercedes close to *Who Cares*. She grabbed a bottle of Tuscan red and hurried towards the barge, admiring the clean well-painted look. Before she had time to clamber aboard, Dex had appeared on deck, arms spread out wide in welcome. "Saw you arrive," he explained needlessly. There were two glasses and an open bottle of Tuscan red on a small table. Tiffany recognised the same label at once as she laughingly handed her bottle to him.

Dex grinned. "Great minds, eh?"

"Or maybe coals to Newcastle?"

"Thanks, anyway. I thought we'd eat up here as it's such a beautiful evening. The food's ready."

"My fault. Sorry to be late." She sat down. "The book-signing over-ran."

"Good crowd, then?"

"Above average. Leadenhall Market tonight was great. Earlier, Chiswick High Street was okay. Big turnout expected in Hampstead but after that cloudburst only six turned up. That included a cocker spaniel with a bandaged leg." They caught each other's eyes and laughed.

"Excuse me while I dish up." Dex reappeared moments later with smoked chicken pasta and mixed salad. They settled and chinked glasses. Beside her, Tiffany had her phone, apologising that twenty-four-seven contact went with the territory. Overhead, as the sun started to lower, the few remaining swallows soared and swooped as they caught flies.

Deliberately, Dex had set their chairs so that their view was across the river to avoid passers-by gawping and pointing at Tiffany's well-known face. Behind them was a steady flow of joggers or couples strolling in the warm evening air, some perhaps heading to *The Dove*, further upstream.

As usual, rowing twos, fours and eights zipped by heading for Mortlake or back to the boathouses by Putney Bridge. A police patrol chugged by ready to prevent anyone exceeding the speed limits and the barge rocked gently from its wake. "So do people come because you're a TV personality or because they really do want the book?"

"Probably a bit of both."

"Your name on the cover helps?"

Tiffany accepted the fact with a smile. "Look, not everyone is *that* interested in the plight of the poverty in Africa."

"I am. I bought a signed copy after your visit to Waterstones. I'd read the reviews. You brought the smell of an African village and the wails of distraught kids into our lives. It opened my eyes. Terrific!"

Tiffany did not look embarrassed at the compliment and acknowledged as much with a wave of her fork. "The royalties are pledged to the cause, so you did your bit."

"It's being described as the number one bestseller."

"To be able to make *a real difference* in just one tiny community, the publishers need to sell me big in the USA."

"You're not known there. In the USA, you'll sell on merit."

"Hype too. There's a good PR machine."

Dex saw she had been about to add something. "Go on. There's more, isn't there?"

"I'm to share a platform with former President Bill Clinton in New York during my US tour. He's done so much about the tragedy of Africa."

Dex raised his glass. "I'm impressed. Here's to more success." Even as he toasted her, Dex was contrasting the shallowness of his past two years. "I'd love to support your cause."

"But we're not here to talk about me. Or at least, not about my book."

"A full stomach and some more red may be a good idea before you…"

"Agreed." Tiffany's sudden sad-eyed look showed Dex a hint of her inner thoughts. For the next hour they chatted about his fishing, Ethiopia and occasional amusing incidents from life in front of the camera. It was long after dusk and only after Dex had cleared the plates away that he prompted her to explain her remark at Bladon "You mentioned *solidarity*?"

Tiffany stood up and took a few slow steps to the rail. She motioned him to follow as if standing looking across the murky opaque surface would somehow make it easier. In silence, they gazed at the dark water swirling by. At last, Tiffany spoke but as if drawing deep from a box usually left shut. "Remember the Bromley rail crash?"

-27-

"Bromley? Hard to forget." Dex recalled the headlines well—thirty-one deaths and countless more injured. "Must have been six years ago."

"Six years next December 15th. I was twenty-five." Tiffany stared even harder at the water below. "I lost both parents and my husband Chris. Miraculously, I survived." Even standing so close Dex struggled to hear her.

"I'm sorry. So…"

"When I met you by the wreckage up the road, I knew there were fatalities. That's why I was so unprofessional in becoming emotional. Having been through my own version of hell, I wasn't just sharing your agony but reliving my own." She turned to him and wiped away a tear. "That's why I went to Bladon." They fell into silence, Dex resting his hand on her shoulder. "My message – the important point *for you* is that *I came back* from that dark place."

"But the ache, the pain?"

She shook her head sadly, her short hair barely moving even with the breeze that had just sprung up. He felt her shiver. "Black holes don't turn white. For weeks, months even, I was like a zombie, trying to find a purpose in life. Trying to work out why such dear people should be, oh God, just slaughtered when they had so much good in them."

"And the answer?"

"I've none. Sod's law. Wrong place, wrong time."

"What got you through it?"

"I took a complete break from journalism and went to Africa. Swamped myself in other people's struggle to survive." She closed her eyes as if revisiting famine and the cries of dying children in makeshift hospitals. "Watching starving orphans eat goats' dung." She sighed painfully. "When I came back, I started the book. But I returned to the day job too, filling every waking moment."

"Is that your solution for me too? To get away? A change of scene."

"Only you can answer that." She looked him squarely in the eye. "But whatever you do, immerse yourself in it. Give yourself no brooding time."

They fell silent as Dex weighed up his determination to destroy Dukes. Was that the answer?

It was Tiffany who continued, this time with her cool left hand clasping his wrist on the railing. "Dex, I'm sorry, ashamed even, but I haven't been entirely straight with you." She saw his look of irritation as if he expected her to say she had recorded their conversation.

"This is off the record?" Dex looked concerned.

"Of course. No, it's nothing like that."

"Go on then, shoot!"

− 28 −

"I know far more about you than you might expect."

"Oh?"

"The journalist in me, I suppose. I googled your father. I read Wikipedia and found plenty about his success in property development. But there was no real mention of you and so I was curious. I dug deeper. I tried the newspaper archives and social media." She saw the wary look on Dex's face. "Dex – I know it all, or at least, much of it. Beth wasn't your first tragedy, was it?" She stopped. "I can leave it there if you like."

Dex stood up straight, changing position. "No. Go on. Talking might help. Caroline and Jamie have been a no-go zone. What Father did – that still eats me up." The moon appearing from behind a cloud caught the streaks in Tiffany's hair as Dex's eyes locked onto hers.

She hit it with him straight. "You despise your father. True?"

"His greed destroyed my life."

"I read the planning documents. You might feel better talking about it."

"Father wanted to build a superstore in Camberley. What stood in the way was land belonging to my company. We manufactured autospares. I was the CEO. I had built it up to over eighty employees. But to grow the company, I'd made a big mistake. I brought in venture capitalists from the City. Foolishly, I became a minority shareholder dancing to their tune." He paused, looking at her in the half-light but other than a slight nod of encouragement, she said nothing. "When I told Father to take a hike, he could have found somewhere else." The head-shake was vehement. "No. He wanted revenge. He vowed to crush me."

"No doubt the VC guys jumped at a generous offer?"

Dex nodded. "I had despised him for many years anyway – for abusing Mother besides knocking me and Beth about when we were kids."

"So, your father bought your company?"

"It made no economic sense. He closed it down. Sheer spite. All jobs lost. That was just for starters. He then deliberately turned the staff against me by starting false rumours."

"Such as?"

"I was accepting top-dog status in his property company. I hadn't cared about the employees losing jobs. Oh, and that I had received a secret multi-million backhander into an offshore bank account. All rubbish. Pure fiction."

"That type of gossip spreads fast."

"Like lightning. The factory-floor workers were outraged. Redundancy money is not a job. Feelings boiled over. My denials were mocked in social media."

"The baying mob wanted a scapegoat?"

"Lynch-mob mentality ruled." Dex faltered, struggling with his emotions. "Caroline, me, and Jamie lived in a remote cottage. One day the word *Judas* was spray-painted across the front. I confronted Father – pleaded with him to quash the rumours." Dex ran his fingers down his cheek. "He refused."

"The bastard." Tiffany's vehemence shone through although the words were almost whispered.

"There's worse yet." Dex spoke slowly, dragging each word from a deep pit "One night I returned from a meeting. It was just after eleven. As I drove along our lane, I saw the cottage was ablaze, the 16th century timbers burning fiercely from top to bottom." He gripped the railings at the recollection. "The fire brigade hadn't arrived but a neighbour across the fields had dialled 999."

"Go on ... if you want?" She squeezed his wrist.

"Somehow, I forced my way in but it was hopeless. The wooden stairs were an inferno. There was no sign or sound of Caroline or Jamie. The roar of the flames and the thick smoke masked everything." He gripped the rail and Tiffany could feel him shaking as past memories tore him apart. "It was impossible." Dex shuddered, not even noticing Tiffany's consoling arm wrapped across his back.

"It was arson?"

"They smashed the windows with rocks and had lobbed in Molotov cocktails both upstairs and down."

"They?"

"Persons unknown. The entire workforce was suspect – call it eighty in the frame. All had alibis but one or more of them had fixed the arsonist. The police never charged anyone." He glanced down and sideways at her, his eyes moist.

"And now ... Beth."

He nodded. "Beth *was* murdered too. I can't prove it – but I bet she was."

Dex saw her mouth drop open. "Who would want Beth dead? Or was your father the target?"

"Beth," Dex mumbled as she removed her arm and turned so that the warmth of her body gently touched him. "Dex, you may be right." She took in his stunned look. "It's getting chilly. Can we go inside? Have some coffee, perhaps? I'll explain."

29

Down below in the cabin, the air was scented by a pair of vanilla spice candles that flickered as they entered. The twin table lights were dimmed and Tiffany was quick to take in an atmosphere of cosy seduction. The door to his bedroom was open, revealing the double bed and a small nightlight that burned from floor level. Feeling sheepish, Dex shut the bedroom door, closed the burnished gold curtains in the galley and motioned her to sit on the sofa.

"Getting a bit ahead of yourself, were you?" It was the sharp directness of the professional journalist but the dig was said with an amused raised eyebrow. Dex's flustered eye movement revealed his guilt at being caught with his hand in the cookie jar. His surrender was accompanied by a sickly grin. Tiffany laughed. "You're not the first optimist! Even after six years and the rutting stags at the studios, I'm in no hurry. I need to know if a book is as good as its cover."

"Me? These days, I'm a well-thumbed library book but always returned within fourteen days." He enjoyed seeing Tiffany laugh but was keen to change the drift of the conversation. "Anyway, how do take your coffee?"

She wanted it black. He watched as she prowled around the narrow room taking in everything with the keen eye of a journalist and bestselling author. When her comment came, it was not what he expected. He thought she would mock him about Princes Diana.

"For someone on the Sunday Times Rich List, you live a pretty simple lifestyle. Why?"

Dex coloured at her mention of his wealth before trying to create a worthwhile soundbite. He watched the percolator on the hob erupting with satisfying plops before speaking. "To Father, making money is or was everything. Winning, screwing his rivals, was his only goal." Dex looked across at Tiffany, his eyes showing his contempt. "After becoming a billionaire, he never *needed* more but always *wanted* it." He offered her crackers and cheese but she declined. "I kicked back at the nastiness he stood for. Unlike him, I treated my employees like friends. I respected people. It really hurt when he turned them against me."

"You thought loyalty worked both ways?"

"The staff believed Facebook and Twitter rather than me." He poured out two mugs. "I'm on the Rich List from family trusts that my grandfather set up years ago. I never needed to work but I wanted to be entrepreneurial. I started the autospares business with Caroline. That was our life, not living off inherited wealth. To me, looking after the workforce and expanding our markets was worth far more."

"You've been very ill? Right?"

He handed her a chunky red and white mug before seating himself about as far along the sofa as he could, something Tiffany noticed with a broad grin as she edged nearer. In return, Dex smiled uneasily as he wondered if there was anything she had not uncovered about him. "It's been tough."

"Your two whiteboards. One is full of JFK's assassination and the other all about the Alma Tunnel. Do I sense a conspiracy theorist?" The heavy sarcasm was not lost on Dex.

"I hate being duped by the Establishment. You don't buy into conspiracies?"

"Like Elvis is alive and well and living in Fulham?" As she laughed, she revealed her beautifully white teeth. "No. But I accept no facts till proven or corroborated." Tiffany's tone suddenly turned sharper. "Beth's death? Your conspiracy theory?"

Dex saw that she was not mocking him but the directness caught him unprepared. He thought of McKay's warning. "I'm sorry, Tiffany but I'm not quite ready to bare everything to you."

"You're an enigma and I'm intrigued. The more I surfed, the more layers of a large onion I unpeeled. I understand now your dislike of the media and disdain for the police." She speared him with an intense yet supportive look.

"After the fire, the trolls and media changed to my side. Supporting me made for a good story. That made it worse." His eyes welled up. "Too bloody late for crocodile tears when I had to bury my family."

"I'm fine about you not sharing about your sister. Remember though, I'm here as a friend, a kindred spirit and not as Tiffany Richmond hunting for a scoop."

"I do trust you – but you had something for me. *You* thought I might be right about Beth."

She turned from profile to full face to catch his attention before pulling up her knees to hug them. Her phone bleeped as yet another text arrived and she glanced briefly at the screen, plainly irritated at being interrupted. She turned back to him. "I've been monitoring the accident. My sources suggest the driver of the truck gave a false name, a non-existent address and produced a fake driving licence. Currently, he is untraceable." She was rewarded with a low whistle as the implications sank in. "Of course, he might have been an illegal immigrant. That *might* explain it."

Dex stared at the black carpet with its deep red piping. Neither said a word as Dex adjusted to the stunning news. Except for the ticking clock and the swish of the river outside, the silence was total. "The police have never even hinted at that." He reached over to touch her knee. "I'm glad you told me but in a strange way, I didn't want to hear that. I'd rather my paranoia had been wrong."

She placed her hand on where his was still resting "Scary, isn't it?"

Had the cabin been larger, Dex would have paced around. As it was, Tiffany could sense his strife. When he spoke, it was as if he were thinking aloud. "Pepe Carmino, you'll pay for this."

It was Tiffany's turn to look puzzled. "Pepe Carmino? *Who* is that?"

"Top, top secret. Off the record."

She laughed. "I'm a journalist. Trust me."

Dex smiled as he stroked his chin thoughtfully and then started to speak.

-30-

Dex had been awake since five but a glance outside had convinced him that sitting under an umbrella beside a windswept pond had little to commend it. The big plus was that a second night had passed without nightmares. He was even feeling better by day without Grierson's pills coursing through him.

After a tasty fry-up, he cleared the table and set up his new purchase of a roulette wheel and chips, his notes about Reverse Labouchère beside him. On his laptop, he saved a page as CASINO but then on impulse changed it to ONISAC. Fired up by reading about Norman Leigh's huge win in Nice, he spun one-hundred times, placing chips on red and black in ever differing amounts with the outcomes recorded on his laptop.

Shit!

Down twenty-three thousand.

But Gus McKay had warned him about patience, so he reached for another book about casino scams. For nearly an hour, he read and re-read the pages on roulette, excited by what he was learning.

With Tiffany arranging her American book tour and with no other plans, he called Adam. "You've nominated me already for membership? Thanks. Yes, dinner there tonight – but not a loose word." He returned to his laptop and tried again to access Beth's back-up programme. As he typed GADECH, which he assumed was her username, he wondered why she bothered with such complex passwords. He had *dexdexter* as a username and *who-cares* for his password, though often he never bothered. He tapped in her password, ZAYBXCWB and then tried by reversing it. Neither worked.

Access Refused!

An online chat with a techie guru about the Cloud proved a waste of over thirty minutes. The company who had provided back-up for Beth's laptop wanted proof of death; proof he was next of kin and a Grant of Probate before even considering helping. Given the speed that solicitors moved, he'd be collecting his pension before probate was granted. He was still scowling when his phone rang. "Yes? Oh thanks." His face brightened. It was international enquiry agents in Bruton Street. "Is that right? You've traced her in Panama? Maria-Elena Sanchez? A blackjack dealer?"

When the call ended, he felt elated at the first big break. But seconds later, a chilling dose of reality hit him.

What am I getting into?
Who ordered the contract-killing?
What would Tavio's sister know?
Could he trust her?
Would she blab after meeting him?

Did she even know her brother was dead – two bullets – one in the head, one in the chest.

Where did she fit into Pepe Carmino's life? Was she still in touch with him? He looked angrily at the words *Access Denied*. All the answers would be there if only her password would work.

He downed a second cup of coffee and grabbed his phone. After more hesitation, he dialled a travel agent on King Street. "Book me a return to Panama. First Class."

I hope I'll need the return segment.
And tonight?
Face Carmino?
Maybe.

Had he known the course he had now set, Dex might have stuck to fishing.

-31-

Whereas less eminent casinos welcomed all-comers ready to lose their weekly wad without membership, Dukes was members-only. Joining had cost Dex £25,000.00 plus having to deposit one million to be held for him in the casino cage. At shortly before 7:30 p.m., he stepped out of the taxi in Mount Street and looked up at his new club. Dukes occupied an imposing five-storey red-brick building, approached by a flight of stone steps. It stood not far from Scott's restaurant and dated back to the eighteenth century. No doubt it had once been home for a lord and lady, with the servants crammed into the basement below street level. The casino had been around for some forty years but Beth reckoned that Carmino had owned it for only five.

Tom, the doorman, touched his black and burgundy top hat in greeting. With his matching frock coat, his image was proof enough that inside was something rather special. No Chinese waiters wearing cheap flip-flops and without socks had ever played in Dukes. They would never even reach the sweep of the staircase down to the gaming-room. Tom would see to that.

The mass-market Chinese gamblers thronged the casinos near Chinatown behind Leicester Square. There, ten or twelve players might be pushing and jostling to place a two-pound bet on their favourite number. Dukes was so very different. Beth had told him that sometimes, there might be just one or two oligarchs betting their millions.

Dex breezed through the heavy black door to be met by the sweet, sickly smell of newly laid carpeting. As he walked down the wide sweeping curve of the stairs, he glanced at the 18th century paintings of rural scenes. Everything was immaculate, classic in style and with ornate gilt to a fault. The décor was French but morphed by a touch of Arabesque styling. At the foot of the stairs, he signed-in at Reception, surrounded by *objets d'art*, giant mirrors and a tasteful mix of original paintings and quality drapes.

In here, Dex felt closeted in a world of serious gambling. Could something so impressive, really be as bent as Beth had believed?

Dex glanced into the restaurant and then peeked at the gaming floor where, in absolute silence, about a dozen members were playing roulette, blackjack or baccarat. He recognised a brilliantined Saudi prince in his *oh-so-western* Ravazzolo suit as he strolled from the roulette, massaging his knuckles as he walked. Dex then saw a tall and slightly stooped figure slip effortlessly between the tables, shooting his cuffs as he did so. With a deferential smile and a slight bow, he escorted the prince to a discreet corner table in the restaurant. *Could the stooped figure be FB?*

He entered the book-lined bar where the Spanish bartender mixed him a spicy Bloody Mary which he placed on a small occasional table. Then, on a silver tray, he was delivered smoked-salmon canapés, a dish of large green and black olives, a pot of crispy biscuits and a side dish of caviar with a tiny silver spoon. Dex had barely sipped his drink before Adam Yarbury entered with the tall but slightly stooped figure he had seen earlier. It was indeed Nigel Forster-Brown. FB was wearing the inevitable black bow tie and dinner jacket. With difficulty, Dex forced a smile as he stood up to shake hands.

"FB, this is Finlay Dexter, brother to dear Beth. I'm his godfather."

Dex gave a very self-assured nod. "Generally, I'm called Dex."

FB stared at the floor, then the wall and then back to the floor again. He was tall, almost bald with a pale pink complexion and a nondescript, forgettable face. It was neither ugly nor handsome, just plain forgettable. It contained no features that made any impression at all. He exuded an air of weary resignation and Dex wondered if he was henpecked at home and bullied at work.

"Mr. Dexter, I am so very sorry. We all *adored* your sister. She was a real charmer." FB flicked an upward look but then quickly returned to staring at the carpet. "A true delight and a sad loss for all."

Dex nodded appreciation as Adam intervened. "FB, if you don't mind me saying so, you're looking rather tired, a trifle jaded."

"Overwork. The usual. Like any business, we always have to work harder for the next buck than the previous one."

"How long till you retire? Not that I'm trying to get rid of you." Adam's trademark laugh was always toothy and this was no exception.

FB looked thoughtful, playing with his hands in front of him before replying. "Two years that will seem like a life sentence. Since the recession, the fun seems to have disappeared."

Adam Yarbury nodded in sympathy. "But when you retire? Devon you once mentioned."

"Correct. A cottage near Dartmouth."

"Sea fishing or sailing?" prompted Dex.

FB managed a weak smile. "Mr. D. I'm a Capricorn – a landlubber." He examined his immaculate black lace-up shoes. "When I retire, I'll continue playing around with computers, writing programmes, y'know the sort of thing."

Dex could now see *nerd* written big across FB's forehead. "Ah! You're a computer geek! That must be fun," he said thinking quite the reverse.

"Microchips beat casino chips any day." It was a line he had often used. "Mr. Y. I saw you had a table booked for dinner. And after that?" The question seemed to be aimed at Dex but their eyes never met.

"I may play roulette," responded Dex. "Unlike Beth, I'm a novice, so maybe I'll just watch for a while."

FB thought of the one million just deposited with the casino. "Of course. Play whenever you feel, er, comfortable." His bleeper summoned him. "Ah! Mr Carmino wants me. Well…enjoy your evening."

-32-

"**I'm moving back** to the family home to look after Father." Until this bombshell, Dex and Adam had been chatting trivia about gambling, horses and fishing. The bottle of Chambolle Musigny was empty. Coffee had just been served.

"Back to St John's Wood? Right by Lord's Cricket Ground. That's a plus." Then Adam's tone turned serious. "But surely …"

Dex raised his hands defensively. "Despite everything, I can't dump him in a care home. Not without trying to do the decent thing first."

Adam looked doubtful. "Charles doesn't deserve decency. Excuse my French but his greed turned him into a total shit. Anyway, how will you look after him?"

"A carer, maybe more than one."

"They're discharging him already?"

"Father's not likely to improve – something called the Glasgow Scale. It measures the severity of the trauma and guides consultants about recovery."

"I never thought you would forgive him."

Dex sighed. "I'll never forget."

"Shall we?" Adam rose from the table, flicking some crumbly cheese from his Savile Row three-piece as he did so. Dex followed him toward the gaming floor while upstairs, Pepe Carmino switched off the feed from the microphone.

Why would Beth's brother join?
She'd once said he was risk-averse.

Was he suspicious?

He bleeped Forster-Brown. "FB? Keep a close watch on Dexter." Stroking his chin and head down, he walked slowly to his walk-in dressing room where he changed from slacks and button-down shirt into his dinner jacket to appear downstairs. By the time he had adjusted his bow-tie, he had a plan. He knew just the person to help over Dexter.

If she would.

-33-

Adam Yarbury bought in at a blackjack table leaving Dex to watch the roulette. There were three roulette players, one being a loud-mouthed American from Houston. The others were from somewhere around the Far East. They were quiet and respectful to the dealer they called One-Eye. None of them were playing the even chance bets of red/black, high/low or odd/even numbers. All were stacking mini-skyscrapers of chips all over the layout and between the three of them, backing almost every number.

Dex tried to monitor One-Eye's fast-moving hands as he placed the dolly, counted out the stacked chips and paid out huge sums at thirty-five times the bet staked. After watching eight or nine spins, Dex had spotted nothing suspicious. But McKay had been right. None of the players was obsessively concerned to check the winnings. They merely glanced at the high-value cash chips, often worth £100,000 each, that sat on the coloured chips below. All three were more concerned to scatter their next bets around the layout.

"It's Finlay Dexter, isn't it?" The voice from over his shoulder startled Dex from his thoughts. Though the tone was silky smooth, Dex spotted a trace of Essex hidden beneath the urbane charm. Dex twisted to find himself confronted by Pepe Carmino. It was a shock seeing the man in the flesh again. "Pepe Carmino. We did meet a few months ago. Now I understand you've joined. Thank you and welcome." Carmino extended a hand in greeting.

-34-

Dex accepted the offer of Carmino's hand, uncomfortable at showing any sign of civility. *Is this the man who had Tavio gunned down and his sister murdered?* As their hands met, he noticed the cold silkiness of the grip from the slender fingers. Hypocrisy did not come easily but he forced himself to be civil. "My late sister signed me in as a guest."

"Everyone here, we was just devastated at the tragedy. The floral tribute was just a small token of our feelings." Dex relived the moment when the wreath had skimmed the churchyard wall and felt his blood run hot and cold.

Say nothing controversial. Stay on message, he forced himself. "Tragic. Beth had so much to live for."

"From memory, I think you never played the tables?"

"Not tonight either. I've been watching. Roulette seems confusing. I need to get the hang of this scene. Adam's helping me."

"May I lay on something to drink? Some Dom Pérignon perhaps? Krug? A Highland malt?"

"Not now, thanks. I may play blackjack. That's easier but before she, er, ... died ... Beth wanted me to learn Reverse Labouchère. She wanted us to play together, backing red and black." The lie came easily.

Carmino thoughtfully stroked his jagged scar. "Interesting system. You need to risk big, big money. Your late sister played the Martingale doubling up losing bets. Players often win most of the time." He pursed his lips and sucked in his breath. "But when it goes wrong, it bites big time."

"A good staking system changes the odds," Dex commented. He knew from McKay that he was talking bollocks but wanted to play the village idiot.

Carmino's hand movements suggested the jury was out on that. "Every system works sometimes. None work all the time." He turned to leave but then added, "I'm not always here because I'm busy with Space City but FB will always look after you."

"Beth reckoned Space City was your millstone." Dex fixed Carmino with full-on eye contact.

Carmino's smile was patronising yet Dex noticed a flash of menace. "Scarcely a millstone Mr D. We see it as a *gemstone*, the jewel in our crown."

Dex wanted to retort but resisted. "Exciting concept anyway. Well, I must watch Adam. I need to brush up on my pontoon days. Adam's mentoring me."

Carmino turned to leave, concealing a smirk at *anyone* learning from that bumbling loser.

Dex positioned himself behind Adam Yarbury who was laughing with pleasure. "Dex. See my cards, an 8 and a 9. I should stick at 17. The dealer has a 5, a bad card. No sane person would take another card on 17. But where's the excitement?" He turned to the dealer. "Card please." He was dealt a 4 giving him a perfect 21. Adam hooted with laughter as the dealer turned over a ten and then another 5. "See, with his 20, I'd have lost if I'd stuck on 17. Exciting or what? Such fun."

Dex joined in the laughter as the dealer prepared to shuffle. Then he felt his phone vibrating. His face lit up when he heard Tiffany's voice. "I've finished early. Fancy a drink?"

"I'm in Dukes. There's a bar here. I'll sign you in as a guest."

"Do I have to play? Remember, I'm a convent girl. Betting on a ball landing on red or black is my idea of madness."

"Madness is not compulsory. See you soon."

It was barely forty minutes later when he led her into the bar. The Spaniard suggested specialty cocktails but both went for soft drinks, Dex feeling smug at his continued moderation. As if by chance, Pepe Carmino appeared. Dex forced himself to make an introduction. "Mr. Carmino. This is Tiffany Richmond, a good friend."

Carmino leaned forward to kiss her hand. "Pepe Carmino. Miss Richmond, such a pleasure. I finished your book on a flight to Las Vegas. Very moving. Punchy stuff."

Dex resented that Carmino had charmed her but loved spotting that he had used Botox on his forehead. Compared to the photo on the website, his forehead was now a wrinkle-free zone. But the scar on his right cheek remained. As Carmino small-talked Tiffany about her work, his hands were at ease, his movements relaxed and he exuded an aura of a tea-matinée playboy. "Come on, Tiffany. We can take the drinks over to the roulette. I'm keen to get the hang of it."

"Do visit us again, Miss Richmond. Perhaps dinner with me?"

"I'd like that. Thank you." Tiffany watched him as he slithered to another table to chat to an Indian couple. "Sexy bastard, isn't he?" She whispered. "There's something edgy about him. Perhaps it's that scar. Is he married?"

Dex was irritated at her readiness to accept dinner and his cheeks had flushed. "Married? I don't know. But gallant to a fault I'm sure." His sarcasm was not lost on Tiffany. They left the bar pausing only to look at the artwork and figurines.

"The décor – too grand. It's overpowering," Tiffany volunteered. "Reminds me of the Palace of Versailles. Awesome but after a couple of days living there as the King's mistress, I'd have run screaming to a cave. I prefer everything simpler."

"Carmino caters for Middle Eastern or Oriental tastes. Everything implies unlimited wealth." He guided her towards the tables. They were comfortably busy and soft chatter greeted them along with the hypnotic hiss of the balls circling the wheels. From the baccarat, Dex heard someone saying *Pay the Bank*.

"The entertainment industry is full of Carminos."

"He's an Essex boy," Dex prompted, as if that explained everything. He leaned over and whispered in her ear, her fragrance pleasingly intense. "Remember – no loose talk." She smiled a response as they reached the roulette. Dex looked at the players. "FB told me earlier. The two women are in that reality TV programme *Party Girls Abroad*. B-List Celebs. They're with Mick Glenn, the footballer and Scotty Brannigan the American Formula One racing legend."

Tiffany raised an eyebrow. "I'd know Amber Murray a mile off. She's the blonde stroking Mick's thigh." She spoke quietly, her mouth close to his cheek. "Does that idiot Glenn have a death-wish?"

35

Dex flinched. "Death-wish? What do you mean?"
"Amber is shacked up with Creole Henry. Has been for months."

"What!" Dex managed to muffle his shocked response. Creole Henry was Jamaican and a kingpin Yardie. Even the broadsheets had profiled him – the dreadlocked playboy in a designer suit and dripping in bling. Behind him were failed prosecutions for murder but a string of convictions for extreme violence. "Glenn must be an even bigger tosser than Adam Yarbury warned me."

"If Creole finds out, Amber's going to need a plastic surgeon."

"That's if she's lucky." Dex nodded and then turned to the revolving wheel. "Let's watch. Mick's playing big money. His orange chips are worth one-hundred each. There's at least ten thousand riding on this spin." He pointed to the 0. "Five orange chips just backing zero. He could win £17,500 but he'd still lose nearly all his £10,000."

And Scotty?"

"He's only playing on red or black – the outside bets. Like Beth did."

Glenn tossed the two women a few cash chips. "Here you are, you little ravers. Have some fun with these."

"No more bets." One-Eye waved his hands across and above the layout.

Dex pointed to the portly figure perched on a high stool at the head of the table. "That tub of lard is Jeb Miller," he whispered.

"18. Red. Even." One-Eye's clockwork English was followed by him sweeping the mass of losing chips into the hole that fed the chipper-machine. Despite covering most numbers, Mick Glenn had lost. Brannigan, using blue chips each worth a thousand, had also lost but only three grand.

Glenn glared at the stick-thin dealer with the big black-framed glasses. "Give over, mate!" One-Eye ignored the comment. "Only backed thirty-three bleedin' numbers, didn't I? Last spin was 22. Now 18. Next door. Only four numbers could lose. That's the second time you've done me over. That is seriously out of order. Shake it up a bit. This place spooks me. Bleedin' magnets in the wheel. 'S-all rigged."

One-Eye shrugged at a loser's typical rant. "The wheel has no memory, Mistah G."

"And we don't use magnets," chortled Miller, trying to add some frivolity.

Brannigan leaned towards his pal whose physique towered above him. "Don't shoot the messenger, buddy." He was amused at Glenn's mounting frustration but under his bullet-head, the footballer's part-shaved face just scowled. "Right now," Scotty continued. "I couldn't hit a dead fly with a banjo – let alone place a winning bet! It'll change. It always does … if you don't go bust first."

Dex watched the compact but fit-looking racing driver double up his previous lost stake and switch to backing red. Meanwhile Mick Glenn had backed thirty-three numbers but this time his orange chips were stacked even higher. "Over twenty grand," Dex pointed. "Looks like the Manhattan skyline out there, doesn't it?" he whispered. Tiffany responded with a despairing shrug and a raised eyebrow.

"No more bets." The ball slowed and dropped. It appeared to land on 22 Black before slowly edging next door. One-Eye spoke like a metronome. "9. Red. Odd." He swept away every one of Glenn's towers.

"Shit! It was bleeding 9, then 22, 18 and now 9 again. All next to each other. Three numbers I ain't bet on."

"Cool it," prompted Brannigan while the two women sipped cocktails with no interest.

"One-Eye, you fixed this, screwing me. I'm down thirty-five grand." He scowled at Miller. "Get this dealer changed. Send him back to China, send him anywhere. A slow boat." Miller ignored him, simply fingering his over-sized moustache. "Yeah, yeah." Glenn burbled on. "Don't say nothing, Miller. Your toad-like face tells me. Your Christmas bonus is the winner. Well I ain't your turkey."

Scotty Brannigan scooped up his winnings and glared. "Shut the fuck up, Mick! Big boys don't gripe. What you've lost – just an hour's training anyway – a few throw-ins and two free kicks. So quit the shit, big fella."

Mick was unreceptive. "When I'm losin', I'll fuckin' gripe until my bollocks fall off. Hey! You! One-Eye! Don't spin yet. I ain't ready. Gotta get more cash."

When Mick returned from the casino's cage, he had plaques worth one hundred thousand. These he changed into chips. Dex and Tiffany exchanged glances as Mick tossed forty thousand around the layout. "Spin me up an' watch me clean you out!" He glared at One-Eye and then kissed a giggling Amber.

Tiffany craned forward to watch the ball. The only sound now was its relentless hiss. The ball teased 22 again before skittering like a stone across the waves. "1. Red. Odd." It was not far from the previous clutch of numbers.

"Done it! I've done it!" Mick's relief was obvious. There was sweat dripping down his muscular neck and his victory snort sounded like a racehorse. In contrast, Scotty Brannigan, who had staked twenty chips on red, showed all the coolness he used when cornering at 160 mph on a wet track at Spa.

"How much will Mick win?" Tiffany prompted.

-36-

Tiffany watched Dex scratch his ear as he did his multiplication. "Thirty-five times his stake of fifteen chips, he wins £52,500. But he still lost £38,500 on his losing numbers. Net profit of £14,000. He needs to win the next two or three spins to recover what he's lost." Dex fell silent, watching the dealer pay out Brannigan's even-chance win of twenty stacked chips. One-Eye assembled his own stack to push across.

Surely, it was raised above the green baize.

As Glenn accelerated into his brash swinging-dick mode, tThe American was too busy grinning at the bottle-blonde next to him to be watching as One-Eye paid him out while. The two stacks came together and Dex did a double-take as he saw a small, sharp but definite movement. Coming in high and bumping had moved Brannigan's bottom chip across to the winnings. One-Eye's forefinger ran across the two stacks. They were of equal height.

Trying to look casual, Dex counted a stack – just nineteen. Whilst Brannigan ordered Sambucas, One-Eye had just cheated him of two-thousand. Tiffany spotted something in Dex's body language, a question apparent in her face. "What's up?" The pleasure of her mouth deliciously close to his ear was lost on him.

"Leave it!" Dex hissed as he forced a friendly smile. He turned back to watch One-Eye again. The dolly was sitting on Glenn's fifteen orange chips but Glenn was far more involved with chugging down a beer while caressing Amber's pert buttocks. Then, after pulling her close for a smooch and snog, he followed up with a noisy belch. "Better up than down," he laughed.

One-Eye broke the orange chips into a tower of three groups of five. The cameras could now verify the stake. "Five-Twenty-Five orange."

"Yes." Miller approved as One-Eye prepared to pay out £52,500.

"What would you like, Mistah G?" enquired the dealer in his robotic style as if he were taking orders in a Chinese takeaway. "Mebbe four purples, some golds, a few pinks and the rest in orange?"

"No. Give us all cash chips. No orange." Mick turned to Amber. "This is where I win big using them golds. They're one thousand each. The purples is ten grand. The pinks is one hundred nicker." He whispered something in Amber's ear and she responded with a poke in the ribs. Dex caught the dirty chuckle as he turned to Tiffany. "Using the golds, he can cover twenty-two numbers, plus leaving his winning orange chips left on number 1. With thirty-seven numbers on the wheel, that still leaves him fourteen losing ones." He watched One-Eye count out the winning chips. They seemed to be correct. As the footballer continued boasting what he was going to do to Amber later, One-Eye steered the winnings towards him. He pushed with his left hand, steadying them with his right on top. Then he withdrew his hands leaving the winnings in front of Glenn.

Christ! I saw that flash of gold.

Under One-Eye's right hand as he drew away, Dex had glimpsed a gold chip. One-thousand pounds had been palmed – surreptitiously stolen from the winnings.

As Glenn scattered his golds around the layout, Dex was counting. There were just twenty-one gold chips – definitely one short.

One-Eye spun the wheel and the ball rolled to a halt on 31 Black – a losing number. Glenn thumped the table angrily. "Heh! Chinky! You're getting' on me tits! 'Ere. Change these for more gold." He pushed the three purples worth thirty grand across the table.

"Well I'm doin' jus' great now," Brannigan tactlessly volunteered. "These kind folk keep givin' me money."

"Shall we sit down," Dex suggested realising that next time, he needed a hidden camera. As he turned away, Dex acknowledged Carmino who had been watching from behind them. In particular, he had been admiring Tiffany's black stockings and the tasselled purple dress, so different from her no-nonsense television image.

"Not tempted then, Mr. D?" Carmino fell into step with them as they left the room.

"Too much to learn. These different coloured chips. Confusing."

"Some drinks," Carmino suggested, adjusting his bow-tie while flashing his teeth and cufflinks simultaneously. "I have an excellent table." He walked them into the bar and settled them at a thick-cushioned settee for two. "Champagne cocktails?" On hearing their agreement, he organized the drinks but then excused himself and headed for his office.

Dex draped an arm across the back of the settee as he offered Tiffany a choice of Belgian chocolates or canapés. "Enjoy that in there?"

"Pure theatre! Glenn is something else!" Tiffany helped herself to a dark chocolate. "So, when are you going to Pa…"

Horrified, Dex jumped in quickly. "To Park Royal? He improvised, hoping that any listener would be fooled. "Tomorrow probably. It's a care home I was recommended but my advert has produced a few applicants. The Bistbury, a specialist unit up in Northampton even contacted me. I'll keep all options open."

"Wouldn't the Bistbury be best?"

Dex looked serious. "I'm not sure. The consultant likes the idea of home environment and daily stimulation, y'know, see how it goes."

Tiffany's face turned toward him, her voice lowered. "What was the matter in there?"

"What I saw…" His voice trailed away as he tried to recover from blurting out an answer. "Shock, mainly. The way Mick Glenn was chucking away money. I kept thinking of those kids in Africa eating shit to survive."

"Me too. Crazy him losing so much. I'll tell you what surprised me though. Everything the dealer did, the fat guy with the moustache checked. Then there was that thuggish looking guy who kept patrolling. Not much trust around, is there?"

"Everybody is watching everybody. Beth told me that one day, the cameras had saved her. Some Peruvian guy had claimed her winnings! The cameras sorted that out." They clinked glasses as Dex enjoyed a moment rewriting history.

Just in case their conversation was being recorded.

-37-

Locked in his office, Carmino produced his box of tricks from the safe. From an array of settings, he selected one. At once, the conversation from the settee was live, picked up from microphones in the armrests. The hidden lens, built into the wall fabric, missed nothing either.

The dimmed wall lights and comfy chairs in the bar encouraged intimate exchanges, not least from guests relaxing on the settee. Carmino listened and watched. She was asking about him going to? To where? Was that concern before he wittered on about Park Royal? From the camera's angle, it was hard to be sure. *Was she about to say Panama?*

Carmino continued listening to the chatter. "What was the matter in there?"

Then came Dexter's reply. "What I saw…" Then there was a pause, maybe a tad too long before Dexter had continued about Mick Glenn and starving kids? Wondering if he were becoming paranoid, Carmino poured himself an Otard Napoleon brandy, larger than normal for this stage of the evening. Then he selected a Padron cigar from his humidor. The cameras and recordings continued.

What's that she's saying about going to America?

"Because of my US Tour, don't build your hopes or plans round me." He watched her touch his hand. "It's a long trip." The mikes fell silent as the camera captured disappointment on Dexter's face. Carmino stretched his arms back above his head and yawned.

Nothing to suggest Beth had briefed Dex about late bets or her trip to Vegas.

He watched them draining their drinks to leave. Carmino switched off and stretched out on his recliner. Then he tapped off the cigar ash. Like everything he did, even this simple act was delicate. The dollop fell unbroken with precision. Care in everything was his creed. Leave nothing to chance.

He thought of a call from earlier in the evening.

A sinister smile crossed his face.

Plenty to smile about.

-38-

As their taxi splashed its route past Harrods, Dex made sure the driver could not overhear their conversation. "Beth was right. I spotted deliberate cheating. What I saw tonight, even without *late bet* calls, could save Dukes tens of millions a year, possibly even one-fifty million."

"You're kidding me, Dex. I didn't notice anything." She wiped the condensation off the window as she gathered her thoughts. "*That* makes cheating worthwhile. *Now*, Beth's concerns make sense."

"From just one spin, One-Eye stole two thousand from Scotty Brannigan – okay that's peanuts. Every day, on just one table, assume only three hundred spins. If they can steal on just fifty of them, that's one hundred thousand. Multiply that by four working roulette tables and you're looking at four hundred thousand a day, or nearly three million a week."

"Equals one-fifty million." Tiffany's enthusiasm seemed to be growing. Her nostrils twitched as she thought it through.

"That's beside stealing from Glenn and whatever else they do on blackjack." He shook his head sadly. "I bet they rob dear old Adam Yarbury something rotten."

"Sorry for nearly landing you in it about Panama. It's hard to believe they may hear every word."

"We don't know that. Just better we play safe."

Tiffany shimmied along the seat to face him better, a puzzled look obvious. "Dex, they must be very desperate to take these risks. You'd need to prove that."

The taxi swerved around a cyclist and their bodies touched. "There's more," he added. "Earlier on, I'd seen a dealer called Andy palm a chip worth one-thousand off a South African's winning stake. That's much more lucrative. On just one spin, that trick saved the casino thirty-five thousand."

"You spotted that?" Tiffany squeezed his arm and sounded impressed. "That leaves one-fifty million a year for dead." She flourished her hand. "Could this just be the dealers stealing? Nothing to do with Carmino."

"One-Eye didn't palm the gold chip for himself. Plus the late bet trick? This is an orchestrated fraud coming from Carmino."

Tiffany felt for his hand, a warmth in her voice. "I meant what I said on the barge. I'm in no hurry to change my life. I'm still getting my head around life without Chris. Before him, other good-looking guys like you had fooled me. My fault – rushing in." She stroked his fingers. "With you, what intrigues me is your strength of purpose. *That* makes me feel close to you."

Dex leaned towards her and softly caressed her wrist. *Strength of purpose*? He wondered what Dr Wilfred Grierson would have made of that assessment. "I won't be deflected."

"I believe you. So, what next? The Gaming Authorities? The Police?"

"Panama and filming." The taxi was slowing up outside Tiffany's mid-fifties block in World's End.

"Don't underestimate Carmino, Dex. I wonder who slashed his face."

"Yeah! Point taken. But it could have been a car crash." The taxi stopped and she unbuckled. He grasped her shoulders so that they faced each other at close quarters in the half-light.

"You're cornering a rat. Never a good choice."

Dex did not dwell on the warning. "Before you head for New

York, please get me contacts for Scotty Brannigan and Mick Glenn. Your Sports Editor will know."

"No promises." She sounded concerned. "But Mick Glenn? Not him. He's a loose cannon. I mean this Amber and Mick thing. If Creole Henry finds out, he will stuff Glenn's balls down his throat."

"Maybe a loose cannon's what I need. For two long years, I've seen every ladder as a snake in disguise. Perhaps it's time to take risks."

She eased herself out after kissing him on both cheeks, arms around his shoulders. "I shall miss you. Take care."

"Good luck with the US tour."

"Cornered rats. Never forget that."

-39-

Dex took a break from practicing Reverse Labouchère to sizzle sausages to add to buttered bread with brown sauce. By his calculations, he had tested the system for over thirty hours with not one winning streak. And every day passing was one day closer to the launch of Space City.

That must never happen.

Never.

Meanwhile, as he was watching the sausages turn golden brown, a barrel-chested Jamaican with a shaven head presented his passport at Immigration Arrivals at Heathrow Airport. It showed his name as Leroy Creole Henry. The sullen look on his face matched the passport photo. He was nodded through and the fixed stare and set of his jaw as he crossed the concourse showed his mood was not pretty. Moments later, he stepped into the rear seat of a chauffeured BMW with tinted windows. Within minutes, the driver was speeding east to take the boss to his mansion in Stonebridge Park, north-west London.

His route took him not far from *Who Cares* where Dex was just settling to more roulette when the phone rang. It was Tiffany. After a few pleasantries, she confirmed that getting Brannigan's contacts was impossible. All approaches had to be through his management company in Delaware but she had a couple of numbers for Glenn, who lived in grand style in the Bishop's Avenue area of north London. "I was tempted to tell you I couldn't get Glenn's contacts. He could be a disaster. But it's your call."

After wishing her a safe flight, he went for a jog hoping to clear his mind.

Do I phone Glenn?

Do I want to lose endless real money in Dukes playing Reverse Labouchère?

Could I ever teach Adam Yarbury to play it?

No.

Maths – not his strong suit!

If not Adam, then who?

How can I trace Brannigan?

Maybe forget Brannigan and Glenn till I've got filmed evidence?

But Space City opening?

Time's against me.

After completing his six-mile run, his mind was made up. He dialled Glenn's number, making sure that Glenn could not use callback. The footballer was lying next to Amber on a giant sun-bed by his indoor pool. He removed his muscular arm from around her neck and answered with casual indifference. "Yeah?"

"Hi, Mick! You don't know me. Name's Johnny. I was watching you and Scotty at Dukes."

"So? I lost an effin' packet, didn't I?"

"Dukes cheated both of you. I saw what happened. We need to meet."

"Them magnets. Bleedin' Dukes! Always said they used magnets."

"I don't know about that."

"I'll fucking do Carmino, know what I mean?"

"No – don't, Mick. You've no evidence. I have. We must meet. Plan carefully with Scotty too."

"Fuck that! I knew I was stitched up by that Chinky. I'll fix Pepe bleedin' Carmino and no mistake. I'll sort him. He is seriously out of order."

Dex could take no more. He cut the connection, wishing now he had listened to Tiffany.

The footballer looked at the silent phone for a moment and then ranted to Amber, who seemed too spaced out behind her headphones to give a damn. "Bleedin' Dukes. I'll fucking sort them wankers. Sod 'em. Anyway, when's Creole back from Jamaica?"

"Lands tonight." Amber did not sound enthused at the prospect. "Least, I think so."

"We got hours yet, then." He leaned across her tanned body and started to remove her bikini top.

– 40 –

Dex drove over to the family home in St John's Wood where he had spent much of his youth. Despite its grandeur, Porcupine House held no happy memories. Father's wealth had ensured that the interior décor was the finest throughout each spacious room of its three floors. Local real-estate agents would have drooled over their prose when describing its perfection.

Dex hated the place.

The bad vibes were over-powering.

It had been from here that his mother had walked out, never to return.

In the kitchen, when he had been eleven, he had shielded her from a rain of blows from his drunken father.

It had been in the sitting-room that he had blackened his Father's eye and broken his nose with a real haymaker. That had been just over two years ago when he had discovered that Father had been stoking rumours round Camberley.

Just days later, his home had been torched.

After Dex had married and Beth had moved into a penthouse overlooking the river near Blackfriars Bridge, Sir Charles had continued to live there alone. Dex entered Beth's old bedroom. It looked just the same as ever. He could almost see his sister as a vibrant seventeen-year-old, doing her yoga in her red leotard, classical music playing softly. He rested his head against the wall and sobbed – for how long he had no idea. Biting his lip, he forced himself to control his emotions and turned to go downstairs.

Give up life on the river?
For this?
Surrounded by a past I'd rather forget?
To look after Father, rather than send him away?
The thought reminded him of his last discussion with Simon Morrison at the hospital. "To be blunt, your Father will never do anything meaningful again. He will never walk, talk, wash or clean himself." As they had spoken, they were standing just outside Father's private room in the hospital. Dex had been able to see the broken figure, Father's head lolling down toward his chest.

"He's not in a coma, though?"

"Oh no! He responds to stimuli. His eyelids fluttered when shown a photo of Beth."

"He's a prisoner, then? In his own body." Dex had been surprised at how moved he felt by the old man's plight. Nobody deserved that type of living death.

"Good carers could be better than a care-home."

Shortly the first of the hopefuls would arrive for interview. He opened the curtains and windows letting the gentle breeze blow away the stale air.

Interviewing the candidates proved to be dispiriting. Two had no relevant experience, the third had been well-qualified but if you asked her the time, she'd tell you how to make a clock. *Drive me crazy in minutes, she would.* The fourth was recovering from a low-level spinal fusion and could never have coped with shifting the old man in and out of bed.

Dex steeled himself for the final applicant, an Australian, who had just rung the bell. Aged twenty-seven with deep copper hair, Jude Tuson had a bottle-brown skin and an attractively strong but angular face. She had a sporty physique, her lean frame and leaner face suggested she worked out a great deal or took care with her diet. Or both. Everything about her oozed self-confidence while still suggesting a cynical awareness of life.

Above her green eyes, her eyebrows were a prominent feature. Overall, her attractive features told the world that she had *been there, done that*. Dex sensed there was something of the brazen recklessness of a streaker about her, an image which Dex found a turn-on. He'd seen her sort clutching pints of lager heading for Twickenham to support the Wallabies. Perhaps too, it was the way she stood – chest thrust forward and shoulders back that emphasized both her physique and strength of character.

After his opening questions, Dex had immediately warmed to her, knowing Jude had precious little competition. Subservient she was not but her answers ticked every box. With her Sydney accent and in her Bondi sweatshirt, Jude explained that she was an Aussie but now living in Earl's Court, the heart of London's Kangaroo Valley.

Every answer exuded confidence in her ability. *Just like Aussie cricketers*, Dex had thought. *It must be an Aussie thing.* With her deep voice, Dex could imagine Jude having no trouble shouting for drinks in the hubbub of the Prince of Teck. Her hair was slightly bouffant adding further to her height, which Dex judged at a good five-eleven. As she spoke, she waved her arms, highlighting hands suitable for wrestling crocodiles in the Northern Territories.

After she had left, he looked at his notes: tough, blunt, cynical, ambitious, sexy, grasping, "efficient, not loving" – her own description. His notes reminded him of the conversation about her experience. "Yeah. Started in Sydney. Full nurse's training including geriatrics. I worked at Westmead Hospital. Brain-damaged victims. Then I went to Saudi. Couldn't stand that. No drink allowed and randy Arabs wanting to sodomize me. Turned my back on that, I can tell you. Well, so to speak."

Dex guessed she had cracked that joke many times before. Her laugh had revealed good teeth, well cared for. "I've nursed everything from koalas to kinkies, babies to baldies. Yeah! Put me down as experienced. Your old man? Piece of cake. He's an in-and-outer, right? Shove it in, clean it out." Her appraisal was startlingly robust.

Dex was taken aback by the summary. "He'll need stimulating too."

"Right on! 'Course he does. Stimulating!" She looked at him slyly over the rim of a can of Coke "That's essential. Who gave you all that stuff about maybe needing two carers? Is he a big fella?"

"He was. Not now. Wasting away."

"No sweat. I could throw a sumo wrestler over the Eiffel Tower."

Dex anticipated her reaction to his next questions. "What about the law? Working hours, lifting weights?"

"Aw, c'mon! Health and Safety crap. Politically correct bollocks. I want the money. I've one aim – get rich quick. That's why I went to Saudi and now London. I'm up for the main chance. Me? Giving bed-baths in five years? Give me a break! I want to meet some rich layabout to keep me in Gucci and champagne. Meantime, don't hire two. Just pay me more and hire in cover for my evening off."

After she'd left, her personality had lingered with a smell of the Gitanes she had asked to smoke and the Gaultier perfume she had sprayed as she was leaving. The house seemed strangely silent and empty without her. Dex went down to the cellar and found a bottle of 1990 Hermitage from Jean-Louis Chave. It was in a section labelled ready for drinking. At five-hundred-and-eighty pounds a bottle, Dex was not used to drinking such great wine, so he decided to sink a glass or two while devouring a couple of Scotch Eggs he had brought in from Sainsbury's. It worked well while he weighed up his decision.

There were only two choices. *The Brummie woman with verbal diarrhoea or the headstrong Aussie with her sexy physique* – something he failed to keep out of the equation. Yet something niggled about Jude. She seemed to have the right answer for everything. As she had handed over her references, she had volunteered that they were *impressive if not sensational, mate.*

Was she as good as she had made out? Did she really tick every box? *Or was I seduced by those eyelashes and flirty smiles?* Each mention of the need for *stimulation* had prompted a suggestive glance. It took a second glass of the deep red Hermitage before he phoned her. "Jude. You're hired. Father will be discharged in a few days. I'll give you a call."

He checked his watch. Time to get packed for Panama.

Within moments of Dex ending the call to Jude, she made one herself. "Great news! I got the job."

-41-

It was early evening and sub-tropically hot as the air-conditioned taxi sped him from Tocumen Airport through the city outskirts and onto the dual carriageway behind the curving seafront of Panama Bay. It dropped him at the Intercontinental Miramar Hotel. Only Tiffany knew of his trip to Panama. Even Adam Yarbury thought Dex was in Vienna with a friend from Harvard. Gus McKay, for all his eccentricity, was a wily old sod and his warning weighed heavily, especially after Mick Glenn's crass reaction on the phone.

Talking to him had been disastrous. The best hope was that Glenn would do nothing.

Don't kid yourself, Dex.

Bulls, china shops and loose cannons all seemed apposite.

It had been a long day involving a change of flights and the usual hassle clearing security at Miami International Airport. Now, it was too late to visit Maria-Elena Sanchez but his plans were ready. He guessed that dealing blackjack, her English would be better than his Spanish. As he sat on the balcony in the balmy air, the view was of lights of vessels approaching or leaving the canal, away to his right.

He enjoyed a simple dinner from room service with no alcohol. Afterwards, he slept fitfully, partly due to the time difference but more because of apprehension of the day ahead.

Would Maria-Elena warn Carmino that Mr Finlay Dexter had been sniffing around?

By dawn he felt as if he had never slept. Even the thundering water from the shower followed by a hearty breakfast did little to revive him. From the map, he knew the Casino Sienna was a short walk away but he wanted to catch Maria-Elena at home. If the enquiry agent were right, she was unmarried and lived with her widowed mother at an address in the Old Town. The *Casco Viejo,* was about four kilometres away and so he took a taxi and was dropped off by the twin turrets of the impressive Metropolitan Cathedral. It had stood for hundreds of years in the heart of the jumble of ancient streets that surrounded it. When he spotted the vultures peering down from the cathedral's parapets, their curved backs reminded him of Forster-Brown, though otherwise anyone less like a vulture was hard to imagine.

Overhead, the sky was clear blue but the air remained humid and he was glad he had not worn even a lightweight jacket. Even in his short-sleeved shirt and jeans, his skin felt clammy. Thunderstorms were forecast but, at present, rain seemed a distant prospect.

He turned his map around until he had sorted his bearings and then headed into the shady back streets behind the Avenida Balboa. The area had none of the trash and clutter that he had expected but there were a few scavenging mongrels sniffing and yelping or making use of the ornate wrought-iron streetlamps. From somewhere, came the sound of salsa music and occasional guttural shouts from open windows.

An old man in a shapeless black suit chewed on a cigarette. From his stool outside his front door, he raised a feeble arm in greeting. No doubt he had done the same thing yesterday and would be there again tomorrow and every day until one morning he would no longer be around. It was a chastening thought.

In these narrow streets, time had stood still. The stone houses, just two storeys high were poorly painted with the stone crumbling after centuries of weathering. The area spoke of folk living in homes where they had spent their childhoods, as had generations of their ancestors. Certainly, when he knocked on the faded blue painted door, the old lady who answered did so without any sign of fear. No doubt this was a close-knit community and she had no expectation of danger or of a stranger dropping by. The pickings for thieves round here would be poor.

Dex judged her to be late seventies. Her iron-grey hair was tied tightly into a bun at the back. She was wearing a grey smock that almost reached her clumpy black sandals. Her face was deeply lined and her narrowed mouth and cheeks suggested she had lost most of her teeth. He gave her an exaggerated friendly smile to allay any fears but her face showed none anyway, just slight puzzlement. Using halting schoolboy Spanish, he asked if Maria-Elena was at home. She shook her head and then responded with a few rapid words of Spanish, which were too fast for Dex to understand. But he got the impression she could be at work. "Casino Sienna?" he asked.

"Si, señor. Si."

"Muchas gracias, Señora Sanchez."

He was rewarded with a toothless smile of pleasure as she closed the door.

Meeting Maria-Elena at work would not be ideal.

-42-

Dex picked up a taxi from the square and headed for downtown, where he saw the glittery façade of the casino with the name lit by flashing neon. As he was paying off the taxi, the entire street was illuminated by searing shards of lightning, instantly followed by a mighty crack of thunder – nature at its most extreme.

The rain started, falling like a wall, bouncing off the roof of the taxi and even worse still, off his head and shoulders. He was soaked even before he got under the casino's canopy. For a few moments, he stood there, awestruck at the flashing, crashing intensity of the storm. The street was now like a river, the water rushing by. He wiped down his face, entered the plush jazziness of the casino and dived into the men's room, where he used paper towels to absorb the worst of the wet from his shirt. His hair he dried under a wall hand-drier, so that when he entered the gloom of the gaming-area, jangling music coming from rows of slot machines, he looked less like something dredged up from the deep.

It was not a busy time. A few tourists – perhaps eight at the most, and probably from a cruise ship, were playing the slots. He strolled between the tables most of which were unmanned. At the only open roulette table, the dealer was a man. Dex noted with relief that he was wearing a nametag. That would make it easier.

The craps tables were closed but two blackjack tables were in operation and he approached them. Both dealers were female. One was only mid-twenties, so he ruled her out. The other was an attractive woman with tight black curls topping the smooth olive skin of her face. Her broad mouth was emphasized by red lipstick. Not wanting to peer obsessively at the nametag, he joined her table where there was an unhappy looking tourist. His multi-coloured shirt had a map of Maui across the back.

As he seated himself at the half-moon table, the dealer turned her head, offering a profile that made a nametag irrelevant. He drew breath because of her eerie similarity to the photo of Tavio in *El Mundo*, a Spanish-language Las Vegas paper. No question, they were brother and sister – indeed, they could even be twins. Then, as she finished the round, he saw the words *Maria-Elena* just below her shoulder. "Hello, sir" she welcomed him with a smile.

He bought in for one hundred dollars as the other player wished him luck. "Maria-Elena has been whipping my ass. If she beats me again, I'm quitting," he concluded staring at his solitary chip. Dex muttered a few words of commiseration. Dex had 19, the American showed 20, and the dealer's up-card was a 4.

"Looking good," Dex volunteered.

"With any other dealer, I'd agree. You watch her." Dex placed the American's accent as the Deep South, perhaps Georgia or Alabama. They watched as she turned over her hole card, which was a 7. "See what I mean? The way she's been playing, she'll hit a 10." He was right. Her next card was a King of Hearts, giving her the winning hand of 21. She swept away their bets with neither pleasure nor regret. The American swung round off his stool. "Good luck, pal."

"Better luck to you too." Dex then slapped out chips worth fifty dollars and waited for Maria-Elena to deal.

She looked at him for a moment. "Ingles?"

"You can tell?"

"After twenty-three years, señor." She shrugged with a smile. "It is easy." She dealt the cards and this time Dex cleaned up with blackjack – an ace-king. She paid him out and, as it was the end of the shoe, she prepared to shuffle.

This was the perfect moment.

Just do it, Dex.

"I have a message from an old friend of yours in London. Pepe Carmino. I'm his lawyer, his *abogado*." He saw her shock change to concern and then to fear all in a flash. "We need to talk. When do you finish?"

"Pepe? He here?"

– 43 –

"No. Pepe's not here." "I see you at 10 tonight. *Bodega El Cuervo*." Her English was adequate but spoken with a Spanish-American accent so that Dex had to listen carefully.

"*El Cuervo*. Tonight. 10 p.m." He saw her nod at his understanding. "I'll quit while I'm ahead," he volunteered as he gathered up his chips and took them to the casino cage to be changed into US dollar bills. Outside, the storm had moved away and steam was now rising from the sidewalk.

He decided to dummy-run *El Cuervo*. He found the bar with no problem in a street with a very different character. It was traffic-free and in almost any big city, one he would avoid after dark. Tonight, there would be no choice. The strip-club on the corner spoke of sleaze and late-night drunks. Sodden trash littered the cobbles over its two-fifty metres length. It was narrow and deserted with little going for it except for *El Cuervo* and the solitary girlie joint.

An optimistic realtor might describe it as up-and-coming. For Dex, it had a long way to go. Most of the buildings had once been lockup facilities or warehouses and were now shuttered and empty. Perhaps a property-developer tycoon, a Panamanian version of his father, had already bought the entire street with plans to rip everything down to add yet another skyscraper to the horizon.

The alley smelled of rotting vegetation and blocked sanitation Feeling uneasy, he headed for *El Cuervo*. He peered into the bar which was almost deserted and one he would have avoided at night in an unfamiliar city. He was glad to reach a small sunny square. Beneath the leafy trees and purple, pink and red flowering shrubs, were shops and several restaurants, some having shady terraces out of the thirty-degree heat. He chose one with freshly painted wrought ironwork and tables to match. Better still, it was offering paella and seafood specialties. After climbing a few wobbly steps, Dex settled under the shade of a giant tree and called for a Miller Lite, wondering what Maria-Elena was thinking.

Had he known that she was speaking furtively on her phone, his paella might not have been quite so enjoyable.

Back in London, another time-bomb was ticking.

– 44 –

Mick Glenn ignored the respectful *good evening* from Tom, the doorman, as he entered Dukes and bounded down the wide sweeping curve of the marble stairs.

Only at the Reception Desk did he stop. The young woman in her black evening-gown, recognised him and greeted him with the same courtesy she gave every visitor. She swiped his membership card but he showed no interest in moving away to the bar or the tables. "Where's Pepe Carmino? I want him here, now." Every word was barked out in a London accent that told of his childhood on a Wandsworth estate. The woman's face showed her shock.

"I'm sorry, Mr. Glenn. Mr. Carmino is not available tonight. I'll get Mr. Forster-Brown."

"That bald-headed coot! Okay! He'll do for starters." He paced the room, ignoring her invitation to sit on one of the Regency-style chairs. She spoke quietly on the phone and a few moments later, FB appeared, forcing a smile despite the warning. As he saw the snarl on Glenn's face, he felt his legs turn to jelly. That same look had intimidated many a referee or opposing defender. FB was scarcely small but he swallowed hard and his eyes blinked as he took in all six foot three inches of packed muscle looking ready to explode.

"Mr. G. How good to see you again! Mr. Carmino is traveling until Thursday but I'm sure I can help. What seems to be the problem?" His eyes avoided the footballer's.

"Fu-uckin' disgrace this place." Mick's voice was raised and a little slurred. "Full of shits like you in penguin suits. You lot – oh, yes, all so la-di-dah – but you're only out to bleedin' cheat us. Rob us blind."

"Do please keep your voice down. Mr G, you really are talking nonsense. This is most…unwelcome." His own career experience in top-end casinos had not trained him for dealing with an intimidating giant like Mick Glenn, whose eyes had the manic gleam of a copulating bulldog.

"Now you listen, rabbit-ears." Glenn moved closer so that his chin hovered close to FB's bald head. He rapped the acting boss on the shoulder. "Listenin', little man?"

FB now felt very small indeed. "We should go into the office. Let's talk in a calm way like gentlemen."

"Ain't no gentlemen round here. You'd be unsold as a used pisspot at a car boot sale, an' that's a fact. And we ain't goin' nowhere. Got it? Anyone mug enough to gamble at Dukes needs to hear this. You tell Carmino I know this place is fuckin' crooked. Your dealers cheat us, that's what. Last time I was in, you shits rolled me over. You lot was seen. Caught in the bleedin' act."

"You must be mistaken."

"Listen, you bald-headed bunny. You tell that ponce Pepe: I'm not leavin' next time without all me money back—all £210,000 I lost. Otherwise, I'm goin' to Scotland bleedin' Yard. I know the fuckin' works on you lot. An' I'm goin' to tell every fuckin' member the way it is. Got it, you carrot-cruncher? I'll be in next Thursday evening. 10:30. You tell Pepe, know what I mean?"

Overhead, the security cameras captured the scene and the mikes were picking up every word. "Please leave. Utter nonsense but of course Mr. Carmino will wish to discuss your concern."

Above Glenn's shoulder, Forster-Brown could see Adam Yarbury faltering as he descended the stairs. He had stopped on hearing the commotion and his frown showed his embarrassment.

FB held his breath as Glenn spun around on his Cuban heels and then ran up the stairs. Halfway up, he glared back down. "The game's up, mate. You're all goin' to jail."

Adam stepped aside for Glenn to rush by before he continued his descent.

FB wrung his hands in embarrassment. "I'm so sorry about that outburst, Mr. Y. Most…unseemly."

"What a bore! Pepe already knows my views about oafs like him being members. A red card, perhaps?" Adam Yarbury chuckled at his joke.

– 45 –

Dex had hours to kill till his meeting so he returned to his hotel and booted up his laptop. There was an email from Doc Grierson, confirming his appointment with a reminder to pay cash or debit card, credit cards not accepted.

That'll be fun – telling the miserable sod about the pills.

He quickly moved on to an email from Tiffany. "How are you? I'm on a train from NYC to Washington. Let's message this evening." Her email had arrived two hours before, so he confirmed he would call. Seconds after pressing the send button, his eyelids drooped and he fell asleep until nearly eight. Following a beer at lunch, he slept deeply, his stomach filled with his paella of chicken, lobster, shrimp, squid, sausage, mussels and onions.

On awakening, a few clicks on his laptop and Tiffany's radiant face filled the screen. It was almost like seeing her reporting on TV, except now it was interactive. "You're in Washington?"

"The Four Seasons, where Washington becomes Georgetown and only a brisk walk to the White House. I'm here for two days—doing more interviews and of course the event involving Bill Clinton."

"How was NYC?"

"Tough! Seven TV slots plus media one-to-ones and four signings."

"You're getting real traction, then?"

"Sales are shooting up the graph."

"That's great! Terrific! And after DC?"

"Atlanta, Miami, Dallas, Houston, Los Angeles, San Francisco, Seattle and back to Los Angeles. Anyway, enough about me. You're… where you expected?"

Dex hesitated. WhatsApp was reckoned to be pretty secure but he decided to play it safe. "Yes, but the joke is that Adam wants a Sachertorte from Vienna."

Tiffany's face showed she had caught on at once. "Is that easy to find?"

"There's a cake-shop in Knightsbridge."

They both laughed but quickly turned serious. "Last night, I found an article written by a reformed hacker. Y'know – access to Beth's stuff."

"Go on."

"I'll scan it to your hotel."

"Please." His face shone with boyish excitement.

"Dex, there's no magic bullet but he explained that nearly everyone uses passwords that are obvious – somehow linked to their life pattern. Kid's name. Family pet's name, place of birth."

"Beth's was more complicated. Random letters. And her username had no obvious link to her life – just a load of letters."

"This guy says that random is rare."

"Beth was smart." He grinned at her. "Sorry. I don't mean to sound negative."

"I'm transmitting now." She leaned across and Dex heard her scanner working and he saw her do a couple of clicks and nod in satisfaction. "It's gone. Anyway, Dex, how are you? Your father?"

"I'm good. Father's returning to Porcupine House next week. I've hired an Aussie carer to look after him." He felt strangely uneasy mentioning Jude Tuson.

"And you? Still no pills?"

"They were frying my brain."

"No more nightmares?"

"Not one."

"And the drinking?"

"I've been a good boy. Not even with the free booze on the flight."

"Sorry, Dex but I must rush. I've got a press conference. You take care." Her face showed a moment of concern before the link was cut.

The article arrived seconds later and for the next hour, he read it before looking yet again at the details – GADECH and ZAYBXCWB.

Why had she chosen GADECH?

Was this truly random or was there some hidden logic?

Had she fluffed the details on the phone?

Or did I mishear?

He jotted down *GADECH equals Georgina, Angela, Dex, Edie, Chrissie and Harriet.* Okay, she knew someone with all those names.

Probably complete crap, he decided, noticing that it was time to go. With a resigned look, he shut down his laptop, thinking that he too should get a less obvious password. As he waited for the elevator, he had another thought. *Hire a hacker* – better still, the guy who had written the article. The thought was still with him as he strode the short distance through the city until he reached the corner of the back alley.

It was not improved by night. A small neon arrow on a derelict building pointed to the distant lights of *El Cuervo*, some two hundred metres away. As he took in the near blackness ahead, a hustler for the girlie club pointed inside the door. "You Americano?

Sexy girls. You make friends. Have good time." Dex laughed away the opportunity, though watching Latino beauties bumping and grinding seemed more attractive than the empty darkened alley. He could feel his heart pounding through the wetness of his shirt as he starting walking.

What had Maria said or done since I met her?

− 46 −

In Mayfair, Pepe Carmino strolled through the bar toward the gaming tables. As he did so, a leggy blonde with a deep-red designer outfit rose from her bar-stool where she had been perched, slinging back vermouth. She approached him with an exaggerated wiggle. As they came face to face, she pouted. Pepe gave her a dismissive glance as if to blank her. "I miss you, Pepe," she said in her rasping Hungarian accent. "Couldn't we…maybe …."

He did not want a scene. In the casino, Irenke was useful. In bed she had been a bore. He was irritated that his discarded mistress had still not got the message. "Irenke, darling, we are done, finished. Accept it. That's the way it is. Just be grateful for the generous pocket-money and free meals you get for opening the blackjack tables." He turned briskly and with no further formality, walked away, leaving her looking pensive before she returned to her stool and ordered another vermouth with an olive.

The previous evening, FB had phoned him at his hotel in the mountainous enclave of Liechtenstein. The report on Glenn had forced him to advance his meeting with the pudding-bowl Swiss lawyer and a shifty-looking overweight banker. He had then jetted home early from Zurich to be able to watch and listen to Glenn's outburst. He had no intention of saying so but FB had been impressive.

He replayed the recording. *You lot was seen*. What did Glenn mean by that? Was that the way Glenn spoke about himself or had someone else spotted something? *I know the fuckin' works on you lot*. Now that sounded as if Glenn himself knew. But was that from what he had spotted or had someone told him? Scotty Brannigan perhaps?

He decided to watch the recordings when One-Eye had screwed both players. He strolled across his office to lean on the ornate Robert Adam fireplace, wondering if a sober Glenn had calmed down. Might he chicken out? No. That notion died instantly. Not a thug who head-butts opponents and swears at referees. Arnie Fisher would need to hire extra security on Thursday.

At about the same time, inside Creole Henry's conservatory, a distressed Amber Murray was on the phone to Mick Glenn. "He knows, Mick."

"What you mean he knows? How?"

"Creole knows." There was more sobbing as she dabbed a cold flannel on her swollen cheek. "Someone told him we was in Dukes." There was more sobbing. "He hit me, kicked me, punched me. Threatened to kill me."

"The bastard." Glenn threw down his snooker cue. He had been practising alone before going to bed. He often relaxed like this after a big match. True, this afternoon's match had been a *friendly* but he had missed a sitter and the manager's blue-language was still ringing in his ears after the no-goal draw. "Amber, love, Creole is so out of order. I'm sorry." He paused. "Where is he? You want him sorted? I know some heavies. He won't father no kids after they've done with him."

"He's out somewhere. Didn't say where. But I'm scared, Mick."

"Leave him. Go to a hotel. I'll pay."

"He said if I wasn't here when he got back, he'd hunt me down... anywhere." She shifted position and caught sight of her blackened face in a mirror and burst into more tears.

"Tell the law then, love. He can't go knocking you about."

"No, Mick. He said any cops, he'd kill me."

Neither of them said a word as they weighed up whether it was an empty threat. Creole Henry's reputation went before him. Mick grabbed the blue ball and jettisoned it round the full-size table. It cannoned off a couple of cushions before smashing into the bunched-up reds scattering them every which way.

Eventually, it was Amber who spoke. "Mick, he said he was gonna get you. Gonna do you. Them was his words. Do you."

"Creole? I'm not scared of him." But even as he said it, he was walking to the front door to set the alarm system, just in case the big Jamaican could somehow beat the security gates at the foot of the drive.

Mick slammed the bolt across the door and fixed the chain. "I'll think of something. Call me tomorrow when you can."

"In Creole's present mood, I'm scared, Mick. For us both."

– 47 –

His eyes flicking from side to side as he checked the shadows for movement, Dex took large strides along the cobbled street. The stone walls of the old warehouses and abandoned lock-ups added to the air of menace. Nobody seemed to be coming from or going to *El Cuervo*. There was no sign of movement anywhere between him and the bar. The smell of cheap scent from the clip joint receded, and now it was just him and the distant pool of light outside the bar ahead.

He had gone nearly halfway when he heard footsteps behind him. He flicked a quick look over his shoulder and realised that someone must have been concealed in a doorway. The shadowy figure was no more than twenty paces behind him. Dex quickened his pace but the footsteps seemed to be closing on him. He broke into a run. Whoever was behind him did the same.

At that moment, another figure appeared ahead from the shadows. He too must have been skulking beyond the lights of the bar in case Dex arrived from the other direction. Now the man ahead was accelerating toward him.

I'm meat in their sandwich.
Not yet dead meat.

Entering El Cuervo was impossible now. He had no choice but to keep going and use his bulk and momentum to crash the silhouetted figure out of his way. Making it to the little square where he had lunched was his best hope – so near and yet so far. From behind, he could hear the man's breathing just a few strides behind him. It had been a mistake to falter even fractionally at the sight of the second figure. Barely twenty metres now separated all three as Dex swerved to sidestep the man ahead. But Dex had none of the subtlety of a rugby three-quarter and the local matched his move and then stopped.

Steamroller him.

Turning his left shoulder slightly, he used his weight to barge into the smaller man. For a fleeting moment, he saw a glint of steel as the light from the bar caught the knife as it flew from the man's hand. With the impact, Dex stumbled. That was enough for the figure behind him to hurl himself at Dex's hip, knocking him completely off-balance. He lurched another pace or two before crumpling to the ground. As he tried to get up, he was sent sprawling onto the cobbles as someone crashed against him. Though Dex was much heavier, when the second man pounced, he was pinned down.

They turned him over before one of them knelt on his chest while the other retrieved the knife. He smelled their hot breath and felt the knife's sharp point against his throat.

One false move, one false word and I'm dead.

– 48 –

The vicious plunge from the knife never came. Instead, one of the men spoke in halting English. "What you want our sister?"

"I must talk to her."

"You no from Pepe. Bullshit."

Trying to think with a knife against his throat and two strangers pinning him down was a novel experience. *What to say to stay alive?*

"I have information."

"From Pepe? You lie."

At least they seemed more interested in talking than killing. "About Tavio. I have news about your brother."

For a moment, neither attacker spoke, both surprised at hearing something unexpected. "Tavio? He America. What you mean, news him?"

"You speak Tavio?" It was now the other man, his face just inches away and his minty breath was coming fitfully.

Not a question Dex wanted to answer. "No. I no speak to Tavio." He found himself mirroring their broken English. "Tavio is dead." He paused to assess their reaction. Both men eased their pressure on him but the knife-point remained. Plainly, they knew nothing. *But why not?* "I will tell you. *Comprendo?*"

"Tavio no dead. He where?"

Dex managed a shake of his head. "Sorry, *amigos*. He is dead. I explain." He lay still as the two men spoke to each other in rapid-fire Spanish. "Take me to Maria-Elena," Dex said commandingly, sensing he had them confused or interested. The two men eased themselves off him and permitted him to stand. He saw he was much taller than both of them as he tried to understand their debate. The older man with a pinched face jabbed the knife at him. "We go Maria. No shit, gringo."

Dex raised both hands in emphasis. "No shit. Me...*amigo*. Friend."

The brothers did not seem convinced as they pushed and prodded him into the bar. It was poorly air-conditioned and smelled of stale sweat as much as from a line of garlic sausages and cured hams that hung from the ceiling. Dex was still panting from the brawl and from fear of the knife still held close to his neck. His hands, shirt and jeans were filthy from the scuffle in the dirt.

There were fewer than twenty people inside the surprisingly large room. As the brothers forced him between the tables, Dex spotted a mural of a giant crow with the words *El Cuervo* beneath it. From the piped music, Dex recognised Christina Aguilera. He was led to a booth with ripped green upholstery where a sultry-looking Maria-Elena was seated alone, a glass of red wine and tapas in front of her. She was wearing a low-slung turquoise blouse and a pair of white figure-hugging jeans. Dex noticed the heavy perfume and the silver jewellery that highlighted her ears and neck. She ignored him, instead looking at her brothers with a question on her face.

Without being invited, Dex sat down opposite her and one brother slid in next to him, the other next to Maria. He said nothing, content to take in the arm-waving and animated discussion, Dex judged her to be the eldest by several years and evidently in command. At the word *muerto*, he saw her mouth drop as they explained that Tavio was dead. He watched her hands open and close as she gave him a puzzled glance before firing off another question in Spanish. The two men looked at each other and then shrugged.

"You no from Pepe," she said. It was a statement of fact. If she had spoken to him today, that was his worst nightmare.

"I know Pepe. In London. My message is not from him."

"You say my brothers – Tavio…he dead? Where he? Maybe Las Vegas?"

"Las Vegas, yes. Till he was murdered." Dex looked at the brothers in turn. They were both late thirties with swept-back crinkly black hair, rather messed up by their exertions. Both were lean and fit with stubble lining their cheeks. Each had a moustache, one of them rather bushier than the other. They had brown eyes similar to their sister, though hers were mellow and inviting.

"Please ask your brother to put the knife away," he invited. He waited while she spoke to the pinched-face man and he withdrew the blade of the flick-knife but let it lie on the table.

Dex nodded thanks, and as a waitress appeared, he suggested a jug of wine and a tray of cold meats. "We must talk plenty." Having ordered, Dex continued. "You still speak with Pepe?" It was a blunt question and there was no response. "You write to him? See him? Maybe this year?"

He could see she understood and this time the response was sharp. "No." But then her eyes flashed a warning message. "Why you speak Pepe? You here talk Tavio or Pepe?"

Dex ducked the honest answer and explained that he would tell them about Tavio.

The oval-shaped dish of ham and sausages with tomatoes and peppers arrived with a jug of red. Maria leaned towards him, elbows on the table, "Tavio, he go USA long time." She brushed her hands together as if to say he had disappeared in a puff of smoke. From his hip pocket, Dex produced a copy of an extract from *El*

Mundo. The Vegas newspaper showed a mug shot of Tavio and reported his murder, describing him as Puerto Rican. There was a quote from his live-in girlfriend confirming he was originally from San Juan, having arrived twenty years before. "That is Tavio? Your brother?"

All three studied the photo of a smiling Latino. They pointed and nodded between themselves until Maria responded. "*Si, si.* Yes. He older. But is Tavio but…" She turned to her brothers and spoke in Spanish again "…why he say he Puerto Rico."

"Maybe he entered the USA illegally?" Dex was unsure whether they understood or whether they were not going to admit that. He spoke slowly. "The cops did not know he was from Panama. Officially, he was from Puerto Rico."

The younger brother topped up his sister's glass, pouring the wine from the litre earthenware jug. "Why Tavio killed? Who kill him?"

Dex was anxious not to go there yet. He answered slowly. "That…is a good question. Let's eat, shall we?"

It would be impossible to ignore the burning question for too long just because there was food. While he munched away at a chunky piece of chorizo, he motioned them to read the long report in *El Mundo*. This led to more rapid-fire Spanish – all spoken in such a strong local accent that he had no clue what they were saying. "You know who kill Tavio?" It was Maria-Elena who had downed her cutlery to ask the question.

Dex was not ready to volunteer what little he knew, or *thought* he knew about that. There was more groundwork to be cleared first. He gave a *maybe yes, maybe not* hand signal. "Tell me about Pepe Carmino."

"He kill Tavio?" prompted the younger brother angrily, spitting a piece of meat onto the table as he did so.

Don't go there yet, Dex.

"Pepe? When was he here?"

Maria-Elena placed her elbows onto the stained table-cloth. Having silenced her brothers with a fierce stare, she told him. "Pepe work here twenty years ago. More."

"In a casino?"

"*Si*. Yes. I see him there."

"You worked with him?"

She nodded agreement using only the slightest possible head movement.

"He was a dealer?"

"Blackjack. Always blackjack."

"And he left here?" Despite another warning look from the brothers she nodded yes. "Why did he leave?"

Maria-Elena looked discomforted as she shrugged. "He go."

"Was he a good friend? Was he special to you?"

There was a short lull before her face showed a moment of wistfulness but then as quickly hardened. "He good friend. I like him, *si*." Dex reckoned she must have been a stunner back then and no doubt Pepe would have been quick to spot her. But had they been lovers?

He debated the next question, before blurting it out. "Did Pepe have a scar," he ran his finger down his right cheek, "just here?" Dex looked at each of the family in turn. The stony looks had returned and silence hung shroud-like between them. He knew then that he had touched a toxic tripwire. The stony faces morphed into wary hostility. There was no point backing off now. "Was Pepe attacked here?"

"Señor, you go." Maria-Elena rubbed one hand against the other in a dismissive fashion. She signalled to the brother sitting across the table.

Dex stood up and dumped thirty dollars on the table. "Let me explain about Tavio," Dex suggested as he shuffled along the bench-seat. First one arm and then his other were seized. His slight bow to Maria-Elena got no reaction, not even the hint of a goodbye. He said *adios* but nobody said a word. Moments later, with a hefty shove, he was jettisoned into the street, once again crashing down onto the cobbles.

It was a slow and painful walk back, his knees and back aching.
What did I learn?
Pepe had dealt blackjack here.
Twenty years ago.
Tavio had left twenty years ago.
She'd had no contact with Pepe.
Do I believe her?
The scar.
That had spooked them.
Even twenty years later.
Why and how do I find out?

−49−

The piping hot bath had eased his stiffened knee but not his lower back. Yet compared to a knife at the throat, he considered himself fortunate as he sat in a towelling bathrobe, an ice-cold beer beside him. Yet again, he stared at the jumbled letters − GADECH and ZAYBXCWB.
Not the months of the year.
Not the days of the week.
Think out of the box.
As the hacker had written − like wartime Bletchley Park.
Like the Enigma codebreakers.
He ordered a cheese and ham platter with a glass of Malbec and opened some cheesy dippers to keep him going. On the hotel's scribbling-pad he wrote the alphabet across the page − all twenty-six letters.
That was out of the box.
Then beneath every letter, he entered every number up to twenty-six. He stared at them, wondering if he had stumbled on something. Fired up now, he wrote down GADECH and beneath each letter, wrote its number. GADECH matched numbers *714538*. He heard the knock and, cursing his swollen knee all the way, shuffled to the door to admit Room Service. The cold platter looked appetising but suddenly he wasn't hungry. Cracking the password now seemed more important and he returned to the desk. ZAYBXCWB. The letters danced in front of his eyes as he tried to penetrate the logic.

Once again, he wrote down their corresponding numbers from the alphabet – 26, 1, 25, 2, 24, 3, 23, 2.

Then he saw it!

Except for the final letter B, there was perfect symmetry.

My God! When Beth told me, I misheard the D as a B.

Changing the B to a D made the last number a 4. The letters zigzagged from one end of the alphabet to the other. With shaking fingers and pulse pounding, he typed in *714538* as the user name. Then, after switching the B for a D he scarcely dared to breathe as he typed in *ZAYBXCWD*.

The vein in his forehead throbbed as he waited for the sound of the computer opening.

Access denied.

Deflated, he took his beer out to the wraparound terrace, where the night air was still pleasingly warm, tainted only by fumes from the traffic far below. He limped around the terrace to look across the Bay of Panama. The inky black emptiness was a soothing backdrop after the disappointment of the near-miss.

What am I missing?

Apply logic.

When trading commodities, Beth had always relied on logic and maths. Computers lived on logic.

What am I missing?

He limped back to the chill of the air-conditioning and looked at *ZAYBXCWD* again. Could this be a possible? He entered the username as *714538*. But this time, instead of *ZAYBXCWD*, he entered their matching symmetrical numbers – 26 1 25 2 24 3 23 4.

I don't believe it!

The laptop's innards started to whirr and within a few seconds he was connected to Beth's backup somewhere in the clouds.

Close to where she now is.

He shivered at the thought.

With her Home Screen showing her laughing face against a background of Canary Wharf, he almost felt she were alive and beside him. Having just been so close to death and now so close to her final moments, from out of nowhere the first tears filled his eyes. There was no fighting them back, so he let himself go, shoulders heaving, tears spattering onto the keys of the laptop.

It was several minutes before his tears ran on empty and he dried his face and wiped his laptop. Then he forced himself to eat – turning to the Manchego cheese and cured ham on dark brown bread.

It provided some comfort as did the wine.

He phoned down for another glass of Malbec.

Had Dex known what he was about to discover, he might have ordered a bottle.

-50-

While Dex had been sleeping off his paella lunch, darkness had fallen over north London. The last chatter of thousands of starlings had died away. The tall chestnut trees were swaying gently in the evening breeze. At just after ten and with no sign of aggro from Creole Henry, Mick Glenn locked his front door and set the alarm, eager for the confrontation with *that bastard Carmino*. There was a spring in his stride as he hurried across the gravel to his yellow Porsche and zapped open the locked door. He was wearing jeans, a black shirt with a red-and-white-striped tie under a black velvet jacket. He wanted to look good, to feel good and had again selected his Cuban boots with the highest heels to emphasize his height.

Glenn settled into the bucket seat of the 911 Carrera and fired the engine. Immediately, Elton John's "Crocodile Rock" resonated from six speakers. On the passenger seat, he saw his agent's reminder about tomorrow morning's visit to the sick kids in Great Ormond Street Hospital. Talking to a famous footballer meant so much to the desperately ill youngsters.

Every month, he donated to the hospital but, to Glenn, the visits were more important. In a bitter-sweet way, he looked forward to them. Every occasion had a sobering effect, brought his feet down to earth. He always promised the kids match tickets for *when you're better*. He knew that some would never make it, their short lives snuffed out almost before they had begun. As he drove away from the hospital, it always struck home that he was a lucky sod to be fit, strong and earning so much.

He pressed the remote to have the security gates open by the time he reached them. His thoughts of tomorrow were now replaced by what lay ahead with Carmino tonight.

Sorting him.

Making him squirm.

It was going to be fun.

Over sixty metres away and beyond the curve in the tree and shrub-lined drive, the heavy gates swung open. With much scuffing of gravel, Glenn accelerated away, the Porsche's throaty roar splitting the silence.

Pepe Carmino – you was so out of order.

I'm getting all them losses back!

He licked his lips in anticipation of the confrontation.

Meantime several miles away in Dukes, Pepe Carmino was at his desk doing paperwork, the cool, jazzy tones of Diana Krall playing from the Bose system. He checked his watch and then phoned FB. "What time is that shit Glenn due?"

"In about forty minutes. Ten-thirty."

"I'll see him in the secure-room." Pepe thought for a moment, tapping his fingers in time to the rhythm. "Have Arnie Fisher's security guys arrived?"

"They're here, boss."

He allowed himself a satisfied smile. Arnie's suggestion of CYA was shaping up just great.

"Have them out of sight near Reception. Tell Arnie's guys – no rough stuff unless essential. I'll fix Glenn tonight. Then we'll throw him to Creole Henry. He'll do the rest." He ended the call with an even broader grin and a slug of brandy.

Thanks, Arnie.

Cover Your Ass

Great idea.

-51-

The remnants of supper now pushed aside, Dex wondered just where to start. Should it be Beth's emails? Her Calendar? Notes? Contacts? Her pdf files? In the end, he opened *My Documents* and then clicked through to *Recent Documents*, all in WORD. There was nothing saved as Tavio or Vegas.

No surprise there then.

A file marked NYNY, attracted his attention. There it was – Tavio's statement taken in the New York, New York Casino on the Strip. It ran to over thirty pages of close typeface. He drained the last of his second Malbec and with a deep breath started to read the dead man's words. Once started, he found himself flicking through the pages quicker and quicker. It was like reading the climax of a thriller. He wanted to get to the end, scarcely believing what he was reading.

Except this was not fiction.

This was all true.

All fact.

Monstrous fact.

No wonder Beth had been terrified when she had phoned from the Cosmopolitan Hotel.

No wonder, Tavio had been gunned down.

By page twenty-three, Dex had to pause. The enormity was getting too much to absorb. Even in the chill of his suite, he noticed his palms turning sweaty and dampness beneath his armpits. Before continuing, he had to wipe his hands dry on his spotted hankie.

Feeling as he had been through a wringer, Dex at last reached the end. He sat staring at the final words, stunned.

My God!

What had Beth been feeling as she learned the truth about Carmino.

And then hearing that Tavio was dead.

He forced himself to explore her other files and was rewarded when he found a pdf version of her interview, this one actually signed by Tavio. She had called this file *9-FI* after the location of the interview.

I'm in possession of evidence that was worth killing for.

Evidence that had got Tavio murdered.

RIP Tavio.

No wonder Maria-Elena had ended the discussion.

Dynamite.

Evidence worth murdering Beth for.

RIP Beth

In the mirror in front of the desk, Dex saw a grey and haunted face.

If Carmino discovers what I now know ... I'm dead.

– 52 –

During the night flight to London, sleep was impossible. Long after starting the second leg from Miami, Dex kept seeing and almost hearing Beth saying *hornets' nest*. They were the last words she had ever typed. After the meal had been cleared and about two hours out from Florida, he ran through what Beth had uncovered. He had thought of little else all day.

According to Tavio, Carmino had worked in the Casino Sienna. Using cheating skills, he had previously been taught in a shady casino-dealing school just off the Vegas Strip, his role in Panama had been to cheat drunken sailors and inexperienced tourists. There he had met Maria-Elena and a passionate relationship had developed.

Using his ability *to deal seconds* and to fix a deck during a shuffle, the management at Casino Siena had valued him highly and rewarded him generously. Over an eighteen-month period, he had saved them tens of thousands by screwing unsuspecting players.

Dex stretched out on the sleeper bed and angled the light before opening his laptop to read Tavio's statement again. His question about Pep's scar? No wonder Maria-Elena had ended their discussion. Her body language had accelerated from wariness to fear.

Now he knew why.

"In this statement, I, Tavio Sanchez, now of Las Vegas but formerly of Panama City (and never Puerto Rico), mainly call the dealer in question Pepe Carmino. This is his real name and I recognise his picture. When he worked at the Casino Sienna in Panama, we knew him as Rick Hensfleet, a young Brit with Vegas training. But my sister Maria-Elena, who dated him, had seen his passport.

"The scar on his right cheek – I know how he got it. It was early afternoon and the Siena, where I also worked, was almost empty. I had one player at my roulette table. Maria was at an empty blackjack table, waiting for players. The only other player was at Carmino's blackjack. This was a young sailor. I think his name was Pancho. Maybe his family name was Torres. For a Mexican, he was a big guy. Carmino was dealing. Maria watched the Mexican lose plenty money. It turned nasty. The Mexican was angry, complaining that the dealer was cheating. I expect he was. Pepe always did.

"Pancho was banging the table with his fist. Maria saw and heard everything and once the fight broke out, I saw everything. I saw the sailor. He leaned across the green table and grabbed Carmino's arms, dragging him close. There was shouting. Carmino broke free. From somewhere, Carmino pulled out a big knife and came around the table.

"The Mexican should have run but he held his ground and Carmino stabbed him in the shoulder. Even then, the Mexican did not flee. Instead, he smashed a glass ashtray on the corner of the table and struck Carmino across his right cheek with the jagged edge. Blood everywhere, Carmino went berserk. He forced the Mexican to the floor. The pit boss, an inspector and me, we ran over and tried to pull Carmino off him. Impossible! Carmino was crazy, snarling like a dog. He then stabbed the guy in the neck and chest. Even after the Mexican was dead, Pepe stabbed him in both eyes. There were over twenty stab wounds, mainly to the face and chest.

"Maria was shocked and screaming because she had been his lover. Later that day, she told me that Carmino must be crazy, a psychopath. I agree. He was a crazy man. Nobody could have stopped him without risking being knifed themselves. Pepe Carmino really enjoyed killing the guy. He was snuffling, snorting and grunting, very excited. When he got up, his eyes were wild and he was laughing saying the fucker had deserved it.

"The owners needed no scandal, so they closed the casino. The cameras had captured everything. The recordings were destroyed but six of us staff were witnesses. The unfortunate gambler at my table saw everything. Tough luck – wrong place, wrong time. He was taken away by the security boys. I guess he was murdered and buried in the jungle, far from the city. Back then in Panama, maybe still now, money talked. The casino owners knew the top guys in the police – all bought.

"Me, Maria and the casino staff on duty were each given five thousand bucks for our lifetime silence. We gave the cops signed statements that we had seen the Mexican attack Rick with a broken ashtray. The Mexican had then pulled a knife after Rick had caught him switching his cards – that's cheating. Our statements said Rick had tried to hold the Mexican but he had bolted from the building. The police accepted our evidence that the Mexican had been unharmed when he had left the casino and other bribed witnesses confirmed seeing him later that day drinking in *El Cuervo*.

"In fact, we watched as the Mexican was wrapped up in the blood-stained carpet. I was told he was fed to the pigs in a farm just outside the city. We all knew that Carmino was treated in hospital for the slash down his cheek. He gave the hospital another false name – South African, I think. From then, Rick Hensfleet never existed, was never mentioned. It was as if Hensfleet / Carmino had never been in Panama. The boss later told Maria that the casino had smuggled him over the border into Costa Rica, perhaps even that same night. He disappeared. Maria and me, we thought maybe he too had been murdered. It was safer to know and say nothing.

"With my pay-off, I quit Panama. I trekked and bummed lifts

up the Pan-American Highway. I paid to be smuggled across the Mexican border into Texas near El Paso. In Vegas, I said I was from Puerto Rico – lawfully in the USA. I got work in a casino and have been dealing here ever since. Then, on TV, maybe three months ago, I saw Rick Hensfleet calling himself Pepe Carmino. I was shocked! He was still alive! I saw the scar. Carmino and this guy Enzo Letizione were talking about Space City.

"I had gambling debts, poker mainly, a divorce. I was desperate. Space City was hiring but they tell me they no want more roulette dealers. I was goddammed mad at this and after too many beers, I spoke to another dealer friend, Diego Rodrigues – boasted I knew enough to convict Pepe Carmino. My big mistake! Diego had a loud mouth. At first, he denied it but then admitted he'd told my story to couple of folks including a guy from London.

"Around that time, I was playing poker Downtown and met Letizione. He seemed a regular guy. I told him I needed to work in a better joint. He said no. I'd had a beer or two and after the game, I told him I had stuff about Carmino murdering someone in Panama. I thought I'd get a good job.

"Letizione played hardball. He said my story was crap – just blackmail. But I could tell – the guy was worried. He warned me – don't go spreading false rumours or you'll end up in the desert. But it was Diego's big mouth led you to me."

As he shut down the screen, Dex again felt shivers ripple down his spine. The word *psychopath* played on his mind together with an image of a blinded and bloodied corpse being bundled up to be devoured by hungry pigs. He poured sparkling water and called for more, forcing himself to resist taking refuge in several large measures of Scotch.

No wonder Tavio had been silenced.
Diego Rodrigues?

Maybe next?
Carmino a violent murderer.
A psychopath.

Before checking out earlier, he had researched the definition of psychopath – *inflated sense of self-worth, constant need for stimulation, lying pathologically, conning others, being manipulative, lacking any remorse or guilt.*

That seemed to sum up Carmino pretty damned well.

As the jet lumbered over Hounslow and into London Heathrow, Dex was still shifting uneasily on his recliner, gathering his thoughts. In his absence, nothing had improved. His Alma Tunnel witness had been killed in a strange and unlikely car wreck in western France. In London, the police were telling him nothing. The expert's report on the DAF tipper's tachograph had still not surfaced. Maybe Mick Glenn had challenged Carmino and fired up Carmino's suspicions?

Do I really want to risk filming in Dukes?
The psycho's lair.

Tired and lightheaded, Dex cleared Customs and Immigration and grabbed a welcome double espresso at Costa Coffee. There, he switched on his phone and saw a text from Tiffany. "Call me. Any time." It was timed 8:05 a.m., just an hour ago. Any time? Intriguing. Or ominous? He dialled at once.

Tiffany sounded tense. "Hi, Dex! Are you still in Vienna?" There were no frilly niceties.

"London. Just landed. Your message sounded urgent. Not the usual Miss Cool. What's up?"

"You haven't heard the news? No, of course you haven't. How could you?"

- 53 -

"What news?"

Dex heard both concern and excitement in Tiffany's voice. "Mick Glenn was murdered yesterday evening, London time. My TV station is at the scene now."

"My God!" Dex was then stunned into silence as his tired mind assessed the implications. Another customer, attracted by the exclamation, craned toward Dex to listen. Pointedly, Dex turned away.

Had Mick challenged Carmino?
Maybe. Maybe probably.
Had he landed me in it? No.
He didn't have my name.

"You still there, Dex?"

"Sorry. Yes. I'm just…I don't know."

"The reporter says he was shot outside his home. A neighbour heard two shots."

"Where was that?"

"On his driveway. North London. Near The Bishop's Avenue."

"This is just *too* awful."

"You didn't speak to him, did you?"

It was a question Dex was dreading. "I did." He faltered. "But… you couldn't talk sensibly to him."

Tiffany was typically forthright. "More bloody fool you. I warned you." Her irritation crossed the miles, no problem. "Did he raise hell with Carmino? You'd better face up to that."

Dex was ill-equipped to defend himself. "I don't know. I told him to do nothing. He flew off the planet, totally ape-shit. He never got my name."

"If Glenn confronted Carmino, you and me, we're up the proverbial creek.. F'Christ's sake Dex, as a journalist, he'll finger me and then you as Beth's brother. There'll be recordings of us watching."

"I'm sorry."

"Too damned right you should be. If a loud-mouth like Glenn had spotted something, he'd have cursed One-Eye there and then. Carmino will know that."

The conversation died, each locked in imagination of what may or may not have happened. Then Tiffany's voice brightened. "Our Sports Editor says the rumour mill is already in overdrive. Remember those four footballers arrested on match-fixing allegations. Y'know, bribed by that Malaysian syndicate? There's gossip on Twitter suggesting Mick Glenn might have been a fixer. Several contributors point to an easy goal he missed in the friendly the other day. Others are speculating that it was the husband of some woman he bedded."

"Twitter's great for peddling lies."

"Like it or hate it, it exists."

Dex lowered his voice even further. "Creole Henry? In the rumours?"

"No but it makes sense."

He tipped his cup nearly vertical to get the last drops of caffeine into his system. "I'm moving into Porcupine House." Then he stopped. "Oh God, Tiffany, I'm sorry. I should have asked. How was your event with Bill Clinton?"

He was rewarded with a throaty chuckle. "That man has charisma in spades. He spoke for forty minutes without a note and I swear every person present thought he was talking just to them. It's something to do with his eye contact."

"And you got to speak to him?"

"We chatted for nearly five minutes. He approached me after I'd done my piece. First, he looked me straight in the eye, boring into me in the best possible way. Oozing sincerity, he held my elbow the way US politicians do and said *my book had done the world a great service*. My legs just turned to jelly."

"That is just so cool. After that type of praise, your book's going to number one." Then, as an unwanted image of Mick Glenn lying on a slab destroyed the pleasure of the moment, he fell silent. "Where are you?"

"Atlanta. I left DC yesterday evening. My head was so big they had to widen the door into the 737."

From somewhere, Dex managed a laugh. "Thanks to you, I cracked the code."

"You mean into Beth's…"

"Right on."

"And?"

"You just don't want to know."

"Try me."

"No. Trust me. You don't want to know. Enjoy your memories of meeting Clinton. There's been enough bad news for one day."

For the next few hours, Dex's imagination ran wild with images of Glenn confronting Carmino.

Perhaps it hadn't happened.

-54-

After a late night shifting his belongings, the following morning, Dex had made Porcupine House ready for Jude and Father. Before heading out to Simpson's, he did a quick catch-up on the Mick Glenn rumour-mill. Glenn's womanising was a constant theme, though most conspiracy theorists linked the murder to match-fixing. Names of ex-girlfriends and women he had been seen with had prompted speculation about angry husbands and even a suggestion he had enjoyed a quickie with the wife of an England teammate. There was just one reference to a sighting of him with Amber Murray.

More would surely come.

In Panama, whilst waiting for his flight, he had tracked down Billy Evans, the blackjack specialist suggested by Gus McKay. They had agreed to meet for breakfast and Dex had chosen Simpson's-in-the-Strand. Billy arrived with his small daughter. "My access day with her," he explained on sitting down in the grand and traditional surroundings of panelling, chandeliers and wall-lights. "I'm taking Emily to the zoo. I hope you don't mind."

Emily was like a china doll with delicate pink skin and an engaging smile. Her hair was like flax and tied in a ponytail at the back. The ponytail was the only similarity to her father who was a walking wreck. Emily pulled off a tartan poncho and sat in the corner of the booth in a pair of red dungarees over a white jumper. To Dex, she had the face of an angel, round and smiling with large eyes that beamed across the table. Yet she bore no resemblance to her daddy who was somewhere the wrong side of haggard, his eyes tired and his cheeks prematurely lined. His clothes were crumpled as if he had slept rough on a park bench.

"Hello, Emily. I'm Dex. Did you bring something to read or play with?"

She nodded and from a Barbie box, she produced a faded but obviously much-loved Winnie-the-Pooh and a Gruffalo story. "These are my favourites," she said proudly. "Pooh goes everywhere with me."

"Pooh will have fun at the zoo. That's if he's not scared of lions, tigers and hissy snakes."

"*My* Pooh is very brave and very hungry. He needs some honey."

"He'll get honey here – the very best. You're a big girl, aren't you? How old you are."

"I'm five. Soon, I'll be six, won't I daddy?" She waited for his proud agreement and then beamed, her face radiating excitement.

"Well, Emily, us grown-ups, we're going to be talking about very boring things. But when we've finished, perhaps we can play I-Spy or Connections."

"What's Connections, Mr. Dex? I-Spy is boring too."

"I'll teach you. Now let's order." Dex turned to Emily's father, hoping his shock at Evans's appearance wasn't too apparent. "I'm going for the Simpson's special – the Deadly Sins. What about you?" As he was speaking, he took in Billy's strange appearance. The man could do with a square meal…or ten. The way his linen jacket hung, it looked as if he had been on a crash diet. For his age, his skin was much too pallid and scrawny. His age? Thirty? Forty-two? It was impossible to know.

"The same please." Billy's accent and somewhat flat vowels suggested an upbringing somewhere in the Midlands. "Sorry to keep you waiting. Late night in the casino. Then I had to collect Emily. We're having pizza and ice cream at the zoo, aren't we?" He was rewarded with a hug and then a nuzzle from Pooh. Billy's eyes were furtive, such a contrast to the wide-eyed innocence of his daughter. "I'll share the Deadly Sins with Emily. Coffee for me, hot chocolate for her."

Dex poured orange juice from a large pitcher as he appraised the figure opposite. The prospect of getting help from Billy wasn't obviously appealing. He wondered what McKay would now make of the man he had rated the best blackjack player he had ever come across. "Do you work locally?"

"Computer Programmer in Eastcheap. Zero-Hours contract." He wiped his hand under his nose and moments later did it again. He glanced at Emily who was pretend-reading the menu to Pooh. "I can see what you're thinking but I'm not an addict. I did have a problem but it's behind me now."

Dex raised an eyebrow, unsure whether to believe him. Shutting any addiction into a locked box was a tall order. He knew that Billy would always be fighting his demons.

Just as I was, just as I am with the booze.

Billy lowered his voice. "Gussie McKay will have told you about the white stuff. Cost me my marriage. Sandie and me – we're living apart, not divorced." Emily was now in a make-believe world of her own, so Billy continued. "I'm not after sympathy. It was my fault and I'm trying to get her back. But beating an addiction?" He shook his head. "My life became a mess. My only friends were pushers and bartenders."

"Any casinos after you for counting?"
"Not in London. I never did it here."
"In America?"
"I was never caught. That's why Gussie respects me. Together,

we toured the USA way back – played Atlantic City, the Gulf Coast, Vegas, Indian Reservations in California."

"That," Dex grinned hugely "is just what I need." He leaned towards Evans. "I want a punter who plays solid Basic Strategy. Every shoe, you count cards" He chopped his right hand across the table. "But never, never ever *playing* as a counter."

"I don't get it."

"I need to know if the decks are fixed."

"You mean if some tens and aces have been removed?" He saw Dex nod a yes. "It happens in less-regulated countries. Some also slip in a few extra 4s and 5s. But in London? I'd be amazed."

"Prepare to be amazed!"

"That's cool with me."

Dex noticed that Billy had chewed the fingernails almost to nothing. His bloodshot eyes were dull, dead even and lurked between prominent cheekbones. Except at the back, his hair was closely cropped so that the black ponytail looked as if it had been glued on. In one ear was a stud and the knot of his wide navy tie hung a full inch below the fraying collar of his shirt.

"I can tell what you're thinking," Billy volunteered, his face suddenly youthful. "You're thinking, my God, he's a bloody wreck. You're right too." Billy looked at the table, his face once again forlorn. "Counting cards reduced me to this." Billy shook his head in self-disgust. "The risk of being caught in the USA got me started. For months, I couldn't live without it, the white stuff that is. I didn't eat properly. Couldn't afford to. My money went up my nose." He shook his head. "Anyroads, six weeks ago, I went to Biloxi to gamble. When I got back, Sandie had locked me out." He shrugged. "I don't blame her."

"But with Gus McKay?"

"I even looked young then. We toured the USA, never playing

at the same table but often watching each other. He was a canny old sod."

"But then?"

"He got caught."

"His gorilla moment?"

Billy's eyes managed a flicker of life. "That scared me. Seeing him dragged away between those two guys." He glanced at Emily, who was now looking at the Gruffalo. "The big wins stopped. Vicious circle, it was. No counting equals no big wins equals more white powder equals cash crisis equals marriage meltdown." He shook his head so that his ponytail swayed. "I went to Biloxi as a last shot at a big win by card-counting. I wanted to treat Sandie to pretty things. I wanted to make her love me again. But I felt too much heat, y'know the gorillas watching me. I chickened out. I lost even more." He cut up a plump sausage for Emily. "This is a real treat, isn't it, Emily. I told you we'd have a fun day out."

"Thank you, daddy. Thank you, Mr. Dex." The little girl wriggled along the bench seat to be closer to the daddy she so obviously loved.

"You have no idea what it's like – card-counting, I mean." He twiddled his fork. "Playing blackjack isn't difficult. Just like Happy Families or Snap. You may win but you'll probably lose over time. But card-counting's different."

"Go on!" Dex wanted to test McKay's comments and advice.

"Casinos aren't charities. No way! They want every last penny and your balls as well. They're always updating wizard technology, real Big Brother stuff like face-recognition software, devices in the blackjack shoes doing player-tracking. Add in automatic continuous shufflers. For card-counters, that's the end. Kaput. Stone dead gone. They've got us beat." He stabbed into the fried bread with an angry movement and then laid down his fork, still chewing rapidly.

"Here's the story. I'm gathering evidence against a casino. I'll fund your membership fee. There are strings attached, mind. You'll join via a friend of mine, not through me. I'll bankroll you and pay for your time. I want you to test the count over two or three weeks."

"Explain."

"A player there was griping that he rarely wins."

"You said this was in London?" Billy stopped his fork in mid-air.

"Dukes."

Billy ran his finger under his misshapen nostrils. "Proper posh joint. You surprise me. But by counting through enough shoes, I'd spot whether they were fixing the decks." He watched Emily finishing the last of her breakfast. "A clean plate, Emily. Well done!" He laughed for the first time. "That must be your good influence, Dex."

Dex waited while Billy wiped egg off the girl's cheek. "Here's the deal." For the next few minutes, they fixed the small print of what was needed. "Your cover is you've met Adam Yarbury and you're teaching him how to play Basic Strategy. Adam's a friend." Dex paused, slightly embarrassed about what he wanted to say. "He's old-fashioned. One of the chaps."

Billy pushed aside the remains of his toast. "You're telling me I must smarten up?"

"Get rid of the stud, the ponytail. Look conventional. I'll pay. Buy some new shirts, ties, jackets Without a giant makeover, nobody would believe Adam would ever have spoken to you."

"You're the boss." Billy did not seem offended.

"You known in Dukes?"

"No. Far too posh."

Dex was pleased at the denial. "Let's meet after the zoo. I'll give you enough cash for everything. Oh, and I'll fix a meeting with Adam. Today, he's at a wine-tasting jolly in France." Dex waved his knife in emphasis. "Get this: if you see me in Dukes, you don't know me. Got it? Not unless Adam introduces you to me. Understood?" Dex waited for the firm nod.

Billy checked his watch. "Time to go, Emily."

"But Mr Dex is going to teach me Connections."

"Next time. We must hurry to the zoo." He grabbed her arm, her poncho and Barbie box.

Dex patted her head. "That's right, Emily. Next time. That's a promise."

"The bears will get you if you don't keep promises," she warned, suddenly all stern.

Dex's eyes welled-up as he thought of baby Jamie and all the fun he had lost. "You're right, Emily. I wouldn't want that."

Emily looked across at Dex, puzzled at his watery eyes. "Goodbye, Mr. Dex."

"You'll have a lovely day." Dex turned to Billy and gave him the address of Porcupine House. "I'll be there later. It's not far from the zoo. Here's a tenner. Come over by taxi this afternoon."

The euphoria he had felt on receiving a tight hug from Emily vanished as he stepped into the noisy bustle of the Strand. The air was filled with the stink of diesel from the steady flow of buses and taxis. Motorcycle couriers raced by as if practising for the Isle of Man TT. He checked the time – he had an hour to get to Harley Street to see Dr Wilfred Grierson.

55

With plenty of time to meet Grierson. Dex decided to walk to Harley Street and was soon rounding the long curve of Regent Street with its mix of touristy memento shops and designer stores. His thoughts were on his visit to Dukes tonight, a chance to use the toys he had bought yesterday from the espionage specialists in Mayfair. He had bought a camera disguised in a tiepin and another in a cufflink.

Would Carmino be suspicious?
That depended on Mick Glenn.
No answer to that.
Yet.
What do I play?
Do I watch One-Eye?
Or maybe Andy?
Or flit from table to table?

The sight of Hamleys Toy Store reminded him of Emily's big smile. Impulsively, he went in and bought her a large panda before heading on to Harley Street. Nearly every Georgian building housed leading medical consultants but, concealing behind impressive qualifications, more than a spattering of charlatans. Dex knew the street well, this being his sixteenth visit. About halfway up on the right, he spotted the too-familiar brass plate – *Dr Wilfred Grierson MBChB, MRCPsch. Psychiatrist.* He used the brass knocker and entered, for once rather looking forward to seeing the dour Scotsman but who was a mad-keen Morris Dancer to boot. With the emphasis on *mad*.

After Dex had browsed through a well-thumbed *Country Life* magazine, he was called in. Grierson was sipping from a bone china cup in a room that might once have seated thirty Victorian gentry for a very long lunch. The cup's contents smelled smoky enough to be Lapsang Souchong but Dex was offered nothing. Presumably the consultation fee of one-thousand pounds was insufficient to cover such generosity.

"How are you feeling?"

Grierson was late fifties and his crinkly grey hair was meticulously groomed. The toffee-nosed accent and the tweed jacket suggested he probably owned a salmon beat in the Border Country. Or a whole river, come to that. Unless he spent all his spare time and money on Morris Dancing, wearing a daft hat, jingling his bells and waving hankies.

Dex enjoyed seeing the consultant look at the panda, a question-mark on his face. "How am I? Doc, this is Percy Panda. These days, I take him everywhere. Such a comfort. We cuddle up every night, along with my Koala Bear." Dex tried not to laugh as the psychiatrist frowned and noted this new quirk on his pad. As Dex replied, he was already rolling up his sleeve to have his blood pressure checked. He knew the drill sixteen times over. As the gadget tightened on his upper left arm, he explained that he was feeling a damned sight better since he had flung every pill into the Thames.

There was a long silence as Grierson watched the deflating arm band and then grunted. "No pills, eh? Since when?" The man's gruff voice made him sound as if he had an anger management problem.

"I forget," Dex prevaricated, "but long enough to know they weren't doing me a damned bit of good."

"You think so?"

"I know so."

Grierson fell silent as he sniffed his tea and sipped thoughtfully. *That silence has probably cost me at least thirty quid,* Dex thought as he waited for a response. At last, after much flexing of fingers and examination of his nails, it came. "How?"

Dex reckoned that single word had probably cost another fifty quid at least. "Not a single nightmare since I fed them to the fishes. Never felt better. On the other hand, the perch and roach feasting on your pills in the Thames are having nightmares about ending up on a dinner-plate and being sprinkled with vinegar."

Grierson gave an expensive grunt. Humour had always passed him by. He leaned across the antique desk and picked up his Mont Blanc pen and made a laboriously slow note. Dex imagined it confirmed that *this patient still presents as unstable. Collection of fluffy toys suggests lack of breastfeeding as a baby.* The doctor then tilted his gold-rimmed spectacles further up his nose before looking over them to stare at his patient. "Your blood pressure…"

Dex feigned surprise. "You never treated me for that, did you?"

"When you were on your, eh, *med-ic-ation* for stress and anxiety disorders," he spoke the words so slowly Dex reckoned he was dreaming of his fee again, "your blood pressure was 112 over 77."

Dex knew that was good. "That bad?"

Grierson ignored the comment. His lips narrowed. "Today it is 155 over 108." He shook his head very slowly, like everything else he did. Dex understood the figures were too high. "Higher, eh! I'm getting better then." Dex rubbed his hands. "The figures are going up at last." He enjoyed winding up the guy and wasting more of the man's time for the fee.

"When you were on that *med-ic-ation* and following my advice to relax, you were coming along nicely, just fine. Another year, maybe two and I could have signed you as fit for work." He shook his head in despair.

"Doing just fine, was I, Doc? The nightmares from your *med-ic-ation* scared the shit out of any young beauty who happened to enjoy my company in bed."

"Really well. Yes, doing really, really well." Grierson had ignored Dex's remark as he gazed at a nineteenth-century painting of a clipper defying a storm. "Are you relaxing like I advised? You're not nearly ready for life in the wider world yet."

"No stress in my life at all." Dex grinned disarmingly as memories flashed by – the smell of the burning limo; identifying his sister in the morgue; the funeral; visiting his father; moving house; the murder of Mick Glenn; investigating a psychopath; being held at knifepoint just three days ago. "No, Doc, nothing stressful, nothing out of the ordinary."

"No alcohol still?"

Dex waved a long arm airily. "Oh no, Doc. Strictly and absolutely off-limits."

Grierson was unimpressed and leaned forward. "I don't *believe* you. Something is pushing up your blood pressure." He looked Dex up and down. "You're lean, fit-looking. Something is doing this. We must start a fresh course of er, eh – *med-ic-ation* – something to reduce the blood pressure. An ACE inhibitor."

Dex shook his head. "*We* are starting nothing."

Grierson ignored this instruction. "And besides taking something for the blood pressure, I want you back on the tranquillisers you so foolishly discarded." He was poised to write a prescription. "Your problem, Mr Finlay, is you see black and white as if they were equal. Black and white may mean blacker or whiter. Small side effects, the black part, you should ignore for the greater good. Your *med-ic-ation* was much more white than black."

"Doc, I've swallowed enough pills to make me rattle." He stood up rather abruptly from his chair. "Pills? No thanks. I'll heal myself." He headed for the door. "Without your fees, I'll be stress-free. Ticketyboo, as you medical professionals say." He picked up the giant panda. "Come on Percy. Goodbye, Doc."

"You're not consulting me again?" Grierson pushed his glasses back up his nose, sounding shocked and close to despair. "Your blood pressure is a ticking time-bomb." He barely paused. "And remember, cash or debit card only."

"Yeah! I remember." Dex nodded thoughtfully as Grierson opened the notes for his next patient. Dex breezed out to the receptionist and offered his Amex card. The young woman told him Dr Grierson did not accept it. Dex leaned across her desk and gave her a big smile and a friendly wink. "You're new here, aren't you? I always pay with Amex," Dex insisted. "He just hates them taking their cut." He watched the receptionist hesitate, so he smiled again. "You'll find the card-reader in the left-hand drawer." He watched her pull it out. "Thanks, darling."

Moments later, he and Percy Panda were gone, enjoying their moment of minor triumph. He wandered westwards to St Christopher's Place where he ordered a latte. Something Grierson had said had set him thinking. He relived the fifteen minutes until it hit him.

Seeing things in black or white.
Perhaps Grierson was right on that.
My God!
Was it doable?
Was this the way to beat Dukes?
A masterstroke?
Or wild, impractical and fanciful?

He drained the coffee and tucked away the idea for later, also making a mental note to get some blood pressure pills on the NHS.

– 56 –

As he sat in his Space City office, the door shut against the drilling and clatter of ongoing work downstairs, Enzo Letizione should have felt happier than he did. He had bought some loyalty from the Union reps. A star-studded celeb-list had accepted for the Grand Opening. Millions of casino profits had been crossing the Atlantic from Dukes with the bankers not suspicious of money-laundering or RICO offences.

What troubled him was this morning's *Las Vegas Review Journal*. The story, on an inside page, had nagged like toothache. He read it again without needing to. A man had gone missing while boating on Lake Mead. The body had not been found and neither had the victim been named. As a local story, it was unremarkable. Countless times, Letizione had read of drownings on the vast expanse of water. At weekends, hundreds and even thousands took to the lake in small boats to fish, to party or to poodle around. Accidents happened. Usually they involved alcohol and a loss of balance or perhaps a drunken argument ending in a fight.

But Letizione remembered when the mob might invite a victim for a day at the lake. Tickets were strictly one-way, concrete jackets and boots supplied. Moments ago, Channel 13 Action News had reported that the body of Diego Rodrigues had been recovered. The name had hit him like a kick in the gut. He sat thoughtful for a few moments, his anger growing. The chiming wall-clock confirmed it was just turning 3 p.m. and 11 p.m. in London. He clicked open

FaceTime, wanting to see Pepe's face during the conversation. The call was quickly answered.

"Yeah. It's all good, Pepe. And you?"

"No problems." Carmino's eyes narrowed as he spoke, something not lost on the American. Then he smiled disarmingly. "Well, that's not quite right."

"Go on!"

"We're keeping a close watch on a new member. He acts a bit strange, like a detective – hanging out round the tables and watching."

"You think he's a cop? Or maybe snooping for the Gambling Commission?"

"Neither. I know his background."

"He's suspicious?"

"Says he's learning. But like I say, we're watching him."

"24-7?"

"Not yet. Only in here." Carmino paused, undecided whether to continue. "Okay. Let me explain. Remember I mentioned an Aussie woman? Bit of a looker?" He waited for the nod before continuing. "I've got her planted in the guy's home. Nursing the guy's father. Smart, eh?"

"I guess." The American was bothered by the need for such an extreme step. "Gonna explain why?"

"Just wanting her to sniff round, get him talking."

"Sure, but what are you looking for?"

Letizione noticed Carmino's pupils shrink as he assessed his answer and then picked his words carefully. "To see what his game is, if anything. To see what he's got on us, if anything. Jude's drop-dead gorgeous. She'll get him talking."

"Pillow talk, huh?"

"Whatever." No way was Carmino going to reveal that Jude

was there to see if Dex had been to Panama. Jude's brief of *just sniffing around*, had never mentioned that. Neither was Carmino going to tell Letizione that it was Beth Dexter's brother who had been acting suspiciously. "Arnie's mate forged some great references for Jude. Fooled the guy a treat." His knowing look showed how pleased he was with himself.

"She's a hooker?"

"For the right guys, I reckon she does tricks for free." Now was not the moment to reveal that he had been bedding her for weeks.

"Hey Get this for coincidence! Guy drowned out at Lake Mead. Name was Diego Rodrigues. Mean anything?"

Carmino looked away, frowned and he shook his head. "How, or maybe why in hell should I know this Diego?"

To Letizione, the frown seemed exaggerated. "He used to hang out with Tavio Sanchez – remember, that dealer who was shot outside his apartment when you were here."

"These names mean nothing."

"Want to know more?"

As he crossed his arms defensively, Carmino was unsure what to answer. "Well, I suppose you're going to tell me. Make it quick."

"Diego also reckoned you were in Panama. Two guys, same story. Both dead."

The American watched for guilt but was disappointed as Carmino swatted away the message. "Don't you get it, Enzo?" The Englishman's tone was sharp. "I've said before, I've never been in Panama. Listen: is someone trying to screw us over our licence? Is that the story? Getting these Latinos to spread crap around your city that I wasn't straight on our gambling application?"

"Not so I've noticed. But hey, something else – what's with all this shit I'm reading about a guy called Mick Glenn, a soccer star, who got himself murdered. They report he was a big player at Dukes."

"Reached Vegas that story has it?" Carmino looked surprised. "Glenn was a member. Big player?" He snorted with derision. "He came in occasionally. Big ego. Maybe a big dick too. The dumbfuck was screwing a Yardie's woman. Bad move! The media are all over that. What's it to you, anyway? Someone bad-mouthing us about Glenn?"

"Uh-uh. No. Nobody suggested Dukes was involved in the murder."

"I'd have had our lawyer onto it if they had!" Carmino laughed as he reached for his espresso.

Letizione stroked his chin wanting to look pensive. "I mean you lost that member, that woman, in the car wreck. Now there's Glenn and there's these two dealers. That's four – all dead, all within a few weeks." Letizione paused for emphasis. "And each had some link to you."

"Not those two in Vegas." Carmino retorted, his voice rising. His eyes were unflinching as he glared at Letizione. "Get this straight. None of these four deaths is to do with me, us, or Dukes."

The American settled his hands across the spread of his stomach. He wanted to come across as calm but forceful. "Just remember what I always warned you – no whacking. It don't pay. I learned that in the eighties."

"Cut this crap, Enzo. Downstairs, I've got princes, billionaires, even oligarchs. We're screwing them all to pay for your fuck-ups." Carmino pointed at his screen. "Never forget that because I won't." Carmino ended the connection with a pointed flourish of his cigar butt.

Letizione stared at the blank screen. Slowly he got up and paced his office, looking at a photo of him with the mayor of Las Vegas and another with a senator outside the Capitol in Washington. Life then had been good. He thought of the skimmed money, drip-feeding his secret account. He was in too deep now to back off. He and Carmino both needed the other. In London, Carmino was thinking much the same – for now.

Letizione stared at a photo of the topping-out ceremony. His jowls quivered as his pent-up frustration took over. "You're a lying lump of shit. This is for you, Pepe." He hurled his glass at the picture. Both broke with a resounding crash, shards of glass scattering over the floor.

He felt better for it.

-57-

As he heard Jude enter his father's study, Dex swung round from his laptop. He was seated at the generous proportions of Father's desk. Despite hating Porcupine House, he relished a room big enough to swing several cats. "Settled in up there?"

"Yeah! No sweat, mate."

He gave her a welcoming smile and a longer look as he took in her change of clothes. She had arrived in faded blue jeans and a grey sweatshirt. Her baseball cap had the fishbone logo of Doyles restaurant at Watson Bay in Sydney. Now, however, her copper-coloured hair swayed over her shoulders and along the top of a clinging silvery catsuit. It was figure-hugging with sex bursting through every stitch. Jude approached, crossing the thick grey carpet with feline grace that matched the outfit.

She looked round the room with obvious approval. Even now, the smell of Father's Erinmore pipe tobacco still tainted the carpet and heavy drapes. Of his father's memorabilia, there was no sign. Dex had dumped everything in the cellar. The study now gave him room to spread out his work on the Alma Tunnel. The roulette wheel he had set up on a mahogany side-table.

"Don't think every day will be this easy," Dex commented. "If everything is ready for Father's arrival tomorrow, you can bunk off – watch TV here or see your mates in Earl's Court."

Jude shrugged *whatever*, a movement that seemed to waft the scent of a subtle perfume closer to him. "What are your plans?"

Something in her voice and tilted head told Dex that a suggestion that he chase her round the room, with her not hurrying, would have been welcome. "I'm going to a casino in Mayfair."

"You're obviously pretty damned expert," she prompted, nodding at the wheel.

"Hardly." Dex stretched his clasped hands behind his neck and leaned back in the expensively upholstered chair. "I'm a novice. But I'd be a bad loser, so I'm practising."

"Roulette's a tough game. Trust me. I used to play at the casino in Sydney. Here's the secret: Think like a winner! Play like a winner Be a winner."

"You didn't always win playing roulette. You must have lost."

"Same as my virginity. Just once, long ago and best forgotten. Nah! Losing's for wimps. I prefer Punto Banco."

"Which is?"

"Strewth! You are a novice! It's cards. Best odds in the house. Or maybe you call it baccarat." She adopted a very upper-crust English accent to say the word.

He looked blank, showing she was talking way over his head. "You ever play in London, Jude?"

"Occasionally. I've had city friends take me to Crockfords, the Ritz."

"Dukes?"

"Dukes?" She thought for a moment. "Is that in Mount Street?" She saw Dex agree. "Sure. Maybe once. Could be twice but after sinking enough vodka-martinis to float a cruise-ship, I sometimes get mixed up." They both laughed at the image as she perched her shapely thighs and buttocks against the roulette layout. "Mind, at Dukes, I was bankrolled by an insurance broker. He lost his New Year bonus playing blackjack. I won him a rhino-sized wad."

Dex thought for a moment and then plunged in. "Well, why not come along tonight?"

"Do me a favour, boss! Me? Gamble?" Her laugh was coarse and raucous. "On what you're paying me?"

"I'll bankroll you. You win at baccarat; I lose at roulette. Balance out. Deal?"

She met his gaze with all the confidence of a poker player sitting on trips. "You mean I don't keep my winnings? You kidding me?"

Dex could see she was enjoying the wind-up. "Christ! You Aussies! Plus dinner on me."

"Gee! I'd love to." Jude seemed ready to jump at the chance but then her tanned face wrinkled. "I'll take a rain-check. Tomorrow's going to be busy with your Dad. I might pop down to Earl's Court but not a late night."

Dex managed to conceal his disappointment. "Okay. Another time?"

"You got a deal, Dex. I love gambling." She paused. "Dukes? Would I have met Pepe someone there?"

"Pepe Carmino."

"What a charmer, eh! He joined us in the bar. That guy! He has some stories!"

Dex could have added one or two that Carmino would not have told her but let it pass. "I'll remember that." He checked the time. "I'll be off soon."

"I'll get everything ready for Sir Charles. Hey? Is that what I call him?"

Dex was floored. "I don't think Father's in any condition to complain if you don't – but on the other hand, why not?"

"Okay! Ciao boss," she laughed as she left with a wave of her hand.

He sent a couple of emails and then, as usual now, checked the web for news from Vegas. The main stories were about casino moguls differing about Resort Fees, car-parking charges and the influence of Macau on the sector. Then he scrolled down and saw another headline – *Missing Dealer Named*. The words Diego Rodrigues jumped out at him. His pounding heart reminded him of Grierson's blood pressure warning but it was too late to worry about that. Diego Rodrigues – he of the big mouth in whom Tavio had confided. He took a deep breath.

Carmino at work again?
Two dealers.
Both fingering Pepe.
Both dead.
Coincidence?

He tried to contact Tiffany, still unsure about revealing Tavio's statement. If she knew what Carmino had done, the worry, her fears, could spoil her tour. That was scarcely fair. perhaps fortunately, she wasn't picking up anyway. Yet, as Reverend Hillyer had said, he shouldn't carry the burden alone – but who to trust, who to confide in?

Perhaps, Adam?
Panama would scare him shitless.
Maybe Jude?
McKay would say no.
Not yet anyway.

On his Sony laptop, he updated his diary to enter the death of Rodrigues and then shut it down. Taking his example from Beth, he now had a complex but memorable password. He closed the lid and left it on his desk beside a scattering of cheap gel pens, a stapler, a calculator, his empty coffee cup and some crumbs from a raisin cookie. His scribbled notes and results from Reverse Labouchère, he left by the layout but his passport and everything about Panama was either in the safe alongside Father's cheque books and share certificates or were password protected in the Sony. He slammed shut the safe's heavy door and set the combination lock.

Time to go.

Upstairs, Jude lay on her bed waiting for the slam of the door. She needed the house to herself.

-58-

Pepe Carmino swivelled the monitor on his desk so that Nigel Forster-Brown could see it. Carmino was in his comfy chair, the picture of relaxation, whereas his deputy stood nervously, eyes looking more at the carpet rather than the screen. FB's restless hands looked even whiter than usual as Carmino wanted to enjoy his manager's discomfort.

Suddenly on screen, Forster-Brown joined the footballer. Moments later, Carmino laughed in a mocking way as they watched: "Listen, you bald-headed bunny. You tell that ponce Pepe: I'm not leavin' next time without all me money back – all £210,000 of it, or I'm goin' to Scotland bleedin' Yard. I know the fuckin' works on you lot. An' I'm goin' to tell every fuckin' member the way it is. Got it, you carrot-cruncher? I'll be in next Thursday evening. 10:30. You tell him."

Carmino let the recording continue until Glenn had bounded up the stairs toward the exit. "So, FB – you finished checking yet?"

FB handed over a typed list with ten names on it. "My take, boss. Glenn saw nothing or he would have shouted the roof off. Anyway, he was too busy groping Creole Henry's woman between spins. Scotty Brannigan? On the racetrack, he's ruthless, tough as hell. Wouldn't have been world champion if he wasn't. If he'd spotted something? He'd have raised hell at once. The recordings support my views. You can discount their two bimbos. That leaves the German guy – Gerhard Hoge, the three Indians - Virat Khan, Zaheer Ashwin, Ajit Badani plus Tiffany Richmond and Finlay Dexter."

"Any of them friendly with Mick Glenn?"

Eyes locked on the carpet and feet shuffling, Forster-Brown said there had been banter between the German and Mick Glenn about penalty shoot-outs. Nobody else had spoken to the footballer. "Mick Glenn might have invented it?" FB did not even convince himself.

"Get real, you bald-headed bunny!" Carmino glared at his manager, enjoying Forster-Brown flinch at the insult. "One-Eye *was* cheating them. Glenn was bang-on correct. The question is who told him. Someone smart enough to spot what One-Eye was doing."

FB wanted to tell his boss where to shove the job but that was beyond his comfort zone. He had to think of his pension. "No likely candidates. Least, not on what we know."

Carmino looked at the list again. "Those three Indians?"

Forster-Brown hesitated, wary about putting his head above the parapet again. "All cricketers. They only played five spins and anyway, there was no sign they recognised him." He saw his boss nod and heard him grunt, so he continued. "Tiffany Richmond? The enquiring mind of a journalist."

Pepe doodled on his notepad. "And she would know how to contact Glenn."

"That chump Adam Yarbury told me Dexter is a novice."

"But Beth was his sister, so we can't rule him out." Carmino looked up, his sucked-in cheeks emphasising the wolf in his appearance. "So maybe for now, it's Tiffany? The unknown quantity."

"And boss, who brought her in?"

"Correct, FB. Answer – Finlay Dexter." Carmino lit his cigar. "So maybe it's them working together, Dexter using her as an investigative journalist. Possible." Then he shook his head. "Nah! Journalists keep scoops for themselves. No way would she contact Glenn and reveal her big story."

"Your instructions?"

"It must be Dexter but business as usual. Keep One-Eye and Andy away from Dexter if he plays. Tell Jeb Miller to keep a special eye on Dexter and her but I think she's touring the USA. Anything suspicious, let me know at once."

"Dexter arrived about forty minutes ago. I'll get back down there." As FB turned away, one of Carmino's two mobile phones vibrated, a signal for him to shoo FB out of the room even faster. When Carmino heard the voice, his face broke into one of his most charming smiles and his voice oozed ersatz friendliness. "Settled in have you?" He listened for a few moments. "Yes, you're fine. Plenty more time. He's downstairs. What's that you said? A roulette wheel where he practices? And documents? What have you found?" Again, he fell silent, listening to the Aussie accent. "Is that all? He's pretty careful? No passport? No diary on his desk? Hmm! Search his bedroom, his briefcase." He was then quiet for rather longer as he listened, his face growing increasingly solemn. "Password protected, is it? Oh, and a modern safe?"

As Jude continued, Carmino fist-thumped his desk in pleasure. "He did, did he? You were right to say no. Keep snooping. Wastebaskets, the trash. Everything." He adjusted the angle of his desk lamp thoughtfully. "But, sure. Come here for dinner another night. While he's here, we'll have someone crack the password. You have your own house-key? Good, good. Know the code for any alarm?" He scribbled down a number on his pad. "That's the alarm, is it? I'll read it back. 19293900. Correct? And where is the control box? Beside the kitchen door? That's down the side? Okay."

He had heard enough and now sounding impatient, he thanked her. "Yes, of course I enjoy our afternoons. We must. We will! Can't wait! Yes – once Dexter's old man is settled in and you can get away. My place again, of course."

~ 59 ~

Dex had deliberately not gone to the wheel where One-Eye was spinning. He settled in next to a cheerful middle-aged German who introduced himself as Gerhard Hoge. The dealer's name was Jasmine. Hoge only played the outside bets and so Dex asked if he would mind if he followed his play, as he seemed to be winning. "*Ja*! Please bring me more of this luck," Hoge replied in good English. "For sure, I'm not always winning like tonight."

"Is that because of Jasmine or is it your lucky underpants?"

"Ha! I guess the guy I shook hands with earlier was a chimney-sweep." Hoge saw Dex look puzzled. "For us Germans, that is the best way to get good luck."

"And a black, sooty hand," laughed Dex, pushing a stack of chips to back even numbers. He was happy to be talking. It took his mind off his secretive cameras. Forty minutes later, Hoge said he had won enough, just over twenty-nine thousand pounds. Dex also eased back his chair and coloured up his chips. "Thanks to you, Gerhard. I'm up nearly eight thousand." Yet beneath his enthusiasm, there was disappointment at spotting nothing unusual.

The German rose to his beanpole height. "So, my friend. Maybe we play again together."

"I can be your honorary chimney-sweep."

"Any time. See you." With that the German headed for the bar while Dex strolled to the baccarat where he rapidly decided that comprehension was beyond him. He stopped by the blackjack and watched a few hands before squeezing himself into a corner seat at

One-Eye's roulette table. The dealer was paying out over four hundred thousand to a Brazilian steel magnate. If One-Eye had cheated him, Dex was too late to find out. He looked around and smiled at FB. *Am I paranoid, or is FB following me like a hungry mongrel?*

He placed his wrist on the layout close to number 34 and aimed his tie toward One-Eye, hoping to catch some sleight of hand on the Indian's next win. He was disappointed. Not only was the Indian paid out exactly right but One-Eye was moved on after the next spin. *Strange or not?* Dex knew that dealers were often moved or given a break, sometimes after twenty minutes but maybe after much longer. For the next hour, the dealer was Cheryl, a new one as far as Dex was concerned. Until he had a partner to join him, he had parked Reverse Labouchère and so played the even-chances but without any luck. "That's me done," he volunteered to Cheryl after he had lost most of his winnings.

In the taxi back to St John's Wood, he was disappointed. He had caught nothing on camera. Worse still, while in the bar, FB had told him that Space City's Grand Opening was on schedule. He had to move faster. *Thank God Adam Yarbury was flying back tonight!* He needed to get Billy Evans playing blackjack. When the taxi purred to a halt outside the white stucco of the double-fronted home, Dex saw a light from Jude's room on the very top floor. He checked the time. It was 2:20 a.m. Not quite the early night she had suggested.

He went into Father's study and opened his laptop to message Tiffany but again she was offline. He left a message and was about to exit his computer when he noticed the second drawer down on his desk was slightly open. Though he was not obsessively tidy, Dex knew that it had been searched. One thing he always did was to keep all drawers tightly shut, a habit from a school trip to Sri Lanka. In the hostel, they had been warned that if drawers were not tightly shut overnight, they might confront a cobra in the morning. That old habit had never died.

With an angry shake of the head and a sense of shock at Jude's behaviour, he checked every drawer but spotted nothing missing or unusual. If she had planted a bug, it was well hidden but he would have to get the place swept when Jude was out.

Was she just nosey?

Or something more sinister?

It was with slow footsteps and deep in thought that he mounted the stairs. By the time he reached his bedroom on the first floor, he was philosophical. At least he knew he had a snooper living in the house.

Knowledge is power.

Wasn't that the expression?

－60－

Three days later, his father was settled in a spacious top-floor *en-suite* with a special bed. Jude's room was next door. As yet, Sir Charles had shown little meaningful responses, his mouth flopped open, his body listless and his head lolling forward. Watching Jude, Dex had been impressed. She had been efficient at dressing, undressing, cleaning, chatting or reading to her patient while he lay on the bed or slumped in his chair.

But she was a snooper.

During those three days, not much had changed. the police had at last admitted that, as Tiffany had told him, the truck driver had disappeared. The tachograph report had still not emerged. The police were still following "a number of lines of enquiry" into Mick Glenn's murder, something Dex had chatted about to Adam Yarbury.

Adam had a small apartment in West London but his preferred pad was a penthouse overlooking the Millennium Bridge. Dex had breakfasted there on the terrace, served by his maid, Ursula in her black uniform with a white frilly headband, a relic from a bygone era. In the chilly breeze, she served them a *full English* as they took in the dome of St Paul's and the murky brown of the Thames far below.

The morning air was scented by sweet peas, petunias and lavender, all tended by Adam and flowering from their alabaster pots. As usual with Adam, much of the conversation was surreal – one of the pleasures of the time-warp he occupied. "I see that fella, the footballer, was murdered. I never liked the cut of his jib but he didn't deserve that. Or perhaps he did. Perhaps he *was* a bit of a cad and a rascal. When I was young, we would have called him a poodle-faker." He paused looking thoughtful. "Don't ask me what that meant though," he guffawed, throwing back his head.

Dex laughed at the outmoded vocabulary but quickly became serious. "I spoke to Mick Glenn. Not long before he died."

"My dear old thing! Whatever for?"

Dex rapidly explained about Glenn and Scotty Brannigan being cheated. Dex could see that although Adam was listening, he was also marshalling his own train of thought. Dex watched him tapping his teeth and then scratching his ear as if somehow that would clarify whatever was on his mind. "Dex, my boy. I wish we had shared this conversation sooner."

"Oh? Why would that be?" Dex put down his coffee cup and rested his elbows on the teak table.

"It all makes sense now. Not at the time, of course. It was all mumbo-jumbo. Jail and all that stuff." Adam was talking more to himself than to Dex, who crunched his wheat toast with impatience. Adam stood up to lean against the balcony railings, taking in the view towards the Tower of London. After a few quiet moments, he turned, nodding his head in recollection. "The game's up, mate. You're all goin' to jail."

"Adam! Come on! What do you mean?"

"I was in Dukes. Coming down the stairs when Mick Glenn rushed past me going up. That's what he shouted down to Nigel Forster-Brown."

Glenn threatening Dukes was not what Dex wanted to hear. He pushed aside the remains of his toast.

"Adam, Glenn is dead along with Beth and two Vegas dealers who blabbed about Pepe being in Panama." Dex paused to deliver a rueful half-smile. "I owe you an explanation. Secret squirrel again? I went to Panama, not Vienna. The Sachertorte I had delivered, I bought in London."

Adam gave Dex a friendly punch. "You sly old dog."

"Panama had to be a secret, even from you. Beth got a statement from one of the murdered dealers." He clasped Adam's arm. "Brace yourself, Adam." He saw that he had Adam's wary attention. "Twenty years ago, Pepe murdered an innocent blackjack player in Panama – slaughtered him with over twenty stabs."

"Well, I'm buggered – if you'll excuse my French." Adam's jaw dropped and it looked as if his bowels would freefall several floors, such was his pained expression. Dex could see that Adam's normal affable bonhomie could not cope as he turned away to look down-river. Dex knew better than to speak, waiting in silence for more reaction.

"Beth was right, then. Dukes *is* bent."

"The attack was described as psychopathic."

Adam adjusted his striped city tie "Dex my boy, this is out of our league. We must bring in the police."

"Not yet, Adam, please not yet. I need much more evidence. That's down to Billy Evans." He checked his watch. "We should be going. We're meeting him in forty minutes."

Adam placed a paternal hand on his shoulder. "Carmino a psychopath? Beth wouldn't want you risking death. As you are, dear boy, as you are. Carmino will be after you."

"Please, don't chicken out now."

Adam bristled at the suggestion. "For myself, I'm scared of nothing. I fear for you with your life still ahead."

"Adam, you won't stop me. Nothing will." They left the terrace, crossed the galleried sitting-room with its picture-windows, thanked Ursula and went to Adam's private elevator. Dex gave

Adam's arm a friendly squeeze. "I'll explain more about your new friend Billy Evans."

The brisk walk across the Millennium Bridge seemed to bring out the bulldog in Adam. "Billy Evans card-counting. Secret cameras in cufflinks, eh? Undercover stuff? Wet raincoats and street corners. Like that movie – *The Third Man*. Spiffing fun – well, so long as we don't get caught."

As they rode the elevator to the 25th floor, high above Fenchurch Street, Dex wondered about the chemistry and whether Billy Evans would now pass muster. He knew Adam's opinion about the fashion for shaven heads and stubbled chins. "Neither fish nor fowl, dear boy. Makes them look like Abel Magwitch in *Great Expectations*."

As Dex introduced Billy, he was relieved. The makeover in Selfridge's had been transformational. His new image was understated smart-casual. In a lightweight grey suit, dark burgundy shirt and no tie, Billy looked like someone that Adam could have met at Royal Ascot or Goodwood. The ponytail had gone, along with the ear-stud and stubble. He might even have had a decent night's sleep too.

Better still, over a pot of coffee and chocolate fingers, an unlikely rapport seemed to be struck between the two of them. For his part, Adam, after initially protesting that nobody could teach an old dog like him new tricks, gradually became enthusiastic. "Billy, dear boy, I'll try, of course I will. Just don't expect me to master Basic Strategy like you youngsters."

"I'll be there, helping with decisions."

"Let's talk about this over a good lunch at Dukes."

Dex jumped in. "No careless talk. Treat every table as bugged."

"We'll chat about horses and women then. Suit you Billy?" Adam volunteered the suggestion with a braying laugh. "We'll play later after the tables open."

"Tables open?" Billy looked puzzled. "Isn't Dukes 24-7 then?"

"Unusually for London, it isn't," explained Adam. "Dukes closes at 8 a.m. offering breakfast for survivors. The tables reopen at 2 p.m."

Billy Evans thought for a moment and his sallow face broke into a grin. "A posh joint like Dukes, I expect that suits their high-rollers. Mornings is when they romp with their women or buy Ferraris or bloodstock."

"I'll leave you to it." Satisfied, Dex rose from the low-level coffee-table. "I may drop by Dukes later." He hurried home because he had given Jude the afternoon off while security consultants swept the house for bugs. She was meeting friends in Bayswater. By mid-afternoon, the consultants had reported that no bugs had been planted, so he returned to Reverse Labouchère, a mug of tea beside him.

Vaguely aware of the 6pm News in the background, Dex hit his first ever imbalance with reds dominating by sixty-eight to thirty-two. His calculations showed a theoretical win of over two million, way more than Beth had lost from cheating. He poured a celebratory G & T. but it was only as he was sipping it that an uncomfortable thought struck him.

I'd already lost 1.7 million.
I need to win more.
Unless I win first time in Dukes.
Fat chance.

As Dex debated another gin, Adam phoned and made the running. "We had a most agreeable lunch talking about blackjack and James Bond movies."

"And Basic Strategy?"

"The afternoon was really rather jolly. Bless my soul if I didn't end up winning!"

"Excellent. Nobody suspicious about Billy?"

"The chap played a straight bat."

"And did he think the decks were fixed?"

"Dex, I'm surprised you even ask. We never spoke about anything like that. You'll need to speak to Billy."

Dex spotted a taxi pull up and Jude climbing out. "I must go. Thanks, Adam. Must be strange taking money off Dukes. They'll soon stop your free lunches!"

"Dex, my dear boy, those free lunches have cost me hundreds of thousands. Cheer-ho."

As Jude breezed into the hall, Dex was not ready to speak to her, so he clasped the phone to his ear. They exchanged cheery waves before she bounded upstairs. During the next thirty minutes, Dex locked away his calculations and then stared at the empty glass, his thoughts returning to the inspired or madcap idea that had struck him after seeing Grierson.

Not just black or white.

Look for the grey.

Time to head upstairs to see Jude.

I've got two plans, maybe three.

- 61 -

After looking at Father when he had been asleep that morning, Dex had been studying on-line about Dignitas. Was the solution a one-way trip to the Swiss clinic near Zurich? Life could be ended with respect and dignity. It seemed better than Father sitting in a chair, slumped and drooling for year after year.

Am I just being selfish?
Or is it the kindest solution?

By early evening, he was still undecided. He paused on the landing on his way up to Father's room to revisit his most immediate plan. From one floor further up, he could hear thumping music from the top floor. Jude had explained that she was using what she called *advanced stimulation techniques*, something she had learned in Australia. Dex had no idea what they might be.

Yesterday, she had certainly worked hard to stimulate him by wearing a mini-kilt and a white tank top with no bra. As she had sat beside his father, he reckoned she oozed porn movie star more than nursing carer. To add to that image, twice when he had entered Father's room, she had, *just by chance*, bent over to pick up something, on one occasion revealing a black thong and, on the other, some skimpy tiger-striped briefs.

But for her snooping, Dex might have found her obvious flirting to be irresistible. Even so, he was fighting a battle between lust and good sense.

Was she simply curious?
Or had someone, perhaps even Pepe, set her up?

Perhaps now I'll find out.

He breezed in. "How's it going Jude? Any improvement?" Despite the air freshener, a faint smell of faeces was still noticeable. Before answering, Jude, who had been standing beside his Father's chair, bent to grab a tissue from her handbag, revealing an expanse of tanned thighs. Less attractive was the sight of his father, a hunched and feeble figure, his eyes only able to stare towards the floor. He knew that even with the volume low, Father would be hating the heavy beat of *Men at Work* from Jude's Alexa.

"Improvement? Give me time, boss," Jude responded with a broad grin. "Occasionally, there's flickers of reaction but I reckon they're nervous ticks." As he watched his father's head loll sideways and Jude wipe dribble from his mouth, Dex stared at the broken figure – the man he had hated for so long he couldn't remember ever liking him. But God! Seeing him like this was gut-wrenching. Nobody should have to endure such a sub-human existence.

"Jude, we're out of milk and cookies. I'd like to sit with Father for a while to see if my voice helps him. Can you pop to that shop on the High Street?" As he spoke, he handed over a ten-pound note and suggested she choose something for herself.

"No sweat. I spent the afternoon downing lager in the Mitre. Y'know in Craven Terrace. Some fresh air would be good." She pointedly brushed past Dex, her fragrance intense. Dex held his breath as he waited for what would happen next.

Would she grab her iPhone? She usually carried it everywhere and was forever tapping on the keys. He was lucky. It was on a shelf, charging. Her instinctive grab changed to a spin-turn and a cheery exit.

Dex had no qualms.

The snooper snooped.

He waited till she had hurried down the two flights of stairs.

Then he was into the iPhone and had opened the App for her Calendar. He reckoned he had about fifteen minutes max to get into the real world of Jude Tuson. Feverishly, he started from eight weeks back, checking every day. Each one had entries. Some made him grin, others made him laugh outright until a single one made him freeze. After letting out a low whistle, he raced on for more, finding seven more damning entries in the past month. The most recent was for this afternoon and she had been nowhere near the Mitre pub in Craven Terrace.

Is this worse than I feared, or better than I expected?
Depends on my next move.

He was unsure. The diary was certainly dynamite, irrespective of references to handcuffs and bondage. To go back further would have been titillating but a luxury. He had learned enough. Any more would be voyeurism. He wondered if the reinsurance broker she called *Mr Littlun* knew her nickname for him. He replaced her phone on the shelf and commanded Alexa to play some waltzes by Strauss, cheery music he knew Father had enjoyed. "Not so loud, Alexa!"

He heard the slammed door and Jude singing as she climbed the top flight of stairs. She appeared, her face radiant. Dex stopped reading to Father about travel in France, something he had had loved. If he were receptive to the description of the Roman remains at Arles, Dex had no way of knowing. "The cookies look good. What's yours?"

"Milk in the fridge. Double-Chocolate cookies for you and this yummy cinnamon bun for me. What is this shit you're playing?" She turned to the mini-flying-saucer. "Stop, Alexa."

"Father likes it. Try Mantovani instead then." Dex rose to leave with Jude wondering who Mantovani was and whether he was joking. "I've got a call to make."

Dex need time to think alone. Lots of time.

- 62 -

Later that evening, when Jude was upstairs putting Sir Charles to bed, Dex shut the study door and messaged Tiffany. The time difference and her punishing schedule had made communication spasmodic at best.

"Knowing Jude's a Judas, changes everything."
"And that she was planted by Carmino."
"Yet I still like her. She's terrific fun."
"Changes everything? Like what?"
"I can play an ace. Turn this to my advantage."
"Carmino is onto you. Dangerous."
"Maybe he knows very little. That's why she been planted." He saw an admiring smile spread to light up her face, her eyes delivering a supportive message. "Jude will be my double agent. But she won't know it."
"That I like." She paused to wag her finger. "But how, why? You going to share with me?"
"It involves a tethered goat." Dex was rewarded with a long silence as Tiffany wrote something on her pad.
"Sounds high risk. And the goat would be?"
"One guess."
"You? Oh God! Dex, just *butt out*." They chuckled at her pun. "If your goat fouls up, crapping in the wrong place, Carmino won't hesitate to … eliminate you. Like Beth."

Even knowing nothing of how Carmino had been scarred, she was right.

Like twenty stab wounds right.
No point terrifying her yet over that.

"Oh yes," Tiffany continued. "The Sports Editor has spent hours watching matches to see if Mick missed too many easy goals."

"And the answer?"

"He didn't. Which then puts Creole Henry as number-one. One of our journalists door-stepped him. He was at a boxing match in Manchester. That's been confirmed."

"Guys like him don't always do their own dirty work." Dex paused to look over his shoulder to make sure he was still alone. "Which puts Carmino into pole position."

She checked her watch. "Almost two p.m. The limo must be here. I'm doing a signing in Santa Monica. You take care. I mean it." Then for the first time, Dex saw her face turn sad. "Anything happened, tethered goats or whatever, I would miss you."

"And I need you. Back here. Soonest."

Father's wall-calendar gave the stark reminder that it was just ten days till Space City would open. Ten days to prevent it. Planning for that goat was urgent.

- 63 -

The next day, just after 7 p.m, the relief nurse arrived to look after Sir Charles. Dex had offered Jude dinner at Dukes. During the afternoon, he had met Gus McKay in his back-room. As ever, he was surrounded by books, parcelled and ready to go. In his reddish tartan trews and yellow waistcoat, he added colour to the drab surroundings. It was a brief meeting, very much to the point.

"A private eye in Vegas?" McKay's tic went ballistic as he racked his memory. "No. Mind, I never needed one but this attorney can help." He scribbled a note in unruly writing. "Mention my name or he'll bill you a thousand bucks just for answering the phone."

"My second request is trickier." Dex ran through what he needed and why. McKay absentmindedly spun the roulette wheel. Only as the ball slowed and dropped onto number 17 did the Scot speak. "17 black – a lucky number." He looked Dex straight in the eye. "I was wrong when we first met. I underestimated you. You can be an evil bastard, can't you?"

Dex laughed. "I'll take that as a compliment, not a question."

He was rewarded with a widening smile. As if reluctant to say anything out loud, the Scot wrote down another name and details. "My introduction or not, he'll skin you alive, I'm telling you. He charges like a wounded rhino."

Dex saw the address in Peckham, southeast London. "Money is not an issue. Time and results are"

On returning from McKay, Dex went straight to his desk.

Terrific!

Before going out, he had left out details of his return flight to Zurich. Next to it, also precisely positioned, was an article about Dignitas. No question, both items had been moved – just as he had hoped. The trap had been sprung.

For the casino. he changed into a navy-blue mohair jacket, pale blue shirt, tie and black jeans. He only wore the tie because he needed the tie-pin. Shortly after eight, Jude appeared on the stairs in a slinky and strapless aquamarine outfit, three-quarter length with her flowing hair beautifully coiffured. "You look great," he enthused like a guy on a first date.

"You too, boss. Prince Charming himself. Let's hit the tables."

After Dex had signed her in, FB appeared and greeted them with his usual embarrassed smile. He led them straight to the restaurant, Dex suggesting they should eat at once to allow more time at the tables. He led them to a circular corner table with a pink cloth, a small table lamp, heavy silverware and the finest Riedel wineglasses. "Great table." Dex smiled encouragingly at Jude.

"Seductive too, tucked away where nobody can hear us. Did you ask for this table, you naughty boss?"

Dex was wrongfooted and looked sheepish as he denied having any part in it. "Anyway, you're right," he blustered, "lots to talk about." Dex threw in a suggestive wink as he forced himself not to laugh at the image of Carmino listening to every word. After a half bottle of Krug had been poured and glasses chinked, Dex got straight to the point. "Jude, this isn't going to be easy. I'll come straight to the point." She put down her glass, looking uneasy. "Since we first planned to come for dinner, things have changed – my thinking has changed. And please don't take this the wrong way. This is nothing to do with you. You're doing a great job but…" He hesitated. "It's about…well, me and Father."

"Go on. Tell me I'm fired."

"Unusually for them, the Americans put it rather kinder. I'm letting you go."

"Strewth! Why?" There was no anger in the question but no easy acceptance either.

"I've agonised about keeping Father alive but I can't take his suffering much longer. Tomorrow, I'm sending him for a two-week assessment at the Bistbury in Northampton while I fly to Switzerland to check out Dignitas."

"No worries, boss. Just pay me my notice." She paused. "But jeez, just when I thought I was maybe getting through to Sir Charles."

"I'll be blunt. Say his condition is 100 percent hopeless. Is it kind to improve him to 98 percent, or even to 90? Just so that he drools rather slower?" He topped up their glasses. "I don't think so. The Dignitas team are in Forch, just outside Zurich."

"Did Sir Charles ever express a wish for this? Like a living will?"

"No. Father considered himself both invincible and immortal." Dex saw her weigh up that answer. "Your call, Dex. Poor you."

"My solicitor warned I could be prosecuted. Well, so be it." He was sure that her sharp brain would be assessing the new situation but her reaction was still a surprise. She leaned across and clasped his hand. "Dex, that's brave. And me? Relax. I'll find another job." She lowered her eyes and moved her bronzed hand to his wrist. "Don't be shocked by what I'm going to say. Despite my nursing instincts, I agree about Dignitas. The law is a load of shite." She squeezed tighter.

"Do you have somewhere you can move to?"

Dex noticed the slight hesitation before she replied. "I've plenty of friends. I'll land on my feet."

"Then leave in the morning. I don't leave till much later."

"That's cool with me. When do you fly?"

"21-40pm. I'm being picked up at seven."

Get that Pepe?

"Right. Nasty bit over. Let's enjoy our evening as friends. You can explain baccarat." She touched his chin to ensure their eyes met. "Do I get to call you Dex now instead of boss?"

"You're on." Jude turned to the menu. "Dex, I could slaughter a whole lobster followed by a T-bone, served rare, blue even."

"Good choice."

Upstairs, Carmino took in every word.

Zurich?

Interesting.

Leaving tomorrow night.

Better than Jude working there.

− 64 −

Through the bug in the table lamp, Carmino continued to overhear their conversation as he opened some spreadsheets. He chewed a delicately cut smoked salmon sandwich and weighed up the new information. Being dismissed was no problem. Short of pillow-talk, Jude had done everything possible but if she gave him a right old dicking tonight, she still might learn more.

Given her assessment that Dexter had *the sex drive of a castrated monk*, the dicking bit looked unlikely.

As the conversation downstairs changed to explaining baccarat, he studied the secret profits from the hot money being siphoned off. Thanks to pudding-bowl in Geneva, most nights he had up to five different high-rollers, always signed in by a friendly casino hostess. The rake of 20%, "lost" by the guests, less the cut for himself and Enzo, was transferred to Vegas. The guests, with their fake IDs, could deposit a casino cheque for 80% as clean money in selected banks in relaxed jurisdictions.

Cheating players and laundering had never been a long-term plan. From his corrupted contacts, he knew the Gambling Commission worked on a risk-assessment formula. An upmarket casino like Dukes was rated low risk for under-age or inebriated gamblers. On the flip-side, because of the multi-millions being wagered, it was rated high-risk for money-laundering. With the success of the scams, Carmino calculated he needed just a few more days before returning to legit gambling.

He returned the bogus accounts to the safe and from under a

wad of fifty thousand US dollar bills, he pulled out his three false passports, credit cards and driving licences. He flicked through them, reviewing his exit plan in case the Gambling Commission got too close. With his network of offshore accounts, Carmino's maths proved he could spend a million a year for life and still have change.

So long as you're not in jail, my old son.

Jude was now explaining Aussie Rules football. He checked the time and quickly polished off a second-round of sandwiches with the last of his chilled Meursault.

Yes, time to drop by downstairs.

-65-

Dex spotted Carmino enter the restaurant, slithering over the thick carpeting. He stopped at every table for a quick word, a friendly hand on shoulders, a kiss on both cheeks or a shared moment of laughter. Dex had to admit that the slimy shit knew how to work a room, schmoozing the men and making women's hearts flutter. When he reached their table, after a friendly word and a handshake, he kissed Jude's hand with a swift brush of the lips.

"Don't I recognise you? It's Jude something, isn't it? You visited us before." He stroked his scar thoughtfully as he tried to recall. "Yes. With Mr G, that Spanish insurance broker, wasn't it?" Dex suppressed a smile at the thought of Mr Littlun.

"You've a good memory."

"Didn't we talk about you working here? Y'know, looking after our members?"

"Strewth! Bang on!" Jude sounded astounded at his recollection. "I'd forgotten that. Too many of your Moscow Mules, I expect." She rolled her eyes in mock shame.

"They do have a kick, don't they?" He paused to let his quip sink in before adding. "That offer stands but perhaps you have a job?"

"Well, mattrafact, no. Dex no longer needs me to look after his father."

Dex caught Pepe's eye. "You know, the crash that killed…"

"Yes, yes. Of course." Pepe was quick to intervene. "And how is your father?"

"Not good. He needs further tests."

"I see," murmured Pepe, looking his most sympathetic, his lowered eyelids adding sincerity.

"And," chipped in Jude, "that leaves me out on my arse, looking for a job."

"Well, think about it. The hours here are demanding."

"Look, Mr. Carmino, I mean I'm as full as a goog, so can we talk now? Like working here, sounds exciting compared to … well, almost anything!"

Dex looked up at Carmino and then at Jude. "Go right ahead. I was feeling bad about letting you go."

Jude blew him a kiss. "Nah, no worries, don't blame yourself."

"I'll play some roulette." Dex watched them head for the bar, chatting comfortably with each other. Replaying their fairy-tale conversation, he sat for a few moments, declining port or brandy.

Christ! Keeping stumm about Jude's diary and Tavio's statement had been tough.

Worth it though.

As he fingered his now empty wineglass, visions of Carmino butchering the young Mexican mixed with Jude's calendar entries about her meetings with PC. After visiting Dukes with Mr Littlun, she had lunched with Carmino at The Ivy. They had then lunched several times, spending afternoons at his apartment in Holland Park, studded leather and all. Firing his imagination, several of Jude's entries about S&M had been punctuated with three or even four exclamation marks.

Dex strolled to the men's room to wash away Carmino's handshake. As the hot water tumbled over his hands, he could still feel no resentment for her deviousness.

Jude's just a young woman on the make.
Not a bad person
I hope she never regrets it.

— 66 —

It was over an hour before Jude reappeared and excitedly brushed her lips on his cheek. He waited till the ball landed in number 10 black, a winning number, before looking round.

"Mr Carmino will tell me later but I reckon, I got the job."

"That's great. You joining me? Or will it be Baccarat?"

"Baccarat. When you've lost your wad here, come and watch me win."

"You might have a long wait," Dex grinned. "I'm up over £17,000. Beat that if you can!" He watched her turn away and saw a number of other men's eyes follow her as she sashayed to the large Baccarat table where the shoe was being passed between six players. His thoughts returned to his stack of chips and the spinning wheel. Almost as soon as he had sat down, One-Eye had been moved away. Ned, a young Cockney dealer, seemed to be playing it straight. After each win, Dex had pretended disinterest, hoping his cameras would catch cheating. Zilch.

FB sidled across. "Given up on your Reverse Labouchère idea?"

"For now, yes. I'm playing the way Gerhard Hoge suggested. Doing okay too."

"Enjoy your evening Mr D."

Later, despite winning £40,000, he still felt deflated.

Yet again, no evidence of cheating.

Or am I missing something?

He had been watching One-Eye dealing at a high-stakes

-212-

roulette game where the minimum bets were a total of £500,000 on the layout and £100,000 on the even-chances. He decided to join it. *Would One-Eye be moved on?* A couple of Russians were playing. Each was accompanied by a young woman, dressed to kill and easily thirty-five years younger. The older man had three chins and cheeks flabby enough to lose a tongue in. The other's jawline was brick-hard, matching his narrowed eyes beneath beetle-brows.

Dex settled in, impressed that winners would receive millions from a single spin. Catching One-Eye *palming* just once would be enough for the cops and mega for casino profits.

Very odd though!

The Russians seemed uninterested in roulette and the dancing ball. It was the young women, both English, who were placing the huge bets for them and scooping back the winnings. The two men seemed happy enough sinking shots and pawing the women.

Perhaps this is what Carmino had in mind for Jude.

Spotting that there had been no red numbers for eight spins, Dex bought-in and was given a single £100,000 chip to back red.

"Getting into it, are we, Mr. D?" Jeb Miller rolled his stomach forward, sounding friendly enough.

"I had a good win on the other table. Hopefully, my luck will last."

It did not. He lost the next two spins but watched the brick-faced Russian's companion being paid out £3.5 million.

Surely One-Eye would cheat the winner.
Easier than stealing candy from a baby.

He spotted nothing.

Does Carmino suspect me?
Or had Mick Glenn's outburst stopped the cheating?

Two-hundred thousand down, Dex strolled over to stand behind Adam Yarbury who was seated next to Billy at the blackjack.

"Dex! What a pleasure!" Adam's chortle was infectious. "Don't laugh but I'm winning – long story but I've my friend Billy here to thank."

"You've got 16, Adam. Hit it," said Billy. "Remember? The dealer has a king as his up-card. You've got to take another card."

"With my usual luck, I'll get twenty-six," Adam volunteered with a resigned smile.

"No. Assume the dealer's hole card, the one you can't see, is a 10. He'll have 20, so…you'll lose anyway. Go on, Adam." Dex watched as Adam, with a despairing roll of his eyes, signalled for another card. It was a 5 giving him a great hand at 21. The dealer then flipped his hole card, which was indeed a 10. Realising he had won, Adam's face looked as if a magician had produced an entire warren of rabbits from a hat.

"Bless my soul! This Basic Strategy thingie has done it again. Dex, let me introduce Billy Evans. We met at Ascot. He's been teaching me some damnably clever thing. Seems kamikaze but blow me down, it works!"

"Hello, Billy! I'm Finlay Dexter and called Dex. You'll have your work cut out teaching Adam!"

Billy laughed. "Tell me about it!" He returned his attention to the table almost at once.

Dex turned away. "See you later. I'm going to the Baccarat." Taking in the freshness of her hair and her subtle perfume, he stood behind Jude and saw that she had lost nearly half of his £200,000. "Struggling?"

"I'm playing for Tied Hands now. This is the sixty-first hand of this shoe without a tie. That's ridiculous! By now I'd expect three, maybe four and sometimes even seven ties." Dex nodded as if he understood as she placed £30,000 in a box marked *Tie*. She lost as Bank won 6 over 1. Without hesitation, this time Jude bet £50,000.

Out came the cards, a total of 7 for both Player and Bank. "Tied Hand!" whooped Jude, turning to high-five him. "See – I'm paid out a tasty 8 to 1. That's £400,000 smackeroos."

Dex looked at her chips. "That covers my losses! Fancy a drink?"

She shook her head. "Can't stop now! Ties may repeat! I learned that in Sydney. No logic but it often happens." She bet £100,000 and they watched as the Player's two cards totalled a perfect hand of 9. "Shit," Jude muttered. The first card to the Bank was an unpromising 3 but with a flourish, the final card was turned over. It was a 6 – a tied hand on 9. Jude half-stood and rewarded Dex with a hug and a squeeze as if it were his doing. The dealer pushed across her win of £800,000.

Even though the wins had been sheer luck, Dex was impressed. "Tell you what. Quit now and you keep £200,000. Deal?"

"You're on!" After cashing in, they settled on the sofa. She gave him a suggestive nudge and a peck on the cheek "Winning always makes me thirsty…and horny. Be warned." Dex raised an eyebrow in mock surprise as he sipped a Spitfire beer whilst Jude downed a couple of Moscow Mules. She was just explaining why sometimes there were three cards dealt to each hand in Baccarat when she received a text. She glanced at it, completely unfazed at Pepe's question about keys to Porcupine House. She replied confirming she had made a duplicate set. "That's Mr. Carmino. Wants me here by 6 p.m. tomorrow."

"So, you landed the job. Tell me about it."

"Later. It's about chaperoning."

"I'm intrigued."

Dex made up his mind.

It was time to tether the goat.

"Amazing the pace of technology," he prompted. "I used to

carry my laptop everywhere. That's my whole life in there. Take tomorrow, when I go to Zurich overnight. Now, I'll only need my smartphone and can synch up when I get back."

Got that, Jude? Listening Pepe?

"Makes sense. Travel light." As she ran her hand up and down his thigh, Jude refused a third Moscow Mule whispering that she had an urge to get home. He sunk the end of his beer while inwardly, his mind was in turmoil.

Christ! Pepe Carmino's mistress – so available.
What did he want her to find out?
Not the length of my aroused dick, that's for sure.
Tonight's her last chance to find out.

-- 67 --

The casino's stretch-limo had collected Jude shortly before 11 a.m., just before the private ambulance had arrived for Sir Charles. Dex had loaded her three suitcases and several colourful tote-bags into the back of the Lincoln Town-Car and after giving her a hug, quite a lingering one, the vehicle moved away. He saw her smile, sad and wistful as she blew him a kiss.

Inside, the house felt still and empty without her. Her personality seemed to linger, her throaty laugh still seeming to resonate down the stairs and from room to room. Despite her lies and deceit, he knew he would miss her zany desire to live life to the full. As he toasted some cheese and brewed some dark brown tea, he thought how life played curious tricks. Until only a few hours ago, Tiffany had played the slow game in their friendship. Sure, she had been a good friend but she had been old-style cool in her attitude, maybe even aloof. Contrastingly, Jude had never concealed her eagerness *to shag you till your bollocks fall off* – as she had so graphically put it during the taxi ride the previous evening. Her wandering hands on the journey had made her intentions very plain.

No sooner had they entered the kitchen than she had flung her arms around his neck and kissed him firmly on the mouth, thrusting her hips toward him. As she had pressed her warm thighs against his lean body, his own reaction was immediate. When she felt the hardening, she pushed even more forcibly, whimpering and simpering into his ear. Dex knew he was close to the tipping-point. To back off now would be a first and his testosterone-charged instincts were being tested to the brink. She leaned back and switched her grip to clench his buttocks, pulling him even closer as she gasped and moaned for him to *come on, come on.*

But he didn't.

He fought to resist every throbbing instinct. He forced himself to imagine Carmino writhing across her breasts, a thought that reduced his erection to *Condition Docile*. He pulled away, gradually releasing his hips from her grip until, in the half-light, she looked at him questioningly. "What's the matter, Dex? Don't you fancy a hot Aussie girl?"

"You felt the evidence."

He saw her eyes change between frustration, fury and understanding. "You mean there's ... someone else?"

Dex seized the welcome escape route. He nodded. "Right now, she's in the USA."

"Jeez! I'm not telling if you're not. Come on! Now ... I want it now. Standing up. On the table, on your desk, in your bed." As she spoke, she pulled up her slinky dress revealing that she had gone commando. Dex did a double-take at the almost irresistible sight of the trimmed bush and tanned thighs. He ached to seize the moment and to hell with common-sense.

But he didn't.

"I promised I'd speak to her as soon as I got back." Slowly, Jude lowered her dress with a sigh of resignation. He grasped her hand and led her through the hall and stopped at the foot of the stairs outside his study. "Jude, you won't believe it after ... y'know just now, but I've grown very, well really fond of you. I'm sorry, so sorry." He gave her an affectionate hug that turned into a long moment before Jude pulled away.

"I shall miss you and being here. We'll both regret that lost moment just now." Even in the darkened hallway her sincerity shone through. "Dex, I've not met guys like you. Loyal, strong, funny, interesting and sexy as hell. If whoever ... lets you down, I'll be there. Remember that, won't you?" For a moment, Dex saw tears in her eyes before she turned to climb the stairs, one slow and grudging step at a time.

Moments later, Jude was up in her room and the relief carer had left. Dex settled down at his desk but it took several minutes before he was calm enough to call Tiffany. To her, he was just a friend. To him, she was...? He was unsure and Jude had made him even more uncertain.

Am I star-struck by Tiffany's celebrity?
Is it only the heat of the chase?
Or do we share something deeper, some two-way magic?

He booted up the laptop and Tiffany appeared, her eyes looking tired from her travels and time zone differences. Her voice though was excited. "Heh Dex, get this! I've been offered a three-book deal and a TV network want a series on my work in Africa."

"Fantastic and well done. Amazing – but deserved! I'll help you in Africa and not just with money. Perhaps we could set up an orphanage."

"That's so very you, Dex! Thanks." For a split-second, Dex saw emotion in her eyes. "And you? You and your tethered goat? What's happening?" Her tired eyes lost their remaining sparkle.

"The stake's in the ground. Besides which, long story, Jude's leaving and Father's going to a special unit."

"Dex, you've still never told me what Beth learned from Tavio. Or what you discovered in Panama. You ready to tell me?"

"It'll keep."

"Surely you've enough for the police?"

"I need Billy's evidence and a clincher. That's why tomorrow I'm tethering the goat."

"Don't sacrificial goats get their throats cut?" She let the words hang for effect. "Dex, this is just too big. Please, for me, Dex. Stop now."

"I'm sorry, Tiffany."

"A man's gotta do – you know the rest." Tiffany trotted out the unfinished cliché and then came the first tears. Her shake of her head revealed frustration and irritation in equal measure "I wish you would listen." She dabbed her cheeks with a tissue. "There's something else I want to say." She faltered with more eye-mopping. "Since we've been apart, I've come to realise … well, how important you've become and that I care about you, so much. I don't want crazy goat plans. I want you safe and with me in Ethiopia, the Congo or Gambia. Don't risk what you can't control."

His stomach churned at thoughts of his plan going wrong. "I'll be just fine. It's a great plan." He fought to look convincing as his thoughts raced ahead to the following night.

Tiffany managed a watery smile as her helpless look changed to reproachful and then to reluctant admiration. "Dex, you're impossible!" She put the tissue aside but still spoke falteringly, her voice breaking. "So … the goat? When?"

"UK time, tomorrow night. Carmino thinks I'll be in Zurich."

"You think he might break in?"

"Let himself in. I bet Jude has copied my keys. Jude knows that my laptop contains secretive stuff and he's desperate to know what I've got on him."

"Like me then," she prompted. "He's in the dark about Panama, about Tavio."

"And whether I tipped off Mick Glenn about cheating."

"And your plan?"

He smiled. "Don't bleat! See you at Heathrow on Saturday. I'll meet your flight. No kidding."

Tiffany laughed for a flickering moment at his silly puns. "Stay safe." Her eyes started to fill with tears as she cut the connection.

-68-

Dex's preparations for the night ahead were interrupted by his private investigator who had been watching Carmino's penthouse, barely three miles away in Clarendon Road, Holland Park. "The target has moved in with her luggage. Carmino is there too."

Running on double espresso, Dex went to St John's Wood Station where he tubed it to Lillywhites, the sports suppliers at Piccadilly Circus. Then, it was a brisk walk to the spy-shop where he was greeted like an old friend following his previous purchases. Laden with his needs, he doubled back on himself to visit a chandler and marine supplies store near Shaftesbury Avenue. For his next purchase, he dropped by an office equipment specialist in the Strand but the final essential was trickier. Dex entered the maze of small streets and alleys of Soho. In Archer Street, he saw the *Naughty Nocturne* sex shop. Trying to look self-confident, he breezed through the open door passing among the giant black dildos, weird chains and leather accessories that helped some customers get their rocks off.

He found what he wanted and shame-faced, took his purchase to the counter. He swallowed hard but the bored-looking woman at the checkout showed no more interest than if he were buying a can of sardines. She reminded Dex of Tina Turner's *Private Dancer – Men come in these places and the men are all the same. You don't look at their faces and you don't ask their names.* She never looked at him as she swiped his card and stashed the purchases in a plain bag.

In Wardour Street he stopped a passing taxi and fifteen minutes later, everything was locked away in the safe at Porcupine House. Then it was time to head for Trafalgar Square where Billy Evans was meeting him in the Sherlock Holmes pub. There was no rush. Jude knew he would not leave for the airport till seven and he doubted Carmino would risk coming unless he was sure the Zurich flight had departed, probably even much later.

Assuming he was coming at all.

As the taxi crawled down Baker Street, an unwelcome thought struck him.

Suppose Carmino was having him tailed?

Today's shopping, even the sex shop –no problem.

But meeting Billy Evans?

It was not a comfortable thought.

For the first time, he glanced behind him. At the next lights, he did it again and then checked each time after the taxi took a left, right and left through some back-doubles. He saw nothing suspicious but even so, he varied the instructions. "Forget the Sherlock Holmes. Take me to the River Entrance of the Savoy Hotel."

When he got out, he entered Embankment Gardens almost opposite the hotel. There was only a scattering of people strolling on the paths between the lawns. Hopefully, if he were being followed, he would spot somebody between here and the pub. He walked with no great speed between the flower-beds for about 150 yards, before spinning round as he chose a chair outside a closed café. He saw only the usual mix of Londoners – office workers in casual clothes and barristers, all suited and booted. There was a handful of tourists, a couple of pram-pushers and several lovers, arm-in-arm. Was there a private eye among them? It seemed not. Nobody paused suddenly to tie a shoelace or stopped to look towards the river.

After a couple of moments, he moved on until he reached the magnificent statue of Robert Burns, the Scottish poet. He stopped beside it and again squinted back – still no reason for suspicion. He hurried up Villiers Street, took the steep flight of steps into the bustle of Charing Cross Station and exited on the far side. Even then, he did not head for the pub, instead returning to the crowded concourse, looking out for anybody he had seen more than once.

As satisfied as he could be that nobody was tailing him, he rounded the corner of Trafalgar Square and entered the pub. Billy Evans was already there.

Oh God!
Had Carmino had Billy followed?
Too late to worry about that now.

Dex looked around the cosiness of the atmospheric bar. Nobody showed any interest as he joined Billy who was looking at the evening paper. Billy declined a drink, saying he was sticking to water. Though he said nothing at first, Dex felt concerned at Billy's appearance. Okay, he was still smartened-up but his face was a train wreck and his hands were shaking.

Was Billy a risk too far?
Another Mick Glenn disaster.

Dex ordered an orange and lemonade for himself and felt pretty virtuous as they peered into the famous "study." It was crammed with memorabilia of Holmes and Watson. Plaster casts of the hound's footprints, a deerstalker hat and Holmes' pipe set the tone. The opening chitchat went well enough until Dex spotted the occasional body twitch. *Cocaine abuse or withdrawal?* Dex had almost decided to pay Billy off when he mentioned Emily's birthday. That changed everything. For no valid reason, Dex felt a sense of responsibility to her.

Not your problem.

You owe Billy nothing.
End it and play safe.
Yet flashbacks to Emily's wide-eyed trust and innocence tugged at his heart. Remembering her with Pooh Bear played on his mind. After just that short breakfast, she was like the daughter he had never had. He glanced away to the life-sized head of the Hound of the Baskervilles. Its huge eyes flashed insanity, almost like Billy's today. A portrait of the great detective showed his shrewd beakiness in a face so calm yet so commanding. The watchful eyes looked into the distance with measured disdain. It was as if he were contemptuous about Dex's choice of associate.

Elementary, my dear Dex.
Billy must go.
Compassion, yes. Involvement, no.

"Billy, before we get into detail, I want a straight answer. Are you back on the white stuff? Are you struggling? Your hands are shaking. You need to shape up."

It was an age before Billy responded. He looked crestfallen. "It's been hard. Much harder than I thought. Cold turkey, that is. If you want to end this, I can't blame you." It was an incomplete answer and Dex knew it.

"You look as if the Gaderene swine have just crapped in your eyeballs. You're no use to me like this."

"Late night after I left Dukes."

"Cocaine?"

Billy shook his head. "Booze. Buckets of it. At my digs, I couldn't sleep. I never made it to the day job."

"When did you last eat?"

"A quick bite yesterday with Adam – a Thai place on Piccadilly."

"How about steak pie and chips now? Soak up the alcohol?" Dex stared hard trying to get across both irritation and sympathy.

"You reckon?"

"I'll order for you. Meantime, pop out for a razor and shaving cream. Spruce up in the Gents'. You can't go on to Dukes looking like this – you owe it to Adam."

When he returned twenty minutes later, Billy looked better for his shave and sluice down. "So, Billy. Let's cut to the chase. Is the blackjack fixed?"

Billy's fork filled with pastry stopped in mid-air. "I'd say so but I can't yet prove it. Not credibly. I need to play longer and at more tables."

"So how do they do it?"

Billy popped a chip into his mouth using his fingers and devoured it with rapid and rabbit-like chewing. "I have a theory. Adam couldn't be there yesterday afternoon, otherwise we could have road-tested it." Some peas fell from his fork as his hand shook.

"Adam went to the Oval to watch the cricket."

"He has not the slightest understanding of what is going on." Billy dipped a long chip in his ketchup and examined it for a moment before chewing hungrily. "Don't get me wrong. He's a real gent, old-fashioned. He's intelligent too but at the blackjack tables, his brain is never in gear. He could have been cheated for years."

"Why the afternoon?"

"I'd rather not speculate. Not yet."

"Say two more days? That would give you two afternoons. How long do you need?"

"See, Dex, it's like this. Firstly, I got to play enough hands, enough shoes to prove that statistically the games are bent."

"By rigging the number of good and bad cards?"

"Exactly. So, if you want me to give a statement that will hold up with the Gambling Commission, I need to know how Dukes can fix the decks. That's where the afternoons come in. Trust me."

"I trust your expertise, Billy. It's your demons that make me shit myself." Dex rose to leave. "You okay for money? A taxi to Dukes?" Just a quick glance at Billy's face gave him the answer. "Here's two hundred to keep you going for a couple of days. Don't piss it against the wall or shove it up your nose." He gave Billy a friendly smile. "And remember, stay in character when you're with Adam." As he left, he found he was chewing his lip in frustration.

Sherlock Holmes was still looking down with disdain.

Billy was a walking time-bomb.

But still essential.

— 69 —

Jude stretched her arms as she lay in the black silk sheets of Pepe Carmino's bed. It was late afternoon and her suitcases were not yet unpacked. After the limo had dropped her off before noon, they had sunk a bottle of Krug before heading for the bedroom.

Now, four hours later, she heard the front door shut as he headed to a meeting promising to be back in a couple of hours. She was alone, free to relax before luxuriating in the jacuzzi. Later, she planned to wear her sheer navy-blue off-the shoulder outfit to host a rich Croatian. Pepe wanted her to entertain him in his hotel suite, hand over his false ID and, if need be, she was *to help him relax* before going through the charade of gambling. Win or lose, he would leave with a Dukes cheque for at least 80% of the millions he had come to clean.

On Pepe's side of the king-sized bed lay his black mask designed to cover his eyes and nose. She had discovered weeks before that Pepe's erection turned on pain, fear and domination. On the floor were his studded leather vest and matching jock-thong. Her thighs were still reddened and sore from when he had pounced before she had ripped the damned stuff off.

In Saudi Arabia, Jude had refused weirder requests involving mirrors and panes of glass but generally she had no problem playing along with fantasists and dressing-up games. Pepe, though, was pushing her to the outer edges. Today, using a spider gag, had been a step or ten too far. Her jaws still ached from being forced wide apart while her wrists and ankles were restrained.

As she lay back now, massaging her jaws and her mouth tasting foul, her thoughts turned to Dex. Until him, men had always found her irresistible but he had been different – old-fashioned really, staying faithful to someone in America. *Face it, girl. You loved flirting and teasing him. Had become infatuated on him, big time. You hated the spying and pretending to care for his old man.*

At first, Pepe's suggestion of nursing Sir Charles had excited her but the more she had got to know Dex, the more she had resented the lying and snooping. She smiled at the thought that they might meet again in Dukes leading to another chance to show him what he had missed.

Maybe tomorrow night?
No. He would still be in Zurich.
Perhaps after he got back then.
So long as Pepe did not find out.

Apart from Pepe's perversions, she had enjoyed his pampering. He had showered rings and bracelets on her with promises of *just you and me* trips by private jet to exotic destinations. Yet listening to him barking and growling on the phone to some guy in Vegas, she had no illusions: Pepe Carmino had a short temper and was not to be crossed.

Restless now, she got up and sorted her clothes into the walk-in closet that lined one side of the huge pastel-shaded bedroom. When she had done, she was intrigued to look inside the other end where Pepe kept his suits and leather paraphernalia. *Besides spider gags, what else lay ahead to turn him on?*

She slid back the louvred doors and saw everything neatly arranged, from casual through to blazers to suits to DJs and an evening suit. Beyond that was the leather – singlets, Y-fronts, bracelets and wrist-grips. On a series of shelves were all types of butt plugs, cock rings, and pink dildos that he had yet to try on her. On the floor lay his whip and a large paddle-slapper, something he had promised would be *a special treat.*

Not on me, it won't be.

As she rummaged in an eye-level shelf, she spotted another gadget that she had never seen before. Seemingly designed as a challenge for an escapologist like Houdini, she pulled at the thick leather straps and metallic rings to take a look. It was heavy and fell with a clatter to the floor. She pushed it this way and that, trying to understand just how she would be trussed up within it. Then she saw the instructions. She pulled out the leaflet and her sore mouth dropped open as she studied the diagram. The paper trembled in her hand at the prospect of being locked into an extreme position, her neck strapped to her knees. Once trapped like that, she shuddered to imagine what Pepe would do next.

She was about to replace the gadget and instructions when she spotted something else, tucked away at the very back. She pulled at a belt and out followed a sheath and in it a knife, a huge knife such as she had only seen in gangland movies. The blade measured at least nine inches with a tip so sharp it could instantly draw blood. Feeling very shaky now, she shoved it back into the sheath and returned everything to where it had originally been. For a moment, she sat on the bed wondering what the hell she was doing with her life but then hurried through to the drinks cabinet and poured herself a large neat bourbon.

She felt no better for it and poured another.

− 70 −

tay safe.

Stay safe. Tiffany's words still rang in his ear. What might lie ahead with a murderous psychopath was scarcely safe. Had he known, Doc Grierson would have been burbling expensively about soaring blood-pressure and unprecedented stress levels. Dex was perched uncomfortably, concealed behind the door into Father's study. As far as anyone knew, he was now far away, visiting Dignitas in Zurich. Instead, he was alone in Porcupine House, a tethered goat awaiting a predator desperate to trawl through his laptop and maybe crack the safe.

Dex was pleased with his planning – like *forgetting* to get back Jude's keys, in case she had not made a copy and revealing that his laptop would be in the empty house.

Surely nothing could go wrong?

As the minutes ticked by and dusk became darkness, his breathing and damp palms revealed his fears. Several times, he had to force himself not to ditch the dangerous plan and dash to a nearby hotel.

Oh my God!
Suppose he doesn't come alone?
Shit!
Maybe brings a safe-cracker.
I'd never thought of that!

He shivered as he waited, dressed in black from top to toe – waiting for something that might never even happen.

Do I really want it to happen?

As he shifted position to kneel uncomfortably in the darkened room, his face blackened and wearing black gloves, he liked the reassurance of the chunky baseball bat from Lillywhites. A well-aimed single swipe would fell Carmino before he knew what was coming. He swigged from a bottle of water and nibbled on a tuna sandwich, his legs numb, his body crying for relief from his cramped position.

Another hour passed. Still nothing.

- 71 -

Pepe Carmino had returned while Jude was reclining in the jacuzzi. Now, having changed to drive to Dukes, he appeared from the bedroom. "Remind me. What time was Dex's flight?"

"21-40. I saw the reservation. The taxi was picking him up at seven. About now in fact."

Pepe then leaned over the bubbling water and kissed her without passion, his mind far away. "We'll catch up later. Ciao."

Moments later, he was in his Aston Martin for the short commute along the Bayswater Road from Holland Park. At this time of day, the journey was rarely more than twelve minutes and as he drove beside Hyde Park, he always planned for the evening ahead. Today was no exception. By the time he rounded Marble Arch, an idea was developing, *a very good idea*. He kicked himself for not thinking of it before.

Back in Carmino's penthouse, Jude towelled herself dry, puzzling why Pepe was so obsessed with Dex.

Do I really believe him?
That Dex is planning to rob or cheat the casino?

It seemed implausible. Well, except for the roulette-wheel he was always using.

What hasn't Pepe told me?
Why is he so obsessed with checking all things Dex?
Like having to search Porcupine House tonight?

"If I can find out what the hell Finlay Dexter is up to, I can take care of it – in my own way." Carmino's chilling words over their pasta lunch today had lingered. What did that mean? Violence? Maybe. The police? Presumably not. A nasty thought went through her mind. Wrapped in the fluffy pink towel she opened the louvred doors and rummaged in the back of his closet.

The knife and sheath had gone.

For a moment, she was rooted to the spot, staring at where the knife had been. Then a tidal wave of relief swept over her. Panic over! Dex is in Zurich. So why had Pepe taken it? She had no answer to that but with Dex safe, she dismissed her concerns.

She dressed quickly and finished her make-up, spraying on the Dior perfume that Pepe had given her. A glance in the mirror confirmed that she was looking her best and ready to be taken to the Dorchester Hotel. There she was to meet the Croatian. Pepe had briefed her that the guy was *a big cheese* and needed cossetting while she laundered his fourteen million. As she saw the limo pull up down below, she hoped he smelled rather better than a previous ageing Croatian she had once bedded. Memories of his stink had haunted her long after he had finished his staccato performance.

~ 72 ~

It was gone 11 p.m. Porcupine House felt chill and Dex noticed the smell of damp rising from the cellar beneath him. Everywhere was blackness, every light was off, every curtain drawn. He passed the time by planning the next day including a visit to Father in Northampton, *assuming I'm alive*. He checked his watch again, stood up, yawned and stretched his aching limbs. He dared not move any further around the room for fear of triggering the alarm.

Except for a rustle from the trees and the old house showing its age, there was silence. He was alone and surrounded only by the ghosts of old memories – of Mother shouting in fear as Father kicked and beat her; of him and Beth playing hide and seek for hours; of Beth calling out, "Ready or not, I'm coming to get you."

But tonight, it was not Beth who was coming.

The creaks, groans and sighs as the house cooled added to his unease. He wished he could unleash some Bruce Springsteen or Led Zeppelin to drown the sounds. He opened and closed his hands. He wriggled his toes and did a few stretches.

Another hour disappeared. Still there was silence. Until…
Hello?
Was that a scratching sound?
Yeah – just branches rubbing on a gutter.
Nothing to worry about.
A click.
Fuck!

No question.

A key had unlocked the kitchen door.

He heard the slightest sound of night air moving and recognized the familiar noise of the dark blue kitchen door moving uneasily on its hinges. There was a creak, followed by another. The alarm system start to buzz. The intruder had thirty seconds to kill it. He guessed Jude had briefed Carmino well.

What a dumb-fuck game this is!
What in hell's name got into me?
Poking sticks at psychopaths.
But he's expecting an empty house.
You're in Zurich, remember?
He'll be unarmed.
You have surprise on your side.
That and a baseball bat.
But was Carmino alone?

The buzzing stopped as the kitchen door was gently closed.

~ 73 ~

Between Dex and the kitchen was the square hall with its parquet flooring. After the kitchen door closed, the sounds from the waving branches of the giant horse chestnut were muted. Carmino was now within thirty feet. Dex felt his stomach gripe and his bowels struggle to combat his panic. His heart was pounding, his mouth now dry, his breathing short and strangulated. His limbs had turned to water. He felt helpless as he imagined Carmino now advancing towards him.

He dug his nails into his palms and by a slight contortion, twisted enough to peer through the crack above a hinge of the study door.

Nothing.
Just blackness.
Then distant breathing.

Then nothing again. Carmino seemed to hesitate, unsure of his bearings.

He must be by the door from the kitchen into the hall.
Waiting for his eyes to adjust?
Debating whether to turn on a light, perhaps?

He heard a few slow, steady footsteps. Eye close to the crack, Dex scarcely dared to breathe as he waited for the first sighting. Suddenly from the blackness, a face appeared but nothing else. Disembodied, it was fearful—only visible were green and white luminous stripes of a Zulu warrior moving slowly toward him. Of the body beneath there was no sign.

He fought down a scream, his sphincter control on the cusp of failure. Again, he dug his nails into his palms and tried not to cry out at the pain.

F'God's sake, Dex.

It's just a kid's mask.

A flashlight clicked on, its beam searching around the hall, its holder invisible. He heard a grunt of satisfaction as the beam steadied and hit on the open study door. Barely ten feet separated them now. He wondered if the sounds and smell of his own fear were a giveaway as the torch advanced across the hall.

Nightmarish.

Sub-human.

Relax, Dex.

Be rational.

Like Sherlock.

It's just a man.

Nothing more.

A man with a kid's Halloween mask.

Just Carmino.

A psychopath.

The footsteps moved unseen now, just the thickness of the door away as the intruder entered the study, the beam pointing ahead at the computer on the desk. "Ah!" It was the sound of satisfaction on seeing the laptop. Then the torch flashed around the outside walls revealing that all windows were hidden behind floor-to-ceiling drapes.

Satisfied, Carmino switched on the desk lamp as Dex peered at the man's back from behind the green fronds of the King Sago. Carmino was wearing thin latex gloves, trainers, jeans and a black roll-neck. He switched off the torch, put down his bag and seated himself at the desk with his back still toward Dex. Then he eased up the mask till it perched across the top of his black beret.

Dex had prepared for two alternatives. Under *Plan Stay*, Dex had left the Sony laptop running so that Carmino could search it on the spot rather than borrowing it. *Plan Go* assumed a remove-and-return job with Carmino taking the laptop away for checking. Under *Plan Go*, he would club Carmino from the rear as he exited with the laptop. He clenched the baseball bat in readiness. Either way, the laptop was not his password-protected. The previous day, he had bought an identical model and had transferred mountains of useless data onto it. Everything sensitive, including Tavio's statement, was stashed away at Waterloo Station Left-Luggage, where he had gone after leaving Billy Evans.

Was it Plan Stay or Plan Go?

From a rucksack on his back, Dex saw Carmino produce his own laptop and a blue cable. He then linked the two laptops.

Plan Stay.

I see what he's doing.

Clever.

He's going to copy what he wants across to his own laptop.

The intruder flicked from screen to screen, searching the programmes and studying the contents. From Firefox, he saw that Dex had been looking at Dignitas, flights to Zurich and at online shops selling fishing tackle. Then Dex saw Word being opened. Scarcely daring to breathe, he knew this was the moment. The two most recent folders were called *Obsession* and *ONISAC*. Both appeared at the top of the drop-down list under *Recent Documents and Recent Places*.

From his crouched and aching position, Dex had a partial view of the screen, obscured only slightly by Carmino's right shoulder. As he looked at him, hunched forward now, he heard a grunt of satisfaction at seeing these two files with intriguing names. He clicked to open *Obsession*. Dex watched as Carmino skim-read but after about four pages, he saw the reader's shoulders sag in disappointment.

With an angry and dismissive movement, Carmino clicked and transferred the folder through the cable to his own laptop.

Dex watched as the next folder was opened. "Onisac? Onisac?" Dex heard the muttered question. Carmino clicked on the mouse and the page appeared. There was a relieved laugh as the word ONISAC appeared typed in large font across the page.

"Ah! Casino." The words were accompanied by a derisive laugh. Dex was puzzled.

Those words?
That snorted laugh.
This was not Pepe Carmino.
Carmino had sent his poodle.
Nigel Forster-Brown.
The computer nerd.
This was FB in a ridiculous kid's mask.
Probably terrified.
Probably unarmed.
More petrified than me.
Just the errand boy counting the days to retirement.
It's just FB, thinking he's alone.

Dex felt his chest muscles relax. His heart, that had been pumping like crazy, started to slow. He thought rapidly, reassessing how to use the unexpected situation. There had been no need for any other plan. Not battering or trapping Carmino as he had hoped was a setback. Dealing with FB would be easier. That depended on what FB did next.

Everything now turned on a single mouse-click.

Would FB simply transfer ONISAC or would he be intrigued and want to read on? Beneath the headline ONISAC was the introduction Dex had crafted. Though he could not read it, Dex could recite every hand-picked word as easily as The Lord's Prayer.

"This folder and the sub-folder are strictly confidential and relate to crimes I and my dead sister have uncovered at Dukes Casino. In the event of my sudden death, my solicitor holds one copy of everything and will draw the obvious conclusion. The sub-folder is listed under SEKUD."

The wait as FB read the introduction seemed endless but in truth was only seconds.

Would he?
Will he click the mouse?
This is the moment.

- 74 -

Click.
FB opened the sub-folder SEKUD, mumbling *feeble anagram* as he did so. A new page appeared. Light-headed with relief and euphoria, Dex fought back a snigger. FB quickly scrolled down the page and then paused. First, he tapped his fingers and then nervously scratched his ear as he started to re-read. Dex could scarcely contain himself at seeing the discomfort. FB now shifted uneasily on the cushioned seat and Dex could imagine cold sweat starting to drip down towards the foot of his spine.

Dex had written the page to shock.
Would Carmino have reacted like this?
Hopefully.

As if being manipulated by a puppet master, FB slowly turned to look uneasily over his left shoulder toward the far corner of the room. Then, he looked directly in front of him and above his head. From the slight profile, Dex glimpsed fear, confusion and bewilderment before he scrolled through the screen again.

"Hello, Pepe! I hope you enjoy my joke. I have caught everything on camera, a bit like you with members. You have been filmed entering my home. Look over your left shoulder. Top corner. There! See that camera? Perfect mug-shot. Look up in front of you, above the desk. See another camera? Get the picture? Well, if you haven't, don't worry, because I have…if you don't mind another little joke.

The microphones under the desk have captured anything said too.

Entering the house has triggered an armed response team to surround the building. Escape is impossible. These heavies will be taking you away for a chat. Well, they'll start by, shall we say, encouraging you to talk. But you are dispensable. Like you dispensed with Beth and Tavio. Know what I mean? If you don't cooperate, they will have a few laughs with your body parts until you do. Maybe you won't see the fun side. But I do think that after their probing, you will be eager to meet my demands and transfer all Beth's winnings you stole and much more on top.

My solicitor advises that if you survive the interrogation, the police will include charges of murder, conspiracy to murder, accessory to murder, keeping fraudulent records, money-laundering, conspiring to defraud members by rigging casino games and of course theft and burglary of my home. Your gaming license will be revoked. Nobody at Dukes can be regarded as fit and proper persons to operate casinos ever again. Space City will not open. You, Pepe, will die in jail – assuming the guys now surrounding you even bother with the police.

Or perhaps you will be extradited to Nevada and face the death penalty.

Your choice.

Fun, eh?

You can surrender, if you prefer.

If you are armed – say with a knife or gun – place any weapon on the desk now. Turn off any lights in the study. You will then walk empty-handed to the French windows. They are nineteen paces to your left. You will stand beside them, open the left-hand curtain and tap on the glass three times. You will then face the window with your arms high up, legs apart, palms against the glass until someone opens the door in front of you. Sorry I can't be with you to see this, especially if the boys get to use the electric cattle prods.

FINLAY DEXTER

PS: If you have simply stolen my laptop without opening this folder, it will be too late to save you from what is coming.

Dex watched FB now sitting as if frozen stiff and lifeless. Dex guessed he was staring at the screen but seeing nothing, hands now gripping the edge of the desk. Perhaps this seemed safer than tapping on the window for a bunch of thugs to take him away. Dex's brain was now on fire, recalibrating the plan. Every detail needed to be changed. For the better. Holding Carmino until he transferred ten million from Dukes was now junked.

Would Carmino pay that for FB's release?

Doubtful.

There had to be another way.

"Fuck you, Pepe Carmino! Fuck you." FB's sudden exclamation was spat out and full of venom. It brought Dex back to FB seated just feet away, confused and transfixed.

What would he do?

- 75 -

Dex watched FB fumble to replace his mask.
Get real, FB!

Reluctantly, FB rose from the chair and stared at the instructions on the screen. As if reluctantly, he removed the mask and dumped it on the desk. He extinguished the light and counting aloud up to nineteen, he walked hesitantly to the distant corner of the room. Out of vision now, Dex eased himself from his niche as he heard three sharp raps on the glass.

Despite the blackness, Dex could make out the shape of FB standing beside the open drape with his hands above his head, palms on the glass, legs apart. Unlike FB, who had moved as if on final steps to the hangman, Dex had a new idea and was seeing and thinking in glorious Technicolor. Of all the options presented by FB, one now stood out. He tightened his grip on the baseball bat and crossed the carpet with soft and silent steps.

FB had no reason to expect Dex to be there, let alone creeping up on him. As if frozen solid, FB never moved, his hands firmly on the window as he looked for the heavies outside. Dex crept to within three paces before he roared – roared louder than he had ever roared. The sound came from deep down and bounced off the walls, the windows and reverberated through the house. In the study, it sounded as if the hounds of hell and the lions of Longleat had been unleashed.

The unexpected noise in the deadly hush scared the hell out of FB. He screamed, not daring to look behind him. Instead, he seemed to press even harder against the window.

"Turn around." Dex's command was shouted as he swept back the second drape. In the shadowy light from the night sky, Dex could now see that his roar had been even more effective than he had dared to hope. FB turned to face him. The guy had lost it and maybe had just crapped himself. His face was hollowed and his eyes saucer-wide. The hangdog look and a smell reminiscent of Father's room upstairs confirmed the effect of the roar.

Dex saw a man pleading to crawl back into his mother's womb. If the Baskerville Hound had been bounding toward him, FB could not have been more terrified. "One move, FB, and you get this." He brandished the baseball bat. "And when you wake, you won't like where you find yourself." Dex switched on the corner table-lamp. "Sit. Back against the wall, hands beneath your knees." He crouched down and, fighting against the stench, handcuffed the obedient figure. Then, also thanks to *Naughty Nocturne*, he used leather bondage straps to secure FB's knees and ankles. Satisfied, he turned to the window and rapped on it four times – in two bursts of two.

"You due back in Dukes?" Dex watched FB wriggle. "Tell me … now?" He snapped out the command as FB nodded, yes. Adam had once told him how to command attention in Board meetings – *speak slowly and to the point*. He did so. "Answer everything I ask or you will go on a one-way journey." He leaned forward in emphasis. "Your body will never be found. The pigs are waiting and hungry."

Dex heard nothing more than a whimper. He grinned, his confidence boiling over, as if on steroids. "You're lucky, FB. I'm giving you a chance. Pepe Carmino would have been dead by now." He prodded FB in the chest with the baseball-bat. "Co-operate or it's fingernail treatment and electric cattle probes for starters." He saw FB shrivel further onto his excrement. "Electrodes will be attached to your scrotum. I'm told it hurts. Shockingly." He alone laughed at his joke. "But I'm told that's not needed so often. Most guys talk after the third fingernail."

Dex waited for the terrified man to look toward him. "FB, there's no cavalry coming for you. Carmino will never report you missing." He saw FB's entire body trembling. If FB could have put a comforting thumb in his mouth, he would have done so. "Nobody else knows you're here, burgling my home. You are so *very* dispensable." He spat out the words and broke down *dis-pens-ible* to make the point. FB stared at the carpet but said nothing, his breathing uneven and his chest still heaving from the shock of the roar. Dex now crouched down so that his face was inches from FB's. "*Nobody* fucks with me. Not Carmino. Nobody."

He saw FB shudder again. Dex leaned even closer so that FB tried unsuccessfully to retreat. Now Dex could also smell warm urine, mixed with FB's aftershave and a hint of garlic. "Unless you help me, you are into the *last minutes* of your life." He prodded his captive again. "*Dis-pens-ible*." Dex enjoyed the contempt he had injected into the word. He leaned across to the window and signalled, five raps and then another five. "There, FB. You have ten seconds. Start talking or I hand you over."

Without hesitation, FB spoke but his words croaked out like an old man's death-rattle. "I'll talk."

"From now, when I give you an order, any order, you jump. Got it?" He gimlet-eyed FB again. "Yes or no?" He barked the words slowly for effect. Dex waited for a few long seconds and then moved to open the French window. "Last chance."

FB's lips trembled. "Okay. But Pepe," he faltered. "That bastard. I'm scared."

Dex said nothing. He gave four bangs, two and two on the window. "When is Carmino expecting you back?"

"Maybe an hour or two."

Dex thought fast. With FB dancing to his tune, there were two ways he would be valuable. Could he be the missing link for Reverse Labouchère? Gus McKay's suggestion suddenly seemed *fuck me good*. He switched on the voice recorder, bought that morning. "Explain the cheating, fixing, laundering. Make it good because otherwise Carmino gets this recording." He smiled in a disturbing way that made FB look away. "Me? I'd rather jump under a train than let Carmino near me with that knife of his."

FB's voice croaked again and he cleared his throat. "That bastard controls me. I was never involved, never wanted to be. One night, I saw One-Eye and Jeb Miller cheat a player. That's when Carmino told me that was the way it was going to be till Space City had been funded. Cheat, cheat, cheat! He's running parallel accounts, false accounts. All these guest players playing big-money – they are all laundering. Dukes take a cut." FB raised his frightened eyes, some dribble slipping over his lower lip. "What more do you want?".

"First, some questions answered."

"What do I tell him when I get back?"

"You mean after you've showered and changed your clothes? I'll help you if you've told me everything." Dex wondered where to start. "On a typical day, how much cash is in the cage?"

"Since the laundering, up to fifty million in sterling, dollars, and euros. But if you're thinking of stealing it, forget it."

"When the tables open at 2 p.m. you have cash?"

"Of course. Many millions."

"And Carmino? What time does he usually appear?"

FB looked shifty but the response made sense. "Most days, between 5 and 8 p.m."

"You arrive when?"

"By ten each morning."

"Is Carmino suspicious of me?"

"He's convinced you're up to something."

"Mick Glenn's death? The murdered dealers in Vegas. My sister. All down to Carmino?

FB's shrug and denial of knowledge were convincing.

"Now, I want specifics. Details. Names of everybody involved. Banking arrangements. How these phony guests reach Dukes." He grabbed a chair for himself. "Talk fast."

– 76 –

As the hands on Carmino's Rolex nudged toward 4 a.m. there were still over forty members and guests at the tables. Carmino was standing close to the cage, chatting to a Lebanese regular. He tried to appear interested in the guy's rant about British culture. He nodded politely, murmuring the odd *of course* and *couldn't agree more* but his mind was elsewhere. FB should have been back by now.

He could see Jude at the roulette with the Croatian in a loud checked-cloth suit. She was clinging to his arm while placing his chips with her other hand. Then from the staff's relaxation room, FB appeared in his working gear of black tie and dinner jacket.

"Ah, FB! How is your brother?"

"Doing a little better, thank you."

"Remind me to send fruit and a card. No, better still, let's go to my office and I'll arrange it now. Goodnight, Mr Doumany."

The charade over, the two men were quickly seated in Carmino's office, either side of the wide desk. Carmino poured himself a generous malt whisky but offered nothing to FB who felt in need of one. The room smelled of Mediterranean flower spray struggling against stale cigar smoke. "Strike gold?"

FB looked at the ashtray on the corner of the desk, his eyes no more evasive than usual. Then he shook his head. "No."

"You left no clues?"

"Gloves on all the time. When I left, I double-checked. Everything looked undisturbed. I reset the alarm."

"Good. And?"

"My expertise wasn't needed. You could have gone as you intended. I didn't have to crack any password. The chump hadn't powered-off." FB hoped he looked disappointed. "If he's up to something, you'd never know from his computer." FB's eyes looked at the carpet and then gazed toward the colourful Lassen original on the far wall. "Maybe there's stuff in the safe. It was beyond me to crack that. It's state of the art."

"No travel plans? Las Vegas, maybe?" Carmino could not mention Panama.

FB shook his head and played nervously with his fingers. "He may have been in Vienna recently. There were some hotel details." FB paused. "Boss, knowing you were convinced the shit was up to something, I didn't give up. After checking the laptop, I took my time – searched every drawer, shelf, bookcase, cupboard from the top rooms to the bottom. If he's got anything on us, it must be in the safe. In a drawer by his bed, there were some notes about his Father. There were medical bills from Harley Street. His recent web viewing history involved a fishing tackle supplier, stuff about Princess Diana and Dignitas and his flights to Zurich. Nothing sinister."

"Dignitas. That's where he now is." Carmino thought back to Jude's conversation with Dex over dinner. He felt satisfied that FB had done a thorough job.

For no obvious reason FB brushed his sleeve. "I did find a folder on his laptop called *Obsession*. That sounded interesting."

"No?"

"Was it hell! It's the name of a novel. Dex is writing a thriller about a student obsessed with beating the casino. That's probably why he has a roulette wheel in the study." He shook his head. "Looked like tripe. Long-winded drivel." He yawned into the back

of his hand. "Can I go now? I'm feeling pretty bushed. Creeping round someone else's house like that."
"No emails between him and Mick Glenn? No links?"
"He uses Outlook. I checked it out. I ran a search. No. He emails that Tiffany woman in the USA – nothing interesting. Just setting up Messenger calls. She's back this weekend it seems."
"Anything about Jude Tuson?"
"Besides hiring her? Nothing. You were so sure there would be something, I even undid his last defrag to see if he'd hidden any old material. The Recycling Bin contained nothing of interest. His recent letters and emails are all about winding up his sister's estate."
Carmino struck a match for another cigar. "No separate password-protected area?"
FB's snort of derision was response enough but he threw in a *do-me-a-favour* look. "First thing I checked – looking for secret areas. That's what I was hoping for, something meaty for me to do. A bit of cryptography." FB then tapped his forehead as if he had remembered something. "Oh, yes! I read his contact list – names, addresses. No Mick Glenn. No Scotty Brannigan."
Carmino topped up his malt. "I'm not sure whether I'm surprised or disappointed."
FB frowned. "Isn't it better that he's not onto us?"
"You'd think so. I was convinced he tipped off Mick Glenn. If not him, who the hell was it?"
"Boss, tonight did not prove you wrong. I just found nothing to prove you're right."
Carmino nodded as he absorbed the comment. He spoke slowly. "Yes, of course. You're right." He was about to dismiss FB when his face brightened. "Downstairs, One-Eye rolled over that fat Swede for 2.3 million. The slob was as drunk as a skunk, a bottle of vodka behind each eyeball. And the Belgian? Y'know, the guy

who worked in agriculture at the European Commission. His 20% was a cool two million. Pudding-bowl reckoned nothing moved in his division without bribes."

Carmino reached across his desk to open a folder. FB knew this meant the discussion was over. He turned away without expecting any thanks or goodbye. Once outside the door, FB paused to take a deep breath. Sweat was gathering on the nape of his neck but somehow, he had escaped unscathed. Somehow, he had got across what Dex wanted Carmino to know.

But the future?
Taking orders from Dex?
His stomach churned at the prospect.

— 77 —

Dex had slept for barely an hour and now, on the train to Northampton, it was a struggle to stay awake. But he had so much to review. Having FB under his thumb was game-changing. This afternoon, he would meet Gus McKay's contact, Larry Jamous or as a fall-back, Max Horobin. Jamous was based in Penarth Street in a tough part of southeast London, about five miles from Tower Bridge and not far from Millwall FC.

More hub-cap thieves than designer shops round there, he told himself as he planned for that meeting. The jolt of the train slowing for Northampton brought his thoughts back to Father. The Bistbury Care Centre was just a few minutes' walk from the station. Dex was impressed. It proved to be clean, modern and smelled of boiled fish, floor polish and disinfectant. The director, Marty Baxter, produced coffee in mugs and a plate brimming with assorted biscuits. He summoned a nurse and Dex soon heard what had become familiar jargon – *stimuli, reaction, responses, deficit, motor function*. After twenty minutes of explanations, Dex knew his worst fears were justified.

"This sounds hopeless. It's tearing me apart. I'm thinking of Dignitas."

"Mr Dexter, give us two weeks for more tests. It is quite early days since the accident." Baxter, who was about thirty, shook his head sadly.

"And in two weeks?"

"We'll know what the future holds." Dex could tell by his voice that Baxter was not expecting miracles.

"Okay then. Deal."

Cursing the steady rain, he splashed his way to the station, thinking now only Larry Jamous. Penarth Street was a forty-minute cab ride from Euston. The route passed between sprawling council estates and run-down commercial premises, tucked under railway arches. The taxi dropped him outside a low-rise brick-built building dating back to the 19th century. It stood around a small courtyard. Vandals had hurled stones through the windows of an empty unit. Across a sign naming about eight different businesses, someone had spray-painted meaningless red graffiti. At the far end, he found Emporium Supplies (Global) Limited, where he asked the bored-looking receptionist for Mr Jamous. She put down her Big Mac and dialled through to him, still chewing.

Moments later, Larry Jamous appeared using small, busy steps. Aged perhaps sixty, he was below average height with narrow-set eyes, a pencil-thin moustache and thick grey crinkly hair. Jamous, who might have been part English, part Egyptian, led Dex into a small office. Not unlike McKay's back-room, it was crammed with files and invoices, at least three dirty coffee mugs and a girlie-calendar showing the wrong month. Dex settled in beside the cluttered desk.

"You phoned this morning. Recommended by that eccentric little Scotsman, was you?"

"Gus McKay said you're the man."

"I might be. What do you want?"

In a couple of brushstrokes rehearsed on the train, Dex explained. Jamous stayed poker-faced, showing neither surprise nor concern as his hands rearranged some computer cables on his desk. "By when?"

"Seven days max."

"Nah. We're busy, mate. Up to our bleedin' necks. Two months."

"Cash payment?"

"Don't cut no ice, mate. We got stuff goin' out seven days a week already. I got my existing customers to worry about, not piss them off by givin' you priority."

"How much for delivery in two months?"

"Forty thousand quid, twenty-five up front."

Dex knew from Gus McKay that Jamous would screw him. He didn't care. "Look, Larry, here's the deal. Sixty-grand in cash tomorrow. Forty more on delivery in seven days or less." Dex rose to leave. "Gus McKay gave me an alternative. Max Horobin." Dex was now by the door, hand on the frame. "Okay. Suit yourself. I've an appointment fixed for later in Morden."

"Horobin, eh? That duffer's second-rate. I'll do it… but what you want mate, is a work of art. Bleedin' van Gogh wasn't pressurised like this."

"Van Gogh cut off his own ear. In your case, if you don't deliver on time, it won't be your ears I cut off. Get this straight. You *will* deliver on time."

Jamous flinched in his tubular chair. "You're a hard man, Mr… er?"

"Cornelius. Jake Cornelius. The courier will deliver the cash by ten tomorrow."

"How do I contact you?"

"You don't. I contact you."

-78-

During the taxi ride back from Penarth Street, Dex received a text from Tiffany. "Flying tonight from LAX." He replied promising to meet her at Heathrow. As he typed *Heathrow*, memories of Beth flooded back. Tears welled-up as he imagined her clearing Immigration, waiting at the carousel and climbing into the limo for her final few minutes of life. He wiped his eyes with the back of his hand. Reliving her final moments was a recurring theme. He wished it were not. It gave him an eerie feeling, similar to viewing the clip of Princess Diana leaving the Ritz Hotel in Paris on her fated journey.

After he had composed himself, he made a call to the Las Vegas attorney. When he heard Gus McKay's name, his enthusiasm was obvious. "The best private eye? The guy you need operates from Summerlin in the northwest valley. His name's Otto Schneider. Tell him I recommended you. He hangs out below the radar, specialising in commercial espionage. Don't ask about his methods. Just whoop at the results. Oh, and give my best to the little Scotsman. He's something else, that guy. We had some wild parties in Binions."

Dex rang Schneider at once. The private eye sounded like an American Dutchman and assured Dex he could move quickly so long as the fee was immediately transferred to his bank at the Trails in Summerlin. "And the fee?" enquired Dex.

"Three hundred dollars an hour. Minimum billing of fifty hours. Your account must be maintained evergreen at this figure."

Dex swallowed hard. "I'll transfer $15,000 today." For the next ten minutes he explained what Schneider had to do. No sooner had he ended that call than his phone rang again. He heard the gloomy Wolverhampton accent of the policeman in charge of the accident investigation. "The DAF's tachograph had been tampered with. I am not permitted to tell you the details. We have yet to trace the driver."

"So, there's no evidence the DAF accelerated deliberately? To go for murder?" It was like a rerun of the useless investigations of Caroline and Jamie's murders.

"A couple of independent witnesses might help. Wait for the Inquest."

Dex got the taxi to drop him off in Sloane Street, a few hundred metres from the Bulgari Hotel on Knightsbridge. Adam had suggested they met there with Billy. Taking no chances in case of a tail, he entered Knightsbridge Tube Station at the Sloane Street entrance and bought a ticket. He dropped deep down to the Piccadilly platform, walked its length and then resurfaced at the western exit. Satisfied now that he had no pursuers, he rounded the corner and entered the hotel.

The public areas were crowded with international dealmakers. Dex heard Arabic, Russian, broken English and American as he strolled through the lobby and into the crowded bar. As he rounded the burnished copper curve of the bar-counter, admiring the clever blend of colours in the décor, he saw Adam and Billy seated on the far side.

Adam offered him a champagne cocktail but after the roller-coaster of the past twenty-four hours, he settled for a spicy tomato juice. He appraised Billy. "You're looking better than yesterday." *But not by much*, he told himself. "How's Emily? How's Sandie?"

Billy shrugged with a touch of despair. "Maybe Sandie's softening but she won't have me back." Then he brightened. "Emily's got a new bike for her sixth birthday. Pooh goes everywhere in the little basket."

"She's a fun kid. As for you and Sandie – if you avoid card-counting, cocaine and booze, hopefully she'll forgive you." Dex then looked at each of them in turn. "Productive afternoon?"

"You tell him," prompted Adam, looking at Billy.

"Adam and I hit the blackjack when the tables opened at two."

"I've never done that," explained Adam. "Normally," he added with a chuckle "I would be in the restaurant with the chaps till way gone three. We would be limbering up to watch the nags with a schooner of port. Or twain."

"Use the cameras?" Dex had lent Billy his cufflinks but Adam had declined to risk the tiepin. He saw Billy nod and then grin, very much a cat that had got the cream.

"Nothing caught on camera yet but I know how they *can* fix the decks."

"Can?" Dex look puzzled and wanted an explanation. "Or do?" In the early hours, FB had headlined him about fixing but he could say nothing of that.

"Look, when the tables open, the joint is empty. Unlike most London casinos, which are twenty-four-seven, Dukes is barely coming to life at 2pm."

"Most of the chaps, the regulars that is, we're still lunching," explained Adam.

Billy took up the story. "But there's a woman, early thirties, all alone at one of the blackjack tables, waiting for the first hand to be dealt. When we joined her, the cards were already in the shoe."

"This popsy looks just like Charlotte Rampling back in the seventies." Adam's tone was lyrical. "Penetrating eyes and a proud, almost supercilious look. Stunning gal. Not English." He sighed. "If I were thirty years younger! I've seen her in the bar of an evening.

Name is Irenke. She's all touchy-feely with Pepe. Too damned familiar I'd say. Less so recently. Last night, she was helping some Belgian fella. She often plays roulette or blackjack with older men. But never with me." He looked disappointed.

So far this fitted what FB had told Dex. "Showing your age there, Adam but I get the picture. Go on Billy. Explain."

"At the start of play, or whenever the cards are changed, typically perhaps six new cellophane-wrapped decks are opened. Then all the cards should be semi-circled on the table, face up, so that the players can see all fifty-two cards from each pack. The dealer then shuffles up. A player then cuts the cards. Then they are put in the shoe."

"You mean this had been done before you arrived?"

Billy scoffed. "Or not!"

"You think this woman is stooge?" Dex saw Billy's nod in agreement.

"Anyway," Adam leaned forward as if someone might overhear them, "as soon as we joined her, she played one more hand and moved to the next table and had that one opened up."

Billy continued the explanation. "We could scarcely switch tables to check what she was doing. That would have looked suspicious. Her dealer spread out the six decks before shuffling but she never even looked. Were they full decks or fixed?" He shrugged.

Dex knew the answer from FB. It was reassuring. FB had told him the truth. "If she's on Pepe's payroll, some missing tens and aces wouldn't bother her."

"And maybe a few extra fours and fives might be added." Billy was quick to agree.

"Yes – and next?"

"She played a couple of hands and then moved to another table and opened that."

Dex whistled quietly. "So bloody simple! Players like Adam drifting in later would assume other players have already checked the decks."

"Damnable fixed decks." Adam sounded hurt more than angry.

Dex laughed. "Adam, you kept losing because you played like a trout." He saw Billy give a quiet smile.

Adam looked severe for a moment but then laughed too. "Oh, alright! I lost *even quicker* because of their fraud." Adam's voice still showed indignation as he continued. "She opened four tables. The fifth one rarely opens until late evening anyway."

"We're nearly there, Dex," Billy confirmed.

Dex waved his hands calmingly. "Billy, how many shoes have you played?"

"After playing again tomorrow, one-hundred. Nice round number for the stats. Based on ninety, they're rigging the decks." Billy helped himself to a smoked salmon tartlet. "Every time the card-count tells me the odds favour the player, it doesn't happen. Sure as hell, the remaining cards are crap."

"Meaning that Dukes has a huge advantage?"

"I'd say." Billy opened his ancient BlackBerry. "My notes and calculations." He read from the screen. "Right now, I could tell a judge that at least five aces and maybe nine face cards or tens are missing."

Just as FB told me.

Dex clasped Billy's sleeve. "Sensational! Don't go tomorrow."

Billy ran his hand over the fuzz on his head. "I want to reach one hundred shoes. Secondly, I want to see if this Irenke woman opens the tables. Most importantly, I want to open a table myself for comparison. That way, I'll know every deck is kosher."

"You reckon they have legit packs if someone else gets to open a table?" Dex saw Billy agree but watching the way Billy's tongue flicked in and out, made him wary. Though Billy's logic was impeccable, Dex sensed he was not getting the full story. "Adam?" Dex was interested in his take.

Adam looked at Billy and then at Dex. "If Billy played ten shoes with decks Dukes couldn't rig, that would clinch it." He looked to Billy for confirmation. "Wouldn't that be a double whammy?" Adam beamed, proud to have picked up some modern jargon.

Dex was uneasy. "I guess filming this Irenke could be valuable." FB's recorded admissions had been secured under extreme duress. *Would that stand up in court?* Filmed evidence from Billy would tip the balance "Every time you play it's a risk. But okay, play on a legit table but try to film this woman opening a game without checking the decks."

As he listened, Billy adjusted his bottle-green jacket. From beneath the sleeves, his pastel green cuffs appeared. "Agreed then." Absent-mindedly, he rubbed a patterned cufflink while Dex ordered another round of drinks. "Adam, you'll be with Billy tomorrow?"

Adam finished chewing on a blini before explaining that he had a charity meeting involving a spot of lunch. Dex did not say anything but he had expected his godfather to be there as a valued witness. After Adam had for a dinner engagement at Le Caprice, Dex leaned across to Billy who was about to leave as well. "Look – tell me straight. Are you back on the drugs? I've got to tell you, I think you are. If I'm right, tomorrow is off."

"No, Dex. I'm still clean. Honest!"

While Dex waited to pay for the drinks, he watched Billy walk away slowly. *Had Billy been lying his arse off about drugs?* After settling up, Dex checked his phone for messages, taking no interest in the two men and one woman seated quite close by who had been drinking sparkling water.

- 79 -

"I expect to go to Vegas. Later tomorrow probably." Pepe Carmino threw in the casual remark as he dusted his black loafers.

Jude's face lit up at the thought of a few days chilling out on the Strip. "When do we leave?"

"Not you this trip, sorry. Busy, busy, busy. Anyway, I need you here, looking after these rich geezers." He came over and kissed her on the cheek. "Once Space City is flying, then we'll be hitting the hotspots. Promise."

Jude didn't buy his excuse and she pouted as she sat at the dressing table. She now suspected that Pepe was all bullshit and she would be dumped when he got bored with her. The previous evening, she had chatted briefly to Irenke who had been waiting for her Belgian to arrive. Too many cocktails had loosened the Hungarian's tongue. She too had been promised exotic travel, only to be discarded. She had never got to Tahiti, Fiji, Curacao or the Far East.

Devious bastard, Jude thought as she checked her eye-liner. *All promises*. "Will you be away long, Pepe?"

"One night, maybe two. Depends if Enzo Letizione has stopped fucking up."

"Get rid of him."

"After the launch, I'm going to…" He was interrupted by an old-style American ringtone on his phone. "What's news?" He took the phone into the sitting-room next to the bedroom but Jude could still hear him. "Good job! Like it! Yeah, that's all I need for now." He returned to the bedroom, punching the air. In a few jubilant strides, he stood behind Jude and cupped his hands under her generous breasts and kissed the top of her head.

Jude looked in the mirror and gave Pepe a questioning look. "Good news? What was that all about?"

"This rather strange friend of Adam Yarbury – he's called Billy Evans. I've had a tail on him and my guy only copped a photo of him buying coke on the corner of Gerrard Street in Chinatown."

"Okay, so he takes drugs. What's the big deal?"

"Finlay Dexter met up in the Bulgari with Adam Yarbury and Billy."

"That's no crime. Dex didn't do drugs. I asked him."

"Dexter's up to something. The guys watching the monitors were suspicious about some of his body movements in the casino."

"Tight trousers and his huge tackle, Pepe."

Carmino did not see the humour. "The way Dexter holds his left arm and sometimes twists his body. They reckon he's almost certainly been filming. They suspected a tiepin or his ornate cufflinks. Who wears tiepins these days?"

"And?"

"Billy was wearing the same cufflinks today at the tables. And guess what? He too held his left arm in a similar way. He was followed to the Bulgari Hotel. He was caught rubbing the cufflink."

"Cleaning a lens maybe?"

"You betcha."

"What are you going to do?"

"Maybe cut Dexter and Evans a bit of slack before pouncing. I'm not sure."

"But," Jude hesitated, her open-looking face puckered into a slight frown. "Don't take this wrong but Dex is a regular guy.

What's your problem? That he's friendly with Billy? You know he's friendly with that old guy, Adam."

"Why would Dex be filming? I'll tell you why. I'm convinced he's the guy who thought Mick Glenn was being cheated. As for Billy Evans – face it! Billy's scarcely the type Adam Yarbury would normally ever notice, let alone talk to." He saw Jude's tilt of the head in agreement. "Tonight, if either Dexter or Evans is in, keep an eye on them. But this Greek politician you're looking after, he's priority. Make sure every last drachma, euro, pound or whatever is squeezed from him. He's top, top loaded."

"Who is he?"

"Vasilis Eliades, a former prime minister aged about seventy-eight. His pockets are stuffed with untaxed wealth. A right slippery bastard."

"Seventy-eight? Not, please not, a bedroom job?"

"Do what it takes." He gathered his jacket, watch, wallet, keys and small change while she adjusted her hair. "Ready? I'll drop you off at the Westbury. Eliades has the best suite."

"Well, I hope I don't see much of it." She twirled round in her new red halter-neck midi-dress by Balmain. "These old guys are all the same. I blame Viagra."

"Whatever it takes, Jude, whatever it takes. I'm paying you well." Jude could not disagree as he grasped her hand and led her toward the garage. "I'll be home for breakfast. Then I've some interesting gadgets we can play with. I think you'll enjoy them."

Jude thought of the money and forced a smile. "You, Pepe, are a lusciously evil bastard."

- 80 -

Dex was surprised how edgy he felt as he waited at Terminal 5. When Tiffany appeared with her trolley, although she could not wave, her excited smile was reassuring. Once into the concourse, she stretched out to wrap her arms around him. "Thank God you're safe!" She buried her face into his neck and for a few moments they were lost in each other, oblivious to their surroundings.

"Hopefully, I don't smell as bad as when I was a tethered goat," Dex laughed. "The car's in short-term parking." He led her to his open-top Audi and once inside, flipped back the roof. "It's a beautiful day. Fancy lunch in the country, somewhere far away from it all?"

"Sounds like bliss after the Los Angeles freeways. Thoughts of humdrum and drudgery in my kitchen doesn't do it for me right now. I'm still on too much of a high." She leaned across and kissed him gently on the mouth. "Anyway, we both need to unwind, relax a little and catch up."

"I know just the place." He stroked her cheek before returning her kiss. "The Sir Charles Napier at Chinnor."

"Great but no phones. Mine's been clamped to my ear for weeks. PR people and journalists hounding me."

"Journalists? That's rich coming from you."

"*Touché*. I got sick of touring – everywhere, journalists asking the same questions." She mock-yawned. "You get to feel a bit sorry for Brad Pitt or Madonna." Tiffany watched him switch off his phone before continuing. "Today is *us time*. You and me but mainly you. These past weeks," her sigh turned into a real yawn, "have been too much about me. Give!"

Dex looked thoughtful before changing the subject. "This pub, well gastropub really, is in the back of beyond. Well worth finding." Dex fired the engine and soon joined the M25 and the M40 west. Just under forty minutes later, they were standing in the garden taking in the tranquil beauty – an abundance of trees, lawn and a colourful mix of blues and purples. Late summer scents surrounded them as they settled at a table under the spreading branches of a huge tree, the air filled with birdsong and the sound of bees in the shrubs.

Tiffany leaned across the table and held his hand. Her bare arms were tanned and her elfish face radiated a glow that belied her long flight. "I couldn't have dreamed of somewhere better. The stinking fumes of La Cienega Boulevard seem a million miles away." She yawned again, stretching her arms above her head, emphasising her shapely figure.

"And no job to go back to. A good feeling?"

"It was time for a change. I can't wait to get my feet back in the hot African dust. What's not to like? But after we've ordered, this is about you. Tell me all."

Tiffany listened well as Dex told her about Northampton, Panama, Tavio's statement and FB's luminous mask. "In espionage jargon, I've turned FB." Only the description of Carmino murdering the Mexican spooked her. "This Jude woman – she sounds quite a character."

Dex had Tiffany laughing as he explained about her bogus references, the snooping and having to fight off her advances. "She doesn't know I rumbled her. I'm really fond of her, despite what she did for Carmino."

"And destroying Space City? What's the latest on your madcap plan?" Tiffany took a spoonful of Eton Mess.

"I leave for Vegas tomorrow. Then, everything depends on what Otto Schneider digs up."

"When does Space City open?"

Dex's eyes hardened as he answered. "Five days, but if Otto does his stuff, never." Dex lowered his fork. "You never did a signing in Vegas, did you?"

"My book? Sell in Vegas?" She laughed. "Not enough four-letter words and too many long ones. Why?"

Dex had been building to this moment. "Come to Vegas. I have an outrageous idea to nail Enzo Letizione and I need your help." He saw the dubious upturned eyebrow. "Hear me out. Please?" She managed a half-smile, so he continued. "You told me you were a convent girl. Have you ever done anything *really* naughty? And I'm not talking sex."

Dex was rewarded with a laugh while she stroked his hand. "As a journalist? Absolutely. Naughty goes with the job. You have to be brass-necked or tell the occasional fib."

"Yeah, yeah!" Dex grinned. "Like door-stepping a funeral in Bladon, maybe."

She rewarded his dig with an impish smile that dimpled her cheeks. "But when I'm not a journalist? Goody-two-shoes, that's me! Oh! There was once. When I was fifteen, we did creep out of the dorm one night to smoke ciggies. We felt very naughty doing that."

Dex leaned back, hands clasped behind his head. "A perfect CV. It's the journalist in you I need. Let me explain what I have in mind for Mr Enzo Letizione."

-81-

It was pushing three o'clock when they reluctantly left the shaded warmth of the garden. Their mood was mellow until Dex broke the magic by switching on his phone. "Sorry but this is urgent. I need to know if Billy has the evidence." As they sat in the Audi, he read the three text messages, each increasingly panicky. Dex looked at Tiffany, his eyes narrowed. "Bugger! Bugger and sod it! Everything gone in a flash."

"Big problems?" Tiffany's prompting was unnecessary. She had seen Dex chewing his lip as he read.

Dex hesitated before explaining. "That was not Billy. It was FB. Like I told you – he's reporting to me now."

Tiffany cottoned on. "So … the problem is …?"

"A security guy in Dukes challenged Billy about carrying drugs. Someone had seen Billy buying in Gerrard Street. Billy panicked and bolted but dropped his BlackBerry and never stopped to pick it up. Just kept running."

"Check with FB what's happening. With the Blackberry. With Carmino."

"Too risky. In his words, they're on damage limitation, checking out the Blackberry."

"Bad?"

Dex thought for a few seconds. "The worst. They'll find Billy's notes on crooked decks for starters. There'll be emails and texts I exchanged with him. Carmino could never link us before this. Now he knows I'm deadly serious to get him."

"Then go to the police." Her voice was raised. "Now."

Dex recognised her solid advice as he revved up and sped away. "Think of Mick Glenn, the two dead dealers in Vegas. Add in Beth's death – murder, whatever the cops think." He twisted slightly to catch her tight-lipped glare. "Carmino will fight like a cornered rat."

"Will the Blackberry reveal what Carmino did in Panama?"

"Tavio's statement? Not on there and never mentioned. But Carmino was already obsessed enough to plant Jude and burgle my place."

"Your point?"

"We're in danger, deep, deep shit. Me and Billy especially. Even Adam. Maybe you too – anybody who gets in Carmino's way. Even if Billy never mentioned Panama, our lives are in danger. Carmino now knows I intend to bring him down."

"But he wouldn't get away with it, not if he starts murdering…"

"Getting away with more murders? Not the point, Tiffany darling. He's a psychopathic killer with a short fuse. The way the Vegas dealers were silenced shows nothing stops him. We have Beth and Mick Glenn and know how he murdered the Mexican." Dex paused. "If Carmino thinks he's going down for murder, then sure as hell it's worth risking a few more. It might buy him time to escape."

Dex left the thought hanging for Tiffany but she was not buying it. "Why are you so stubborn?" Tiffany's voice was tetchy. "You've enough to bring down Carmino and Dukes. With Carmino discredited and banged-up, the Feds will move in and Space City won't open. He won't be able to take revenge."

Dex was irritated by her oversimplification. "I wish! God! How I wish! Sorry, but I've nothing but a ragbag of suspicious circumstances. FB's evidence was given under duress. Billy's calculations are gone.

In Vegas, what Otto Schneider gets might be dynamite but will be illegally obtained and can't be used in court. We have nothing on film. We have nothing linking Carmino to anything except the Panama murder."

Tiffany said nothing.

"The police, if they do anything, may not keep him in custody. He'll deny everything and may be free to go. What then? While they suck their pencils wondering what to do, he roams free to take his bloody revenge."

The uncomfortable silence lasted for several miles. It ended only when the Audi was approaching Hanger Lane. "Tiffany, Billy is in immediate grave danger. Carmino will have his address from his membership form. I've got to protect him."

"Carmino knows where you live too."

Dex ignored that uncomfortable truth. "With your help and Otto Schneider's report, we can nail Enzo Letizione. Kill Space City. Y'know, my plan we discussed at lunch?"

Tiffany could see from the set of his jaw that he was not to be deflected. "And so?"

"If Pepe Carmino is staying in London, we should not be here."

"We? Meaning, including me?"

"Carmino is not going to have everything destroyed without a fight. You're connected to me." He saw Tiffany flinch. "You, a journalist, were there when One-Eye cheated Glenn." He let that uncomfortable fact sink in. "*Anybody* in his way is a target." Deftly, he swung off the elevated section, turning north toward St John's Wood. "I'm collecting my passport, laptop, some cash from the safe. With him in London, we must be far away. We fly to Vegas today. All of us. But Carmino must not know that."

"Count me out. I'm bushed, sick of travelling. Until he's locked up, I can hide up somewhere far from London – Blakeney or Polperro. Africa."

"Tiffany, a well-known face like yours? Do you really think you'll ever be safe while Carmino is free? Not after Billy's balls-up. If Carmino's jailed, he'll never rest till a contract killer gets me. He'll have nothing to lose."

"You mean Carmino must be…"

Dex ducked a direct answer but to Tiffany his body language was answer enough. "Please. I need your help to nail Letizione," Dex urged as he paused at the traffic-lights. "You agreed. If we can lure Carmino to Vegas and get him arrested there, they have the death penalty." Dex looked up and down his residential street before pulling up outside Porcupine House. There was no sign of anybody watching. Dex gave her a peck on the cheek. "Plus, I want you around."

"Obsessions can be dangerous. Carmino's and yours." She gave him a resigned sigh. "Are you going to phone Billy?" Tiffany saw Dex's eyes crinkle as he gave her a surprised and disdainful grin. "Oh! Silly me. Must be jet-lag. He has to contact you." Dex hopped out of the car and she followed his rapid strides to the kitchen door. "Dex, if Billy's like most of us, he won't remember your number. His BlackBerry did all that for him."

Dex nodded yes. "You're packed and ready. I'll be five minutes max. We've got to get to Billy before Carmino does. Book a big car to take us to Stansted and charter a jet. We're flying tonight."

"Private jet? That'll cost…"

"I'm on the Rich List, remember? Here's my credit-card. There's no limit. I'll ring Adam while I throw a few things together. Every second we're here, we're in grave danger."

Twelve minutes later, a black Mercedes pulled up and they piled in with their baggage. Dex checked in both directions. "We're lucky. Still nobody watching here yet."

"Picking up Adam, are we?" Tiffany enquired.

"We spoke. He was strangely calm. Mind you, he'd had a good lunch. He's either cool under fire or hasn't properly realised we're in shitsville. He was actually planning to *toddle along* to Dukes this evening. We're picking him up by the Tate Modern on the way to Clapham."

"And if Billy is not at home?"

"We wait for a while. If that fails, I leave a message for him to disappear. He should have enough of my cash to hole up somewhere for a few days."

"I've a better idea," Tiffany volunteered as she rummaged in her handbag.

– 82 –

While Dex was enjoying the shade under the tree at the Sir Charles Napier, Pepe Carmino had taken Jude to the intimacy of Julie's Restaurant, near his Holland Park home. Carmino had not felt so elated for a while. The surveillance reports from Chinatown and from Bulgari had been a major break. Based on them, he had ordered that whenever Billy Evans appeared, he should be challenged and searched about drugs.

Better still, the noose around Dexter was tightening.

Or was that worse.

His plans had allowed time for a leisurely lunch plus another hour or two in bed with Jude, before flying to Vegas. FB's call shortly before 2 p.m had changed everything. "Evans arrived. Malky Fuller from security challenged him for carrying narcotics in contravention of Club Rules. Evans bolted for the stairs. Malky's a big lad and was too slow."

"I'll deal with him later." The look on Carmino's face scared Jude as she prodded a lump of goat's cheese.

"Better news," FB continued, his voice sounding flaky. "Evans dropped his BlackBerry. I have it."

"Can you access it?"

"It's an old model and didn't need face recognition."

"I'll come in. Start checking it. I'll delay Vegas till tomorrow." He walked Jude around the corner into Clarendon Road. "No time to get changed," he said.

"Why are you delaying Vegas?" Jude asked.

Carmino's face took on a narrowed foxy appearance as he lied to her. "Depending what the BlackBerry reveals, I could know Dexter's plans for robbing Dukes." He gave her a quick farewell and disappeared into the below-ground parking.

After his perfunctory goodbye, Jude tried to settle, vaguely aware of an American sitcom on the TV. Ever since finding his knife, she had grown increasingly uneasy. Not for the first time, she wondered why he had taken it the other evening. Had he used it? On who? And why? He had never gone to Porcupine House and, anyway, Dex was in Switzerland then. The more she thought about this, the more deeply sinister Pepe seemed. There were too many things she did not understand.

Things he was not telling her.

Unable to relax, she padded through to the bathroom with its mirrored ceiling and ran the jacuzzi. As she relaxed in the hot bubbly water, her thoughts were confused. Why was Pepe interested in his Dex's passport? Why had Pepe really wanted her snooping in Porcupine House? Did she really believe that Dex would rob the casino? Was it believable that Dex was planning a heist? With that delightful buffer Adam Yarbury and a cokehead like Billy Evans?

As she dried herself, she still had no answers. Except that Pepe Carmino was not to be trusted. Life would be better without him. If only Dex would …

83

Arnie Fisher had been summoned to meet Carmino in his office. "We got them bang to rights, Pepe," he concluded. He had just read the messages FB had uncovered passing between Billy Evans and Dexter. "What now? Evans has been gathering some shit-hot stuff."

"Or did have until he dropped the phone."

The carriage-clock on the mantelpiece struck 6 p.m. as Arnie Fisher shook his head, his weasel face screwed up in disagreement. "Billy Evans is dangerous. Dexter too. He's got some of this on his phone. Dexter doesn't need the BlackBerry to cause you trouble. Maybe even that old boy…"

"Adam Yarbury? That chump! Don't worry about him. He couldn't find his arsehole with a torch and map." Carmino tapped his scar before twice circling his office. "Dexter's the danger. We can only guess what else he knows but certainly too much. Beth may have told him about Panama. We know she spoke to Tavio for a couple of hours."

Arnie's voice was thin, matching his angular face and sly lips. His build and creased features were those of an ageing jockey. "Did he go to Panama?"

"Unknown. With Tavio's evidence, Dexter, would have my nuts in a vice."

"You said FB searched his laptop and it was clean. Nothing on it from his sister about her Vegas trip. My guess? Whatever she got from Tavio died with her."

"Arnie, we must assume Dexter is a rogue elephant, know what I mean?" Carmino returned to his desk and sat down opposite. He helped himself to a biscuit and pushed the plate nearer to his loyal lieutenant. "Get Porcupine House and Billy Evans' place in Clapham watched. I want to know where they are twenty-four-seven. No. Better still, once spotted, strong-arm them to that basement in Wandsworth. Ask them a few questions. Nicely of course with a pair of pliers."

"Time for another accident?" Arnie's nose twitched in anticipation.

"After interrogation?" Carmino shook his head They could disappear. A disused Cornish tin-mine or mid-Channel like that other guy last February."

Fisher chewed on a broken fingernail. "Won't Dexter go to the cops?"

"Arnie, I'm banking on you to stop that. If he gets to Scotland Yard, I'm expecting your bent cop contacts to tell you. If I'm warned, I can disappear just like that." He clicked his fingers and then fell silent.

Arnie rose. "I'll get the boys moving at once."

84

The Mercedes Maybach was parked along the street from Billy's bedsit in Lavender Gardens SW11. Between the small Renaults, Hondas and various elderly saloons and vans, it shone like a beacon. With Adam Yarbury now with them, they sat uneasily watching street activity for a few minutes. There seemed to be nothing unusual – several helmeted cyclists, a mother with two kids, a few returning office-workers and someone delivering pizza. "I'll chance it," Dex said as he opened the front door.

"Got the notes?"

Dex nodded yes to Tiffany. He saw no watchers in any other vehicles as he approached the three-storey Victorian mansion building. He knew Billy had the garret room but there was no sign of any light or life from the single front window. From the six bells, he rang the one for Billy's room. No response. He checked the time. It was just turning 6:00 p.m.

How long should I wait?
Billy could be with Emily.
He could be pissed out of his brains.
Snorting cocaine.
He could be anywhere.

He decided to hurry to Clapham Junction station and check the pubs along the way. As he walked, he called Tiffany to explain what he was doing and to let him know if Billy appeared. A quick glance in the Waggoners revealed no Billy. The next two pubs were also fruitless. He was just about to enter the Drum and Whistle when he saw Billy turn out the station exit into St John's Hill. Billy did not notice Dex who fell into step behind him, anxious to see if he was stoned out of his mind. Billy was walking briskly, his short steps busy and his arms swinging. If he had been drinking or snorting, it did not show.

"Billy." At the sound of his name, Evans jumped, his nerves suddenly evident. He twisted his head and was poised to run until he saw it was Dex. Relief flooded his face.

"I couldn't phone. Long story."

Dex hailed a taxi and bundled him in. "I want you outside with your passport. Five minutes turnaround?"

Evans looked confused. "I'm seeing Emily tomorrow."

"If you stay here, there may be no tomorrow." Dex saw that the message had hit home.

"You know about…?"

"The BlackBerry? Yes."

Billy looked puzzled at how Dex knew but said nothing, simply scurrying into his home while Dex thumbs-upped to Tiffany and Adam. It was 6-23 p.m, way behind what Dex wanted. He pulled out the blu-tack and the notes from his jacket pocket. Now that Billy had appeared, one note was redundant but the second he folded and stuck onto the bell marked *Top Floor*. He grinned as he did so, excited that Tiffany's idea just might work and buy them time. Like an anxious father waiting in Maternity, he stood by the front entrance tapping his feet and looking up and down Lavender Gardens for any sign of hostility. He checked his watch. 6-28p.m.

Come on, Billy!
Come on!
For fuck's sake!

In a Ford Focus on Battersea Rise, the driver and passenger were shouting abuse as they waited at the traffic lights. When Arnie Fisher had called, the two men had been settling down for a curry in Borough Market. Leaving it behind, they had used their back-double experience to race to Lavender Gardens but the roadworks for the new cycle lane were screwing up the traffic.

Arnie's instructions had been clear: "If he's there, keep him till I arrive. If not, wait for him. As long as it takes."

Across London, a Subaru had left a council tower block in Ladbroke Grove heading for Porcupine House. The driver and passenger's instructions about Dex had been the same. The third vehicle, a Mini Cooper, had already reached Adam Yarbury's apartment by the Millennium Bridge and reported nobody home.

It was 6:37 p.m. when Jack Shotley, the Ford Focus driver, phoned Arnie. "We're at Lavender Gardens and we're gonna wait. He's not here but he will be."

"Give!"

"Only found a bleedin' note pinned to his bell, didn't we? Get a load of this."

85

Even in the powerful Mercedes, it was slow progress through east London heading for Stansted Airport. The Gulfstream had a 10:30 p.m. departure slot. They stopped at a drive-through Burger King and picked up burgers, fries and drinks except for Tiffany who opted for a salad. "Really rather good," said Adam Yarbury, sounding surprised. "My first ever fast-food." Dex nearly managed a smile at the revelation. It was the first lighter moment in over an hour.

For the first forty minutes, everybody had been too tense for more than sporadic conversation but then Dex felt he had to speak out. The elephant in the room seated behind him was saying nothing, head and eyes lowered "Billy, you told me yesterday you were clean. He twisted to glare into the back of the limo. That was a lie. You bought cocaine from a dealer on a street corner in Chinatown."

Billy flinched at the word Chinatown. He said nothing though his head drooped. "You let me down. I don't deserve that. None of us do." Dex turned further, resting his arm on the seatback so that he could face Billy directly. "Now, I want the truth." The words were fired out with pedantic precision, reminding Dex of his shock tactic on FB. "Firstly, can I believe a word you say? Was the blackjack even fixed?"

"I swear. Everything was on the Blackberry. Carmino has that."

Dex leaned further over the seat. "Look at me." He waited for Billy to do so while Adam peered out of the side window. "You've blown our cover. You've buggered everything. Because of you, we're now running for our lives." There was an embarrassed silence until Billy perked up, for the first time looking more confident. "I've still got the results from those ninety shoes. Here. On my laptop. I copied them across."

"So? I should shout with joy? Dance a bloody jig? That's like dropping a pound coin and finding a penny." Dex lowered his voice slightly. "It was crap, wasn't it Billy? What you told us at the Bulgari? All lies." Dex was backing a hunch. "Your coked-up brain couldn't resist a chance to play the count and win some big money for yourself. You planned to use the straight decks to win big and buy more drugs." He paused to wag his finger close to Billy's pale cheek. "More coke, more visits to that pusher on Gerrard Street."

Dex watched Billy's face contort first one way and then the other as he wiped his hand under his nostrils. Dex let the silence hang for a good thirty seconds. "That's right, isn't it?" Dex eventually barked, adopting a technique used by a QC at the inquest into Caroline and Jamie's deaths. It had proved effective then and again now.

Billy looked at the three occupants in turn and started to shake, his shoulders heaving. "I'm sorry. I needed a big win. You don't ... you can't understand how, how…" His voice trailed away and his whole body shook, out of control.

"Know how hard it is to kick a habit, an addiction? Assume I can. If you hadn't lied, we would not be in this mess. You had no need to be in Dukes today. Not for me, not for us." He pointed to Adam. "Thanks to you, Adam is now facing the prospect of Carmino inserting a Bowie knife into his jacksie."

Tiffany, who had tried a smile of encouragement to Billy, recoiled at the image. Dex had no intention of taking his foot off Billy's throat now. "Because of you, we're running away like dogs in the night or maybe more like scaredy-cats. Carmino will not kiss and make-up. For vengeance, assume Pepe Carmino will slit our throats." He made a sudden jabbing move with his right hand. "I never told you this but a poor sod murdered by Carmino in Panama had over twenty knife wounds. It was a manic attack. *That* is the guy who is now on our tail."

"I'm sorry. I...I was desperate."

"You're not carrying drugs now, are you?" It was Tiffany chipping in. "Because the US use sniffer dogs at the airports. If your bag contains the slightest trace, you'll be in the slammer."

"None since heading into Dukes," he muttered as he started to calm down.

"What else was on the BlackBerry?" Dex took up the interrogation.

"Besides e-mails and text messages? Photos. My Contact List – y'know, names, addresses, and phone numbers. Music, the usual."

"Think carefully, Billy. Is there anything suggesting I'm after Space City?"

"You never told me that."

Dex changed position, relaxing his posture. He thought back to the recorded confession from FB and turned to Tiffany. "Carmino won't tell Letizione about this. Agreed?"

"No. Not show any weakness. What are you getting at?"

"I'll phone Otto from Stansted. We'll still go ahead with Letizione."

"Or," Adam intervened for the first time, "Carmino might vanish, leaving this Lavazione fella to catch all the doodah that'll be flying."

Dex was about to reply when he saw tears rolling down Billy's cheeks. He patted him on the shoulder. "Bollocking over. We now need to be smarter than we've been, smarter than Carmino. Then, after our lives are out of danger, I'm sending you to a clinic in Wiltshire. They'll help control your demons."

86

Standing by the Ford Focus in Lavender Gardens, Jack Shotley speed-dialled Arnie Fisher. "Yeah. The note's timed at 5:45 p.m. It says: *Where are you? Pickup was 5 p.m. We've gone on without you. Meet us in the hotel. We must hit the casino in Monte Carlo tomorrow night. Everything is fixed. Be there!! Adam.* Jack tucked the note into his pocket.

"Monte Carlo?" Arnie was quick to react, his cheeks sucked in. "Serious stuff." Arnie's quick brain struggled with this surprise information. "Must be Yarbury and Dexter are gonna roll over the casino. God knows how. Yarbury's a relic from when dinosaurs roamed. Billy Evans must be the key." He glanced at Carmino who was hovering across the office. "Stay there, Jack. Grab Billy-boy when he appears. I'll have his Thames Ditton place watched in case he's gone there. One thing's for sure. He ain't going to Monte Carlo. Not never!"

At Stansted, after clearing Security, Dex distanced himself from the others. There were no messages from FB so he phoned Vegas. "Otto. I'm arriving at the Wynn Hotel at around 2 a.m. your time. Will you have what I need?"

Otto was cryptic and to the point. "I need one more nugget. I'll have it by eleven tomorrow morning. Let's meet in your hotel – the *Parasols Up* bar, beside the main gaming floor."

"See you there." Dex re-joined the group, sensing an uneasy silence. He saw that Tiffany looked especially sullen, exhausted by her overnight flight from Los Angeles. He glanced at each of them in turn while rubbing his hands to create some enthusiasm. "They're ready. Let's go."

"Eighty thousand for this charter." Tiffany was unimpressed and the sharpness in her tone was obvious as she walked beside him. "That would feed thousands of dying kids, to say nothing of our carbon footprint."

"There'll be millions for them." He walked in step with her angry strides. "When this is over, that is. And I'll donate to a carbon-offset programme. Look – jetting about like this is a first for me too. Any time, I could have *bought* a Lear or a Gulfstream or both. Not my style then or now. We had to escape England, don't you see? Your safety is tops." He wanted to squeeze her hand but sensed from her tone, this would be unwelcome. Eye contact failed too. "At least for now, we're one step ahead of Carmino."

The hostess in her amber tunic and dainty hat led the disparate and dispirited group across the tarmac to the Gulfstream G650. Taking Dex's lead, the group paused at the foot of the steps to admire the jet's sleek beauty, its red, white and gold livery gleaming on the floodlit apron. "Better than a night-flight to Malaga, all crammed in like battery-hens," Dex enthused and the faces beside him showed that the chill was thawing. The two pilots welcomed them aboard and within moments, the whine of the Rolls-Royce engines turned to a roar as the jet accelerated, soaring into the blackness of the night sky.

In the grey leather seats, Adam and Billy were across the wide aisle from each other. Billy was almost instantly asleep while Adam was reading *Wine Spectator* magazine and sipping a pink gin. Dex was across the aisle from Tiffany. He touched her hand, hoping she had mellowed but was disappointed. She was awake but her tightly shut eyes suggested ongoing bitterness. The magic of the pub garden seemed very distant. He turned and could just see

Billy's face, at ease now he was asleep. Despite the mess Billy had created, Dex still sympathised. Battling his own need for alcohol had been tough. Less than two years before, he had been sinking shots of vodka before breakfast, though he had never considered himself an alcoholic.

I knew Billy would be a risk. I took it. It nearly paid off.

Dex slid his hand up Tiffany's bare arm. "Can you believe you only landed at Heathrow this morning?"

She stretched her legs, her eyelids opening just slightly. "I'm not even sure what time zone I'm living in."

"Vegas and Los Angeles are both eight hours behind England. Ideal for you."

She turned towards him, a hint of supportive body language. "First Class on BA was pretty special but this is pampering and then some." The smile was tired as she absorbed the muted shades of greys and blue – designed to ensure calmness and relaxation. Just in front of them was the dining area, the rectangular table carved from the finest light oak. It was laid up for when the meal was ready. "I'm sorry, Dex. Maybe I've been a bit harsh, unkind even." She flicked her head in embarrassment at the admission. Then her free hand clasped his.

Dex left his seat to perch on her arm-rest. "Look, I understand. None of us wanted this, least of all you. But with Carmino, I'm convinced our lives are at risk." He ran his fingers over her wrist to grip her hand as her eyelids drooped. "If I could have convinced the police, believe me, I'd have seen them today."

"You got me scared, Dex."

"About Carmino being a permanent threat?" Dex draped an arm over her shoulder. "I meant it. I wish I hadn't. Getting him arrested in Vegas would be far more … effective."

Tiffany absorbed the unsaid subtext. "I need a snooze. Wake me for supper." Seconds later, her head slumped against him and her hand slipped free. For several minutes, Dex perched beside her, running his fingers across her hair as her breathing grew deeper. Even when he returned to his seat, he could not unwind, so he seized the silent moments to finesse his plans for Letizione. He reached for a scribbling-pad and started his list.

Under an hour after take-off and as the jet raced 33,000 feet above the Isle of Man, the hostess served their meals. Tiffany had chosen the menu on the phone and so Dex shook her awake. On the table was a choice of hot and cold pasta, cottage pie, cheeses, salad, carved meats and a selection of smoked fish. It arrived on fine china plates with a bamboo-leaf motif. Despite the burger and fries, Adam declared himself to be *rather peckish* as he looked approvingly at the bottles of Nuits St George and a chilled white Sancerre. "Splendid vintages. Renowned even. Should help a chap sleep despite the threat of a knife up the jacksie." He gave Dex a friendly pat on the shoulder. Dex responded with an admiring smile, delighted at the way the old boy was taking everything in his stride.

After the plates had been cleared, Billy and Adam returned to their reclined seats and fell asleep almost immediately. Once they were alone, Tiffany clasped both Dex's hands across the table. Her eyes were fixed on him. "Dex, I'll be blunt. I don't agree with all this. It's madness. If you had told the police, we could still have holed up in secret."

"Suppose Carmino has bent coppers in his pay? Suppose they tipped him off where we were? FB explained how he had fixed the guys from the Gambling Commission. Why not the cops too?"

Tiffany had no immediate answer to that. "Considering Doc Grierson wanted you to be stress-free, you're keeping remarkably calm. After all …"

"Don't remind me of Grierson! My blood pressure would blow his gadget apart."

Tiffany laughed, the first time since the pub garden. "You mean the sphygmomanometer? I had to say that word once on live TV! Try saying it without your teeth in!" She helped herself to a Belgian chocolate and then clasped his fingers tighter "Actually, I was thinking of your drinking. Despite what happened today," she waved her hand airily toward Billy, "you seem to be under control."

"Thanks. My mother used to say to me – *never do panic*. When she abandoned us, it was a calm, orderly decision. Carefully planned."

"You resented that?"

"Beth and I hated her for it. But from her selfish viewpoint, her decision was impeccable."

"Good advice from her about not panicking. Headless chickens never achieved anything."

"Dumping the pills. Best thing I ever did. As the saying goes, *they was doing me head in*. The alcohol?" He raised his glass of red burgundy and looked at it lovingly. "Working in a pub was Adam's idea. It was a gamble but it paid off. I'm pacing myself." He twirled his hair as he played for time. Then he produced his scribbled notes. "Look Tiffany, I know you hate all this but I'll need your journalist's experience. More than that, I need support – someone to fight with me, not against me. Your idea to leave that message for Billy. Brilliant! That's bought us twenty-four hours, maybe more – enough time to play the Letizione card."

Tiffany rubbed her eyes and then stretched her arms high above her head whilst stifling a yawn. Dex could see she was fighting more than exhaustion. Then she glanced at Dex's notes and a surprised but admiring look broke through. "Despite my wiser instincts, count me in." She looked at him sharply. "Letizione. Is he a Mafioso?"

"You mean Lavazione, as Adam calls him." They both laughed. Dex shook his head. "Gus McKay said not. Otto agrees but rates him powerful with plenty of juice. That's why he won't crack if we use normal methods."

"Your trap for him ... far from normal." It was said with respect but in a sleepy tone.

Dex saw she was forcing herself to stay awake. "Your eyelids are crying out for help. Time for some kip."

For the first time since the pub garden, Tiffany's eyes softened as she looked across the table, her head tilted to one side. Then her hand ruffled his hair, running her fingers along his neck in a way he found almost irresistible. She spoke in a whisper. "When I was zapping round America, I realised that you're different to the rest of the pack. That I like." She stood up before placing her arms around his shoulders and for the first time gave him a deep and meaningful kiss. "Not always different in a good way. But different. Goodnight, Dex."

87

After a few restless hours in which he was oblivious to the warm curves of Jude's body, Pepe Carmino had surprised the cleaners and kitchen staff by arriving early at Dukes. For him to appear much before 5 p.m. was rare. To be there at breakfast time, when Dukes had just closed was so unusual as to set tongues wagging.

He had coffee, V8 and toast delivered and then Facetimed Enzo. It was shortly before 2 a.m. in Vegas when he ended the discussion. Letizione had been upbeat, reporting that everything was ready for the launch or *lift-off* as he was now calling it. He cut the call after assuring Letizione that everything in London was *just fine*. Carmino though was still on edge, his lips tight and revealing his tension.

His troubles were no longer in Vegas. They were right here. Or in Monte Carlo.

Dexter has evidence.

Evidence that could destroy Dukes.

Destroy everything.

Yet the bastard was swanning about in Monte Carlo. Doing what? Carmino's eyes searched for a solution from the walls and ceiling of his office. He needed action, an outlet, a human punch-bag, someone to feel the heat of his simmering fury. He stared at the remains of his coffee, wondering how long Arnie Fisher's team would take to track down Dexter in the Monaco hotels.

For a contented moment, he imagined his knife plunging deep

into Dexter's eyes followed by a torrent of deadly blows to the torso, face and neck. Snapping out of his thoughts, pleasing though they had been, he pushed aside his breakfast-tray and sat doodling, desperate for a strategy.

Billy Evans had not yet returned to his garret-room or to Thames Ditton.

Had he never made it to Monte Carlo?

He took some deep breaths, forcing himself to be calm. He could empty the safe, grab his false IDs and disappear. With a plastic surgeon already lined-up, he could live a new life flitting between Montevideo and Dubai. Every small detail for a quick departure was in place, leaving Dukes to collapse like a soufflé.

Shed no tears for bankers!
Jude?
Surplus baggage.
But Dexter wins.
Do I accept that?
Has he told the cops?
Not if he's in Monte Carlo.
He can't help them there.
So – no cops yet.
Why Monte Carlo anyway?
Have I got this all wrong?
No.
Dexter intends to destroy me.
Billy Evans' BlackBerry proved that.

He called Arnie. "Yes, right now. And bring that note too." He returned to jotting ideas – lots of underlining and deletions between the meaningless shapes and curved or straight arrows. By the time Arnie arrived, clutching a takeaway tea and a hot-dog in a brown bag, his thoughts had developed. In clipped terms, he outlined

Plans A and B. On hearing them, Arnie wriggled uncomfortably but said nothing.

Carmino looked at his jottings. "But before we consider either of them, we must decide this. Do we fuck off right now? Disappear? Or can we fix that shit Dexter and disappear *after* I've sorted him?" Carmino then picked up the note from Lavender Gardens. He read it over and over. The words *Monte Carlo* seemed to dance before his eyes. They made no sense. He raised an eyebrow toward Arnie. "So? Stay or go now?"

"My guy in the Met. Police checked. He's not been to them. For now, I reckon we stay. I know you've fixed my new ID and a place in South Africa, blah-di-blah but I've got that tasty bit of stuff out in Chingford. Anyway, I like London."

"Sod that. Sod her. You do what I tell you. If you get charged, you could bring me down. I can't risk that."

Fisher's already shifty eyes looked away. "Put like that…"

"If and when I go, you go."

Fisher knew better than to risk stopping this juggernaut. "What now then, boss?"

"To nab Dexter, I vote for Plan A. Plan B is too slow. We've got to move fast. Even from Monte Carlo, Plan A will make Dexter move faster than fucking Concorde."

"Plan A sucks. You can't do that. It's…" He fought for the right word. "…even by your standards, it's horrible, grotesque." Arnie screwed up the brown bag and dismissively chucked it into a bin.

"Fuck that!" Pepe enjoyed the chance to let rip. "Plan A's not meant to be tea with Auntie. That is the fucking point." His eyes bored into Arnie. "Plan A will make Dexter wish he'd never been born."

Arnie wriggled uncomfortably. For over twenty-five years, he had fixed everything, mostly without question. He knew better.

He looked across the desk at the Pepe who had strangled a pet rabbit *just for a laugh*. This was the Pepe who, at eighteen, had swerved his beaten-up jalopy to hit a King Charles spaniel and laughed as he had watched its squirming death-throes.

Arnie sensed the deep ugliness of Carmino's mood. This one scared him. He had noticed Carmino's strangulated voice, catching in the back of his throat. That always occurred when he had murder in mind. One false move and he could be in line for Carmino's violent temper. At moments like this, their friendship counted for nothing. With Pepe's eyes showing no emotion, someone was going to suffer and Arnie had no intention of being the one.

He heard Pepe's knuckles cracking the way they had done before ordering the murders of Mick Glenn and the Vegas dealers. Uncomfortable under Pepe's stare, he squirmed on his leather chair knowing that, like it or not, he had no choice. "Plan A then."

Carmino stood up and leaned across the desk, his features looking even swarthier, his eyes boring deep into Arnie. Then he edged even closer and thumped his fist on the desk. "Good call, Arnie. No back-sliding." His lips twisted into a snarl. "Plan A. Just fucking do it."

— 88 —

During breakfast at the Terrace Pointe Café in the Wynn Hotel, Dex fixed for Billy and Adam to go on a helicopter trip to the Grand Canyon. After they had left, he briefed Tiffany on what he wanted her to do while he was meeting Otto Schneider. In her matching pink T-shirt and shorts with a white gold bracelet on her tanned arm, she looked very much at home in Vegas.

"You really think this could work?" Tiffany's brow was unusually furrowed as she spoke. She sounded doubtful – and was.

"You can do it. As the Americans say, we attack Letizione from left field." He checked his watch. "Time for me to meet Otto. If he's delivered, we press the button." He gave her a fleeting kiss. "I'll come to your room when I'm done."

Otto Schneider had no photo on his website, presumably a deliberate move for someone operating in the shadows. Dex spotted him as the guy sitting alone in a tailored suit with a slim leather briefcase. After minimal pleasantries and a couple of coffees ordered, Dex looked enquiringly for answers. Schneider was aged well into his sixties, with knitted greying eyebrows. His eyes were deep-set, his forehead and cheeks crinkled and his nose aquiline. His mane of silvery hair was swept back into a duck's arse. Overall, he oozed experienced street-smart but Dex reckoned that thirty years before he would have been a handful in a fight. Now, he looked better suited to his industrial espionage. Schneider opened the briefcase and produced a sheaf of perhaps forty sheets tucked into a blue folder. "I guess this is what you wanted?"

The coffees were delivered as Dex read with unusual care. After the third page, he looked up. "Amazing." He read to the end while Schneider browsed a copy of the *Review Journal*. "Otto, I cannot believe you obtained this. It is authentic? No chance we've been set up?"

"Nix. I know and value my sources here and in the Caribbean."

"Astounding. Thanks. Now I've another job for you – very different. I guess I'm still in credit with you by a country mile."

Schneider's face showed no reaction. "Tell me what it is."

After the explanation and Otto's demand for another ten thousand greenbacks to be transferred, Dex ended the meeting and dashed up to Tiffany's room on the forty-eighth floor. His room was on the forty-ninth, looking over the Strip. Tiffany let him in with a swift hug and kiss. Their rooms were identical except that she looked east towards Henderson. "My room has a much better view, especially at night," Dex suggested and was rewarded with a tap on the nose telling him not to get ahead of himself. They sat down on the sofa by the picture window, Tiffany grinning from ear to ear, her almond eyes wide with excitement.

"Guess what?" Tiffany shook her head in wonderment.

"Go on!"

"The publishers just sent me a message – I'm number one on the New York Times Bestsellers." Dex leaned across to swamp Tiffany in a bear-hug, revelling in the smell of her hair and perfume.

Dex looked out towards the distant mountains, his sadness obvious. "I'm sorry to ruin your big moment. Thanks to me, we can't celebrate just yet."

"We'll get our chance." Tiffany looked at her notes on the coffee-table. "I found just the place. But Dex, are you really sure about this?" She looked even more doubtful than she sounded.

"With this stuff from Otto? It's dynamite. Please help me!

Then, after Letizione, I want to get Carmino here. Surely, he must still come for the Grand Opening."

"Unless Adam was right and he's done a runner. Do you really want him here? Near us? We left England to be safe from him."

"Carmino has not done a runner, not if I believe FB. He's sent a text saying that besides Carmino arriving very early, there's no sign of panic. Anyway, with what we may get from Letizione, the Feds will nail him for offences we never knew existed. Jail sentences topping a hundred years. And the death penalty too." The set of his jaw showed his determination.

Dex watched Tiffany check her notes and then reach for the phone by the bed. He placed a reassuring arm on her shoulder. "You can do it. You'll be just great. You're a journalist. Brass-necked." He laughed as he sat back on the sofa, swinging one leg up onto its length.

"Is that Mr Letizione's PA? Ah, good! My name is Shani Sharp of Alacrity TV Productions. I'm in town from Europe doing a big feature on the opening of Space City. The editor wants me to interview Mr Letizione at Haldeman Facilities on South Rainbow Boulevard."

Dex watched as Tiffany listened to the PA, her face impassive. "Of course, I understand he's busy. But your boss, he'll really appreciate this opportunity. You must know how many Europeans visit Las Vegas every year. With our audience reach, we'll be profiling Space City in over thirty countries. If Mr Letizione declines, my editor will spike the entire piece."

Dex tried to catch Tiffany's eye but she was looking firmly in the other direction. All he saw was the side of her shoulder and the shapely curves underneath her shorts. "Fifteen mins tonight at 7? That'll work. He's been to Haldeman Facilities before? Ah! Excellent! He should ask for me, Shani. I'll be doing the interview."

"Brilliant!" Dex stood up and clutched her close to him, almost lifting her feet off the carpet. "Otto is putting three men on standby. Let's get to Haldeman Facilities. Otto says I ought to get some paperwork signed."

For a moment or two, they stood by the window, she with her hand round his waist. They watched as a helicopter flitted across the clear blue sky. "Perhaps that's Adam and Billy," she suggested. "You're not keeping them in the loop?"

Dex shook his head. "You've seen how Billy was this morning. He's struggling. He needs help. The sooner he's in a clinic, the better." He turned away and headed for the door. "You know, I wasn't joking. My room has a much better view."

"You must know better chat-up lines than that." Tiffany raised her slanted eyebrow. "One ceiling looks much like the next." She rewarded him with a cute sideways glance. "I'll meet you downstairs in twenty minutes."

Back in his room, Dex phoned Larry Jamous, imagining him surrounded by the clutter and chaos in Penarth Street. It was nearly noon and way down below, the traffic on Las Vegas Boulevard was starting to back up as the city gradually awoke from its usual late night. "Jake Cornelius here. I assume you've finished?"

89

South Rainbow Boulevard lies a twenty-five-minute journey by taxi from the hotel. Despite the colourful name, Rainbow Boulevard proved to be significantly unpleasant, crammed with six lanes of traffic speeding in each direction. It was a mix of commercial premises, showrooms, endless fast food joints and unkempt waste-ground. The fumes of thousands of semi-trailers, trucks, four-by-fours and speeding Japanese saloons left the air hazy and polluted with the desert sun beating down on the tarmac.

As the taxi switched from lane to lane, they passed a digital sign showing a temperature of 108°. Overhead were criss-crossing cables. Huge billboards for Firestone, Subway or Wendy's and countless gas-stations made everything pig-ugly. The taxi pulled up outside their destination. Haldeman Facilities proved to be in a two-storey block about a hundred metres long and entered through double-doors, like several others units of similar size.

Dex and Tiffany went into the chill of the air-conditioning, telling the receptionist they had an appointment. Almost at once Mel Willmer appeared and showed them around the suite. Tiffany was impressed. She looked at the lighting rigs, the camera positions, the microphones and video monitors that circled the studio floor. "I'm getting a real buzz from being back in a studio. I shall miss this way of life," she whispered to Dex as they moved the two chairs and had the cameras repositioned. "And the control-room?" she concluded.

As they followed a few steps behind Willmer, she told Dex that this would be where he would be positioned, well out of sight. Once behind the glass-screened zone looking down to the studio-floor, Willmer sat Dex behind a hi-tech control panel. "This is where you will need to be." He saw Dex's jaw drop at the array of controls. "Relax. You'll only need to use this one rocker-switch. My guys will take care of the rest."

"Thank God for that," Dex laughed as he fingered the control. "So, let's fix the paperwork." He turned to Tiffany. "You sort the technical side, lighting, recordings, whatever. Mel and I will sort the legals."

It was another forty minutes before they were finished, the driver then taking them even further from the Strip to Marché Bacchus, a French-style bistro overlooking a lake some ten miles from the Wynn Hotel. The contrast to the nastiness of Rainbow Boulevard was striking. Otto had recommended the restaurant as a great place to chill out while watching the ducks, moorhens and swans. For a second, Dex contrasted watching the wildlife while sitting by the lake on wet London nights, waiting for a carp's powerful tug.

They sat on the shady terrace, cooled by a misting system, looking across the translucent blue of the lake. "The power of money," Dex had enthused to Tiffany. "Willmer doesn't know the detail of what lies ahead – all he knows is I've paid his fat and oversized fee. Short of us trashing the place, he'll put up with anything." For the next two hours, over a bottle of chilled Sauvignon Blanc and grilled salmon, they flirted, joked, and scripted the evening ahead, the fine spray cooling them while a small turtle occasionally broke the surface as a backdrop.

At about the same time but eight hours ahead, Pepe Carmino had dropped off Jude at the Ritz Hotel on Piccadilly, where she was meeting the widow of a former Lebanese politician. Later, they would head for Dukes. As soon as she had gone, he called Arnie. "Plan A? Are you taking the piss or what?"

"I'm onto it, Pepe but easy it ain't. I'll deliver as soon as I can."

Carmino changed the subject. "That Monte Carlo note. It's cobblers."

"Meaning?"

"Adam Yarbury never wrote that. I compared it with the membership forms he signed for Dexter and Billy Evans. Whoever wrote that was not Adam." Carmino made a left and then a right turn as he fought the one-way system toward Mount Street. "And that means Monte Carlo may be bollocks too. It never made sense."

"None of them are at home. Where are they? Rural Wales? A Northumberland fishing village?"

"That, Arnie," growled Carmino, "is for you to find out. Dexter's been pulling my plonker for too long. Plan A. That'll fix the odious shit." He cruised to a halt at the foot of the steps up to the grand entrance to Dukes. "Action. Now."

"No chance tonight, Pepe. Tomorrow morning."

As 7 p.m. approached with the sun on South Rainbow still relentless, Dex, Tiffany and Mel Willmer were ready for Letizione's arrival. Tucked away out of sight were Otto's trio, all briefed on what to do and when. A solitary cameraman and a sound and lighting technician were making last-minute adjustments. Under Confidentiality Agreements provided by Otto, all the crew had been paid $3,000 for their silence with liability for unlimited damages for any loose word.

"He's just arriving," Willmer told Dex.

– 90 –

Enzo Letizione's stretch limo pulled up at 7 p.m. precisely. The Space City logo of a golden spacecraft, ringed by the words Space City, was prominent on both sides. He was feeling ebullient, having just chaired the final executive meeting. The board members had been excited by his upbeat report for the opening just seventy-two hours ahead. It was with a confident stride that the burly figure bounded along the corridor to be greeted by Mel Willmer.

Seconds later, Dex, watching from the control-room, saw Enzo Letizione for the first time as he came under the glare of the studio lights to be greeted by Tiffany. He was wearing a lightweight suit, expensively cut to conceal his spreading stomach. The shirt was pale lemon but the tie was overstated and multi-patterned. Tiffany stood, a clipboard in her hand and greeted him. "Hi! I'm Shani. Thanks for sparing the time, Mr Letizione."

"My pleasure, Shani. Call me Enzo."

As Willmer positioned him on a dark blue moquette chair with generous armrests, Dex felt the tension mounting in the dry air. It showed in his throat which he had to clear more than once. The high-risk game was about to start. The trap was about to be sprung.

What Tiffany had first described as *a wild and crazy plan* was now hard reality. As he looked at her from behind his smoked-glass screen, he saw the very model of a cool professional. No doubt Letizione would be unpredictable but with their attention to detail over lunch, Dex was now eager for action. He swallowed hard, wondering if he could handle his own role. For the umpteenth time, he checked his notes.

A member of the studio team clipped the microphone to Letizione's tie. From the control-room, Dex could hear every word from the studio floor and by pressing the rocker-switch, he could make himself heard when required. Now was not the time. Not yet. Willmer joined him among the wizardry as the cameraman moved in for his head-to-foot opening shot of them both. Willmer spoke into the tiny microphone. "Can we do a sound test, please? Get the levels."

"Hi," said Tiffany. "My name is Shani Sharp and I'm about to interview Enzo Letizione about the Space City opening."

"And I'm Enzo Letizione." On the monitors circling the studio, Letizione's strong but heavy features were on display.

Willmer's voice came from the speakers. "We're good to roll."

Tiffany checked her clipboard. "Mr Letizione, as CEO and President of US Operations at Space City, I bet you're pretty excited about what's going to hit the Strip."

"We're not talking of a launch. Being Space City, this will be *lift-off*." He shot his clenched fist into the air to demonstrate. "We've invested nearly five billion dollars. Space City's gonna be the hottest hangout on the Vegas Strip. So, sure! I'm excited. *All Vegas* is excited. You can feel the buzz. Everybody's talking Space City."

"What makes it so special?"

"The gaming room atmosphere will be *terrific*. The shows, the outer-space experience, the mock-up of a Space Shuttle. Awesome! Mind-blowing! Space City will be uber-cool, the best bar none. But bars we have! And then some!" He rocked back and laughed at his rehearsed joke.

"And when is the Grand Opening?"

"Lift-off is Saturday. 7p.m. Y'know, despite the challenging global economy, we're booked solid. Every room has been sold out for weeks. We're booking through Christmas and New Year, months away."

Dex wiped his palms, knowing what was coming next. Earlier, his heart had been racing. Now it was pounding, thudding as if trying to burst out from his ribcage. Despite sipping water, his throat was parched, his eyes fixed on the two people just below him.

He saw Tiffany shift in her seat, almost imperceptibly, so that she could lean rather more toward Letizione. "So not opening this weekend, that would be a huge disappointment." Letizione's time-weathered face showed puzzlement rather than concern. "Excuse me? I'm not following your comment. We're good to go – and right on time."

"I mean, if the Feds closed you down. Arrested you for conspiracy to murder and fraud."

Dex enjoyed watching puzzlement become concern and then confusion bordering on panic. Letizione's jowly face seemed to darken and age in seconds. It reminded him of TV clips of President Richard Nixon when he'd been pressurised over Watergate. "What in hell you talking about? What is this? I'm outta here."

As he saw the American start to fiddle with his microphone, Dex knew this was his moment. Volume turned up, Dex flicked the rocker-switch. "Sit down, Mr Letizione. You're going nowhere." Dex's voice boomed out from the wraparound sound-system, filling the studio floor. The sharpness of tone caused Letizione another moment of doubt. Dex enjoyed watching confusion spread across his weathered brow as Letizione looked in every direction to spot the speaker.

"Let me introduce myself. I'm Dex – Finlay Dexter from London, brother of Beth Dexter." Dex paused to watch the reaction and then continued. "Beth Dexter, *deceased.* I can see you know my name and who Beth was. As you should."

Letizione crossed one leg over the other and then as quickly uncrossed them.

"I'm here to talk about your conspiracy with Pepe Carmino. Cheating the players in Dukes to finance Space City. Money-laundering. The Racketeer Influenced Corrupt Organizations Act. RICO to you and me." His chuckle reverberated round the compact studio. "Though it is more pertinent to you." Dex laughed, suddenly finding he was enjoying himself. "The murder of Mick Glenn. The gunning down in Vegas of Tavio Sanchez. The death of Diego Rodrigues in Lake Mead." Though he had spoken with studied deliberation, he still paused before adding the final thrust. "And the *murder* of my sister."

Still with the microphone clipped to him, trance-like, Letizione stood up again. "I'm outta here."

"Mr Letizione, until I say so, *you* are going nowhere." At that moment, Otto Schneider's three bruisers appeared and circled him. "Pepe Carmino will go to Death Row. You may be joining him. Whatever, you'll spend the rest of your days in a federal penitentiary. The other prisoners will just love the CEO and President of a casino group that cheats and robs gamblers." He paused to make his point. "Gang-rape and sodomy in the showers to enliven your punishment, wouldn't you agree?"

Dex watched beads of perspiration forming on the lined forehead. No doubt the heat from the powerful overhead lights did not help but he knew that he was now deep under Letizione's skin. The lemon shirt looked as if it was soaking up nervous sweat as Letizione tugged it away from his chest. The American stared toward the camera and tried to sound defiant. "Quit dreaming. This is garbage. Utter bullshit."

Dex spoke slowly to articulate every word. He glanced to his right and saw Willmer's jaw had almost dropped to the floor. "Bullshit, you reckon? Here, I'll help you. Laundering money through banks in Montserrat, Panama and the Cayman Islands." Dex read from the notes in front of him. "Caymans Account XCEHZY6398401. Recognise it? It's your account, Mr Letizione. The balance is just over fifteen million dollars." There was now shock and panic flooding Letizione's face. "Think I'm bullshitting you now?"

Dex saw Letizione run a finger around the collar of his shirt as the perspiration soaked every line and wrinkle of his face. His cheeks had turned ashen. "Want to hear something else? How about the felony of concealing from the Nevada Gambling Commission that Pepe Carmino, your colleague and CEO in London, murdered someone playing blackjack in Panama? You knew, didn't you? Tavio and his pal Rodrigues had to be silenced. Both murdered."

Letizione pulled a silk handkerchief from his pocket and started mopping his face with jabbing movements. From above and all round him, the unrelenting glare and heat from the studio lights added to his discomfort. "Quit this fuckin' crap. I knew nothing of this. Nothing to do with me."

Dex ignored the denial. "The death penalty. Nevada still has the death penalty." He stopped to let silence hang heavily across the studio-floor. "Mr Letizione, you are in line for it."

"Not me. Pepe never told me nothing."

"That's for the Feds. Wait one! How about conspiracy to fund Space City with laundered money?" Again, Dex stopped to enjoy the meltdown as Letizione again looked around, trying to spot where the voice of the interrogator was coming from. In contrast, Tiffany was expressionless. She looked unruffled, sitting motionless, glued to the discomfort just in front of her. "These jail sentences are racking up against you, Mr Letizione."

Letizione tried to speak but his voice was croaky from the dry air and tension. He grabbed for a bottle of water. When he did speak, the confident baritone voice had gone, replaced by a nasal whine. "Whaddya want?"

"I want Pepe Carmino here, tomorrow. I'm offering a deal for you both. I want you to phone him now."

"It's 3:30 a.m. in London."

"I don't need you to tell me the time of day, Mr Letizione. We can all join in the call. When he answers, you speak, introducing me."

Letizione pulled out his phone, checked the number and read it off. Dex dialled from the phone in the control-room. Mel Willmer switched it to loudspeaker so that everyone could hear. Moments later, Carmino's falsely cultured voice came on the line. "That you, Pepe?"

"Hi, Enzo. Board meeting go well?"

"Pepe. I have someone with me wants to speak to you."

"It's Finlay Dexter here. I've been chatting with Mr Letizione. In particular about murder, money-laundering and bank accounts. No doubt the number LMKPZB407993 is familiar."

"No."

"Cut the crap. That is your personal account in George Town, Grand Cayman. You thought it was hidden under the corporate name of Dykeside Global Inc. The present balance is seventy-one million dollars."

Even as he read out the details, Dex quickly switched to watching Letizione. The sweaty unease now showed his irritation as he heard how the lion's share had been siphoned off to the Brit. "Here's the deal, Mr Carmino. Meet me at the Galleria Bar, Caesar's Palace at 4 p.m. tomorrow. Mr Letizione will join us. He and you will give me evidence that twenty million dollars has been transferred to my account. On top, I will also want cash handed over. I'll give

Mr Letizione the details of that. In return," the disembodied voice explained, "you receive the evidence I got in Panama concerning the murder of the Mexican at the Casino Sienna. I will also include the signed statement of Tavio Sanchez taken by Beth plus the statement made by Diego Rodrigues before he was dumped in Lake Mead." He enjoyed that bit of bluff before continuing. "I will hand over all films proving cheating at blackjack and roulette. Finally, you can have my report on money-laundering through Dukes."

"Pepe, you gotta go for this. We got lift-off on Saturday," prompted Letizione who seemed ready to clutch at the flimsiest of straws. From Carmino, there was just silence as he inwardly cursed Arnie for not delivering on Plan A.

Dex let the American's plea linger before going on. "My security guys will take the cash from the Galleria Bar. We can then discuss the future of Space City and Dukes. By then, I will have Mr Letizione's signed confession. You can write yours on the flight over. Both confessions will be kept by a Las Vegas attorney. They will only be handed to the Feds if I or anyone known to me is harmed. Understood?"

Before Carmino could reply, it was Letizione who spoke. "Pepe, the guy's got the nuts. It's our only chance. You gotta get here or I'm going to the slammer. If I go, sure as hell, you are joining me. I'll see to that."

-91-

"I'll be there. Enzo. See you at 4 p.m. Caesar's Palace." Carmino's heavy breathing could be heard around the control-room and studio floor until Dex ended the call. For the next eighty minutes, Dex worked on the confession, Letizione only denying prior knowledge or involvement in the murders. Tiffany sat opposite the sweaty figure, chipping in with questions. Throughout the Q&A session, Dex never appeared. Everything was controlled by his hidden voice probing and prodding toward the truth. After every paragraph, Dex read back the details, asking Letizione to agree the accuracy.

Even after the confession was complete and Willmer had taken it down to Letizione for signing, the camera was still running, the recording continuing. Only after the sullen and unsmiling figure had been escorted off the premises did Mel Willmer end the session. "Never had a day like this in near thirty years. Shit fucking hot." Willmer breathed the words as he shook his head in wonderment. "It's all…so goddammed unreal."

Tiffany joined them, her cheeks glowing with excitement. She grinned at Dex. "As the Americans would say, *like, I mean, wow.*" She gave him a hug. "Brilliant."

Dex gave her a huge boyish grin before placing an arm around her waist. "You were just great." He turned to Willmer. "I want you and your guys each to sign this statement confirming you were here and heard every word. Also, you must all confirm the authenticity of the recording."

Formalities completed, Dex handed over cash for the facilities plus the hush-money for the technicians. He took duplicate copies of the recording and the statements and spoke to Willmer and the crew. "Otto Schneider will inform you when, if ever, you may speak about today. Till then – absolute confidentiality."

Moments later, he and Tiffany exited into the evening air. Darkness had fallen but the ugliness of the surroundings remained, though the fumes were less obnoxious. "The Forum Shops, Caesar's Palace," Dex instructed their limo driver. He turned to Tiffany and gave her a squeeze. "I want to check out the Galleria Bar and then maybe dinner?"

"Billy and Adam?"

"Billy texted me earlier on his new phone. They were going to a magic show somewhere. The MGM, I think. But anyway, tonight's about the two of us – celebrating you being number one in New York and you being my number one – *anywhere*. For an answer, he felt her reach for and hold his hand.

As the black Lincoln cruised sedately down West Flamingo, their shoulders shared their body-warmth as Tiffany asked a question that had puzzled her. "You won't hand over the evidence, will you?"

In the darkness, Tiffany did not see the sly look. "If Letizione brings my two million cash and twenty million is transferred to my bank, sure, I'll hand over what I said."

Tiffany looked puzzled. "You would do that? Let these bastards off the hook?"

"I didn't quite say that. I never agreed to hand over Mel Willmer's evidence, everything now recorded in the studio. I never said I wouldn't keep true copies authenticated by Otto Schneider."

"You, Finlay Dexter, are even more devious than you look." She breathed the words, heavy with admiration. "Every base covered.

But I can sense there's more." She prodded him playfully in the ribs. "Come on, Dex, what am I missing?"

"I said *if* Carmino comes. He won't."

Tiffany took a sharp intake of breath. "He won't?"

"Not the way it went back there. Carmino despises Letizione. Would he risk a Nevada death penalty? Would he risk his skin just to save Letizione? Would Letizione truly expect Carmino to save him?" He draped his arm over her shoulder. "No way. They won't come to the Galleria Bar, neither of them. And I doubt we'll get any money."

"In which case," commented Tiffany, "what does Letizione do? Cut a deal with you?"

"I bet those two are on the phone right now. Carmino will say, no way you make any transfer. Letizione will then be shit-scared for himself." Dex looked up as they passed the multi-coloured Rio Casino towers. "What would *you* do in his position?"

Tiffany looked out of the limo window at the Rio's giant marquee. "Look after number-one. Dump Carmino. Make a run. Empty the Caymans account to somewhere else. Quit the USA."

"Right. He'd be scared shitless if Carmino appeared. He's in a lose-lose."

"Unless Carmino still needs him? For some reason, we don't know. Possible?" Tiffany's words were almost whispered in his ear.

"We can only guess."

"Might Letizione cut a deal with you?" She did not sound her usual confident self and seemed content to be led by Dex, a subtle increase in her respect since the interview. She sensed rather than saw Dex shake his head. "Okay. Tell me, what would you do?"

"If I were Letizione? Accept Space City is finished."

Tiffany paused, ready to exit as the limo slowed. "Game, set, and match. But Carmino?"

"He *should* run, shift his hot money and disappear."

"Should?"

The limo pulled up under the sweeping curve of the entrance, fountains, water and statues everywhere – all magnificent under the spotlights. "Carmino? What he *should* do and what he *will* do are different. Surrender? Be defeated by me? I doubt that's in his DNA." He looked across the darkened interior and then eased Tiffany out of the limo. He put his arm around Tiffany's shoulder and led her into the chill of the casino. "He'll want his cake and eat it."

Tiffany understood. "Vengeance first, then disappear."

"Right now, he's more dangerous to me than ever."

-92-

In the Galleria Bar, they took a seat in a corner close to the high-rollers' room. It was dimly lit and slightly raised above the main gaming floor with a scattering of comfy chairs and low tables. The chairs were deep, large and relaxing – well enough set apart for private discussions. They sank a couple of large Hendrick's.

"Otto was right." Dex clinked glasses with a rather sombre Tiffany. The euphoria of the control-room had gone after his warning about Carmino. "Look around. Tomorrow, I'll have the casino's cameras on me plus the hotel's own security guards and Otto's men. If Carmino does show, it would be lunacy to murder me here." He pointed to the sprawling casino-floor, packed with noisy gamblers playing craps, roulette and blackjack.

"Except for the satisfaction of course," Tiffany chipped in. "He's got nothing more to lose now."

Dex lowered his eyes in acknowledgement. "Unless he wants to disappear, I agree."

Tiffany placed her goblet on the table. "Dex, the guy's a psycho. Killing you for destroying everything could be a price he'd pay."

Dex sipped thoughtfully, his eyes watching the non-stop army of gamblers thronging the surroundings. "If he is going to kill me, it won't be here." He managed a lopsided smile. "The timing is his to choose."

"He is unpredictable."

"Then we must be smarter. You, me. Our joint intellects.

We must predict." He stroked her cheek. "Come on, I predict we have dinner." He stood up and when she followed, their steps were slow, heads bowed in thought. They paused briefly between the crowded tables to watch a noisy group playing craps. Further on before they reached the Forum Shops, a tide of people was leaving a Rod Stewart concert. Dex noticed the intensity of her grip on his arm. No question. She was shaking. Tiffany, the cool TV journalist and best-selling writer was scared.

Not for herself.
Terrified for me.
That scares me.
A drink.
Not just one.
Not even two.
Several large anythings.
For Beth.
Fight that urge.
No alcohol.

The celebration meal was muted, a shroud of uncertainty spoiling their linguine and mineral water. "Assuming a no-show tomorrow," continued Tiffany, "promise me, you dump everything on the Feds and the Met Police."

"That's my intention. I can't see the cops screwing this up."

His answer seemed to satisfy her though she sensed he was still determined to fulfil his promise to skin Dukes.

"Don't let your promises to Beth become an obsession. You have Carmino's empire right here." She slowly ground her thumb on the table. He said nothing as he settled up.

Heading back to the Wynn, they window-shopped between the designer stores of the Forum and then outside. The hot air of the Vegas night was lit by the dazzling neon from every direction.

All along the Strip, noisy revellers were trudging slowly in both directions – either toward the junction at Flamingo or to take in the volcano eruption at the Mirage. Beside a small fountain, Tiffany paused to look at him. "This must be how a US President feels."

"Hunted? When everyone around you is a potential assassin?" Dex agreed and pulled her head closer to his. "The best security can't protect you from someone prepared to die for his cause." He kissed her lightly on the mouth. "Carmino's too cunning to want to die. For us, *carpe diem*. Live every moment for what we have." They continued toward the Fashion Show Mall but had barely gone a few paces when Tiffany stopped him in mid-stride. "Was that your idea of a subtle message?" She kissed him full on the mouth for a lingering moment before they crossed the packed street and entered the hotel.

At that same moment, still distraught from his visit to Haldeman Facilities, Enzo Letizione was sinking another bourbon, his hair tousled and his eyes screwed up. He had heard nothing from Pepe, maybe an ugly omen. Beside him were his fake passport and driving licence. Yet, he was still undecided about taking the first flight out to Mexico City. By midnight. he was no closer to a decision.

Maybe even now, Pepe is on his way.

He was not.

In London where it was now 8 a.m., Carmino was pacing his office. It had been a night without sleep since hearing from Dexter. Arnie Fisher had still not delivered Plan A. His worst fears about Dexter had been proved right. Or even worse.

F 'Christ's sake!
The bastard had been so well informed!
Who had been leaking?
About the Caymans account?

One-Eye?
Jeb Miller?
Someone in the cage?
FB?
Jude?
None of them could have known the account number.
Had Enzo squealed under pressure?
He hadn't known those details.
Nothing made sense. Jude only knew about the hot money from the foreign guests. FB knew of the frauds but nothing of the Caymans. O'Keefe? The accountant? Maybe him? He knew of the second set of casino books. Would he have blabbed to Dexter? Unlikely.

He checked the time. By chartered Dassault, he could still meet Enzo Letizione and be in the Galleria Bar by 4pm.

But why go to Vegas at all?
To save Enzo?
Fuck that.
Unsavable anyway.
To pay off Dexter in a deal not worth shit?

He sipped his third espresso since dawn, his turmoil oscillating between personal salvation and revenge.

Could Dukes and Space City be saved?
No.
Can I trust Dexter to hand over the evidence?
No.

He crossed the Wilton carpet and helped himself to a ridiculously large Baron Otard.

Letizione deserves a one-way to the desert.
I don't need to be in Vegas for that.
Except for the pleasure.

Dexter needs silencing.
For the pleasure.
But where?
And how?
What in hell was Arnie doing about Plan A?

Carmino checked the time again and dialled the charter company at Biggin Hill Airport. Then he left a cryptic message for Arnie to meet him there in one hour.

Without fail.

− 93 −

"I didn't tell you before," said Tiffany as they entered the elevator to whisk them high up the Wynn "but, on the flight, my nightmare was just too vivid. Carmino was waving a huge machete and we were running, running but he was catching us."

"But he didn't." It was no time to laugh or scoff and he tried to look reassuring as he held her waist. "Just a bad dream. Mine were always of the past. Like I said – *let's live the moment.*"

"I don't want to be alone. Not after tonight." Tiffany spoke softly into his ear. "Prove to me your room has a better view."

Dex smiled though Tiffany never saw it. "The ceilings are identical."

She managed an unconvincing laugh. "I want to stay close to you. I'll join you in a minute."

It was actually several minutes later when she reappeared, dressed now in an American Flag onesie and carrying a tiny vanity bag. "What do you think? I picked it up in Santa Monica."

Dex, who had changed into a fresh red sports shirt and white shorts, nodded approvingly. "Maybe we should play the *Star-Spangled Banner* and place our arms across our chests."

"Hold me, please hold me tight," she commanded as they stood beside the floor-to-ceiling window. "I need you close, closer than you've ever been." She kissed him, their bodies touching from top to toe like never before.

Dex noticed both urgency and fear as she clung to him. It was as if she thought this night together might be their last.

Perhaps it would be.

He responded, trying to calm her, stroking away her worries, running his hands gently up and down her spine, stroking her, reaching down to the tight curve of her buttocks.

"Carmino is going to kill you. And you're too stubborn to see it." Her voice was now breaking up with emotion. "I can't bear that this, I mean us, you and me, might end before we've really begun." All her pent-up fears were unleashed as she sobbed into his chest. The more she sobbed, the tears soaking Dex's shirt, the stronger and more protective he felt.

"I'll be okay. Trust me. FB would have told me if Carmino was coming," he explained with more confidence than he felt. "Together, we can see this through."

Tiffany leaned back, her cheeks soaked and her gentle eyes still moist. She arched her back and stood tall, forcing herself to be defiant. "You think so?" She wanted to be convinced and forced herself free from him, the room lights bouncing her colourful reflection off the window.

For a moment, this was the Tiffany he had first encountered – strong and determined. Her eyes flashed pleading as she tried to reason with him. "He's a killer. You're not. Not even close. You won't win. Your intellect, our intellect, won't cut it. Not with him, Dex. You've beaten him. Quit now." She threw herself back at him, as if to prevent him escaping. "This mustn't end badly. We can walk away this minute. Forget Dukes, Space City, Carmino. Leave it to the Feds and Scotland Yard. Right now. For God's sake, we can … get a life. Do great things in Africa." Tears once again rolled down her cheeks.

"I won't let Carmino break us." Gently, he led her to the bed and stretched her out. Then he lay down behind her and held her close to his chest, her back nestling tightly. "Tiffany, my sweet, let's live for this moment." He kissed her neck and he felt her pushing back, responding to his message.

When at last she replied, her words were husky. "Dex, darling, you sweet, stupid, crazy man – make me forget everything. Make tonight never end."

The night did end but not till they awoke at 9 a.m. after pleasuring each other into an exhausted sleep, bodies still entwined. As Tiffany pressed the wall-rocker and the curtains swished open, reality and bright sunlight flooded the room. Las Vegas already looked hot, dusty and arid, ready for another day. Down below, the Strip was almost traffic-free as Dex swung into immediate action. He phoned Adam. "Enjoy yesterday?"

"Brilliant. Unbelievable show," said Adam. "And we won at blackjack. What's not to like?"

"Adam, you're sounding more American by the minute. If we don't get you back to London soon, you'll be saying *cool dude* and high-fiving."

"When do we fly?"

"5-30pm. You, Billy and Tiffany will meet me at the airport."

"And Carmino? Where is he?"

"Long story."

"He'll be here for the opening?"

"There'll be no opening. I'll explain later." He heard the sharp intake of breath at the other end of the line. "But he might be here. Breakfast in twenty minutes. Get Billy there."

Tiffany, still lying on the bed, had pulled the pure white sheet over her head to shut out her fears. Dex returned to her and eased it back to kiss her on the mouth. "Tiffany, darling – in front of the others, be strong for me. Please. I'm going to be well protected. But if I don't make the flight, take the evidence to London.

Otto will look after this end with the FBI." He kissed her again. "Get Scotland Yard and the Feds to blow them out of the water." He waved his arms demonstrating a huge eruption and was rewarded with an unconvinced smile as she disappeared back under the sheet.

— 94 —

Otto took a picture of Dex seated in the Galleria Bar with his Cartier showing 4 p.m. Then Dex sent it with a WhatsApp text to Carmino. "I'm returning to London. Your last chance. Meet me in the lobby of the Hilton, Park Lane, at 7p.m today, London time. The amount demanded is now twenty-two million. Letizione has the account details."

Twenty minutes later, Carmino had not responded when Dex joined the others at McCarran's Executive Jet Terminal. Tiffany dashed forward and clung to him in relief as he appeared, hands in pockets, whistling nonchalantly and tunelessly. "No show." He checked the time. "It's nearly one in the morning there now. I've offered to meet him later today."

"You think he'll pay up? Show up?"

"No to both. I'm second-guessing he won't even be in London by then. I think he's hoofed it." He whispered to Tiffany. "FB messaged me. Carmino went to Biggin Hill Airport. Destination unknown."

Tiffany looked anxious. "And the Grand Opening? No news?"

Dex shrugged. "We know Space City is doomed. Why would Letizione tell the world? We have our fingers on the trigger. He's left guessing when we open fire."

Tiffany's eyes were tired. "And Carmino?"

"On his way to Vegas now? With me returning to London? With no Grand Opening. The death penalty. He'll not come near the USA." Dex went to a water-tower and filled a disposable cup while breaking his own rules by phoning FB. "I said never phone." Forster-Brown was almost whimpering like a toddler, his voice a whisper.

"Too urgent."

"He's back. Reappeared a few minutes ago. I was about to message you."

"Back? Didn't fly after all?" Dex's voice rose several octaves. "You know his plans?"

"No."

"If he's not there, I'll play Reverse Labouchère this afternoon, London-time. 2pm. Understood?" Dex ended the call, hoping that Carmino had not spotted FB looking furtive on camera.

A few moments later, under the anvil-like heat, the attractive hostess escorted them to the jet, its fuselage shimmering in the afternoon sun. After settling around a table laid out with finger-food and their choice of drinks, Dex turned to Billy, who had a dead-eye look, his face expressionless. "I've been in touch with the clinic in Wiltshire. Your treatment can start next week."

Billy's sunken eyes showed a glimmer of enthusiasm. "I don't deserve your help." He paused to control his emotions. "All this mess…because of me." He waved a limp arm vaguely across the table at nothing whilst, with a sudden surge of full power, the Gulfstream accelerated along the runway to soar away from the hot desert dust.

Dex enjoyed the satisfying clunk as the wheels were raised. "Billy, they reckon you may be there for some long time." He patted Billy's arm reassuringly. "But don't worry about Sandie and Emily. I'll see them right."

Dex then produced a notebook and tore out blank pages for Tiffany and himself. "Billy, Adam -watch a movie if you want. I'm going to teach Tiffany Reverse Labouchère. If Carmino is not around, we're taking on Dukes."

Tiffany's brow furrowed. "Poking bears with sticks? Madness." Dex could see she was torn between loyalty and good sense.

Now, it was Adam sounding concerned. "Is that wise? Banking on Carmino not being there?"

"By this afternoon, Carmino could have bolted. He was at an airport this morning but then never flew." He selected a pickled onion. "I don't know why."

"Maybe he'll be sharpening his knife for the meeting," prompted Tiffany.

"I don't expect him at the Hilton."

Tiffany helped herself to a shrimp. "Anything from Otto?" Dex could tell that Tiffany was hoping for a big yes.

"His team has Letizione under surveillance. He went to Space City and has not left. Not that they've seen."

"Neither of them is showing concern, let alone panic." The listeners could spot confusion in Dex's tone. "I don't get it."

"They're like swans, I'd say," Adam intervened. "All serene on the surface but frantic action out of sight."

Dex poured himself a mango juice. "Neither of them has done what you'd expect."

"Something's going on. Carmino must be up to something." Tiffany saw that she had their attention. "He must have said something to soothe Letizione."

"Or to dupe him. If Letizione goes walkabout, Otto's guys are handing him over to the Feds. With the evidence." Dex looked at each in turn. "Suggestions? What are we missing? Anyone?" Nobody responded. "In that case, Adam and Billy, you relax or watch. We'll practise this staking system."

"Must we?" Tiffany sighed." I don't want to go near Dukes ever."

"FB will tell us if it's all clear," Dex whispered in her ear. "It'll be safe. Here goes. Don't be scared about huge bets. I can afford it. You will only bet on black. I always back red. If either colour dominates, then we win back everything they stole from Beth and much more." He grinned boyishly. "Plenty to help in Africa."

"You haven't been lucky yet."

Dex looked away. "I'm overdue a big win," he replied. "Win or lose, I'm going to build that orphanage. My solicitors will see to that."

Dex steadied his glass of Santenay as the plane struck a small patch of turbulence on climbing through 22,000 feet on the way to its cruising height. "Our starting bets will both be £20,000, but hopefully we'll get to stake much, much more."

"This is dumb. Absolute madness."

"This will be my last chance before Dukes closes for ever. I owe it to Beth."

"You'll rub your rabbit's foot charm?" There was no humour in the comment, heavy on aggressive sarcasm.

"Better than that. Call me Warren," Dex winked and squeezed her hand. "Here's what you do." He pointed to the sheet of paper. "Across the top, you write 10, 10, 10, 10. Each one represents £10,000. Your first bet is the total of the two outside numbers – 10 plus 10 equals 20 equals £20,000. My first bet is identical. The top of my page are the same numbers. "Red wins. I add 20 to my line so it reads 10, 10, 10, 10, 20. Because you lost, you strike out the first and the last 10s. You have the two middle ones remaining." He watched whilst she struck out the two numbers.

"I'm with you."

"We now bet the total of our outside numbers. I bet 10 plus 20 equals 30, equals £30,000."

"But I bet only 10 plus 10 equals 20 equals £20,000." Tiffany showed she had picked up the idea.

"The next number is also red. I win again. I add 30 to my line so it becomes 10, 10, 10, 10, 20, 30."

"Okay! You will then bet 10 plus 30. £40,000. But me?"

"You strike out the final middle 10s. That line is dead and you start over, with another 10, 10, 10, 10."

Billy lost interest and returned to his seat to watch a Star Wars movie but Adam was still there, struggling to understand. "Deuced if I get the drift. Tiffany is down £40,000 but you are up £50,000."

"If red goes on winning, my bets keep increasing whilst Tiffany keeps betting the same basic bet of £20,000. Let's take it much further, with all red numbers. Of course, it won't be like that but Tiffany's line would always be 10, 10, 10, 10, but mine might be 10, 10, 10, 10, 20, 30, 40, 50, 60, 70, 80, 90, 100, 110. If I win again, I pocket £120,000 on that one spin and Tiffany only loses £20,000."

Tiffany looked at him suspiciously. "Okay Warren, or should I call you the Mad March Hare? Suppose your rabbit foot fails and black wins. What then?"

"I cross out my two outside numbers, which are 10 and 110. My next bet is my outside numbers of 10 and 100 equals £110,000."

"My next bet is 10 plus 20 equals £30,000."

"Trust me, if either colour dominates for an hour or so, we win big."

Adam pushed aside his glass of port. "Spiffing theory, old chap. But suppose red and black come up around fifty-fifty. Even a duffer like me can see you must lose."

Dex chose to say nothing in reply. "These figures crank up hugely. A bet of £500,000 is perfectly possible. Dukes accept outside bets up to one-million." His eyes shone as if the money had already been won. "Even higher by special arrangement."

"Bless my soul! The penny's dropped!" Adam exclaimed.

"You're using winnings, the casino's money, to bet bigger. Not chasing losing bets like I did. Or Beth did." He looked at Dex admiringly but then his tone changed. "But red or black dominating? On 12th August, do the grouse surrender before a gun is even fired?" He put a fatherly arm on Dex's elbow. "Dear boy, real life is not like that."

The hostess reappeared to clear away the debris of the meal. Adam returned to the *Wall Street Journal*. Billy was still gazing mindlessly at his movie while Tiffany was playing around with the staking system. Dex did little except top up his wine and stare at it, his mind wrestling with what Carmino was thinking. Occasionally, he clasped Tiffany's hand or smiled reassuringly. More often though, he was deep in thought, gazing out of the small window as the jet cut through the night sky toward Canadian airspace.

Much later, after kissing Tiffany goodnight and as the jet cruised over Winnipeg, Dex was the only one awake. His tired mind was still struggling. What had Carmino been doing? Why hadn't he disappeared? What happened to stop him flying from Biggin Hill?

Do I get the cops to the Hilton?
No.
Get them to raid Dukes?
They can't rush that.
Quite rightly.

In-between the tumbling thoughts, one uncomfortable theme kept recurring.

Maybe I'll be dead before the day's through.

At last, still with more questions than answers, he fell into an uneasy sleep.

Five hours later as the Gulfstream was approaching Irish airspace, Carmino was at Clarendon Road. After showering and shaving, he had taken his phone into his small office to ring Arnie but instead spotted Arnie's text. *Plan A delivered.* For a flickering moment, he looked pleased before muttering *forty-eight hours too late.*

It was approaching noon when the Gulfstream taxied to a halt at Stansted. In the Terminal, Dex checked for messages. There was one from Carmino. He read it to Tiffany. "Hilton Hotel unsuitable for serious discussion. Meet me 7pm – the Chairman's apartment. 2nd Floor, Ardberg House, Cadogan Square."

Dex knew the Knightsbridge area well enough. Going there sounded like a death-trap. "Don't go." Tiffany shook her head. "Say no deal, Dex. You? In an apartment with Carmino? There's no mention of the money either." She saw he was receptive. "Forget screwing money from him. Go straight to the police. Better still, tell Carmino you'll be there and have the cops arrest him at Ardberg House."

Dex could see she was right. "FB says Carmino's not expected till late afternoon. We'll head for Dukes first." Outside the Terminal, they saw Adam and Billy beside the waiting Mercedes. Adam had his arm around Billy's shoulder. It was obvious something was wrong. Billy seemed to be out of control, having some sort of fit. His arms were flailing and they could hear despairing wails.

As Dex and Tiffany drew close they both heard Billy's fearful groan. "Oh my God! Oh no. Not that. Never!"

95

Billy's hands were shaking. If it were possible, his face was even paler than ever. He flourished his new phone. "It's Emily," he struggled to get out a coherent message. She's gone. Newsflash."

"No, surely not," said Adam, a silly remark which he regretted at once.

"What do you mean, Billy?" Dex spoke gently to coax some more from him.

"Someone seized her while she was riding her new bike."

The journalist in Tiffany got straight to the point. "When was this?"

"According to Sky News, just before nine." Billy's head slumped as he started to howl uncontrollably. Somehow, he snivelled out more details. "Her friend … was left behind." Dex eased Billy into the back seat. No sooner were they moving than Tiffany phoned her TV station.

"It can't be coincidence," Dex said as his mind flashed back to the little girl clutching her bear during breakfast. "This has to be Carmino. Oh God! Dear little Emily. Your poor wife. My fault. I'm to blame." The words tumbled out.

There was silence while Tiffany clung to her phone. Then Billy looked up, his face tear-stained and haunted. "No. No, Dex," he muttered between sobs. "You gave me a chance. It was me. I screwed up. But Emily, what do we do?" His voice rose to a wail. "What do we do?" His fists pummelled the leather seat as he started to howl again.

The noise almost drowned out Tiffany's conversation with her news-desk. She ended the call. "I can't add much. It happened by her home in Thames Ditton." She leaned across the seat to clasp Billy's hand. "But Billy, my take…it could be much worse. There were two men. This was not a lone pervert enticing a child into a car. It looks like a kidnapping. Much better than a pervert."

Dex glanced at Tiffany. "That makes my decision easier."

She looked at him, taking in the shadows beneath his eyes and the determination in his voice. "No Dex. No Cadogan Square. That achieves nothing. He won't be alone in there."

"So what?" Dex thought only for a split second. "Carmino wants me there. I must go. He wants my evidence. He can have it. He wants me dead. So be it." He fingered his phone, poised to message Carmino. "I'll do any deal for Emily. Give him everything he wants, money and more."

"Then the cops must be outside."

"If I tell the cops and somehow Carmino is tipped off, well …" He left unsaid his conclusion as to Emily's fate, before continuing. "I'd be dead before the cops would even know. Them arresting him with me laid out on a slab, somehow doesn't do it for me. There has to be something better."

Adam muttered some meaningless platitudes "You could refuse to go. Tell the police and trigger Otto Schneider You don't *have* to see him."

Dex rubbed his chin thoughtfully. "That's not going to get Emily back. Now, everything is about her. I must take my chances and go there." He looked at Adam and Tiffany while Billy wrapped his head in his arms, sobbing uncontrollably.

Dex texted, *Confirmed. Meet Cadogan.*

Almost instantly came a reply. "Wise move. I have the nuts. Bring evidence. No law." Dex showed Adam and Tiffany the response before turning to Billy. "You must get home. Sandie needs you. Adam, you please go with him."

"Of course," agreed Adam. "Billy, Emily won't be harmed. Dex will do a deal."

"Now we know why neither he nor Letizione bolted. He still thinks there's a chance of survival." Dex was almost thinking aloud, not expecting any response.

"Your conclusion, Adam?" enquired Tiffany.

"Pepe's no fool. Alive or dead, he'll understand that Dukes is finished. He'll murder you because that's the man he is but Emily will be freed. Then, he'll run."

"Nicely put, Adam. Thanks a bunch!" Dex tried to sound flippant but failed. He looked through the window as the Mercedes cruised past Euston Station. Outside, it was just another London day – people of all races and nationalities scurrying about their business, all unaware of the life or death drama now being lived out so close to them. "Billy, you'll be home in under an hour from here. I'd join you, but Tiffany and I…"

"Dex, no! Emily changes everything. Not Dukes."

"Unless Carmino is there, yes we're going to Dukes. Right now, there's nothing else we can do. We dare not risk the police." Dex's tone was adamant. After the limo pulled up outside his lawyer's office in Berkeley Square, Dex gave a final glance at Billy huddled on the backseat. As he and Tiffany stood beside the vehicle, he hated the sight of the tormented face. "Ring Sandie. Tell her you'll be home soon."

After he and Tiffany had removed their cases, the Mercedes pulled away into the traffic. In his solicitor's office, the receptionist recognised Dex at once and agreed to store everything including the evidence.

"We'll be back late afternoon to collect everything."

"That's fine, Mr Dexter. We're open till 6:30 pm."

"Perfect." Dex forced a smile, thinking that at 7.00 pm he was likely to be slashed to death with a Bowie. Then, as they stood outside looking across the square, a text arrived. He nodded in satisfaction. "From FB. Carmino is not expected. We're good to go." Clutching Tiffany's hand, he led her past the Connaught Hotel and into Mount Street. Ahead of them, along on the right, he saw the familiar steps leading up to Dukes' imposing facade.

It was exactly 2 p.m. Beside the door was Tom, standing tall and upright. As ever, Dukes looked so *establishment*, so permanent. Nothing gave a hint of the turmoil behind the spanking white walls.

"Beautiful day, Tom."

"Going to rain later. Might be thundery tonight, sir."

"Pepe arrived yet, has he?"

The doorman shook his head. "He left an hour ago."

Once inside and standing at the top of the stairs, Dex kissed Tiffany and gripped her small hand. Jude's words rang in his ears. *Think like a winner. Play like a winner. Be a winner.*

96

Dex led Tiffany between the tables, almost all silent and empty. Nobody was even opening the blackjack. From the bar and restaurant came laughter and the aroma of rare beef on the trolley. However, the familiarity of the sights, sounds and smells provided no welcome. Now that he was down here, Dex found he was fighting to control his nerves.

He headed for the cage and collected a large stack of plaques. Everything seemed so mundane, so normal. He spotted FB hovering close to the empty baccarat table. "Mr D! Good afternoon! Oh, yes and Miss R, isn't it? So good to see you."

"Not going to Vegas for the opening, FB?"

"The Cinderella role suits me well. Las Vegas, like Southend, is so vulgar. Will you be lunching?"

Dex shook his head. "Remember I discussed Reverse Labouchère? We want to try it today."

For a brief moment, FB raised his eyes from the carpet. "Remember, Reverse Labouchère can bite." He led them toward the tables. "We've one open but if you wish," he coughed into the back of his hand, "we'll open a high-stakes table for you. What stakes did you have in mind?"

"Twenty thousand minimum."

"I see. In that case, yes, of course. I'll get a table open."

"And if Jeb Miller and One-Eye are on duty, I'd like …."

"As you wish." FB smirked discreetly. He slipped away to the house phone. Moments later, Jeb Miller's fat bottom was sagging over the sides of his high stool while One-Eye was sorting out the chips.

Dex nodded to Miller. "Table limit of two million max on outside bets, right?"

"No, Mr D." Miller's brown-toothed smile was both disarming and obnoxious. "Today, the spread is twenty thousand to one million."

"Christ! No wonder you casinos make money. That maximum is far too low. Who decided that?" Dex looked and sounded aggressive. "Get FB over here."

"I'm sorry, Mr D. It was FB that instructed me."

"Mr Carmino, then?"

Jeb Miller enjoyed playing his trump card. "Is not here yet."

Dex looked irritated as he turned to Tiffany. "Stitched-up as usual but seeing as we're here, let's go on." Now that he was at the table, Dex found that his palms were no longer sweating and his pulse-rate was settling to something like normal. As to his blood-pressure though, he hated to imagine it.

He called for two glasses of orange juice as he and Tiffany settled in front of their chips. Their sheets of paper both showed 10, 10, 10, 10. Dex had yellow chips, each worth £10,000. Tiffany's were blue at the same value. Between them were a stack of clunky plaques from the cage, each worth £100,000.

"Let's go for it!" Dex smiled at Tiffany and admired the firm way she pushed out her chips to back black. One-Eye spun the wheel with a deft flick of the wrist, the small white ball speeding round under the rim.

"Labouchère?" One-Eye questioned Dex.

"Much better. *Reverse* Labouchère." Dex watched the ball bouncing around the wheel. Now that the fuse had been lit, he was seeing everything in slow motion, even though the vein in his forehead was pounding. As he looked around, it seemed unreal to think that this gaming-floor, this whole building, was doomed. Jeb Miller, One-Eye, Andy, O'Keefe and probably several more would soon be destined for jail.

"8. Black. Even."

Tiffany swooped on her winnings and added 20 to her line of 10, 10, 10, 10. "Start as we mean to carry on," she laughed to Dex. "Twenty-thousand up already. I should quit but I could get to enjoy this. Plenty more black numbers, please."

"We haven't actually won at all yet." His words were smiled at Tiffany who looked puzzled for a moment before her slow nod acknowledged he was correct.

Dex turned to Miller. "I told Tiffany. My stars said my luck was in today. So far, it looks more like business as usual." He crossed off the two outside tens.

"Perhaps the luck is in having me here." Tiffany raised her delicate eyebrow.

Dex looked unconvinced. though he admired the confident way in which she placed her next bet, staking £30,000.

"I'm on a roll, Dex."

"Swallows and summers," retorted Dex but his reference to Aesop was lost. Tiffany was now focused solely on the hiss and clatter of the slowing ball.

"32. Red. Even."

"Hmmh! That didn't last long then." She crossed off the outside 20 and 10 from her line. "I'm losing now."

Dex turned and gave her a gentle kiss on the cheek. "We're *both* losing. A zigzag. Red then black. Last thing we want." He ran his finger across his throat but the next four numbers were all red. "Hey!" Tiffany protested. "I'm well down, just crossing off tens."

Dex pointed to his chips. "But between us, we're winning."

"My winning feeling lasted one spin." Tiffany re-stacked her chips and crossed off more tens.

Dex looked at One-Eye. "A few repeat numbers would be good." He saw the dealer shrug without interest. "Yeah, yeah, yeah. You don't have to say it, One-Eye! *You can't control the ball. The wheel has no memory.* I've heard that crap." Dex shook his head as he stuck to his script. "I bet you can make the ball do anything you want. Make it land where you want."

"On just reds or just blacks? Dream on, Mr D!" The dealer's small dark eyes met Dex's stare. His moon-like face was inscrutable, his ivory-coloured features revealing nothing beneath the mop of jet-black hair.

"He can, can't he, Mr Miller?" The inspector did not reply beyond shaking his head, as if Dex's suggestion were mad. One-Eye spun a red number again – and then again. "Give me cash chips please. Big ones."

Tiffany looked uneasy and she shifted on her chair. "You've won a lot. Let's go to the bar and celebrate."

"Not yet." He turned to the dealer. "One-Eye, you see, I knew you were trying to help me. Keep those reds coming."

Miller made a dry kissing noise used by casino staff to attract attention. The shaven-headed Maltese pit boss responded at once. His skin was deep olive. The guy would have looked more comfortable in a wrestler's leopard-skin than a dinner-jacket that barely contained him. He leaned close for Miller to whisper to him.

The pit boss left the table and spoke to a serious looking man in his fifties. Despite his well below average height, he still had a *don't mess* image. His grey *en brosse* hairstyle topped a pockmarked face which could have been chiselled from granite. His appearance scarcely invited a friendly word and Dex had never spoken to him, something that had worked both ways. He guessed this was the floor manager who reported to FB. Even when talking to the pit boss, he seemed to be a man of few words and no charm. After listening to the Maltese pit boss, he disappeared but returned a few moments later to stand right behind Tiffany.

Dex sensed a developing gorilla situation. His whisper to Tiffany was intended to be overheard. "Casinos *pretend* they like winners – until you start winning big. This guy standing behind us – that's what they call *giving us heat*. They want to make you uncomfortable. Ignore it."

Moments later, FB himself appeared with a worried frown.

- 97 -

Jude Tuson sprawled crossways in an armchair, her legs dangling. She was wearing a white T-shirt and bikini panties, her hair tousled. The day had started unpleasantly and the way it was shaping up, promised not to be much better. Her mind was in turmoil, wondering and worrying about what to do as she gazed at a rerun of *Friends*.

Ever since Pepe had mentioned that Dex and some guy called Billy Evans had been planning to screw Dukes, he had grown hard to talk to. Since going to Biggin Hill and then changing his mind about flying to Vegas, he had been positively distant. When she had asked about the sudden change of plans, he had snapped at her *to mind her own fucking business*.

She had seen Evans a couple of times. He had seemed harmless enough, playing blackjack next to an older and rather distinguished looking gentleman who was somehow linked to Dex. At first, she had taken Pepe's story of Billy and Dex at face value but the more she thought about it, the more unlikely it seemed. Dex was rich with a sick father and a dead sister. Would he really be planning a heist in Dukes? With this Billy Evans? Or the urbane old guy?

Or, more probably, was Dex somehow a threat to Pepe?

Earlier that morning, while Pepe was showering, his phone had been beside the bed with his wallet, keys and small change. She had heard the bleep of an incoming text. Interested in why he was so on edge, she had taken a quick peek. "Plan A delivered. Emily at my place. Arnie." After wrapping a pink shortie dressing-gown around her, she had padded through to the kitchen to make a cup of coffee. The name Emily meant nothing and Pepe had never mentioned any Plan A but she felt uneasy. The message seemed both sinister and secretive.

She had heated herself a croissant and loaded it with butter and marmalade. Reluctantly, she decided to do the same for him, carrying a tray through to the bedroom. He came out of the bathroom in a black towelling robe, his hair slicked back and damp. Without speaking to her, he grabbed his phone and went into his office. When he returned, he helped himself to the croissant without thanks, pacing around the room as he ate, his mind elsewhere. Suddenly he glared at her. "You didn't tell me a message came in while I was showering."

"What message, Pepe? In case you didn't notice, I've been getting your breakfast." She took in his dismissive shake of the head as he stood in front of the mirror, fingering his scar. "Pepe, pretty please, take me to the Grand Opening." She laid back on a purple chaise longue. Her dressing gown was untied and her long legs were apart. She moved slightly so that a nipple appeared and she licked marmalade off her fingers, her invitation obvious.

Pepe continued pacing, showing no interest in the tanned thighs or anything on offer. "I pay you to look after the high rollers. I need you here. Anyway, I may leave the opening to Enzo." As he finished eating, his tone was as abrupt as his aggressive movements.

Jude crossed her legs and gathered the gown back around her. "When I've finished looking after these guests, all that stuff, we'll jet-off? Like you promised?"

"That's what I said." Pepe looked and sounded disinterested as he slipped into some tailored slacks and a navy-blue polo top. "Right now, just shut the fuck up. I don't need you wittering. I have important calls to make." He slammed the bedroom door after him and Jude then heard the door to his bijou office banged shut too as he entered it from the sitting-room.

While he was closeted away, she too had showered and dressed. Even after varnishing her nails, he was still behind the closed office door. After completing her make-up, she settled down in her T-shirt and panties. Having turned on the TV and with a second coffee, she flopped over a chair, waiting for him to appear. When he did so, he ignored her, going straight into the bedroom, grabbing a sports-coat and his essentials before heading to the front door. "I'm going to Dukes and the bank. I may fly to Vegas after all."

"Fancy a leisurely lunch?" Jude adopted her suggestive smile, still hoping for an invite.

"I expect to be back soon after two."

Moments later, as she stood by the window, she saw the Aston Martin exit the underground garage and glide toward Holland Park Avenue. With Pepe in this foul mood, she was unsure whether she wanted to be around when he returned. Wandering down Kensington Church Street and taking in the antique shops, or along Bond Street with brunch in Richoux, seemed more attractive than being trussed up in studded leather gear for his pleasure.

Still sprawled over the chair, she switched TV channels and picked up the *Daily Mail*, one of two morning papers just delivered. A jingle for Sky News came on in the background followed by a reporter standing in the rain outside New Scotland Yard. She skimmed the paper, looking for items about fashion, Australia or exotic destinations but found she was taking in little. Pepe filled her mind.

Do I really want a future with him?
Want to travel with him?
Is all his S & M a price worth paying?
Just for exotic destinations?

Do I believe he'll really take me anyway?
Do I give a damn about him?
Does he give a damn about me?
Ha! That's a no, a big no.
I'm just his plaything, his blow-up doll.
I'm here to be used or abused at his pleasure.
Maybe I should move on.
Quit.

She reached for an expensive chocolate truffle for comfort. Her thoughts, as they increasingly had done, drifted back to Dex. He too was an enigma – a tad mysterious but funny, kind and intriguing. Maybe when Pepe was away in Vegas, *if he went*, she could make another pitch and see off that American woman. Just imagining Dex's uncomplicated smile started some aching feelings that needed satisfying. She was considering taking her fantasy further in the bedroom when the change of tone from the TV caught her attention.

"We have more on the breaking story of the six-year-old girl who was dragged into a car near her home in Thames Ditton, Surrey. Emily Evans had been riding a bike with a friend. The vehicle may have been a small red saloon. First reports suggest two men were involved. Our reporter is now heading for the scene in Sugden Road, in southwest London."

The word *Emily* jarred. Emily in Arnie's message? *Emily Evans? Billy Evans? The timing matched the text message.*
Could it be her?
Like fuck me, yes it could!
Billy Evans's daughter?
Surely not?
But why not?
Had Plan A been orders from Pepe to snatch Emily?

Why would he do that?
Because of something Billy had done at Dukes?
Maybe.
So, who is Arnie?

Further fantasies about Dex or of going window-shopping were blown away. She jumped up, eager to search Pepe's office. There was plenty of time and a chance to discover something about Arnie. She put the chain across the front door and went into Pepe's cubbyhole of an office. She had peeped in a couple of times but had never before gone in. The air stunk of cigars and one was stubbed out on an onyx ashtray on his small desk. There was a well-padded chair and a small rear-view window. There was no clutter, essential given its size.

A large monitor, a keyboard, a pad of paper, a mouse and mat almost filled the desk. She turned her attention to the three-drawer filing cabinet. The top drawer was marked *Dukes* and was locked with no sign of any key. She hurried to the bedside but his keys had gone. Her attention then turned to the lower two drawers. One was labelled *Space City / International*. It too was locked but the bottom one, marked *Sundry*, opened at once. It contained about a dozen or so green folders, each labelled and filed alphabetically. She riffled through them quickly, hoping for the name Arnie to jump out. It did not. There were files for *Accountants, Car Tax, Cleaner, Council, Electrics, Insurance, Neighbour Dispute, Oil, Old Blunkensoppians, Solicitors* and *Water.*

She quickly dismissed most of them as irrelevant and so started with the accountants but nobody on the notepaper or in any document was called Arnie or Arnold. The solicitors' folder was bulky and took a while to study. It too proved useless, as did the file for the *Cleaner.*

Neighbour Dispute did not sound too promising, so she tried what she assumed was his old school association. The folder contained a directory of members of a school near Chelmsford. She flicked through the list of names to *Carmino* and there he was – *Carmino – Pepe Rolando (1974-1980)*. There was his email address and a mobile phone number.

Quickly, she decided to search for anybody called Arnie or Arnold from the same era. There were over sixty pages but she found she could skim down the years quickly and then cross-check to the name. And then she found one: *Arnold Harold Fisher (1974 – 1980)*. There was no email address but there was a London area phone number, which she entered into her smartphone.

She hurried on through the directory, one eye on the clock, even though there seemed no reason to expect him back. By the time she reached the final entry for Edward Zachariah, there had been no other Arnold. She returned the file and almost ignored the one marked *Neighbour Dispute*. Then, for completeness' sake, she decided to take a look.

A quick glance showed that Pepe had been having trouble with an Indian family next door. He had been irritated by the constant smell of curry wafting across his roof terrace but had been even more pissed off by the Indian music, played too often and too loud. The Council had done nothing about his complaint. She turned to the next letter. It was addressed to Arnold Fisher Limited and read: "Dear Arnie. Copy self-explanatory correspondence herewith. Fix this. Free rein. Just do it. Whatever."

She tapped Arnie's address into her smartphone – *37 Pinesta Crescent, London SW1 4GF*. There was no sign of what Arnie had done about the Indians but it must have been effective – she had never heard Indian music nor smelled curry.

She returned the folder, closed the drawer, double-checked that there was no sign of her visit and unchained the front door. Having grabbed some crackers, cream cheese and poured a large measure of Marlborough County Pinot Noir, she returned to her chair and ran a search on Google for 37 Pinesta Crescent. Up came the name Arnold Fisher Limited, so she checked again with Google Maps. She soon saw that the address was not too far from Victoria Station in a confusing mass of small streets known as Pimlico. She turned to Google's street view and took in the details before honing in on number 37. This was it then – this was "his place" as referred to in the text. *Where Emily had been taken.* Not an office block. Pinesta Crescent was a residential street and seemingly, Arnie Fisher ran his business from home. Her fingers flying over the keys, she trawled the web for more on Arnold Fisher Limited. Nothing more came up. It had no website.

Over a second glass, she was still pondering what next to do when Sky News at 2 p.m. came on. Emily Evans was now the lead story. A sad-faced journalist in a fawn Burberry was standing outside a suburban three-up and two-down semi-detached property. It had a small unkempt garden and there was a policeman at the gate. The reporter pointed down the road to where there was considerable police activity. "Down there is where Emily was seized just around five hours ago. Scene-of-Crime officers are at the spot where she was thrown into a small red car. Door-to-door enquiries are continuing as police seek witnesses. About ten minutes ago, Emily's father arrived in a large black Mercedes, refusing to say anything except to confirm who he was. He entered the house with another gentleman who would not give his name."

The screen filled with a shot of the car pulling up. Instantly Jude recognised both Billy Evans and the distinguished gentleman from the casino. She swallowed hard as her fears had become hard facts.

Pepe and Arnie had kidnapped this sweet-faced kid.
The bastards.
But why?

After a moment or two, she switched to an entertainment channel so as not to give Pepe any sign that she even knew of this horrible crime. It seemed better.

But what to do?
Go to the police?
Would Pepe discover who had told them?
His phone had the damning text message.
Had it been deleted?
Could experts retrieve it?
What would he do?
Would he be arrested and jailed till his trial?
Or would he deny, deny and be bailed?
And what then?
What might he do to me?
She thought of his vicious-looking knife and shuddered.
Why did he have that?
She swung her legs back over the chair's arm as she tried to decide.
That poor kid!
Maybe I should tell Dex.
Pepe links him to Billy Evans.
To hell with the consequences.
I must do something.
As she reached for her phone to call Dex, the key sounded in the lock and the front door opened. Her chance had gone. Pepe breezed in, looking no more relaxed than when he had left.

"Hi, darling! So, do you know yet? Are you going to Vegas?"

He barely smiled, replying over his shoulder as he headed to the bedroom. "I'll decide later. For now, I want you in bed. Afterwards, I've things to arrange." Reluctantly, she swung her legs down and stood up, knowing that it was *fun-for-one* time.

~ 98 ~

A few uncharacteristically brisk strides brought FB to the table. He looked at the number display board showing that recently, red numbers 7, 3, 34, 16, 16, and 27 had all hit. There had been a solitary 29 black. Dex turned and saw FB reach for the floor-manager's arm before the duo took a step or two further away and out of earshot. The Maltese joined them in an intense debate. Dex managed to catch One-Eye's name but the context was unclear.

"What a buzz, eh?" Dex looked at the dealer and the inspector in turn. "Plenty more reds coming, One-Eye?" Dex checked his sheet of paper. "That's only nineteen spins." He pointed Tiffany to his stacks of cash chips. "We're way over a million ahead" He made as if to high-five One-Eye who backed away. "Keep spinning reds and you and me, we can really clean up. I'll see you right – a generous tip."

To Dex's delight, One-Eye's lips curled into a snarl. He was wanting his patter to irritate and distract. Occasionally, as the ball hissed round the wheel, he thought of Emily but there was nothing he could do about her just yet. Now was the time to confuse and disturb management by playing the role of cocky winner. McKay's advice had been for him to *piss-off* the casino staff. It seemed to be working.

He could see that Tiffany was hating his bumptious drivel but he had no intention of stopping. As planned during the flight, he started murmuring Dire Straits' big hit *Money for nothing and your chicks for free*. This, at least, produced a smile from Tiffany even as she pointed to her chips. "Me? I'm losing like a drunken sailor."

"Relax! My pal One-Eye – him and me, we've really got it going! Look at my line: 30, 40, 50, 60, 70, 80, 100, 120, 150, 180. My next bet is £210,000." Dex turned to Miller. "What's the longest run you've seen of all reds or blacks?"

Miller coughed into the back of his hand before responding. "Me personally? I've seen twenty-seven. Just the once, mind."

"See, Tiffany. We've been nowhere near a run of all reds without a black." The ball landed in 9 red, odd. Dex swept in the big win. "One-Eye. You the man! Keep helping me!"

The floor-manager changed position so that he could glare along the table at Dex and watch One-Eye more closely. Dex enjoyed the penetrating look as he pushed out £240,000 for his next bet. He nodded toward the dealer but addressed the Maltese pit boss and shift-manager. "He's some guy, this One-Eye!" He hummed more Dire Straits to fuel their irritation and loved being rewarded with a Maltese glare. Miller too was now watching One-Eye more intently.

"34, red, even," said One-Eye, looking uncomfortable as he pushed across nearly a quarter of a million pounds. Dex made a big point of checking he had been paid out correctly. The next two numbers were black but then came another four reds.

"Let's quit," said Tiffany. "You've won enough."

"You can never win enough. Keep them coming, One-Eye!" He turned to Jeb Miller. "Can you order us some Earl Grey tea and smoked salmon sandwiches, please? And if the kitchen can manage French pastries? Thanks! We shall be here for a while."

- 99 -

In Clarendon Road, Jude eased herself from the bed, her arms and legs aching from the contorted position in which she had been strapped for the last *God knows* how long. Pepe had now dressed in smart-casual and was packing a carry-on sized case. She glanced at him. He was engrossed in sorting his washing-kit, so she slipped into the bathroom, feeling soiled and abused. As soon as he heard the thunderous torrent from the shower, Carmino laid out a change of clothes, three false passports, three wigs, three different pairs of tinted contact lenses, hair dye, a false moustache, cheek padding, two different pairs of glasses and some charcoal pills. Then he added facial makeup to mask the scar or to age his face to suit the image. All he needed now was the stash of cash from his safe in Dukes.

As he gathered the final essentials, his mind was on Dex. Using the garotte on the bastard would be clean, quick and effective. *Less pleasurable but job done.* In case Ardberg House was being watched, he could exit looking nothing like Pepe Carmino. Disguising himself as an old man with a limp would fool the cops, even if Dexter had gone to them – something he reckoned unlikely. With thirty apartments served through the front entrance, there was plenty enough foot-traffic.

The kid?
What to do with her?
Two wasted days!
If only Arnie had nabbed her before Letizione had been crucified.

Would Dexter stay stumm?
Nil chance.
Her only value was bait.
After that?
She was redundant.
Or even before that.
She didn't need to be alive.
Dexter only had to believe she was alive.
He looked at the garotte and nodded in satisfaction. Throttling the kid would teach Billy Evans not to mess.
What's still bugging me?
Who had been leaking?
How had Dexter known so much?
For fuck's sake, Dexter had even got bank account numbers.
Who knew about the hot money being laundered?
Who had the chance to tell Dexter?
The sound of Jude exiting the shower set him thinking.
My God!
She knew of the hot money…and she was cosy with him. Had probably shagged him, if the truth were known.
But had she tipped him off?
Could she have found his secret banking details?
Possible.
If she had been into his office.
But I keep the drawer locked.
Have I ever left the keys lying about?
Possible.
Who else could it be?
He felt mounting dryness at the back of his throat, a sensation he only got when an inner urge started to take hold. When it peaked, it was almost like being choked. His breathing would

change into short animal grunts and his blood would race as waves of fury consumed him. Feverishly, he scurried round the bedroom looking for her phone. Nowhere. He raced into the sitting-room. Nowhere. Kitchen. Nowhere. Then he spotted her cavernous Louis Vuitton handbag lying beside the chair she had been using. In a violent move, he unzipped every pocket and shook out every last item – tissues, make-up, eye-liner, hair lacquer, credit-cards, small change, a wad of notes, a couple of matching pens, a notepad, a pack of condoms. But no phone.

He hurried back to the bedroom, his fury and certainty mounting in equal measure. She was now beside the bed and holding his flight reservation for Singapore. His suitcase had been flipped open. She waved the ticket, "You're not going to Las Vegas." It was not a question but Pepe ignored it anyway. His mind and his eyes were on the phone in her other hand.

"You devious bitch!" he snarled, his voice guttural. "Contacting your pal Dexter from the bathroom, were you?"

"Dex? Why would I phone him?" She stood fiercely defiant. "You lying devious sod! You're dumping me, not coming back." She pointed to the passports. "Mr Ralph Dawkins. First Class ticket to Singapore. You're doing a runner, you bastard."

Carmino stared at her cocky face. His throat was now parched, tinder-dry. Looking at her, he no longer saw the beautiful young woman he had just bedded. Now, he saw only someone who was a danger, someone visible through a red mist. His tipping-point had been passed and a time-bomb inside him had to explode.

The lump in his throat swelled, silently instructing him what he had to do. His pupils widened while his nostrils flared. In a sudden move, he was beside the built-in wardrobe. Seconds later, his back to her, he had unsheathed the Bowie's nine-inch blade. When he turned to face her, Jude was fumbling through the wigs. It was only on looking up that she flinched at seeing his manic stare and heard his open-mouthed grunting.

Then she saw the knife clenched in his hand. At first, Jude stood mesmerised, seeming not to understand, a puzzled look on her face. Then panic hit home. Her hand flew to her mouth and her terrified eyes were transfixed.

"Your phone." Pepe somehow forced out the order but there was a dry rattling throatiness to both words. She saw the tip of the knife now pointing toward her. She screamed, backing away as he advanced across the several paces that divided them. "The phone, you snooping bitch. Double-crossing me. You and Dexter – telling him…"

"No. No. Pepe, you've got it wrong. I've told him nothing. Nothing about anything." The words tumbled out as the blade drew closer. Jude saw the lips, narrowed and mean. She heard his primeval grunts that reminded her of feeding-time on the farm. "Leave me alone. Please. Please, Pepe I've done nothing wrong."

Her plea was ignored. She saw nothing but hatred in his face. At that moment, she realised that she had to escape from those unflinching eyes. They reminded her of a cobra that she had encountered in Thailand. The intense and unblinking blackness of his stare was an unmistakable warning. He was blocking her path to the bathroom, where she might have locked the door. Her only chance was through the sitting-room to the front entrance. Still in her bare feet and defying the pain in her thighs, she turned and ran, the towel falling away. She had a dozen or so metres, nearly forty feet, to cover to the front-door. As she sped beyond the dining-table and between the settee and an armchair, she hurled her phone through the open window to crash onto the street far below.

With each pace, she heard his grunting even louder and more inhuman. He was closing on her, just a few steps behind. In the compact hallway, she grabbed at the door-handle, hoping to open it and slam it shut before he reached her. "Shit! Oh God!" she shouted as she realised that he had double-locked it when he had returned. As Jude screamed and fought with the deadlock, he was onto her. Mustering all his force, he jabbed his arm forward so that the vicious knifepoint savagely entered Jude's throat, penetrating deep and beyond her windpipe. Her scream died and was replaced by a gurgling sound, blood pumping from her throat and mouth. As her eyes flickered wide for an instant, he jerked the knife upward to ensure certain death. Jude's knees buckled and she slumped against the wall before collapsing onto the carpet.

As he snorted with pleasure, his eyes wild with excited satisfaction, Carmino withdrew the knife and stabbed her again, first in the chest and then once in her stomach. Breathing heavily with satisfaction, he looked down at the bloodied and lifeless body. With a snarl that came from deep down in his diaphragm, he grasped her hair, tilting her head. Using a vicious horizontal cut, he ripped open her neck, nearly severing her head. Satisfied, he stood over her before giving her inert body several vicious kicks, grunting each time with the force of his exertion.

Breathing hard, he looked at the walls and grey carpet, everywhere sprayed and soaked with blood. For a moment, as he had savaged her throat, it was the glorious frenzy of Panama-relived. His clothes were saturated as, with a toss of his head, he returned to the sitting-room, leaving a trail of bloody footprints. When he reached the window, his breathing was still far from normal. Lying in the street, way below, he saw her phone, looking as if it had burst open. Whether the data would have survived from three floors up, he had no idea. Looking like he did, with bloodied face, arms, hands and clothes, going down to collect the remains was not an option.

I was right.
The bitch had leaked everything.
Jettisoning her phone proved that.

For a few anxious moments, he wondered if anybody was reacting to her screams. It seemed not and anyway, was unlikely. The Indian neighbours had moved and their apartment was still empty. The young couple on the ground floor were never at home during the day. Down in the street there was no sign of activity.

Having wiped the Bowie clean, he showered, the piping hot water sluicing away her blood until the water running off him ran clear and clean. Then, as he selected a change of clothes from the closet, he changed his mind about using the garotte – the prospect of slitting Dexter's throat was irresistible. He strapped the studded belt around his waist and tucked the blade into its sheath. He was ready to go, using the kitchen door leading to the bare concrete of the emergency stairs. Outside in Clarendon Road, he checked for Jude's phone. The remains had been scattered by passing traffic. There was no point scooping up the crushed remnants. As he drove away, he dismissed the phone from his mind as a minor inconvenience. In a few hours, Pepe Carmino would no longer exist.

The clock on the dashboard showed it was not yet five pm – ample time to empty the office safe, visit Arnie in Pimlico, strangle the kid and be at Cadogan Square before seven.

One down, two to go.

-100-

Another forty minutes passed. The Earl Grey tea, sandwiches and strawberry tartlets had been cleared away. Despite six more black numbers, red still dominated, hitting a further twenty-two times with just a solitary zero. By now, Dex was into the Beatles and was irritating the watchers by quietly singing, *Now give me money, that's what I want.* As the casino staff hovered, watching his fortune stacking up, he was enjoying infuriating them with continuing silly chatter. Rapidly, he counted his chips and deducted Tiffany's losses.

"We're just over nine million ahead. Let's make it ten before we quit." He grinned at Tiffany and then at the stony-faced floor-manager as he switched to Abba's lyrics, breaking into *Money, Money, Money, always sunny in a rich man's world.* He enjoyed the Maltese emitting a dismissive sniff, so he decided to wind the guy up even more. "Fair do! You're right! Not everybody likes Abba." He watched the ball nestle into 25 red and waited while One-Eye pushed the huge win across the green layout. "How about Liza Minnelli in Cabaret? *Money makes the world go around, the world go around.*"

His brows knitted together in a furious scowl, the Maltese pit-boss muttered angrily to FB who was fiddling with his hands and staring at the carpet. Jeb Miller nodded toward Dex. "Funny old game, roulette. It can change suddenly. Don't go losing it all!"

"I didn't know you cared, Mr Miller. But with my pal One-Eye helping me like this, I'm good to keep this rolling." Dex gave the

Deadline Vegas

dealer an unsubtle wink. As he had hoped, One-Eye looked embarrassed, his narrow eyes flicking left and right as the heat of management once again turned to him. Dex was just about to place his next bet when he felt his phone vibrating in his pocket. He took it out to check the message and was shocked to see not just one message. There were three. In the heat of the action, he had missed the first two.

"Move away please, Mr D. No phones at the table." Miller's tone was polite but firm. Dex took a few steps to read them quickly. The most urgent was from FB – *Carmino heading for Dukes*. He turned to Tiffany and spoke so he could be overheard. "Father's nursing home. He's sinking fast." He turned to One-Eye. "Cash us out, please."

FB broke off from his conversation with the floor-manager. His agitation was obvious. The conversation had been increasingly animated with shaken heads, glances at One-Eye and now irritation at the winnings Dex was sweeping from the table. "FB – I must dash to Northampton. My Father may not survive the day. Have the cage cash me out – US dollars, sterling and euros. Big denominations, please. Oh, and FB. Remember, I joked that one day I'd need a suitcase playing Reverse Labouchère?" He saw FB agree, his face grim. "Today's the day, so have the guys in the cage fill one up." As an afterthought, Dex tugged FB on the sleeve. "And please sign a letter certifying these are casino winnings."

It was nearly nine anxious minutes before the cash mountain had been counted and cross-checked. He was struggling to keep calm knowing that Pepe Carmino might even now have entered the building. Then FB appeared trundling a suitcase and the letter. "I'll bring it back," Dex grinned cheerily as he grasped the handle. "Empty, though." Then he lugged the heavy suitcase up the stairs, Tiffany a couple of strides ahead of him.

Dex spotted a passing taxi. "Berkeley Square and then the Goring Hotel in Victoria. Thanks."

"The Goring?" Tiffany's mind was all at sea. The size of the win, the panic over Dex's father and the suitcase of cash had left her dazed.

"I think we can afford it," he joked, nodding at the suitcase. We'll hole up there tonight." He gave her a peck on the cheek before his deliberate bravado evaporated. "We need somewhere safe for the money and I need to make some urgent calls."

Even as the taxi was pulling away, Tiffany saw an Aston-Martin appear behind them and slowly ease to a halt. Pepe Carmino was talking intensely on his phone and never noticed Dex departing. "God, Dex! What a win. But you were so bloody annoying in there."

He tapped the suitcase. "It worked too. I wanted *heat*. And I got it." Again, he kissed the side of her flushed cheek and changed the subject. "Forget Dukes. The priority is Emily. Then maybe meeting Carmino."

"But Northampton? Your father?"

"Ah! Yes. I was coming to that."

He pulled her as close as the seatbelt allowed and his eyes told Tiffany that something was afoot. At that moment, the taxi pulled up outside the solicitors' offices and Dex was gone, hurrying towards the large brown doors.

-101-

No sooner had FB finished with Dex than he was back on the casino-floor with the Maltese pit boss and the floor-manager. "I saw almost every spin," said the pit boss. "Dexter seemed too damned familiar with One-Eye. Even winked at him." FB wrapped his hands around each other as the Maltese continued "Winked twice in fact."

FB stroked his chin. "Is that so? Curious. He had asked for One-Eye." He saw he had their attention. "It seemed harmless. Now I'm less sure. Plus, he was so damned cocky. You'd have thought he knew he was going to win. Can we trust One-Eye?"

"It seemed like he was in Dexter's team."

FB was not persuaded. "Look – One-Eye's our top guy at cheating players. No way can he *deliberately* land on so many reds. Anyway, why cheat us, even if he could?" FB continued, mainly talking to his feet with the occasional glance at the motionless wheel, the ball lying in 3 red, odd. "Okay, we know One-Eye can land the ball damned close to any number he wants. But nobody's going to convince me he can mainly pick reds – or blacks. Not possible."

The hatchet-faced floor-manager agreed. "Impossible. But in fact, he didn't. He hit several blacks but just not enough. I've seen these imbalances before. It's hardly unique."

FB looked up sharply. "What about the wheel? Could it be faulty? Or gaffed?"

The Maltese shook his head and spun the wheel in a sudden,

irritated move. "One-Eye was spinning sometimes slow, sometimes quicker. I can't see how he's to blame." He tried to catch FB's downturned eyes. "To me? The guy just got lucky. This was nothing like a record run of all reds. Shit happens."

FB scratched his silvery hair for a moment. "Well, if it's not One-Eye, I'm having the wheel examined and tested. What spooks me is that the first time Dexter plays Reverse Labouchère really big, he cleans up. Who wants to explain this to the boss? He'll explode."

The Maltese scratched his backside. "Yeah! That wheel looks perfect to me but send it to John Huxley's for checking."

FB nodded. "Good call. A top manufacturer. If we do nothing, God help us when the boss finds out. He doesn't like Dexter anyway." His voice sounded wary. "I expect the boss is up in his office. We must be seen as decisive I'll have security remove the wheel at once." He started to move away but then stopped to give the two listeners a meaningful stare. "Get One-Eye to my office in five minutes. And Jeb Miller."

–102–

Dex googled *Police Belgravia* on his smartphone and found there was a police station on Buckingham Palace Road, just a quarter of a mile from Pinesta Crescent. He tapped on the glass behind the driver's head and slid open the partition. "Change of plans. Take us to 202 Buckingham Palace Road, the police station."

"Ain't so comfy as the Goring, mate," the driver laughed.

"Cheaper, though." Dex slid the partition shut. "Jude sent a text suggesting Emily is at 37 Pinesta Crescent. Belongs to someone called Arnie Fisher. She's included his cellphone number."

Tiffany puckered her pink lips. "How would she know? Is it a set-up?"

Dex had to admit there was no explanation. "That's all I know."

"Surely, she'd dial 999, not tell you. You can't trust her. That's why you got rid of her. This could be a trap."

Dex tilted his head left and right as if weighing the balance. "We've nothing better. In Sydney, she did kids' nursing. Perhaps she loves kids." His flow was interrupted by the taxi braking sharply to avoid a motorbike courier as they swung into Grosvenor Place. "Why would Jude want to trap me? I'm meeting Carmino anyway." He gave her a reassuring hug but got neither reaction nor response. He looked ahead at the stop-go traffic heading towards the river. Then his tone brightened. "At least while Carmino is in Dukes, Emily should be safe."

"The journalist in me says this is too flimsy for the cops. They'll want to contact her."

"If they ignore this and Emily was there, all hell would break loose." The cab's diesel engine purred as it waited at the junction of Buckingham Palace Road with Bressenden Place. "Living with Carmino, Jude could have found out." His thoughts were interrupted by a text. "Shit!" he exclaimed. "Shit, shit, shit." He saw Tiffany trying to read the message. "It's from FB. Pepe has just left Dukes."

"Any reason? Destination?"

"None given." Dex thought rapidly. "Suppose Carmino's going to Pinesta Crescent to collect the girl." Unsaid was his fear that he might harm Emily rather than taking her to Ardberg House. "You fire-up the police. You've got the credibility. I'm going to number 37. We're much closer to Pinesta Crescent than Carmino. I can't risk him getting there before me. When I see him arriving, that'll be the clincher. I'll dial 999 and somehow stop him entering."

"And if he's no-show?"

"Then he must have gone to Ardberg House."

"If Emily's there, this Arnie won't let you in." Tiffany grasped Dex's hand and gripped it tight. "Don't even try. Leave it to the police."

Dex shook his head. "I may have to. The cops may be too late and I've got to get to Ardberg House as well. With Carmino elsewhere, this may be a great opportunity." He checked his screen again. "Puzzling. Jude hasn't replied to my message."

"Take care," she said, as she piled out of the taxi with the suitcases, the winnings and the evidence.

Dex waved back as she blew a kiss goodbye. "Be quick," he called through the window.

Dex told the driver to take him to Winchester Street. This was just around the corner from Pinesta Crescent. After juggling with the one-way system, the driver pulled up a few minutes later. "There you are, guv."

Dex got his bearings. Pinesta Crescent ran off to his right and the corner house was numbered 93. Despite several parking places, there was no Aston-Martin. He hesitated before walking past the lowering numbers towards 37. Because of the one-way system, Carmino would have to enter Pinesta Crescent from the far end, so he loitered beside number 53. Seven minutes passed, enough time for Carmino to have arrived from Mayfair. No sign of him. He dialled Arnie Fisher's number. Wrapping a hankie over the phone, he spoke from a distance when it was answered.

"Arnie. Bad line. Can you hear me? Be with you in two minutes." He ended the call, hoping he had done enough to be admitted. He looked down the street. A nanny was pushing a pram, a West Indian couple with bags of shopping were heading in the other direction. Cycling toward him was a man in royal-blue lycra. Otherwise, the street was quiet and no cars were moving.

He hurried to number 37. All curtains were closed and if any lights were on, it was not apparent. The property was mid-terrace, dating back to the nineteenth century, and probably gentrified. He guessed it to be either two or three-up and two-down, designed with a sitting-room fronting onto the street and the kitchen somewhere to the rear.

He looked at the solid white front door with a large brass dolphin for a knocker. It was well kept, even prosperous-looking. There was no security camera and no spyhole. He was about to rap on the door when a nasty thought struck him.

Two men had handled the kidnap.
Will Arnie be alone?

He hovered uncertainly, torn between immediate action and waiting for the police to come roaring into the street.

What orders might Carmino have given Arnie?
Or what if Carmino had somehow got here first?
Just suppose he's in there now.
Maybe even killing her?
While I'm waiting outside.
That made up his mind. He banged the knocker twice and after a slightly longer wait than he had expected, the door opened. By now, Dex had tucked himself out of the immediate line of sight, flat against the wall to the side of the door. For a moment, Dex saw nobody but then a slim, short and thin-faced man took a step outside. Dex pounced, grasping the man in a bear-hug and twisting him so that his back was pinned to Dex's chest. He shoved the man into the house and used his own backside to shut the self-locking door, something he instantly regretted.

It was not pitch black but it was gloomy enough in the small entrance area with no lights on. The air smelled of cooking fats. His captive's grey sweatshirt was stale and damp with nervous sweat. *Was this the gofer who had fixed Beth's accident and who had murdered Mick Glenn?* His anger mounting, he tightened his grip. The door to the front-room was slightly open, providing what little light there was. It revealed that Dex was in more of a corridor than a hall. Directly ahead was a straight set of stairs with a handrail fixed to the wall and wrought-iron bannisters with a wooden rail on the right side.

If Jude were to be believed, then somewhere in here was Emily. But where? Dex guessed at a bedroom though there was no sound of any other occupant besides the man who was wriggling and kicking. To the right of the stairs the unlit narrow corridor led to what Dex assumed was the kitchen.

"Where's the girl, Arnie?" Dex shook the man and snapped out the words but got no answer. He then yelled. "Emily! Emily! It's

Mister Dex. We played with Winnie-the-Pooh. Remember? Where are you?" There was no response. No real surprise. She was probably gagged and petrified. "I'm here to save you from the wicked men."

Still not a sound from upstairs. Instead, the front-room door swung open, revealing Pepe Carmino, his Master Bowie in his left hand. In the half-light, his skin looked even darker and his cheeks were hollowed, his face locked in a moment of triumph. The sliver of light from the front-room widened so that the menacing point of the Bowie flashed and glinted for a fraction of a second. Dex flinched as recollections of the butchered Mexican filled his mind.

"Mr Dexter! Thanks for telling us you were coming, though of course our meeting was not until seven. A welcome visit." The sarcasm in his tone was heavy.

Dex looked at Carmino and his tight grip on the handle. As the vicious blade pointed downwards just a few feet from him, he wondered what the hell the police were doing and how Carmino had reached here so quickly. He must have beaten the one-way system and parked in a different street. Dex's second thought, immediately dismissed, was to retreat through the front door.

No way.

Not with Emily here.

Not if there's any chance of her being alive.

At least, for as long as Dex could hold him, the lightweight man was something of a shield. He felt his legs being kicked as the man's trainers hacked back into his shins. He fought to ignore the pain, desperate to keep the prisoner's arms pinned to his side. As before, Carmino spoke slowly but with a bite in each word. "Let Arnie go or I'm going up to take care of the girl."

Ah! Emily is upstairs.

And alive too.

And this is definitely Arnie.

Dex looked at the narrow gap between where he was holding Arnie and the bottom step of the stairs. Carmino could only go up by squeezing through it.

If only I knew which room Emily was in.
If I could get to it.
If I can stop Carmino climbing the stairs.

The plan had gone wrong, horribly wrong. Carmino arriving first with no sign of his Aston Martin had not been in the script. Now, he was confronting the man who wanted to kill him.

Would he murder Emily?
Probably.
Certainly.
Now I'm here, her value is nil.
I need time.
Buy time.
Do anything to buy time.
Wait for the cavalry.

He narrowed the gap by edging sideways towards the bottom step, all the while shielded from the Bowie by the struggling Arnie. Dex yelled again, even louder this time. "Emily! It's your friend Mister Dex. We're going to play Connections soon with Mummy and Daddy. Where are you? Make a noise, any noise."

For a few agonising seconds, there was no response. Then came a loud thump from upstairs, seemingly at the rear of the house. Dex leaned his head sideways and flicked the light switch. The whole area was suddenly illuminated. He could now see Carmino's hatred, his dark eyes as deadly as the knife. He was inching closer, hoping to be able to lunge around Arnie and slash into Dex's side.

Still no sirens, no thundering feet, no door being broken down.
Nothing.

The air was heavy with Arnie's laboured breathing as he panted a strong smell of a Chinese takeaway, his clamped chest heaving beneath Dex's powerful arms.
Carmino would soon be in striking distance.
I must make sure that he stabs Arnie by mistake.
Where the hell is the cavalry?

－103－

Had Tiffany not been a familiar face to the duty sergeant at the police station, she might not have received the supportive reaction she did. In a few pithy sentences, she captured his attention and was quickly seated in an interview room with two detectives who appeared almost at once. Det-Supt Bob Wylie took control and a chain of command was established. Calls were made to New Scotland Yard and to the local team in Surrey.

Tiffany discovered that instant action could never be instant enough. Procedures had to be followed to ensure the safety of the officers involved. The armed-response unit had to be summoned. Someone contacted a Child Support Unit. The ambulance service had to be alerted. Ideally, the surrounding houses had to be cleared and the street cordoned off.

Tiffany described Dex in his navy blazer, pale blue shirt, chinos and loafers. A detective-sergeant was deputed to get ID on Arnie Fisher and Pepe Carmino. "When you get there," she briefed them, "if Dex is not outside, ring this number. If there's no answer, he's inside. Oh…and watch out for Carmino's powder-blue Aston-Martin. The number is DUK something. If you spot it, he's there and both the kid and Dex are in deep trouble."

After that, Tiffany was left alone with a cup of coffee while the detectives disappeared to plan the details. It was a few minutes before she heard the commotion as over twenty officers in combat gear gathered with more expected from across the river.

Det. Supt Wylie refused to take Tiffany on the raid but

nothing was going to stop her from being as close as she could get. Following the map on her phone, she started running into the maze of streets around Pinesta Crescent. As she drew close, her heart stopped. Parked in the next street to the Crescent was Carmino's Aston-Martin. She rang Dex.

There was no reply.

-104-

The standoff had seemed like an eternity. Dex's arm muscles screamed protests as he fought to keep his grip on Arnie. Fortunately, or maybe unfortunately, Arnie was exhausted too. He was struggling less but now his shield provided less protection from Carmino's jabbing knife. Defying his muscles, Dex started to pivot so that Arnie's body swayed to-and-fro, making a lunge riskier.

I can't keep this up much longer.
Do something!

In a sudden but decisive move, he shifted his hands to grip Arnie's elbows. At the same moment, he kneed him in the back and flung Arnie forward. The small figure slammed into Carmino and the blade ripped into Arnie's forearm before it fell to the floor with a clatter. Arnie howled as blood flowed from the wound and Carmino reeled back against the door-frame.

He was still standing though, the knife right by his feet, making it impossible for Dex to reach. He seized the alternative option, bounding up the stairs. As he did so, his phone started to ring and he recalled his instructions to Tiffany.

If I'm not outside or don't answer, I'm in deep shit.
And I am.

At the top of the stairs was a tiny landing giving straight onto the rear bedroom. There was a bathroom and seemingly two other bedrooms to his right. Above Arnie's howls of pain, he heard Carmino somewhere behind him and imagined him about to climb the stairs. The door straight ahead had a keyhole but no sign of a key, a mixed blessing. A locked door and he would be cornered, helpless against Carmino's knife plunging deep into him.

Impulsively, he spun round at the top step and saw Carmino was still only just above the bottom step. Dex's unexpected move made Carmino falter but only for a moment. "Arnie. The gun. Get your gun." Carmino's calm authority had not been shaken.

"My soddin' arm's bleedin' to buggery."

"Just do it."

Dex heard Arnie's rough London accent. "It's out the back. I'll fetch it." Dex waited for a second, a plan forming and knowing now his best chance. He had to let Carmino get closer. Not nice, not pleasant at all given Carmino's grunting noises as he now advanced, one step at a time, the knife in his left hand. Dex waited on the landing, hands by his side like a Western gunslinger about to draw a pair of Colt 45s. Carmino's advance continued, his teeth bared and eyes full of hate. Dex stood his ground, waiting for Carmino to get closer, dangerously close, almost to within striking distance.

Now!

In a swift move, Dex gripped the banister with his left hand and the handrail with his right. Immediately, legs together, he kicked out, swinging himself horizontal, pivoting on his arms. Both feet slammed into Carmino's chest just as he was lashing out with a vicious upward swipe. Like a kick from a mule, the massive impact was decisive. Carmino rocked momentarily before tumbling backwards, head-first, thud, thud, thud down the stairs. Dex heard an impressive cry of pain as Carmino slammed onto the cold tiles at the foot of the seventeen steps. Dex paused only to check that Carmino was still conscious before he turned and tried the bedroom door.

It was unlocked!

In a trice, he was inside the darkened room and slammed the door shut. He found the switch and turned on the light. On the floor was Emily, bound and gagged, where she had bumped herself off the bed. Dex saw her tear-stained cheeks. The tiny helpless little girl looked petrified. Her blue eyes were wide with fear but there was no time for big hugs. To his relief, he saw that the lock was operated by an old-style iron key. He turned it easily enough, knowing that he had bought time.

Not much.

Enough until the police arrived?

A glance revealed that once Carmino had smashed in the door, short of a miracle, he and Emily were trapped. The door was wooden, painted white with two panels centred within the frame. In a sustained attack, they would not last. Besides that, a few shoulder barges would smash the lock from the frame.

A white sock was rammed into Emily's mouth but there was no time to remove it. Her wrists and ankles were bound with cheap blue rope. He looked around and found he was standing by a single bed with a small dressing-table, a faded violet and blue carpet and a solitary chair. The full-length brown curtains were drawn. The wardrobe was empty and of no interest to Dex. Dying in a coffin smelling of mothballs and a sprig of lavender was not on the agenda.

"Emily, everything's going to be just fine." He hated raising her hopes but it seemed better than saying that an armed psychopath was about to kill them both. "Let's play hide-and seek-from the bad men. Do what I say and I'll fix the nasty men." As he spoke, he moved her into the far-right corner, away from the cheap bed with its tubular steel headboard. He briefly stroked her cheek as he concealed her tiny body using the thin mattress and an old army blanket. "Don't move. Be as quiet as a little mouse."

With a noisy crash, he then tipped the bed to stand on its end to straddle the other corner straight ahead of the door. With its solid wooden base, he hoped it looked like obvious protection for people concealed behind it.

He heard more shouting from somewhere but what was being said was muffled. The phone rang again but he had no time to answer. At that moment too, the door shook with a mighty impact. The noise reverberated round the small room and Emily whimpered in fear. "Stay still, Emily. Stay quiet. I'm here but the bad man is trying to break down the door."

The door bulged as it was struck again.

That shouting!

Was that Arnie or the cops?

Dex looked around the simple room. He saw an ornament, a cheap-looking vase in multicolours with the word Benidorm on it.

Perfect!

I can crack Carmino over the skull with this.

He picked it up.

Useless.

It was lightweight, made of *papier-mâché*. A glance around the rest of the room showed no other weapon. He looked behind the curtains for ornaments on the window ledge.

Nothing.

Then he saw that hanging from hooks at either end of the curtains were knotted tie-backs made from cheap cord. Each was looped and about thirty inches long. He ripped one from its hook and hurried to the solitary forty-watt bulb set in a dusty pink shade that hung from the ceiling.

He saw the door bulge again as it was blasted with another shoulder-barge.

Use surprise!

Trick him!
But how?

Ignoring the pain from the heat, he removed the bulb and the room was instantly blackened. Then he got into position, bulb in one hand and the cord in the other. As the door bulged just beside him, he removed his shoes and stood in his stockinged feet. From Emily, there came not even a whimper.

Two, three, four more times the door was buffeted and he heard the wood now splintering. Dex knew that in just a few seconds, Carmino would be into the room. But where would Arnie be? Next to him with a gun? Guarding the stairs? There was no way of knowing.

The shouting had stopped.
So where were the cops?

From his position beside the door's hinges, Dex waited for the wood around the lock to splinter. That happened with the next impact, the door flying open with a shudder. Carmino burst in.

- 105 -

The distant light from the hall downstairs still left the bedroom darkened and shadowy. Dex heard the click of the light switch and Carmino's muttered curse. Before Carmino's eyes adjusted to the gloom, Dex hurled the light-bulb, 10-pin bowling style, skimming it a few inches above the floor toward the bed. It crashed into the far wall. Now he could see Carmino's back, because he had taken a couple of steps into the room towards the upturned bed. The noise from the exploding glass stopped him dead.

Instead of looking around the room, his attention was instantly focussed on the source of the noise. Carmino remained motionless for another moment, staring towards the bed. Then with a slight nod of understanding, he took another step away from Dex's position behind him. Dex tried to see if Carmino was still clutching the knife in his left hand but he could not be sure.

It was now or never.

Carmino must not see the nothingness behind the bed.

Carmino was perhaps a shade taller than Dex and slim and fit but except for the knife, he reckoned they were well-matched. In his stockinged feet, he took a silent pace forward, positioning himself slightly more to the right of Carmino's back.

Avoiding that left hand was essential.

Arms crossed-over and outstretched, he held the cord well above head height. Before Carmino had any idea of an attack from behind, Dex dropped and looped the cord around his neck. To tighten the grip, he viciously yanked his arms apart, forcing his elbows back and compressing his shoulder-blades. The cord instantly bit around Carmino's throat and the lumpy knot dug deep.

For a fleeting moment there was no reaction. Then came a short jabbing move from Carmino's right hand. Dex felt the sharp point of the knife plunge deep into his right thigh.

Christ that hurt!
But surely Carmino had been left-handed?
Shit!
He must have injured his left hand falling down the stairs.

Dex yelped at the searing pain and fought to ignore the sensation of blood gushing from the wound. He shifted his position, moving his body much further left and away from the blade. "Drop the knife."

Carmino did not, one leg kicking back, right arm swinging again, desperately seeking another strike. Dex summoned up what strength he still had to gain more traction on Carmino's neck. There was only one way to do that. He twisted and pulled so that they both moved backward in tandem, Carmino being dragged by the neck.

After one more huge effort, Dex achieved his aim. He braced his back against a wall for support and forced his left knee upward, pushing it into the small of Carmino's spine, adding torque to the throttle.

Success!

Immediately, he could yank harder, forcing the cord deeper into Carmino's throat. The smell of shampoo filled Dex's nostrils as he listened to the strangulated gasps.

Can I hold on long enough?
Render him unconscious.

But this pain, this agony. The loss of blood was making him dizzy.

I can't hold him much longer.

His right leg was losing sensation as his blood still spurted around him. Standing, stork-like on his wounded leg was becoming impossible.

"I said drop the knife."

Dex felt only the slightest response from Carmino's right hand as the strangulation took effect. He heard the knife thump onto the cheap carpet. Waves of nausea were sweeping through him. He fought to keep his balance but still wobbled. Soon his balance would be gone.

Carmino had started to go limp.

Risk it.

He lowered his good leg.

The pressure around Carmino's neck eased

Where was Arnie?

Had he got the gun?

Where were the sodding police?

As Carmino's struggles almost stopped, Dex heard Arnie's rasping accent. "I'm coming up, mate." Then he heard more noise, this time from the street. But Arnie must be close now.

Doing nothing was not an option.

He could be shot before the police had battered down the door.

Defying the pain, his left leg struggling with the two-for-one burden and his right leg now almost useless, he tottered, dragging Carmino the few paces to the top of the stairs. There he saw Arnie, silhouetted by the downstairs light. Instantly, there came the crack of a 9mm Beretta but the bullet flew over Dex's shoulder and embedded in the ceiling. With a hefty shove, Dex jettisoned Carmino down the stairs as Arnie fired again. Carmino's one-eighty pounds crashed onto him.

Dex leaned against the wall, gasping for breath, his shoulders heaving as he saw them both tumble down the stairs in a confused series of bumps. They ended up motionless in a heap by the front entrance. Then, his head spinning and delirious, his knees buckled as he slumped into the small bedroom.

The knife!
I must get the knife.
Emily!
I must get to her.
Must defend her.
Must stop the blood.
Thigh wound.
Not good.

After landing on the carpet, the room was spinning. He saw bagpipers marching on the ceiling.

Or were they on the floor?
Was that Gus McKay with them?

As if from miles away, he heard more shouts but was helpless to reach the knife just a foot or two away. For a second as the bagpipers changed to dark dancing shadows, he blamed Doc Grierson's pills, his fingers clawing feebly on the bloodied carpet.

The shouting seemed very distant now.

The cops have given up.
Never have helped me.

The room did cartwheels before he felt himself slipping, slipping deeper away.

Silence.
Not a single bagpiper now.
It was so very quiet.
Nothing.

As the armed police rampaged through the house, bounding up the stairs, their shouts of *Armed Police* booming everywhere, Dex heard nothing.

-106-

Dex hobbled to a bench-seat at Banjul's Yundum International Airport. It had been almost three weeks since he had dodged death from blood pumping from his femoral artery. Only the arrival of the paramedics had saved him. Now, against medical advice, he and Tiffany had just landed in The Gambia in West Africa. In the spacious and vaulted Arrivals area, he watched her fixing the rental of the Toyota Outlander. In lilac T-shirt and loose-fitting white slacks, she was dressed for the steamy sub-tropical heat of Gambia in the rainy season. As she haggled over the cost for the next week, he enjoyed her dismissive arm movements and mocking laugh.

It would be a five-hour journey heading up-country by a road running close to the mighty river Gambia. Their base was to be Bansang, a small community with over seventy-percent living in poverty. A friend of Tiffany, with the splendid name of Churchill Mwanga, was hosting them during their fact-finding mission.

"Gambia is less corrupt than much of Africa," Tiffany had explained during the flight. "I learned the hard way about corruption, thieving and fraud when I was helping in Ethiopia. We need to be sure that our help reaches the right people, especially the kids suffering from malnutrition. Cash in Africa disappears like snow in a heatwave."

"And ends up paying for lavish apartments in London and Paris, no doubt. So … we send them furnishing, bedding?"

Tiffany had looked doubtful. "If it can be sold or bartered, too often it will be. No. My plan is to arrange accommodation locally for international students to come and build a new school, one classroom at a time. They'll do some basic teaching for kindergarten age every afternoon too. When the school's finished, we'll send school books, kit out the class-rooms. Sustaining what we achieve is even harder – supplying teachers and catering for the differing needs as the kids grow." She flourished her notes. "And I'm not talking of just one school. Economy of scale means we need to get four or five started pdq."

"And the orphanage. I'd really like to get that moving." Dex saw Tiffany's grateful smile before he continued. "Immediate needs? Food? Medicine. Surely they need that to survive till our schools open?"

"Correct, within a month, we'll send in trucks with food and medicines. We'll use Churchill."

As their descent had started, Dex twisted in his seat. "You trust him?"

"Churchill? One-hundred percent. He was a neighbour and friend living close by me in World's End. He was a lecturer at the London School of Economics. Solid business brain. He'll set up a network. Even with our backs turned, I'd trust him."

Now, as he looked through the Terminal's windows, Dex could hear the crashes of thunder and could see the monsoon-style rain sheeting down as Tiffany returned, jangling the keys. "We're all set. In this weather, Mr. Kebba over there did not recommend trying to make Bansang tonight. Too risky after dark when we're carrying passports and valuables."

"So?"

"His cousin runs an animal refuge with huts or tents and he's booked us a hut. About an hour inland. Rated it basic but clean enough. Called Salamanca."

"A hut sounds okay," Dex grinned. "No way am I playing guides and scouts with you in a tent, not in this weather."

Tiffany laughed. "He did say the straw roof might leak but there's a bar and usually big pots of goat stew with rice."

"Sounds better than facing a bunch of thugs armed with knives. Call me chicken but I'm over that type of excitement for now. Salamanca it is. If the roof leaks, I'll put up my brolly over the bed."

Tiffany gripped his wrist to help him off the bench. For a couple of seconds, he swayed unsteadily. "Kebba explained about driving here. Rule One is to forget all manners when driving. Rule Two is use the horn constantly and Rule Three is to regard stopping at red traffic lights as only for wimps."

"Sounds like stress-on-a-stick." Dex managed a feeble smile. "Maybe I'll need to return to Doc Grierson for more pills."

As suddenly as the cloudburst had started, it was over. Outside, as they piled everything under the tailgate, a clammy, damp shroud hit them. The smell of steaming vegetation was mixed with aviation fuel and sure enough, after they joined the exit road, at least a dozen motorists were blasting their horns. With Dex not allowed to drive, Tiffany headed for the South Bank Road leading to the interior. They fell silent as she deftly steered around wandering goatherds, wrecks of abandoned cars, speeding taxis, trucks belching acrid diesel and the occasional cart pulled by a donkey.

Nothing was said for nearly fifteen minutes "You're very quiet, Dex. You brooding about Bladon again? Carmino? Or is it these crazy drivers?"

Dex stretched his arms and massaged his right leg before answering. "None of the above. Pneumonia taking Father was no surprise."

"But him wanting a small funeral at Bladon?"

"Unexpected for sure. Father's solicitor told me that, a week before the crash he had changed his will and had wanted reconciliation. That was emotional, I can tell you."

"So?" Tiffany took her eyes off the traffic ahead for a moment to give him a reassuring smile. "If none of the above? Give."

Dex spoke softly. "It's now dawn in Sydney. Madge and Brad Tuson bury Jude today." He lowered his eyes as tears welled up, something immediately spotted by Tiffany.

"You really wanted to be there, didn't you?"

Dex nodded. "I owed it to Jude … but her folk said no. They wanted a small very private ceremony."

"And with you there …"

Dex nodded. "A media scrum. TV, photographers and maybe a jeering mob."

"I reckoned you had a pretty good press down there. Most Aussie journalists loved you bringing down Carmino."

"But a few plus the trolls crucified me." Dex thought of the abuse and death threats on Twitter.

"Not Jude's folks?"

"No. Absolutely not. We videoed on WhatsApp. They told me not to blame myself."

"Sincere?"

"Yes. I like to think so." For a moment, Dex's face contorted as he pictured the terror on Jude's face as she had tried to escape. His voice cracked as he continued. "But naturally I still blame myself. Too many deaths. Emily's kidnap. All this suffering." He paused to control his emotions, watching some women beside the road, blue baskets perched on their heads. "Did I tell you? I sent Madge Tuson a message from Emily's dad."

"No. Go on."

Dex flicked through the messages on his screen before reading.

"Dear Madge and Brad, Billy Evans asked me to pass on that every time he looks at little Emily's smile, he gives thanks to Jude for the sacrifice that saved her. Jude did not die in vain. God bless her and all sympathy to you both"

Tiffany was about to comment when the lights changed to red and she brought the Toyota to a shuddering halt. She was rewarded with a fierce klaxon blast from an impatient timber-truck for not racing through. "I've said this before, Dex. None of this was for you. You had no wish to make the front of Time magazine, the Sunday papers, as a hero. But for your promise to Beth, you'd have been working in the pub and fishing."

"And finishing the book on Princess Di." He stroked her bare arm. "Thanks. Sure as hell, it doesn't always feel that way. Keep reminding me. I need it. Hate-mail is so cruel."

"Of course, but out here, I can do better than that. Here, you're immune from all that craziness." She pointed to a group of under-sevens, all bare-footed, sitting, standing or sprawling on the red sandy earth. Dex picked out a boy of five in a torn orange shirt and shorts. He was clutching the hand of a younger sister aged about three, her hair tightly plaited. "This is the best therapy you can get."

Dex nodded agreement. "Seeing these kids and their daily lot make me feel bad, so self-centred."

"Dex, you and me – we're going to make so much difference. But never enough. With your winnings, my charity, *our* charity, will help hundreds of kids like these to be fed and educated. We'll give them a fair chance in life. University in England even." Tiffany glanced across and saw the turmoil leaving his profiled face. "How far now?"

"About a kilometre. Turn left towards the river."

Sure enough, just beyond a street-sign that had been twisted and bent by an errant vehicle, a faded yellow arrow pointed to the

Salamanca. She swung the car into the single-track road. Between the dense undergrowth that lined both sides, the red surface was pitted and rutted. Almost at once, the sides of the 4 x 4 were splashed from the puddles in the pot-holes. As the collection of ramshackle buildings came into view, Dex gave a rare laugh. "Five stars, just like the Wynn in Vegas, Better still, not a journalist or camera in sight." Set around what could loosely be called a courtyard, were a rectangular building, made from unpainted breeze-blocks covered by a corrugated-iron roof. Around the perimeter were about twenty circular huts, all with unkempt straw roofs. A pick-up truck that looked as if it had not moved this century, had several hens clucking on its flat-bed. A goose stood on a rusting oil-drum whilst a mongrel cocked a watchful eye from a shady corner, not far from a faded yellow sign saying *Welcome to Salamanca*. Of human life, there was none visible but a welcome smell of hot spicy food drifted towards them.

Before stepping out into the embrace of the 30-degree heat, they slapped on more mosquito protection. "And not a roulette wheel in sight, no. But I just love it here, Dex. Love Africa. Love all this." She pointed to a pushchair without wheels and to a rusted wheelbarrow. "Welcome to the *real world*. Welcome to Africa."

After a dinner of lamb stew followed by dark chocolate cup-cakes and frozen yoghurt, they stayed at their bamboo table to sink a couple of gins, served by a smiley woman in a turban and multi-coloured wrap. They were alone on the veranda. It was thronged with cheap ornaments and artefacts. "Gin, or maybe the tonic, helps keep the mozzies away," explained Tiffany above the Gambian tribal music coming from the sound-system. Under the black night, in the dense foliage surrounding the compound, the chattering monkeys had now fallen silent but from the trees and shrubs came occasional shrieks or eerie sounds of predators at work.

Tiffany saw the glazed look in Dex's eyes as he stared across the black emptiness. She had seen the haunted look too often. "Thinking of Jude again?"

Dex shook his head. "Fighting with Carmino, remembering Emily huddled on the floor."

"It's over Dex." Tiffany clasped both his hands and moved her head closer to him. "He's dead, gone, finished. Arnie Fisher saw to that." She pulled back for a moment as if unsure whether to continue. "When you were showering, I had a message"

"Go on."

"Enzo Letizione has been found – buried in the desert just outside Las Vegas. The FBI are now officially linking Carmino and Fisher to his murder and to the deaths of Tavio Sanchez and Diego Rodriguez."

"The desert?" Somehow, Dex found one of his old-time grins. "After all those years of mobster violence, I'm surprised they could find an empty spot." He squeezed the lime into his tonic. "Pity the Feds can't extradite Arnie Fisher. He'd have a far tougher time in Nevada."

Tiffany shrugged. "Agreed but he'll get life-sentences at the Old Bailey. Besides manslaughter for shooting Carmino, he's charged with Beth, Sir Charles, Mick Glenn and for kidnapping Emily."

"Amazingly, Emily seems just fine. We played Connections a couple of days ago. She was all smiles and giggles. Of course, I let her win."

"And Billy is reconciled with Sandie. That's something else you've achieved. That … and paying for his rehab at that place in Wiltshire." She draped an arm around his shoulder. "Journalists can be callous bastards but they've a job to do. Editors want stories that sell papers or command screen time. Some editors wanted a hero. Others went for the villain."

"I'm neither."

"Whatever. Soon, the media will move on. There'll be another hate-figure, a different story. Out here, you can forget all that. Now, it's just me and the man I'm learning to love." She pulled him close and kissed him on the cheek. For a moment or two, he clung to her, saying nothing.

"I'm glad," he eventually said. "Glad to be with you. Glad to be here. Glad to be having your love and support. Excited by what we can achieve together." Dex wiped some condensation from his glass before picking it up. "But I feel bad about Vegas." He was thinking of the thousands who had lost their jobs with Space City. When they had talked on Facetime, Sheriff Baptisto, the Las Vegas Metro police chief had been blunt. "Those death threats? They're for real, son. I can't guarantee your safety here." Dex had seen the sheriff's convincing stare. They had made his message unarguable. "Don't even think about returning until new owners have launched Space City. And perhaps not even then. Better still, maybe never."

"Dex, you never wanted to go there anyway."

"I'll never be playing roulette or gambling again."

For a moment they were locked in their own thoughts. "Dex, talking of roulette, there's something I've needed to ask you for too long."

On hearing the intro, Dex flinched. "Yes?" He tried to sound more relaxed than he was feeling.

"Our win. Well – your win in Dukes. It was just too good to be true. Y'know, of all the days, that was the one when Reverse Labouchère came good."

"Time for me to move around. Keep the circulation going in

my leg." Tiffany's eyes followed him as he hobbled a few paces along the creaking boards. By the flames from the flickering candles, she could see his shadowed face upturned as he stared into the black sky. Then, for just a fleeting moment, she spotted the slightest of smiles. "Tiffany, darling. It was 85% red – 15% black. Gus McKay had experienced something similar when he won big. The world record is reckoned to be twenty-seven consecutive reds. That's 100%." He shrugged. "This was … rare but nothing unique. We got lucky. Deservedly."

In too many quiet moments, she had relived the excitement of winning mixed with fear of Carmino appearing. Each time, she had been troubled by the massive size of their success. "Come on, Dex. Highest truth." There was an edge to her voice.

Dex avoided looking at her. His brain was in overdrive and was now racing. Thoughts of the casino books he had read swirled around, mixed with the nuggets of advice from Gus McKay. He recalled his meeting with Larry Jamous. Could smell the stale air in his cluttered back-room. In there, using his brilliant craftsmanship, Jamous had created a perfect replica of the wheel used in Dukes. Perfect, except that the eighteen black pockets and zero were narrowed and shallower – not obvious to the naked eye yet sufficient to give red numbers the advantage he needed. For a moment, he was tempted to tell her; to boast about his plan.

But he held back.

No way must Tiffany ever know how he had screwed the casino.
Cheating?
Call it poetic justice.
Justice for Beth too.
Dishonest?
No more than Dukes deserved.

He thought of FB who was now out on bail awaiting trial.

Before the casino had opened that day, he had switched the wheels. As agreed, they had avoided all contact ever since. FB knew his reward would await him after he had served a couple of years or so in Ford prison. For now, Dex could only assume that after paying him out, FB had done what he had been ordered. His task had been to ensure that it was Dukes' own wheel that reached Huxley for testing and not the Jamous masterpiece which was destined for destruction.

Slowly, Dex shuffled back along the veranda to stand beside her. Clasping the edge of her chair, he stroked her cheek with his other hand. "Tiffany, I once saw a pair of illusionists called Siegfried & Roy, maybe the greatest ever. From right beside me, they made an elephant disappear. For days, even weeks, I *really, really* wanted to know how they had done it." He leaned down to give her a kiss. "Then on second thoughts, I decided that knowing would spoil the magic. Sometimes … it's better not to know."

©

THANKS

Thanks for reading Deadline Vegas. It would be terrific if you would put a review on Amazon:

UK: https://amznbook.co/2YsrHHF
USA: https://amznbook.co/3f7f9v8

MY OTHER BOOKS
Webpage: https//www.DouglasStewartBooks.com
I hope you will enjoy my other books – details below.

About Douglas Stewart

Born in Glasgow, Scotland, Douglas was brought up in England and practised as an international lawyer in London and the USA. In tandem, he has also developed a long and successful career as an internationally widely read author, with two number one sellers and a WH Smith Paperback of the Week to his credit. He is married with three children.

DOUGLAS STEWART'S BOOKS REVIEWED

"This book engenders the same get-to-the-end compulsion for the reader as does a Harlan Coben crime suspense or a Simon Kernick or Mark Billingham police novel… the prose is easy to read and the plot is enthralling."

"Couldn't stop reading, this was worth 5 stars."

"Each chapter leaves you eager to continue reading. This was the first of Stewart's novels I have read but I will definitely read more."

"Wow! What a page turner! I can't wait for the next release. A definite five-star from me!"

"Douglas Stewart has done a great job and has created in

Detective Ratso a character who is quick-witted, clever and a worthy addition to the action thriller genre."

"Fantastic read, great characters, gripping storyline. Definitely want to read more adventures from Ratso. Roaring success Mr Stewart!"

"I read a lot of thrillers and Hard Place is high up on my list of favourites."

"It is as if the author has inside knowledge of these characters and places; their portrayal is simple, effective and truly insightful."

"Hard Place is inspired by a real-life event, though Douglas Stewart has transformed this into an entertaining crime thriller."

"... A very enjoyable read. It's a fast-moving thriller in which you feel you really get to know the characters.... Each chapter leaves you eager to continue reading."

"The plot was fast paced, characters well-constructed and believable. There are many twists and turns which makes the book very difficult to put down."

"What a fantastic read, and it's had some awesome endorsements from some of the best crime writers around including Peter James and best-selling author Simon Toyne."

"Fantastic storyline and very believable no super-human

stunts just good believable action – roll on the next one in the series."

"What a treat!! Douglas Stewart is a brilliant author and word craftsman."

"The book races along at breath-taking pace throughout with unexpected twists and turns which end up with a terrific finale!"

"The novel is well-crafted ... and zipped from place to place as it led to a frenetic denouement that kept me glued."

DET. INSPECTOR TODD "RATSO" HOLTOM SERIES

Have you read the *Ratso* thriller series? He is a London detective but his investigations and adventures regularly have him heading for the USA, the Bahamas, Spain or wherever the trail leads.

ABOUT HARD PLACE
– the first in the Ratso series.

In HARD PLACE, Ratso is on the front-line against a ruthless international gang that imports drugs into the UK and Europe. His nephew has died from drug abuse and Ratso is obsessed with bringing down the drug-baron who seems immune from arrest.

The trail leads to the USA and the Bahamas where he is helped by Kirsty-Ann Webber, a Florida detective who has troubles of her own. Mayfair club-land and the Mediterranean feature as Ratso's investigation races to a climax in a series of dramatic confrontations.

Based loosely on the facts of a true crime and set against the background of the war in Afghanistan from where the drugs are coming, Ratso enters a political minefield involving London and Washington D.C.

ABOUT DEAD FIX
– the second in the Ratso series.

Inspired by real events and highly topical, Ratso investigates international sports match-fixing, perfect for this sport-loving London detective. Billions are being staked on fixed results using a global black-market. Following a vicious attack on seeming innocents, he finds himself up against more than bent players as he tackles the shady and murderous world of criminal gangs.

The trail points to a mastermind operating from Dubai and India. But are Ratso's instincts failing him? Once again, he is supported by colleagues, Jock Strang, Tosh Watson and Nancy Petrie. As the investigation twists and turns, fresh evidence points to the USA. Here, his long-distance lover, Det. Kirsty-Ann Webber of the Fort Lauderdale Police Department yet again proves her worth as the scope and scale of the investigation race to a dramatic climax.

ABOUT DEADLINE VEGAS
Deadline Vegas was inspired by my thriller **Late Bet** first published in 2007. To match a requested movie plot, I re-wrote it and, after fundamental changes, a very different and suspenseful thriller has emerged in 2020 as **Deadline Vegas**.

Printed in Poland
by Amazon Fulfillment
Poland Sp. z o.o., Wrocław